ORDER AND CHAOS
BOOK ONE
RAINING EMBERS

JESSICA DALL

Raining Embers

Copyright © 2015 by Jessica Dall. All rights reserved.

First Print Edition: October 2015

ISBN-10: 1-940215-88-9

ISBN-13: 978-1-940215-88-4

Red Adept Publishing, LLC
104 Bugenfield Court
Garner, NC 27529
http://RedAdeptPublishing.com/

Cover and Formatting: Streetlight Graphics

To my mother, my most dedicated reader,
and my father, who accepts I really like this writing thing

CHAPTER ONE

I N THE NEAR DARKNESS, THE *frightful sound of shouting people and clashing swords echoed around the wooden book chest. The battle raged on outside even as the city burned. The little girl curled up more tightly, too afraid to leave the relative safety of her hiding place. Voices rose and fell, some familiar, some with accents she'd never heard. A man cried out, but the cacophony swallowed the noise before it could finish.*

Smoke began to filter into the cracks of the chest, turning the air thick, hazy. The girl swallowed, blinking too quickly as her eyes burned. Her father had been gone by the time she had made it through the havoc to the library. But he had to come back. He was always in the library. Day or night, she could always find him there. Even in all of this chaos, he would have to be somewhere.

The smoke grew thicker, the heat of it making the girl's lungs burn with each breath. Her head swimming, she couldn't wait anymore. She pushed the chest open with the soles of her feet, and a fresh wave of smoke rushed in at her. Mostly by feel, she climbed out, trying to find something familiar, some landmark to show her which way to go in the fiery nightmare. Spotting a patch of lighter smoke, she crawled forward, the normally cool marble of the library floor scorching.

Something creaked. A beam fell, blazing, in front of her. The air shimmered with heat. She had to stop, her mind too sluggish to find another route. The smoke attacked her, working its way inside her lungs. Her heart tried to race but couldn't manage. After a few more inches forward, her body failed, refusing to move. Her eyes fluttered shut, firelight dancing on her eyelids.

Darkness descended. The haze turned to black, nothingness racing in on her.

And it felt... right.

Palmer's eyes flew open as he jerked back to reality, the burning library replaced by the dark classroom under the temple. Shaking his head, he focused on the fire in the center of the ring of acolytes' chairs. Certainly, learning this type of divination could have waited until winter. With summer at its height, they might as well have been in an oven with the entire class of acolytes packed inside the windowless room, along with a fire pit. Between the heat and the smoke, even he was going to start thinking he was having "visions," as the Seers wanted them to believe. Fire, battle, and little girls indeed. Perhaps their classes were truly a study in mass hallucination.

"Um... a bird?" One of the other acolytes' voices clicked somewhere in Palmer's head, his bizarrely focused hearing jumping from the crackle of the fire to the boy's words.

"What kind of bird?" the Master coached, standing behind Danilo Danati as they both stared into the accursed fire.

"A black one?"

Palmer rolled his eyes and looked back at the fire. A log broke, and the voices disappeared, giving way to the new sound. In any other class, Palmer might attempt to force his mind to focus, to accept that the words were what he should hear over any other sound in the room. After being forced into an oven to learn more about false prophesying, however, he was inclined to filter out whatever imagined bird Danilo and Master Franco were discussing as background noise. Since he had to live with the odd affliction of being able to hear only one sound at a time, at least he could use it to his benefit now and again.

"I think it's the city burning," Gianni's voice broke in from his spot in the circle next to Palmer. "Like in Sage Chmela-Parrino's vision."

"That's supposed to be an earthquake." Luca looked up from whatever he'd been carving into the side of his stool. "'The ground shall open, and buildings shall fall'?"

A buzz arose as more and more acolytes debated. Palmer let his mind filter it all out as he wiped at the sweat attempting to trickle down the back of his neck.

"That is *enough*," Master Franco cut through the din. "As it seems we are not going to regain focus for today, we will have to pick up again next week. I expect an essay on what was learned today, in my hand before the fire is lit."

Unhappy groans resonated around the room, but no one debated, packing up their books. Palmer couldn't escape that sweltering room quickly enough, shoving everything into his own sack before moving out into the maze of passageways beneath the temple and toward his little cell.

Palmer couldn't decide if the underground complex was a blessing or a curse during the summer. Generally cooler than upstairs—when the Seers didn't light blazing fires in some weak attempt at fortune telling— the dampness in the air always soaked into the cells below the temple floor, the rooms flooding if the rains came too long or too often. He had long before put everything in his room on stilts, trying to save what meager possessions he had from rotting.

Pulling his cell's door open, he stepped into the small space, barely looking around as he dropped his bag on the cot and pulled out his spare set of robes. They were slightly soiled but at least not soaked through with sweat.

Someone knocked, and Egidio's voice sounded through the door. "Palm?"

"It's open," Palmer answered, pulling the damp brown robes off over his head before spreading them over the small desk. They wouldn't likely dry fully in the musty cell, but at least they wouldn't likely mold, either.

The door swung out with a creak, and Egidio stepped through only enough to let it close again, leaving Palmer enough room to maneuver in the small space. "I'm going to fail."

Palmer sighed. This conversation again. It *was* that time in the semester. He pulled the new robe over his head. "You're not going to fail."

"Another couple bad marks, and I will." Egidio skirted Palmer, sitting next to the bag on the cot. "My father is going to kill me."

Releasing a breath, Palmer took a seat on the low stool in front of the desk, readying himself for the familiar exchange. After six years, Palmer could nearly do both parts. The subject always changed, of course, but it seemed Egidio Dioli had yet to find any part of being an acolyte that suited his skill set. Palmer had to imagine that if Signore Dioli, semiprosperous merchant, hadn't managed to scrape together full room and board, his son would have long been ejected from study at the Church.

"What class now?"

"Master Agnelli's." Egidio rested his mousy face in his hands. "I have no talent in charts."

"Give it here." Palmer motioned toward Egidio and picked up his own stub of a pencil.

Egidio fished around in his bag and pulled out a slightly crumpled paper. He held it out for Palmer to take. "Did you already turn yours in?"

Palmer nodded, not feeling the need to bring up the fact that he had finished while still in class.

"It isn't fair." Egidio slumped forward. "You don't even try, and you have at *least* betas in everything."

"Lucky for me, or I'd be out on the street." Palmer shot Egidio a look before scanning the chart, looking for errors.

"Oh... sorry, Palm." Egidio stumbled over his words. "You know I didn't mean—"

Palmer waved the apology away, rubbing out a few wrong marks with his thumb before replacing them. Even if Egidio had the tendency to end up with his foot in his mouth, he never truly had a bad thing to say about Palmer's circumstances. Maybe that had allowed them to become friends in the first place—Egidio, the talentless son of a family who could barely afford to keep his place; and Palmer, the parentless Ward of the Church who had managed to stay on when most of his peers had aged out, through some combination of dumb luck and an innate talent at astrology. Compared to the grand—or at least wealthy—families most of their classmates came from, Palmer and Egidio were only slightly better than the beggars who wandered around the slums by the river, well outside the walled complex that was the Augarian.

After a few more corrections, Palmer handed the paper back. "Trace that over. It should be more than enough to pass now."

Egidio mumbled some thanks, shoving the paper back into his bag as though the powers that be would know he'd cheated just because Egidio was touching the chart. He tied the bag shut then looked back at Palmer. "Did you hear about Sage Chmela-Parrino's vision?"

Somehow, Palmer refrained from groaning. "Parts of it. Something about the world ending?"

"He said he saw the Augarian destroyed, the ground opening up, a god wreaking vengeance on us all."

Palmer barely managed not to roll his eyes. "Gio, some Seer or another predicts the end of the world once a decade. I don't think we need to worry about this one any more than any of the others."

"If you say so." Egidio rested his arms on his knees. "But I know if the sun suddenly goes dark, I'm going to be a little worried."

"Goes dark?" Palmer frowned.

"Supposedly, that's how it starts. The sun goes dark. Then it's only a matter of time before the gods destroy us all."

Palmer pressed his lips together as he recalled one of the mistakes he hadn't corrected on Egidio's chart, for the sake of believability. A potential solar eclipse, not that far away.

The Seers were going to have a field day.

CHAPTER TWO

GATHERING THE THICK SILK OF her skirts, Brier hurried through the Augarian Palace, passing one painted hall after another on her way out to the piazza. Turning a corner a little too quickly, she nearly lost her footing on the polished marble floor. Stopping just long enough to regain her balance, she continued at a slightly more reasonable pace.

Nico would certainly be hearing from her if she ever made it to the university, where everyone was meeting. He'd nearly finished off the last bottle of liquor they'd stored in her room before he'd left last night, and after twelve years of summers together in the Augarian, witnessing Brier suffer from the same mysterious rotting smell every year as soon as the weather turned warm, he should have known she would need far, far more to drink in order to deal with the crowds and heat.

At least, knowing Nico and the rest of his friends, they would no doubt have something alcoholic where they'd holed up at the university. She just had to make it that far.

Stepping through the gilded front doors, Brier grimaced. The entirety of the Augarian seemed to have turned out on the piazza in preparation for the eclipse, joined by everyone in Latysia who could press through the gates that morning. Taking as deep a breath as she dared against the stench of rot still lingering in her nose, she descended the steps into the mess, doing her best to maneuver through the mass of bodies, aiming for the university towers visible over the heads of students, acolytes, and families. She groaned internally, grabbing her skirts once again to pull them out of the way of a pair of muddy boots. Some of the Latysian merchant women had it right with their straight, colorful muslins not in nearly as much danger as the layers of Augarian silks.

Someone moved, blocking the towers from view. Not for the first time, Brier wished to be taller. She ducked around, moving as quickly as possible and praying she wouldn't be crushed in a sudden shift of bodies.

She survived the courtyard and hurried up the steps of the university. Brier slipped inside, closing out the low roar of the piazza with the heavy double doors.

Of all the large buildings in the Augarian—the high, domed temple, the wide palace with its marble arches striped in black and white— the university with its two tall brown towers still seemed the most intimidating. Perhaps that was simply because it had never been hers. She knew every inch of the palace and spent holy days in the temple, as was required of a good Augarian, but the university... She still wasn't completely sure she was supposed to be inside it at all. Of all the boys' clubs inside the Walls, the university was still the strongest. Her kind had no place within its hallowed halls.

Not that restrictions had ever stopped her from going anywhere before.

Brier stopped just inside the door, orienting herself. With afternoon classes cancelled, for the obvious reason, the building seemed deserted, every noise echoing off the tile floor down the dark wooden hallway. Brier had been to the tower before and vaguely remembered where it was, but she had never gone alone—and very rarely while so sober. Perhaps if she had been able to find that second flask she'd thought they'd stored in her dresser before leaving the palace, it would have helped her get there more quickly.

She scanned the hallways for any sign of life. Satisfied she was alone, she shut her eyes and tried to retrace the path in her mind.

The sound of the ever-growing crowd outside pressed against the door. Footsteps echoed in the stairwell.

Her eyes flew open. The boys were already inside, from the sound of things. Her gray skirts swishing over the smooth tiles, Brier followed the noise, feeling as silent as a shadow, stalking the unseen voices.

The thick mahogany door to the tower room wasn't quite enough to silence the noise coming from inside. Deep voices rumbled and laughed, and glasses clinked. She'd found the party.

Pushing the door open, Brier stepped inside without preamble. "Hi, boys."

Leone hopped up. "Chas!"

Brier just smiled at the nickname.

"I thought you locked the door." Firth looked over from a table that seemed to have been turned into a makeshift bar.

"I thought I had." Leone shook the handle to test it, twisting the key in the hole to stop the door short.

"Congratulations. You *do* know how to lock a door." Nico snorted, grabbing a glass full of deep-red liquid off the table and offering it to Brier. "Happy eclipse."

Brier stepped forward and took the drink, warm from sitting out in the summer heat. "What is it?"

"Just wine," Leone answered instead of his cousin. "Got back into the cellars."

"So, sacramental wine." Brier took a drink.

"Fitting for the occasion, I would say." Nico led her to one of the well-worn couches—which looked entirely out of place in the otherwise very academic tower—no doubt more of the boys' handiwork.

"I'm surprised you made it across the piazza in one piece." Rush looked over from his place at the window, his face already flushed with wine. "The great leader sent out the call, and it seems the masses have responded in droves."

"No kidding." Brier made a face. "I should have made one of you come and get me."

"We were busy putting things right for you here, Chas." Firth leaned against the not-bar, shooting back the wine remaining in his glass.

She hummed, her eyes flitting between the men in the room. As different as each was, from dark Firth to the pale Adessis—Nico and Leone—something about them seemed nearly interchangeable: the easy way they took over a room, the stylistically careless way they wore their silk shirts and trousers. They practically dripped privilege.

She took a long drink from her glass. For as long as she had reaped the fringe benefits as the lone girl wandering around with the rest of the boys in the city, the setup worked for her.

"So what have you been up to, Chas?" Firth finally strode to another chair.

"What am I ever up to?" Brier asked. "I'm about to start cross-dressing and sneak into your lectures. I think I've nearly run out of hobbies."

"Don't think any of my courses would make you any *less* bored," Rush said. "How about you, Firth?"

"Not mine." Firth shook his head, leaning back in his chair. "Have you even been to all of your classes yet, Guillroy?"

Nico pursed his lips in thought. "I think so. Wait. What's that morning one? I may have slept through those."

"Every class for two months?" Brier looked at him.

"You know I'm not a morning person, Chas."

She rolled her eyes, but neither the innuendo nor the nickname was worth arguing at that point. As "discreet" as Nico had always been when staying in her room at night, she had to imagine that was common enough knowledge among the others in the room. And with the way the boys used odd combinations of their last names to address one another, it had only been a matter of time before her own, Chastain-Bochard, had become Chas after Nico had begun letting her tag along.

"Alchemy's actually not bad." Leone fished for something in his pocket. "Maybe you should pick that up, Chas."

"Would have all the books for it." Rush laughed.

"If not the patience," Brier said, glancing at Rush before looking back at Leone. "I'm not sure I have the mind for alchemy."

Leone found whatever he'd been looking for and pulled a cube out of his pocket. He tossed it to her. "But look."

Brier fumbled, just managing to catch the cube while keeping her wine from spilling. She looked at it with a frown. Even though it was solid in her palm, the cube was barely visible. She took it between her fingers and held it up to the light, seeing straight through the blue haze as though it were nothing more than fog.

Nico reached out.

She let him take it, glancing at Leone before looking back at the cube. "What is it?"

"Frozen smoke," Leone said.

Brier's eyes snapped back to him. "What?"

Leone shrugged. "It's frozen smoke. You know, smoke... that's frozen."

"How?" she asked.

"I don't know," Leone answered. "They didn't say."

Nico tossed it back to Leone, settling back on the couch. "What's it do?"

"Not much, as far as I know." Leone caught the cube easily and held it between two fingers. "It's mostly a novelty, from what I can tell. Makes the professors downright giddy, though, let me tell you."

Brier stared at it. "It's fascinating."

"I thought so." Leone smiled.

Firth raised an eyebrow. "That why you pocketed it?"

Leone slipped it away with a shrug. "They didn't miss it."

"But you don't know how they make it?" Brier asked.

Leone shook his head. "Guess you actually have to *be* an alchemist to know that."

Brier nodded, glancing at the window when a cry went up from the piazza.

"First of the Seers are on the balcony," Rush reported.

"Must be getting close." Brier stood, finishing her glass in two more gulps while walking to the not-bar.

Rush looked up at the sky, shielding his eyes as much as possible. "Nothing yet."

Brier poured more wine and took a sip from the fresh glassful, looking out the window. Her stomach fluttered as a Seer started speaking, his voice too distorted to properly make out. She pressed her free hand to her middle, looking out across the piazza. "Do you think anyone can actually hear them?"

"I'm sure there are people who've been camping out right under the balcony all night who can"—Nico moved next to her—"spending their night preparing for the end of the world and all."

"Well." Brier stepped back from being sandwiched between Rush and Nico, suddenly feeling too confined. "If it is the end of the world, I think we're preparing much better than anyone down there. Could only be more perfect with hard liquor. I'm not sure we'll be drunk enough for the end of life as we know it in time, this way."

"Not unless we double our efforts." Nico followed to pour himself more.

"Hear, hear," Leone said.

Brier smiled. Her stomach fluttered again, stronger that time. She shuddered.

"You all right?" Rush looked at her.

She nodded, downing half her glass at once. She held it out toward Nico. "Need more wine, I think."

Nico studied her carefully before nodding, topping off the glass.

A roar rippled through the crowd but hushed quickly.

"The Augur," both Rush and Leone said from opposite sides of the room, neither having to look to know.

Nico popped another bottle open.

Brier looked out the window. Across the piazza, the Augur was just a speck standing on the palace balcony, a flash of gold in the middle of the red College of Seers. Brier nursed her drink, the wine finally reaching her head and beating out the last of the lingering rot filling her sinuses.

The light began to dim just enough to be noticeable.

The fluttering in Brier's stomach turned into a buzzing, the alcoholic relaxation fighting the tension in her body.

"It's starting." Rush leaned against the window frame.

The remaining men moved to the windows, squinting up into the dimming sunlight.

Brier couldn't move. A whispering in her ears battled the wine in her head. Her body vibrated with it, feeling tense and rubbery at the same time. Her eyes flicked toward the glass of wine in her hand. She'd never felt anything like that from wine before. Perhaps something was in it. Her eyes flicked back up to watch the dark disk moving farther and farther in front of the sun.

"Does it always take this long?" Rush took a drink, bringing him dangerously close to the bottom of his glass.

"It's a celestial event, not a horse race," Leone said.

"I need more wine then." Rush retreated toward the not-bar.

Half the sun disappeared... two thirds. The whispering grew louder, and the buzzing strengthened, shaking Brier to her core—as though her very soul were trying to break free. Brier blinked, her vision starting to blur.

Flashes. Black. Red. The tower. Black. Fire. Stars.

She fought to stay in the present. The flashes threatened to overtake her, passing too quickly to make sense.

"You're going to miss it," Leone called.

"I'm coming, I'm coming," Rush answered.

The buzzing radiated outward. Brier's hand began to shake, the nearly full wineglass threatening to spill.

"Chas?" someone asked. A beat. "Brier?"

Her name filtered in above the whispers, faint, distant.

"Brier? Are you all right?"

The wine sloshed over the edge, and she lost her grip. The glass dropped and shattered on the wooden floor. Her body shook, feeling as though it were coming apart.

Black, light, black, water, light, fire, nothing, everything. Images slid past her eyes.

Her body crumpled to the floor, lost. Her mind felt fuller and fuller, close to exploding...

And then nothing. Calm. A heady sense of perfect power.

An explosion. Compression. Everything falling together, frozen in the darkness.

An end. A beginning. Everything and nothing. Together.

"When the darkness descends, the end shall begin. The old gods awaken to mete out our doom. Uncontrolled, uncontrollable, their vengeance will know no bounds until the land cracks open and the vessel succumbs, inside the walls of the city."

Palmer stared at the scrap of paper, which had been making its way through the halls under the temple. He didn't know how much of the scribbling was original and how much was embellishment by some acolyte who thought an already apocalyptic tiding could use more drama. Glancing at a patch of bright sunlight coming through the small window along the roofline of his cell, Palmer scoffed. The eclipse had come, the eclipse had gone, and the world continued to turn, with no gods or quakes or doom—nothing but the sharp headache Palmer hadn't been able to shake since morning.

Rubbing his temples, he shut his eyes, trying to will the pain away. The odd flashes returned, and his eyes flew back open. Maybe he had hit his head against the wall in his sleep or something. That would explain the ache and the flashes trying to take hold every time he closed his eyes.

Someone knocked.

"It's open," he answered, dropping his hand again. The door swung outward, the sight of red robes making Palmer freeze. The Seers rarely, if ever, came down to the maze of cells. One had never come to see Palmer personally.

"Tash?" the Seer asked.

His surname snapped Palmer out of his shock. "Yes, Sage?"

"Palmer Tash?" he clarified, whether or not it was necessary. Palmer was the only Tash in the Augarian—or in the rest of Latysia—as far as he knew.

"Yes, Sage," Palmer repeated all the same.

"If you will come with me..." The Seer swept an arm toward the hallway, his rich red robe fluttering after it.

Surprisingly calm, Palmer just nodded as he followed the Seer out into the hall.

The Seer didn't say a word as he led Palmer down the hallway and out the door. He remained silent even as they walked across the little courtyard set between the temple and the younger boys' dormitories.

Palmer let his mind wander, ignoring the dull ache starting behind his eyes as he tried to determine just where the Seer was leading him. Something, or someone, was waiting for them, Palmer had to assume, but it didn't feel necessarily bad, at least not yet. All he could really do was follow.

Rather than heading for the temple proper, or even any of the nearby rooms Palmer knew, the Seer turned off to one side, leading him to a small door into one of the auxiliary buildings. The Seer turned its latch, and it creaked open. The Seer ducked inside, and with nowhere else to go, Palmer stepped through after, blinking as his eyes tried to adjust to the darkness. The room inside seemed enormous compared to its doorway. A soaring ceiling hung above them, with windows around the moldings letting light down into the otherwise shadow-filled room.

Palmer scanned a group of men sitting at a table at the far end of the room, all eight in red Seer robes, watching him. For the first time, Palmer's muscles tightened with trepidation.

The Seer next to Palmer motioned toward a chair at a smaller table in the center of the room as he passed to take his place with his peers. "Please have a seat, Tash."

Palmer did as he was asked.

The Seer took his place in the last empty seat at the end of the high table.

The room fell silent as the Seer in the center finished reading a piece of paper in his hands. Finally, he set it down and studied Palmer over his half-moon glasses. "Palmer Tash?"

Apparently, they hadn't properly established his identity yet. Palmer nodded. "Yes, Sage."

"Do you know why you are here today?"

Palmer didn't even properly know where *here* was. "No, Sage."

The Seer motioned to the men on either side of him. "Do you know who we are?"

Palmer hesitated but saw no point in lying. "No, Sage."

The Seer actually looked surprised before he recovered, his face returning to the same lofty expression. "We are the Tribunal. We serve our solemn duty as decreed by the gods, deliberating over the moral judgments of men."

Palmer just frowned. "Have I done something wrong?"

"No, Tash," the Seer said. "At least, we do not have any charges for you. No. You have been called here regarding some of your work."

Palmer took a moment and then realized he *still* had no idea what they were talking about. "My work, Sage?"

"Your charts, specifically," the Seer said.

The rest of the men mumbled in agreement.

Palmer looked at each one in turn and finally just shook his head, trying to hide his growing annoyance. "What about my charts?"

The Seer finally turned around the paper he had been reading and hung it over the edge of the table for Palmer to see. "Do you recognize this, Tash?"

Palmer looked, his own writing staring back at him around the arcs and symbols of a star chart. "Yes, Sage."

"What is it?"

"My chart," he said, "the one I completed for Master Agnelli's class, I think."

"Indeed." The Seer turned it back toward himself, straightening his glasses to get a good look. He hummed, passing it down the line of men to the right of him. "I must say, it is incredibly detailed."

"Is it not supposed to be?"

"More detailed than even many of our own astrologers' charts." The Seer returned to studying Palmer over the spectacles. "Tell me, Tash, where did you come up with the second rotation?"

Palmer frowned, trying to remember the chart, trying to understand what made it so important even though he had made the thing in five minutes at the end of class. "I saw it, I suppose. I've always been good with charts."

"Very good, it seems," another of the men said.

The middle Seer barely glanced at the other man before looking back at Palmer. "It seems you were correct, Tash, and succeeded in being the sole predictor of this morning's eclipse, save Sage Chmela-Parrino himself."

Palmer hesitated, his muscles taut as the long table of Seers continued to stare at him. "I was just following the trajectory Master Agnelli instructed us to use."

"Ah." The middle Seer leaned forward. "But neither Master Agnelli nor the rest of your class saw the predictors for the eclipse. It must have been something you saw yourself?"

Palmer remained silent, unsure how to answer. He sighed, trying to hide the sound as an afterthought. "I'm sorry, Sage, but I still don't understand why I'm here. I was just doing my coursework."

"Have you shared any of Sage Chmela-Parrino's other visions?" a Seer down the table asked. "The destruction of the city? End times?"

A more ambitious acolyte might have agreed. As it was, Palmer was counting the seconds until they would let him leave. He'd endured thirteen years of being inundated with the absurdities the Church attempted to pass off as fact with some sense of logic still intact. He wouldn't let himself get swept up now. "No, Sage. I'm just good with charts."

The Seers at the table seemed to physically deflate at his denial. A few began to murmur among themselves.

Looking disappointed himself, the Seer at the center of the table tapped his hand, and the rest of the men fell silent. Adjusting the spectacles at the end of his nose, the center Seer studied Palmer for a long moment before finally speaking. "Tash, it is our job to determine the gods' wills for the daily doings of their people. As it seems your skills are currently being squandered in Master Agnelli's class, we believe the gods have smiled on your placement to train with Sage Chmela-Parrino from this point forward."

Palmer gave up answering and just waited for more explanation.

"Starting immediately, you are to report to Sage Chmela-Parrino's offices each morning from now on. Your courses at both the university and the temple will be adjusted accordingly. There seems to be no reason to delay assigning your future vocation in the Church when it is already so obvious where your talents lie."

Palmer still didn't speak. After one stupid assignment, they wanted him to spend the rest of his life making star charts. Maybe he should have lied about having visions. At least then he might be doing something a little less mind numbing while they waited for him to take his Seer vows.

The center Seer looked at the men on either side of him. They all nodded in agreement. He looked back at Palmer. "So it is decreed. Congratulations, Tash."

CHAPTER THREE

Brier's eyelids fluttered, attempting to open. Her eyes felt too tired, her head too heavy, her body too sore.

Inexorably, quiet voices forced her awake, men's voices talking in quick, worried tones. She blinked, finally managed to open her eyes, and tried to focus. She was certainly in her room, lying on her bed, able to feel her thin summer sheets under her palms. The large floor-to-ceiling window by her desk was even still open from that morning's attempt to get a breeze through the hot, humid air, but the way light was shining through indicated sunset was near. Her mind raced, trying to remember how she had gotten there. Nothing came to her. She couldn't recall leaving the university, much less returning to her third-story room in the palace. She shifted with a light groan, trying to see where the voices were still coming from.

"Brier!" Nico moved from the other side of the room and sat in her desk chair, moved over by her bed.

"You gave us all quite a scare, signorina," Dr. Cario-Hakim said, his familiar, dark face coming into view.

Brier blinked at him. Something awful had to have happened if they had called in the head physician rather than Dr. Cino. She studied the rest of the group across the room: another physician, her father, and even a Seer complete in his red robes. Slowly, the sinking feeling that she was dying settled in her stomach.

"What happened?" she asked.

"You had a fit, child." Dr. Cario-Hakim patted her hand, offering a kind smile. "Took quite a fall for it. Luckily, Signori Adessi-Guillroy and Uberti-Magalhaes managed to catch you before you slid down the entirety of the university steps and ended up in the piazza."

Brier glanced at Nico, confused. His expression told her to keep quiet. She just nodded even though, of all the possibilities, that scenario didn't seem likely.

"Do you remember anything of the fall, signorina?" The Seer stepped forward.

Brier blinked. The vibrations, the power, the darkness—it all flashed through her mind. She shook her head, not ready to share the absurdity of it all. They hardly needed another reason to think her mind was going. Illness was one thing—they could force her into bed and try to treat that—but madness...

"Nothing?" the Seer pressed.

"I..." She tried to think of what to say. "I've been feeling poorly, Sage. I do most summers. I think the heat and the people... All I remember is my mind going fuzzy. Everything just became so loud, and then... I don't know."

The men looked between each other.

"Do you know what it is, signori?" Citron Chastain-Bochard finally asked from his spot in the corner.

Dr. Cario-Hakim looked back at him. "Has your daughter ever had symptoms like this before, signore?"

"Not that I know of," Citron said, looking at Brier for confirmation. She shook her head.

"Though you've been dizzy," Nico said.

Dr. Cario-Hakim nodded. "Is the dizziness worse at any particular times? Possibly at a particular time of the month?"

Brier felt her face flush at the implication. She shook her head. "No, signore. Just in the heat."

The doctor placed a hand on Brier's forehead, waited for a moment, and then turned back to her father. "I would request to examine the girl, now that she is awake, if I have your permission, Signore Chastain-Bochard."

Citron nodded, his arm fluttering in a half motion of permission.

Dr. Cario-Hakim looked around the room. "If you would give the child some privacy...?"

The room's occupants began to shift, moving toward the door.

Nico reluctantly stood. "I'll wait outside, all right, Bri?"

Brier nodded.

The room emptied beyond the doctor and the Seer.

"Sage?" Dr. Cario-Hakim looked at the man.

"I would like to ask the girl a few questions myself if you approve, Doctor."

The men stared at each other, and the doctor finally nodded. It hadn't truly been a request.

Dr. Cario-Hakim looked back at her. "You have a few cuts from your fall, signorina. Glass, it seems. If I may?"

Brier didn't protest, letting him roll up her sleeve without protest. She watched the Seer.

He watched her as well. Finally, he moved forward. "Do you know who I am, signorina?"

Brier shook her head. "No, Sage. I'm sorry."

"I am Sage Gimondi-Parrino," he introduced himself. "One of the Augur's College."

Brier nodded, hissing as Dr. Cario-Hakim wiped one of the cuts on her arm.

"My apologies, child," the doctor said.

Sage Gimondi-Parrino looked at her arm then back up at her. "The Augur has asked for me to speak with you briefly."

Brier frowned. "The Augur?"

"Yes, signorina."

"Why is he concerned with me?" Brier asked.

The Seer moved next to the bed, looking down at her. "Have you had any visions before, signorina?"

Brier's mouth opened, but she didn't answer. The question didn't fully make sense. She repeated, "Visions?"

"Predictions. Sights."

Brier shook her head.

"No?"

"No," she clarified. "I'm sorry."

The Seer nodded slowly, his dark eyes remaining on her as if he were trying to read her mind. Brier's insides squirmed under the scrutiny. Still, she forced herself to look back. Enough times barely escaping trouble with Nico had made her an expert at looking innocent. The level of interest she had suddenly generated with this Seer, however... that was something new altogether.

Finally seeming to realize she wasn't going to continue, no matter how much he stared, Sage Gimondi-Parrino pressed, "Did you see anything today? When you fainted."

"Like what?" Brier asked.

"Anything."

Brier glanced at the doctor and then back up at the Seer, debating how much to say when she didn't understand any of what had happened herself. She relented. "Flashes, I guess. Nothing that made any sense."

"What sort of flashes?" The Seer sounded a little too eager.

"I'm going to look for lumps on your head, child," the doctor spoke. "Let me know if you feel any pain."

Brier nodded, letting him prod her through her hair, welcoming the pause.

"Flashes, signorina," Sage Gimondi-Parrino insisted.

Brier looked at him and blinked once. "They weren't anything, signore. Black. A fire."

"Perhaps the library fire in the Reclamation," the doctor ventured. "When the mind fails, it often falls back on past experiences. I imagine the remembrance of nearly dying would be something especially strong."

"Maybe." Brier dropped her eyes, trying to ignore the childhood memory—the smoke, the hot marble, tiles falling.

The Seer finally reached out, tilting Brier's chin to force her to look at him.

Brier met his eyes, lost for what else to do.

He searched her face, squinting slightly before he dropped his hand. "Thank you, signorina. I will leave you in Dr. Cario-Hakim's very capable hands."

Brier didn't answer, entirely unsure of what had just happened.

CHAPTER FOUR

BRIER FANNED HERSELF, FIGHTING A losing battle against the summer heat. Long after dark, it was still there, the stagnating air turning the entire city into one hot, stinking mass. The perfumes people used in the Augarian to cover it only made it worse, in Brier's opinion, and the packed ballroom became a throng of sticky body heat, poorly hidden by the smell of wilting flowers and musk. Combined with the lingering rot Brier hadn't been able to drink away, she was amazed she'd been able to stand inside the grand ballroom at all.

Leaning against a pillar at the top of the front steps of the palace, Brier looked out at the empty piazza. She did her best to keep from fantasizing. What she wouldn't give to be away from the party inside and out of the heavy dress demanded by formality. Somewhere alone. She took as deep a breath as she dared through her mouth, even that tainted by the rot. Smelling it or tasting it, she would just have to survive until fall, the same way she had every summer since childhood.

"There you are."

Brier glanced back. Nico looked like nothing more than a tall shadow against the brightness of the doorway. Still, the shape was unmistakably him.

He moved toward her. "Was beginning to think you'd ditched."

"My own party?" she asked.

"I've done it."

She snorted and regretted it. "Well, you are more skilled than I, Nicodemo."

He smiled, leaning against the pillar next to her and facing across the piazza. "Needed air?"

Brier nodded. "I just had to get out of there. Too many politicians."

"Smell worse than the rest of us?" He twisted his head to see her.

"More than many," she said.

Nico nodded, clicking his tongue. "I suppose it makes sense. Full of shit, the lot of them."

Brier finally laughed, caught off guard.

"There we go." Nico turned fully to face her, tucking behind her ear a strand of hair that had escaped from its elaborate set of braids. "Smile a little. It's your birthday."

She rolled her eyes. "If only I had been born in the winter."

He kissed her forehead then glanced back at the party. "Are you going to come back in soon? I think they want to start in on their oddly self-congratulatory toasts to you having survived another year."

Brier groaned. "I always forget about those."

"And be worried." Nico glanced back at the party. "My father looks especially excited this year."

She couldn't bring herself to look, focusing on fanning herself instead. "I blame you for all that, just so you know."

"Me?" Nico lifted an eyebrow.

"Your father would have no interest in me or my birthday if we weren't friends."

"You think my father needs me to find opportunities for self-aggrandizement?"

Brier couldn't debate that.

"Anyway." Nico slid an arm around Brier's waist. "Who would be quite so perfect in giving my father an excuse to show just how magnanimous Orris Adessi-Guillroy really is, if not you? Kind, beautiful, well-bred enough not to be an embarrassment while still needing his money—"

"I don't *need* his—"

"Come back in," Nico cut off her objection. "Sooner the toasts happen, sooner we can get out of here."

Brier pressed her lips together, finally chancing a look back at the hot, packed room. "Just another minute."

Nico nodded understandingly, pulling a flask out of his coat pocket.

He pressed it into her hand. "Not much left after Rush got to it. Make it count."

Sticking his hands into his pockets, Nico strolled away casually, leaving Brier with the shining metal flask.

Even warm, the liquid went down in two gulps, making her cough as it hit the back of her throat. She flushed as the heat came over her first, then the dulling. Perhaps Nico hadn't given her enough to fully kill the smell, but she'd drunk enough to make it bearable, not as overwhelming.

She tossed the flask back one more time, shaking out the final drops before she screwed the top back on. Opening one of the small pockets in her skirt, she slid it away, checking to make sure there was no sign of the silver flask in the delicately embroidered gold fabric. She released a tense breath and turned back toward the party. If only she had more to drink. But hopefully, with a little luck, she'd be able to make do.

Palmer shifted uncomfortably between the balls of his feet, looking around the lavish party. "What are we waiting for?"

"I can't see her." Egidio scanned the crowd, rising and falling awkwardly as he tried to see through the mass of suits and dresses. "She has to be here."

"We *shouldn't* be here," Palmer said, trying to straighten his lapel once again. His suit didn't seem to fit him correctly. The pants felt too tight, and the rigid collar chafed. Even though he hated his acolyte robes, at least they had long since been broken in.

"Just wait until you see her." Egidio wrung his hands. "She is the most beautiful girl I have ever seen."

A shape moved into the doorway at the top of a short staircase. Palmer froze, looking at the woman standing there. Light caught the gold fabric of her dress, glinting off the beading on both the dress and in her hair. She seemed to be giving off light herself, glowing.

He blinked, forcing a cough. "Her?"

Egidio glanced at Palmer and followed his line of sight to the grand doorway. Egidio shook his head. "No. That's the librarian's daughter. Carmella's taller. Dark hair."

"Librarian's daughter?" Palmer asked, tearing his eyes away from the girl to look at Egidio.

"Yeah. You spend enough time there. You must have seen her before. She's... what's it?" Egidio returned to searching the room. "Chastain-Bochard. Brier Chastain-Bochard."

"Brier," Palmer repeated, mostly to himself, as he looked back at the woman, who was descending the steps to the main floor. An odd sense of recognition hit him. He knew her—knew her in some concrete but fleeting way he couldn't place. She gathered the folds of her dress in one hand, holding them out of the way just enough to navigate the stairs smoothly. Palmer tried to make out her face, small and delicate under the weave of blond braids wrapping her head. He didn't have enough time. She reached the party floor and disappeared into the crowd, not tall enough to peek out over the old men, her dress not wide enough to clear a path for her among all the other colorful skirts.

"There!"

Palmer jumped as Egidio's voice snapped him out of his thoughts. "What?"

"There." Egidio pointed to their left. "Carmella Huerta-Rey."

Palmer spotted a girl surrounded by a ring of suited young men. He had to admit she was beautiful, with dark ringlets framing her sweet face before falling down over her bare shoulders to the neckline of her pale-pink gown. "She's pretty."

"Pretty?" Egidio repeated. "*Pretty?* She's a walking *goddess*. I've never seen anyone else like her. She's just... perfect."

Palmer crossed his arms, studying Carmella for another moment before looking at Egidio. "So?"

"So?" Egidio looked at him.

"So... go talk to her." Palmer motioned.

Egidio blinked. "Talk to her?"

"Well, yeah."

"I can't talk to her."

Palmer finally frowned. "We snuck out just so you could *stare* at her?"

"What would I say?" Egidio asked.

"I don't know." Palmer sighed. "Tell her she looks nice."

"Looks nice," Egidio mumbled, releasing a breath and swinging his arms before starting toward her. "Looks nice... You look nice... nice..."

Palmer gritted his teeth, scanning the crowd again as he attempted to avoid seeing the inevitable wreck waiting to happen to his left.

There. His eyes found her, Brier Chastain-Bochard, at the far wall, talking to an old man. Rather, an old man talked at her while she seemed to tilt away from him.

Palmer's legs moved him forward before he could reconsider it, bringing him directly up to the pair.

Their heads turned to him in unison.

Palmer cleared his throat, his mouth not working as quickly as his feet had. "Signorina..."

Both waited for him to continue, not even a faint sense of familiarity on either of their faces.

"You look..." Palmer floundered. "You look nice tonight."

A small smile appeared at the corners of Brier's mouth, something more amused than flattered. "Thank you very much, Signore..."

"Tash," Palmer supplied, the lack of prestige in his single name suddenly seeming damning in the room of grandees. Feeling the need to continue before they could comment, he added, "How is your father?"

"He's very well," she answered. "Are you an apprentice of his?"

Palmer just nodded, watching the old man grow bored with their conversation and wander off out of his peripheral vision. He finally offered Brier an embarrassed smile. "Sorry. You looked a little trapped."

Brier's grin widened. "Oh, I was. It was very astute of you to notice. Signore Sanna-Rey likes to think himself the most amusing person in the room. Unfortunately for the rest of us, that is far from the case."

"It wasn't a problem." Palmer shifted, forced himself to stand still.

"So you work with my father?" Brier asked when he failed to continue.

"Uh..." Palmer hesitated. "Well, not really work. I just use the library quite a bit."

"You go to the university, then?"

Technically, he did, for some of his classes. Since he'd seen many of the wealthy full-time university students scattered around, that would likely be the best answer to explain his presence. He nodded.

She nodded back, her eyebrows knotting after a second as some thought struck her. "Are you friends with someone here?"

"Oh." Palmer checked over his shoulder for where Egidio had gone. They really should have thought through showing up more than they had. No doubt, all those other university students had their own double names that said they belonged. Of course she would wonder where this singular *Tash* had come from. He said the first thing that came to mind. "Yes, my friend is... over with Carmella Huerta-Rey?"

"Ah." Brier's tone cooled as she looked the direction Palmer had. "Of course."

Unsure what he had stepped into by invoking the other woman's name, Palmer remained silent.

"Well, Signore Tash." She offered a genteel, if tight, smile. "It was Tash, yes?"

He nodded.

"Thank you very much for saving me from Signore Sanna-Rey. I hope you enjoy the rest of the party."

"Oh..." The rest of whatever he was going to say died in his throat. "Thank you. I'm sure I will."

She began to move off.

"Signorina..."

She turned to look at him.

"It's Chastain, yes?" He inwardly grimaced. Stupid question.

She narrowed her eyes slightly, as if confused, but answered anyway. "Yes. Chastain-*Bochard*."

"Of course," he said before she fully finished, trying to recover. "Brier Chastain-Bochard. The head librarian's daughter."

"That am I," she said and waited for him to continue.

"I..." He swallowed. "I just couldn't completely remember. I thought I would ask before it became too awkward to ask."

Her eyebrows rose, but the half smile returned to the corners of her mouth. At least she seemed to find him amusing. "Fair enough. I don't believe I ever got your given name, then, Signore Tash."

"Palmer," he said. "It's Palmer."

She put his name together. "Palmer Tash."

He nodded.

She waited another beat and finally motioned toward the rest of the party. "If you'll excuse me, Signore Tash...?"

"Of course," he said too quickly, attempting some sort of half bow he'd seen the other men perform. He was entirely grateful she turned away before she could see him make a mess of it.

Brier Chastain-Bochard slipped back into the crowd, seeming to fade from view almost instantly as the suits and dresses swallowed her once again. He watched the spot where she'd disappeared all the same, left with the feeling he had missed something. Something incredibly important. But nothing came to him, and he was left unsettled. He shook his head, trying to rid himself of the feeling as he looked for Egidio.

Wide-eyed and silent, Egidio looked terrified, hovering on the periphery of Carmella's entirely male court. Palmer sighed and walked forward.

Carmella looked up at him, her honey-brown eyes meeting his.

"Good evening, signorina." He attempted the half bow again, managing one nearly passable that time.

She looked at him for another moment. Apparently, he passed inspection. She rewarded him with a pretty smile. "Good evening, signore."

Egidio still stood seemingly frozen on the far side of the circle.

Palmer cleared his throat. "Are you enjoying the party?"

"Very much so, signore."

Another man across the circle studied him. "Don't I know you from somewhere?"

Palmer looked back, barely refraining from wincing as he recognized Firth Sanna-Rey. Firth had to be even less alert during classes than Palmer had suspected, to not recognize him straight off. Or maybe Palmer really did look that different out of his acolyte robes.

"I believe we've had class together," Palmer said, sounding much less tense than he would have expected.

"Ah." Firth nodded, still studying Palmer.

"You're a student as well then, signore?" Carmella asked, touching Palmer's arm lightly.

"Yes," Palmer said, flicking his eyes over to Egidio. "But I apologize, signorina. I need to borrow Signore Dioli from you quickly."

"Whom?" Carmella's brow knotted.

Palmer motioned toward Egidio.

She turned and blinked, as if just noticing a man there. "Oh! Of course. Please."

"Thank you, signorina." Palmer gave another half bow. Perhaps he was overdoing it.

Egidio didn't move.

As quickly as possible, Palmer grabbed Egidio by the upper arm and shepherded him toward the grand doorway.

Egidio didn't seem to recover until their feet hit the tiles of the piazza. Then he jerked away. "What? What are you doing?"

"We have to get back before someone notices we're gone. Or recognizes us in there." Palmer pushed Egidio toward the temple.

"But..." Egidio looked back at the lit door behind them.

"What happened, anyway?" Palmer pushed him forward again.

"What?" Egidio looked at him.

"With Carmella. What did you do?"

"I... I told her she looked nice," Egidio still stumbled over the words, as if the very memory of the woman made him lose his senses.

"And?"

"She said, 'Thank you.'"

Palmer nodded, waited. "And... that was it?"

Egidio groaned. "Oh gods, Palm, I didn't know what to *say*. She's just so magnificent. My tongue ties itself in knots when I try to speak to her."

"Maybe you'd be better off with a letter." Palmer shook his head as he removed his formal jacket and took a deep breath of the hot night.

"A *letter*," Egidio yelped. "I'll write her a *letter*."

Palmer started to speak then just grabbed Egidio's arm with his free hand. "In the morning, Gio. Right now, we get back without waking the Seers."

"Chas!"

Brier spun, refraining from shaking her head. Off balanced, red-faced, Rush was, beyond a doubt, drunk. Someone would have to get him out of the party soon, at least before people could no longer pretend not to notice.

He caught Brier in a hug, nearly taking her off her feet before Leone appeared through the crowd and pulled him back. Rush nearly fell over entirely.

"Sorry, Chas. He got away from me." Leone gave an embarrassed smile, propping Rush up.

Brier smiled, attempting to smooth out her skirts with her palms. The metallic fabric fought back but eventually gave in. "You've been put in charge of him?"

"Happy birthday, Chas!" Rush caught himself as he began to tip, wrapping an arm around Leone's shoulders for support. "Our little girl is all grown up, Leo."

Leone dropped his voice. "Downed most of Nico's flask before we could stop him."

"I heard." Brier brushed her hand against the lump still hidden in her pocket, still tightly in place, before she crossed her arms. "Barely left me any. On my birthday, no less."

"Sorry, Chas." Leone forced Rush to stand straight again—at least as straight as Rush could manage. "I think Firth's still holding if you want to find him."

"Might do that in a bit." Brier nodded, scanning the crowd. "Know where he is?"

"Was with Carmella, last I saw him," Leone said. "She's in town, you know."

Brier scoffed. "Oh, I know."

"You're still the prettiest girl at the party, Chas," Leone assured her.

"Are you kidding?" Rush looked at Leone then Brier. "I mean, no offense, Chas. I'd do you—you know, if Guillroy wouldn't kick my ass—but, Leo, have you *seen* Carmella tonight?"

Brier slid her eyes toward Leone, arching an eyebrow.

Leone sighed. "I'll get him out of here. Be back once I get the kid to bed."

"What? I'm not... what?" Rush stumbled as Leone pulled him along, a full sentence never fully materializing.

Brier shook her head as she looked around the room. She easily spotted Firth, standing with the circle of men around a pink dress. She'd need more booze soon, but she didn't need it enough to head over there. Perhaps she'd make Nico get it for her. He actually seemed to be a man who could control himself with Carmella Huerta-Rey in the same room.

She looked for him, scanning the crowd for Nico's blond head. Near the stairs at the front, she found him, seemingly cornered by his father. Oh well, she could handle Orris Adessi-Guillroy better than Carmella Huerta-Rey. That was saying something.

Orris spotted her first as she approached, offering her a smile. "And there's our birthday girl. I was worried we had lost you to the crowd."

"It is quite a turnout." Brier smiled back sweetly.

"Of course, *dolcezza*." Orris took her hand, leading her between himself and Nico. "Have you been having a good time?"

"Of course," she lied.

"Good, good." He patted her hand. "Why don't you wait here for just a moment? We've been waiting to start the toasts."

"Wonderful." That lie didn't come as easily, but Orris didn't seem to notice.

Nico waited for his father to move away before talking. "Finish it?"

"Yeah." Brier turned slightly toward the wall, working the flask out of her pocket with as little movement as possible and sliding it back into Nico's hands. "Just enough, I think. Could use more."

"Yeah, Rush went to town."

"I saw." Brier looked out across the party.

"Bad?" Nico followed her gaze.

"Leone's taking him to sleep it off."

"Probably for the best."

She finally turned back to face him. "Word is Firth still has some."

Nico raised an eyebrow. "He didn't say he did. Have you asked?"

"He's fallen prey to the lovely Carmella." Brier frowned, finding the circle of suited men across the room.

"Ah, right. I heard she was around."

"I hadn't." Brier fixed him with a look.

Nico held his hands up. "Wasn't like it was my idea. I only heard about it this morning."

"From whom?"

"I don't remember," Nico said. "One of the guys. She came in for the party, I think. The Signora Huerta-Rey is around too."

"Interesting." Brier pressed her lips together.

Nico smiled, placing his hand at the small of her back. "I'll go see if he has any, all right? It's your birthday; I think you have commandeering rights."

Brier gave a tight smile, letting Nico work his way across the room. Taking a deep breath, she forced herself to release the fists she hadn't realized she'd made. As if getting up early to put in an appearance at the temple hadn't been bad enough, she'd also had to sit there, in her pew, after being blindsided by the Huerta-Rey clan in the front row. Perhaps she was feeling jealousy or something else, but whatever it was, Carmella's presence in the same room grated.

The circulating refreshment trays caught the light. Brier grabbed one glass and then another as an afterthought before the tray left. If she couldn't properly drink, she'd at least get her fill of the sweet iced juice they provided. She took a long sip and smiled. If only *zerbet* weren't so expensive, she'd just have it all summer to try to keep cool inside, at least.

More trays glinted as they caught the light, moving across the floor. Brier downed the rest of the first glass and drank the second more slowly as she studied the room. The number of trays seemed to be greater than it had the previous year, more than the glass per person Orris Adessi-Guillroy generally paid for. They'd gone all out, perhaps trying to impress the Huerta-Reys.

Her eyes swung over once again to the impromptu court being held across the room. Nico had Firth off to the side as they spoke, heads curved in toward each other for privacy. She glanced at Orris, beside the main doors, gathering his group of toast-givers, which included Gaspar Huerta-Rey this year.

She glanced back at Nico. Perhaps Orris had his sights on marriage. Nico wasn't through his schooling yet, but the Huerta-Reys would be a strong match. That would explain all the flash. Orris had tried to use his annual sponsorship of her birthday as a political statement every year since she was ten: *Look at how charitable we Adessi are, how connected to those* Innato *families who have been here since long before we* Savrio *swept in to save them thirteen years ago.* It would be just like him to try to use her birthday to marry Nico off to Carmella Huerta-Rey. That would also explain the man's exceedingly good mood.

Her stomach tightened at the thought. She gulped down more of the *zerbet*, praying Firth would come through. As nice as the ice was, she needed liquor, and she needed it soon. She placed the empty glasses on a passing tray and grabbed a third, earning a slightly skewed look from the waiter. She ignored it.

A clinking of silverware on crystal snapped her attention back to the top of the short set of stairs. Orris stepped forward, leaving the others, including her father, behind him. When Citron Chastain-Bochard had pulled himself away from the library was anybody's guess—likely not more than a few minutes before he had been pulled up there, knowing him. Brier could barely remember the last time she had seen her father anywhere but the rebuilt Augarian Library. Possibly at her last birthday. Catching his eyes, she offered a small smile. At least she could find a little comfort in always knowing where he was, even if it meant she'd be seeing him less and less, the more time she spent out with Nico rather than surrounded by books.

The room slowly fell silent, leaving just the sound of dresses sweeping over the floor as everyone turned to face the doorway.

Orris smiled, easy in front of a crowd, once again making it obvious just how much his son looked like him—tall, blond, and entirely self-assured. "Thank you, everyone, for coming to celebrate the birthday of our lovely Signorina Chastain-Bochard. Her father, Signore Chastain-Bochard, has asked me, as one of the backers of this event, to say a few words."

Brier took a sip of *zerbet*, glancing back to search for Nico and finding him still with Firth. The boys looked to be passing something off, though. At least she had some hope for liquor in her immediate future.

"As one of the first *Savrio* to take up residence in this lovely palace," Orris continued, as he did every year, "I have had the uncountable pleasure of seeing Signorina Chastain-Bochard grow from a bright little girl into a beautiful young woman. Thirteen years now." He took a dramatic pause—as if he couldn't comprehend how it had been so long—

perfectly timed for theatricality. "It seems like just yesterday we would find this little blond girl scampering into our reemergence meetings with my Nicodemo, seemingly trying to get themselves into trouble.

"Well, those times are well behind us now. Everyone has prospered under the peace that we have built from the ashes of the *Bugiardi*'s cruel reign, and Signorina Chastain-Bochard has left her scampering behind, becoming a beacon of grace, beauty, and decency, a reminder of what all of us should strive for in our daily lives, be it serving the gods or building a government capable of protecting such ideals."

Somehow, Brier refrained from rolling her eyes. She thanked the alcohol lingering in her system.

"And so, Signorina Chastain-Bochard," Orris continued, finally looking at her and lifting his glass. "We wish you yet another joyous year in your capital. May it be as bright as the last. *Salute*."

"*Salute*," the room echoed, glasses rising in whatever direction the drinker seemed to think Brier was and falling again as everyone drank.

Orris moved back to the group of men behind him, speaking to Citron in a low voice and allowing the room to absorb the toast before moving back to his place at the top of the stairs. Brier frowned. Orris always did enjoy hearing himself speak, but even he didn't normally monopolize the toasts with two in a row.

That time, he didn't bother clinking but simply stood, overlooking the crowd until they fell silent themselves. He took another moment, seeming to look from person to person before speaking again. "If I may steal your time for just another moment, Signore Chastain-Bochard has asked me to speak once more to add to this joyous occasion. Signorina Chastain-Bochard, if you wouldn't mind joining us?"

Brier froze for a moment and then slowly started up the steps, gathering her skirts in her free hand. Why had Nico taken so long getting her more to drink? Whatever the second toast was about, she had a feeling she would need more liquor.

Orris took her elbow lightly, leading her up beside him, and spoke low in her ear. "Smile. We have good news, I would hope."

Her stomach twisted again, unhappily, but she managed a smile all the same.

Orris looked back out at the crowd. "And my son? Nicodemo?"

Brier could see confusion flash over Nico's face, even across the room, before he coached it back into something he would find more fitting. He made his way through the crowd. As he shifted his arm slightly, she saw a bump smooth out in his coat pocket. So Firth had been holding out.

Nico took the steps two at a time, giving his father a questioning look before offering Brier a small shrug.

Orris glanced at Nico's empty hands and grabbed a glass for him before turning to speak again. "With this gathering of friends and family, Signore Chastain-Bochard and I have decided that we would take the opportunity to announce what we have long been discussing between ourselves. Long have the Chastains been a fixed staple in the Augarian, *Innato* scholars from long before the occupation, great enough to survive under the cruel *Bugiardi,* brilliant enough to thrive under the *Savrio* restoration. They are a great family, an old family, a noble family."

Brier slid her eyes from Orris to Nico to where her father had to be just past the corner of her sight, carefully keeping her smile in place. She had never heard Orris quite so laudatory about a "lower" family.

She wasn't sure she liked it.

"From our long discussions, we have come to one logical decision, that our children—as good friends as they have come to be, from such great families—could not be better suited for each other. With their permission"—Orris took Brier's hand with his right and Nico's with his left—"we announce their impending nuptials."

Brier's head snapped to Orris, the smile finally slipping under the chorus of *'salute'* and *'cin cin.'*

Orris didn't seem disturbed by her expression. He simply joined her and Nico's hands and then stepped back to his own drink.

Nico looked at his father, at the crowd, and then at Brier. She held his eyes, silently questioning. He offered another barely there shrug, apparently just as lost as she was, and lifted his glass. They would have to talk later.

CHAPTER FIVE

B RIER LANDED ON HER BED, hard, motioning Nico over.
"You know, you're going to have to say something sometime." Nico took a swig from the flask.

"I've said plenty," she said. "For example, 'Hand it over.'"

He went to hand her the flask but pulled it back. "How drunk are you?"

"Not yet enough." She grabbed it, took another swig, and made a face. "Firth always has the strongest stuff."

"That he does." Nico sat next to her and kicked off his shoes before sliding back onto the bed.

Brier sighed, and the room went silent for a long moment.

"But you are really going to have to say something."

She rolled her eyes, the room spinning with the movement. She nearly giggled. "About what?"

He gave her a look.

Brier fought the giggle away. "I just don't know what to say, Nic."

"In a bad way?" Nico watched her carefully, taking a quick drink when she met his eyes.

"Not necessarily." She waited for him to finish before taking the flask back. "I just don't know what your father's game is."

"His game?" Nico frowned.

She took a healthy drink and looked back at him as the entire room shifted around them. She smiled. "All right, I think I'm getting suitably drunk."

Nico rolled his eyes, took the flask, and set it aside. "What do you mean, my father's 'game'?"

"Just..." Brier kicked off her slippers and pulled at the laces of her dress as she sat up. "It just doesn't make any sense."

Nico waited for her to continue.

"I mean..." She stood to get the heavy dress off. She turned to face him as she fought with the laces, a little unsteady on her feet. "There's no reason for us. Why, when you're a Guillroy, would you marry your only son off to the librarian's daughter? Bochard is nothing to discount, I mean, but there's nothing advantageous to it. You marry a Rey. A Magalhaes, even, if there's something wrong with the boy and you're desperate. You don't marry a *Bochard*. What's the goal there? Extended reading hours?"

Nico still didn't answer.

She shrugged off the bodice, slipped out of her skirts, and hung the dress over the baseboard of the bed before looking at him. She placed her hands on her hips, over her thin shift. "Well?"

He shrugged. "I really don't know, Bri."

"Exactly." She pulled out her braids one by one, nearly tipping over when she lifted her arms too quickly. "It makes no sense. And, correct me if I'm wrong, but your father isn't known for doing things that don't make sense."

"I'm sure it will all become clear eventually." He looked up at the ceiling.

"I just don't like feeling as though I'm being played." She studied him when he didn't respond. "Why aren't you looking at me?"

His eyes came back to hers, though he didn't move his head. "Because we are both very drunk, and that means I'm going to have to be the responsible one."

"Because 'responsible' and 'Nico Adessi-Guillroy' have always been undeniably linked." Brier rolled her eyes, flopping back down on the bed. That was the way it had been—the two of them treading some invisible line they'd yet to cross—ever since they had been twelve or thirteen, whenever the childishness of Nico's sneaking into her room had suddenly evaporated. She had stopped it at kissing—and just very slightly more, if she was entirely honest—then and for months after.

Eventually, the point came when they had finally gotten drunk enough for her to stop saying no, but Nico had taken up the cause. Exactly why that was, she still didn't know.

The silence between them stretched on.

Brier let her head loll to the side as she looked at him. "You can't tell me any other thing in the world where you'd be worried about 'responsible.'"

"You want to be any other thing?" He cocked an eyebrow.

"Obviously, I'm not." She turned onto her side, almost giggling as the entire room felt as if it shifted. She tamped the laugh back down. "Orris Adessi-Guillroy wants me to marry his son."

"You don't think that's a good thing?"

"It makes no *sense*." Brier motioned widely, nearly hitting him. He caught her wrist as she continued, "Why? Why me?"

"Are you really expecting me to have any insight into what my father is thinking?"

Brier pouted, freeing her wrist from his grip. "I don't like it."

Nico studied her. "Hopefully, it isn't a problem with to whom you are intended."

Brier snorted. After years of being Nico's tagalong, the idea of suddenly being engaged—of being *married*—to him seemed nearly too absurd to even consider.

"Bri?"

She snapped back to their conversation, his face blurring for a moment as she tried to get her eyes to focus. "I've put up with you the past thirteen years, signore. I fully believe I could manage."

"Only put up with me, signorina?" He raised an eyebrow.

She grabbed for the flask, nearly rolling off the bed.

"Whoa there." Nico grabbed her shoulders. "I think you're suitably gone, Bri. Save a little for later."

She giggled, flopping onto her back once more. "All right, I'll give you that."

Nico nodded, the motion slightly uncontrolled. "Me too, I think. I'll have to ask Firth what he got."

"And have him get more." Brier pointed sharply into the air with her decree.

Nico looked at her for another moment then finally smiled. "Did you have a good party, at least? Barring my father's impromptu announcement... and the obvious."

Brier nodded, moving closer to him. "Thank you for finding me outside. I don't think I would have made it without that."

"You know I look out for you, Bri."

"You're good like that." She rested her head on his chest, feeling his hard body along hers.

Nico let her lie there for a long moment before speaking again. "Bri?"

"Hmm?" she asked.

"What did you see?"

She frowned, lifting her head. "See when?"

"During the eclipse," he said. "I know you told everyone nothing, but I was there. You saw *something*."

"I had a fit," she said, playing with his collar lightly, loosening his tie. "What do you think I saw?"

"Bri." He gave her a stern look, catching her hand as she moved to the top button of his shirt. "I may be drunk, but I know what I'm talking about."

Brier released a breath, not fighting his hold on her hand, taking a moment to formulate her thoughts. "Nothing, honestly."

He snorted.

"It's true," she insisted, meeting his eyes. "I saw the most literal sense of Nothing."

Nico frowned, raising an eyebrow.

"I don't know how else to explain it, Nico." Brier sighed, lying flat on her back again. "It was like the beginning and the end of the world all at once. A gaping abyss. Nothing. That's what I saw."

Nico continued to frown, either trying to digest her words through his drunken haze or simply not believing her. He studied her face. "A vision, you think?"

Brier yawned. "You think I'm a Seer now?"

"Well, what do you think it was?"

"I don't know, Nico. Something wrong with my head, I imagine. You're getting a broken woman for a wife, I hope you realize. The rot, seizures, some vague vision of destruction and creation? There's something wrong inside of me, Nic. I don't know if there's much more explanation for it than that." She rolled back toward him, feeling her body moving too loosely to be normal. "I don't know. Perhaps I'm dying."

"Don't say that."

"What if I am?" She looked at him. "I've thought it before. What if part of me died a long, long time ago? What if it's been rotting away inside of me while I keep on living? Perhaps that was the fit, that vision—the world trying to correct something that should have wilted away a long time ago."

"You aren't rotting, Bri." Nico frowned, his eyebrows knotted with more concern than she liked to see. "For one thing, if you were, I think people would smell you more than you them."

"Perhaps it's just not bad enough yet."

Nico touched her face, his thumb grazing her bottom lip. "There's something special about you, Bri. There's no doubt about that. I don't think it's that you're dying, though. Not more than in the sense that we all are, at least."

She finally smiled. "That's downright philosophical of you, Nic."

"Must be the liquor." Nico dropped his hand to grab the flask. He took a sip then looked at her. "You've really thought about that? That you're smelling yourself?"

She shrugged. "Your mind can get away from you when you're stuck spending every summer like you're in the back alley of a slaughterhouse."

He set the flask down, stroking her hair gently as he leaned against the headboard. He cleared his throat but then didn't actually speak.

"What?" she asked.

"I was just thinking..." he started then paused. "Do you think it comes from the fire?"

"The rot?"

He nodded. "Maybe not something dying in you but something that happened when you..."

"*Nearly* died?" she supplied.

He hummed. "Maybe something happened to your head then, something that's making all of this happen."

Brier's mind flitted over the pictures in her memory. The roof falling. The smoke. The painted tiles cracking. And nothing—the nothing that existed between the crack of the beam above her breaking and someone lifting her little five-year-old body out of the wreckage of the half-burnt library. She made a face. "You know, it undoubtedly did."

Palmer wiped at the sweat on his forehead, doing his best to refrain from scowling at the fire once again blazing in the center of the circle of chairs. The Tribunal—and whatever other powers there were—had his entire schedule turned around to get him making charts morning after morning, and he still had to sit around a fire in the middle of summer to learn "fire divination." Master Franco droned on, repeating the same things he had said the last time they had been in the room, the same things he had said every time they had been in that room—focus, clear minds, and visions. Palmer tuned it all out, focusing on the fire crackling. His eyes tried to drift shut, but he caught himself. Last time he'd let that happen, he'd drifted into battles and burning buildings. The last thing he needed was to hallucinate more fire.

Palmer's chair jerked, snapping him out of his thoughts. He looked at Alon next to him as he realized the man had kicked his chair's leg.

Master Franco's rather annoyed voice cut in, showing Palmer had missed something before Alon had alerted him. "Tash?"

"Yes?" Palmer asked, decorum lost for a moment with surprise. It had been a while since he had entirely filtered out his own name.

"If you would?" Master Franco motioned to the fire.

Palmer looked at the flames, gritting his teeth.

"What do you see?" Master Franco prompted.

Palmer stared, trying to come up with something that wouldn't lead to some grand analysis for symbolism.

"Focus."

Palmer opened his mouth, ready to spout whatever Danilo had said the last session about a bird. A log cracked. His vision shifted, throwing him out of the room. Heaving gray shapes surrounded him. Shadows swirled, fighting themselves. Metal clanged. Ghostly figures attacked and withdrew in waves. More shapes, more metal, a little girl. At least, it seemed to be a girl, a child at least. Everything swirled too much, refusing to become clear and offering nothing to latch onto.

The metallic clangor rose, becoming deafening.

Someone shouted.

Palmer realized it was himself.

The shadows retreated, blown away as if caught in a gust of wind, leaving him doubled over in the silence, clutching his ears.

"What was it?" Master Franco finally asked, his voice sounding a pitch too high.

Palmer blinked and lifted his head, looking at the faces staring back at him, shifting and grotesque in the firelight. He tried to catch his breath but couldn't in the heat.

"What did you see?" Master Franco asked, his voice stronger. He dropped down in front of Palmer, searching his face.

Palmer took a deep breath and choked on the smoke. "I'm sorry." He shot to his feet and ducked out of the room before anyone could stop him.

He rushed down the dark hall, threw open the door, and ran up the steps to the side yard. Feet crunching on the dirt, he blinked in the blinding daylight. Something clanged, making him spin, squinting into the distance. Nothing. Someone had dropped something in the bell tower, possibly. Nothing strange.

Still, his body remained on edge, waiting for some unseen foe. Something was wrong, something he knew just past the back corner of his mind but couldn't grasp.

A bird cawed, making him spin again.

"Tash?"

Turning a final time brought him face to face with Sage Lee-Parrino. Palmer froze. Master Franco peeked out from the doorway.

"If you wouldn't mind joining me?" the Seer asked kindly.

Palmer strongly suspected it wasn't truly a question. He nodded, not trusting his voice.

CHAPTER SIX

S AGE LEE-PARRINO'S SECOND-STORY OFFICE TOOK up the entire back wall of the temple offices, giving him a commanding view of the garden and dormitories otherwise hidden against the east wall of the Augarian. The sound of children, no doubt Wards of the Church, echoed up to them.

Sage Lee-Parrino didn't spare a second look, snapping the window shut before taking a seat in the large, cushioned chair behind his desk. He motioned to a smaller chair across from him. "Please, Tash, have a seat."

Palmer didn't argue, sliding into the carved chair like a scolded child. The carvings ran smooth under his palms as he looked around the room. Maybe it wasn't as opulent as the palace, but the richness still stood in stark contrast to the cells the bulk of the acolytes and lower Seers called home.

Sage Lee-Parrino looked at Palmer for a long moment, sizing him up before finally speaking. "Master Franco tells me you've had a vision."

Palmer didn't respond immediately. Finally, he said, "I don't know if I'd call it a vision, Sage. I think the heat and the smoke—"

Sage Lee-Parrino opened a drawer, pulled out a stack of papers, and let them land on the desk with a thump.

Palmer snapped his mouth shut midsentence.

"Do you know what this is, Tash?" Sage Lee-Parrino asked at Palmer's silence.

Palmer just shook his head.

"We keep files for each of our wards, start them before they even arrive." Sage Lee-Parrino laid his hand on top of the papers. "There are so many unfortunate, it is the only way we are able to decide whom we will train and who will return to Latysia once they reach their age."

Palmer looked at the file and then looked back at Sage Lee-Parrino.

"How old are you, Tash?"

"Nineteen," he answered.

Sage Lee-Parrino tented his fingers. "And you're hoping to complete a full course at university before you become a Seer, is that correct?"

Palmer took a moment and saw no reason to argue. "I have been."

Sage Lee-Parrino nodded, looking at the papers. "You don't seem to be doing poorly in any of your courses."

"I get by." Palmer didn't elaborate.

"You have been working with Sage Chmela-Parrino as well." Sage Lee-Parrino looked up at Palmer without lifting his head. "Doing charts?"

Palmer's shoulders tightened, suddenly defensive. "I was recently placed with him, yes."

"Do you know why?"

The question hung between them uncomfortably.

"I'm good with charts," Palmer finally said.

"And more than that, from what I see here." Sage Lee-Parrino motioned to the papers. "You have been with us since the Restoration?"

Palmer gritted his teeth. "Yes."

"After your father died in the battle."

Palmer nodded once.

"Such a shame." Sage Lee-Parrino shook his head, sitting back in his chair. "We took in quite a few wards after the battle, I'm sure you know."

Palmer didn't answer. It hadn't been a question.

"Not many have stayed." Sage Lee-Parrino put the file away. "It speaks to your talents that you have."

Palmer remained silent.

The Seer waited, sizing Palmer up once again. "You had visions as a child."

"No, Sage." Palmer didn't hesitate this time.

Sage Lee-Parrino frowned. "More than one caretaker reported you having predicted happenings in the dormitories. You have no recollection of that?"

Palmer shook his head. "No, Sage."

"And you've often scored well beyond your peers in divinations," Sage Lee-Parrino said. He waited for Palmer to speak then continued when he didn't, "None of your other classes score as highly, Tash. Do you have any explanation for that?"

Palmer paused. "I just end up being... right."

Sage Lee-Parrino leaned forward. "There is no reason to hide your gift, Tash."

Palmer sat silently, rubbing his hands in small circles against the chair's carved pommels.

The Seer released a sigh and sat back again. "Tell me what happened with Master Franco today."

Palmer looked away, trying to push the odd hallucination out of his mind, lest Sage Lee-Parrino try to convince him it was anything more than it was. "The heat and the smoke were too much for me, I think, Sage. I haven't been feeling well."

"What did you *see*, Tash?" By the sound of his voice, Sage Lee-Parrino's patience was wearing thin.

"Nothing," Palmer answered. "I didn't see anything."

Sage Lee-Parrino searched Palmer's face but finally nodded. "Why don't you take the rest of the day off, Tash. Go lie down. I'll alert the rest of your Masters."

Something snapped Brier awake, leaving her heart racing.

She sat up, looking around. Nothing seemed out of place, the shadows of her desk and chair and bureau all exactly where they had been when she had snuffed out the little oil lamp by her bed. Even the pair of overshoes Nico had gotten her for her birthday remained where she had kicked them off to one side of the bed. Her room didn't look as though anyone but her had been in it all day. Still she listened, her mind trying to understand what had woken her—someone outside or one of the cleaning girls trying to polish the marble palace floors much too late... or perhaps early. She glanced out her open window, trying to judge how close it might be to morning. Nothing made a sound, just her breathing in the silent night.

"Nico?" she finally asked, barely managing a whisper.

No. No matter how late or early it was, he'd likely not returned from Latysia yet. The boys rarely came back before dawn on nights when they went out into the city. She could go check his room a few halls away, she supposed. But even if he were there, he'd just laugh at her for getting scared enough of nothing to go running to him in the middle of the night.

A sound outside her window made Brier jump, the noise too loud in the quietness. She released a breath as the sound placed in her mind. Wings. An owl perhaps. Maybe that had woken her.

Scanning the room, Brier stood cautiously, padding across the tile floor to the window. The rest of the Augarian sat quietly outside, lights dim or nonexistent out as far as the Wall. If any people were up, they were getting their fill out in Latysia.

She leaned out the window, looking along the line of the roof, but saw no sign of a bird—at least, not that she could see.

Brier turned back toward her bed. Her mind had to be playing tricks on her. Or perhaps she really was going mad.

She froze. Something sharply astringent assaulted her nose, breaking through everything else. Her heart raced. *Smoke.*

Rushing to the door, she pulled it open. Dark, thick smoke poured in, engulfing her.

She stepped back. Her mind reeled, clouding over. She couldn't think, couldn't move. Something oddly sweet was mixed in with the acrid smoke and lingering rot. Her sight flickered, but rather than suffocating her, the cloud nearly left her feeling... drugged. She tried to turn, the world flickering around her.

Someone shouted. A door slammed. The world faded, and Brier's legs crumpled under her.

Palmer dreamed fitfully, the shadows haunting him into the night. He tried to focus, to understand, but they continued to change, shifting anytime he tried to get a solid look. The sensation felt like watching shadows on a cave wall. The objects were familiar and would make sense if he could get a proper look, but they just wouldn't hold still long enough for him to make any sense of them.

"You think his visions are real?"

Whispers broke through the dream. Palmer blinked in the darkness, trying to reorient himself in reality.

"They're... different, at least. The boy had an uncanny ability to predict happenings as a child. I spoke with a caretaker who was there when he first arrived. He would answer the door before people knocked, just know they were there before they had even made it to the steps."

"He hasn't made any predictions," the second voice said.

"His charts, though. He's a completely average student in his astronomy classes—not struggling, but no more than betas. But when it comes to astrology, plotting these predictions, he's more accurate than Seers who have been practicing forty years."

The second voice didn't respond.

"It is my estimation that the boy has gone so far as to repress his visions in his older years."

"But why?"

"Our training encourages their visions, anything that can be given. It doesn't teach them to control visions that come without being sought. I imagine they've overwhelmed him."

Moving as quietly as possible, Palmer slipped out of bed, cringing when the frame creaked. He waited a long moment before daring to stand. He moved to his door.

"So what do we do?" the second voice asked.

"We have to take this higher than you or me."

Palmer pressed his door open, just a crack.

Nothing.

He swung it open, looking both ways down the hall. Still, no one was in sight. Palmer looked up at the ceiling. Were they talking *above* his room? Or was he still dreaming? He squeezed an inch of skin between his fingers. It stung. So he was awake.

Maybe he was just losing his mind.

Something rustled. He leaned back out the door, squinting down the dark hallway. A low rumble filled his hearing. *Water.* He grabbed his robe off its hook and threw it on over his loose pants, not bothering with more clothing.

The rough stone floor scraped the bottom of his feet as he walked, growing damper and damper as he reached the door to the stairs. He stopped, looking at the door. Water glistened, seeping under the old oak. He grasped the handle and pulled it open, against his better judgment. The small stream trickled down the stairs, falling from the temple, not enough to soak his robe but enough to run over his feet and cold enough to make them cramp.

Palmer shivered. Sure, the cells were known to flood, but never when the Rumano River was running so low.

Palmer started up the stairs, careful to fully plant each foot before shifting his weight to the next, the stones feeling too slick under the stream of water.

He pressed against the door at the top of the stairs, half expecting a torrent to rush down upon him from the sanctuary on the other side.

Nothing was there, just the same trickle of water, running down the wall from even higher up the stone wall. He slid his eyes up the seam of the wall, trying to see the source. The sanctuary was too dark. He couldn't see high enough.

His robe caught, throwing him backward. He landed hard in the water, stunned. A shadow descended and grabbed him. He slid, kicking, trying to recover.

Rolling, he broke free and pulled himself upright. He looked around but found nothing.

He was losing it.

Palmer's robe jerked back again, sending him into a wall with a sickening crack. Pain shot from his left shoulder, and he nearly doubled over. His legs were swept out from under him. He fell forward. Unable to move his arm, he felt his body twist and crashed face-first into the floor. His arm flopped beneath him, bent unnaturally, useless.

Pain filled his head, making the room spin. He blinked, sinking, drowning in the pain. His vision dulled, the shadow moving over him as his body went limp.

CHAPTER SEVEN

T HE SOUND OF FLAPPING WINGS made Brier stir. Wings again. Slowly, her eyes blinked open, forced to focus. She froze. Something wasn't right. Sweeping her eyes around the room, she felt a pressure building in her chest. Though the same size, with a similar large window to one side and a door to the other, the room she was in was certainly not hers. Smooth wooden boards had replaced the carefully tiled floor. The posts around her bed were missing, leaving just a large headboard. Even the sheets were wrong, the linen heavier, rougher than her summer silk.

Carefully, Brier slid out of the bed, letting her feet rest on the wooden floor for a long moment before attempting to stand. Barefoot, in just a shift, Brier felt remarkably... light, bouncy, even insubstantial. A breeze made her shiver, and a realization hit her. The air was cold.

She rushed to the window, her heart catching uncomfortably for a beat at the sight. The tall walls, grand buildings, and even the gentle green and brown hills she had seen over the Augarian walls were gone, replaced by jagged mountains, white peaks gracing the tallest of them. And she was high off the ground. She couldn't bring herself to step onto the small balcony outside the window-door, afraid of seeing just how high.

As she backed away from the window, her legs bumped a low chair, a cheerful maroon robe folded in the middle of it.

She picked it up, wrapping herself in the thick fabric without question. As the chill abated, she stood silently, debating what to do. The room was nice, and the clothing given her was the right size, expensive clothing at that. If she had been kidnapped, her abductors at least seemed to be planning on treating her well.

She wondered if she hadn't been kidnapped at all. Thinking back on the eclipse, the doctor, the smoke, the new lightness she was feeling... Perhaps she had died. Perhaps this was the gods' plane. The hereafter.

Unsure of any other options she might have, Brier moved toward the door, the robe whispering lightly on the floor. The handle turned easily, and the door opened with a light creak at not much more than a touch. Hesitantly, Brier stepped into the hallway.

"H-hello?" she called, her voice barely breaking a whisper.

A raven flapped over her head, making her shout. She ducked, watching it fly down the hallway and around the corner.

Brier pressed a hand to her chest, her heart racing. Perhaps she wasn't dead after all. Peering after the raven, she turned, staring down the hallway in the opposite direction.

The building felt old. Outside the room, the floor turned to stone, cold against her bare feet. Matching, rougher gray stones lined the wall, curving to a point directly above her in an oblong arch, wooden beams supporting each side high above her head. The architecture was nothing like the square, airy buildings in the Augarian, yet for all the stone and wood, it didn't feel dark or even closed in, just old... and chilled. After the heat and rot, she couldn't find herself begrudging the temperature in the slightest.

She came to another hallway, hers intersecting it at a T. Pressing herself up against one of the rough walls, she slowly stuck her head around the corner. Nothing seemed distinguishing about either side of the hallway, just more stone and a few doors. She took a step forward, leaving herself visible from all three ends of the halls.

Gathering her courage, she tried again. "Hello?"

Just barely her normal volume, the word seemed too loud. She half expected it to echo. She looked around. No one was there, not even the bird. Perhaps she wasn't dead but just trapped in a nightmare, a dream of being lost in a cold maze—a castle with nobody and nothing in it, just a never-ending set of twisting halls.

She turned, the robe swinging around her feet, and tried more loudly. "Hello?"

A rattle made her jump, followed by a muffled voice from one of the rooms down the hall.

She moved toward it. "Hello?"

"In here." The voice became clearer the closer she drew to the room. It seemed nearly familiar.

A feeling of trepidation washed over her. If she was in a nightmare, opening the door would undoubtedly lead to nothing good.

She called back, "Where?"

"Here." The door shook again. "I'm locked in."

Then again, a shock might be enough to wake her up. She reached out and touched the curved handle. Again, it turned without issue. She pulled, finding herself face to face with that young man from the party. She searched for his name, but as he was short with dark hair and eyes, he looked like half the *Innato* men she had ever met.

"Brier?" Her name seemed to come out of his mouth before he could consider it.

His name came to her much more slowly. "...Signore Tash, right?"

He hesitated before nodding. "Palmer. They got you too?"

"They who?" Brier frowned.

"The..." He seemed to be at a loss for the proper word and just shook his head. "How did you get the door open?"

"I just turned the handle." Brier looked at the door blankly.

"Must have locked it from the inside." Palmer went to try the inner handle, but his hand stopped short with a hollow thump as if running into an invisible drum. He pulled his hand back sharply, carefully trying to reach out again. His hand stopped, just in line with the doorframe. "What the...?"

Brier watched in something between fascination and terror.

Palmer shifted, favoring his left arm.

Brier looked, noticing the simple sling. "Are you hurt?"

He didn't address her question, using his good arm to push on whatever was keeping him inside the room. Even leaning all his weight into the doorway, he remained in place, supported by an invisible force.

"What is it?" Brier asked.

"It..." He straightened, looking at the empty space, perplexed. "Feel. There's... something."

Brier reached out hesitantly, inching her hand forward toward the doorway. She felt only air, pushing forward until her hand was properly inside the room. She pulled back, looking at him.

"You don't feel it?" Palmer swung his right hand forward, hitting whatever was keeping him in the room with his palm. Another loud thud resounded.

"No." Brier moved forward, putting her hand through again before finally stepping into the room.

"Don't!"

Brier froze, just inside the doorway, looking at Palmer.

"You… may not be able to get out," he mumbled.

Brier looked back at the doorway and then at Palmer. "Did it hurt to touch it?"

He shook his head.

Brier reached her hand out, ready to hit something solid at any second. She still felt nothing. Her hand went straight through. Brier stepped through the door, back into the room, out again. She looked at Palmer and shrugged.

He reached his good arm out. It rebounded with a twang.

Brier looked each way down the hall and stepped back inside the room. "I don't like this place."

"Can't imagine why," Palmer said sarcastically.

She flicked her eyes over at him.

"Sorry."

They looked at one another.

"What happened to your arm?" Brier finally asked.

He opened his mouth.

Another flapping of wings made Brier spin. The same raven landed outside the door, its head bobbing.

Brier frowned at it, waving her hands. "Shoo, shoo."

It flapped.

"Get!" She moved to the doorway, batting at it.

The bird cawed once, the sound echoing down the hall before it finally flapped away.

"Damned bird's been stalking me." Brier brushed her hands on her robe, turning back to Palmer. She frowned at his raised eyebrows. "What?"

"Just, I didn't take you for the type of girl to swear."

She cocked her own eyebrow in a way that would make Nico proud. "What kind of girl did you take me for?"

"More..." Palmer hesitated. "Genteel, I suppose."

Brier snorted. "With the boys I grew up with, I assure you I can swear much more than that."

Palmer gave a tight smile and looked away.

Someone cleared his throat just outside the doorway. Palmer tensed as Brier spun.

The man in the hallway studied both of them. They studied him right back.

Brier had to admit the man was well built. In his mid-thirties or so, he had a strong face with striking blue eyes and dark hair going gray right around his temples. Still, something was unsettling about him. Nearly subconsciously, Brier took a step back toward Palmer as if he would be able to fight with his arm in a sling.

"I'm going to have to request that you move a little farther back into the room," the man said, a good-natured smile on his face.

Neither Palmer nor Brier moved.

"I'm afraid I'm really going to have to insist," he said.

Without looking at each other, Palmer and Brier shifted, each taking just a few steps toward the far side of the room, not getting too close to the large window.

"Thank you very much, signore, signorina." The man held a hand out as if he were going to bow. He touched something on the wall, soft whirring buzzed in the room, and the man stepped through the doorway. "Very sorry to have kept you. We believed it was for the best to allow you to sleep. You have both been through a lot."

Palmer and Brier just looked at him.

"Would you care to have a seat?" The man motioned toward the bed.

Brier hesitated.

"Not until you tell me what's going on," Palmer said, his jaw clenched.

The man studied him for a long moment. "Tell me, what can you hear?"

Brier watched as the dark look on Palmer's face turned to surprise then turned dark again.

She just frowned.

"No need to look so serious, signorina," the man said. "We certainly do not mean you harm."

"What are we doing here?" Palmer asked, his hurt arm angled back, his stance defensive.

The man took a moment then finally spoke. "Simply put, you are both here because you are special."

"Special," Palmer repeated.

"Yes." He smiled, showing a line of straight, white teeth. "Special." The man didn't seem to think more explanation was necessary.

Brier cleared her throat. "I'm sorry, but... what?"

The man released a breath. "Are you sure you wouldn't care to sit, signorina?"

"We're fine." Palmer didn't give her a chance to say differently.

The man looked between the two of them but nodded again. "Well then, first I have to say that we have been looking for you both a long time."

Brier clenched her hand, bunching the robe tightly inside it, but otherwise didn't move.

"We have been trying to find you to enlist your help."

"Our help doing what?" Brier beat Palmer to the question that time.

The man caught her eyes and held them steadily. "I need you to remember, signorina."

Brier frowned. "Remember what?"

"Remember who you are."

Brier tensed, moving a little behind Palmer. "I know who I am."

"And who is that?"

"Brier Chastain," she said. "Brier Chastain-Bochard."

"No," the man said simply.

"What do you mean 'no'?" Brier bristled, her voice becoming stronger. "That's who I am."

"Do you remember a fire, signorina? About a decade ago or so?"

Brier's chest constricted. She didn't trust herself to speak.

"Amazing that a young girl survived it, don't you think?"

"Tiles fell," Brier said. "They shielded me."

He looked at Palmer. "And you, signore. You nearly drowned, no? About the same time."

Palmer didn't answer, instead eyeing the man cautiously.

The man looked between the two of them. "Simply put, the both of you are not who you originally were. The original Brier Chastain died at five, Palmer Tash at six. And in those deaths, you were reborn. A freak chance of tragedy and need."

Brier moved back farther, noticeably placing Palmer between them now. "You're mad."

The man seemed unperturbed. He looked at Palmer's arm. "That must hurt."

"I assume I have you to thank for it." Palmer continued to glare.

"No," he said. "I have reprimanded Cerise, though. I believe she was a little rougher with you two than need be."

"A girl didn't do this." Palmer motioned toward his shoulder.

"You haven't met Cerise," the man answered.

"What do you mean we died?" Brier asked, wanting to take another step back but concerned about backing herself into the wall.

He looked at her, his blue eyes seeming to freeze her to the floor. "Brier, the original Brier, suffocated in that fire." His eyes flicked to Palmer. "The original Palmer drowned." He looked back at Brier. "Normally, that would have been the end of it. People die every day. But something happened in your case. With everything crashing down around you, your souls were unleashed, melded into the life you still found in the children."

Brier's brow furrowed at his nonsensical words. She glanced at Palmer, trying to judge if he understood any more than she did.

Palmer spoke before she could catch his eye. "Who do you think we are?"

"Everything," the man said, looking at Palmer. Then his eyes slid to Brier. "And Nothing."

"Goebel, darling, you're going to frighten them." A tall, blond woman strode into the room, petting the raven, perched on her forearm.

Brier narrowed her eyes. With a hop, the raven cawed and flew away back down the hall.

The woman watched it go before looking at Brier with a raised eyebrow. "Making friends already, I see."

Brier pulled herself up to her full height, trying to match the tall woman while meeting her unnaturally dark eyes. "Is that... thing yours?"

"Rocco?" She looked after the raven again. "I think he'd be very insulted at being referred to that way."

"I told you I would call when we were ready for you," the man, Goebel, said.

"Well, you obviously need me. Look at the child's face. You're scaring her."

"I'm not a child," Brier said, finding something irksome about the woman's easy demeanor. The woman couldn't have been more than five years older than Brier anyway.

"Cerise." The man gave the woman a withering look.

"Cerise?" Brier frowned, glancing at Palmer and back at them. "*She* broke his arm?"

"Clavicle," Cerise said, looking downright amused by the fact. "He took a bit of a harder hit to that shoulder than I'd planned."

"That certainly wasn't you," Palmer said.

"Oh, don't feel too bad, Kos." Cerise winked. "I take many forms."

"Cerise," Goebel hissed.

She lifted her hands innocently and held her peace.

The room fell silent.

"You kidnapped us," Brier finally said.

Goebel took a moment. "*Kidnapped* is an ugly word."

"What word would you use?" Brier watched him, her voice stronger, certainly stronger than she felt.

"*Saved*, I would say."

Brier raised her eyebrows. "Saved us by kidnapping us?"

"Signorina, you are free to go, should you like. We would not be able to keep you captive if we tried."

Brier frowned.

Goebel turned to Cerise. "Set the barrier."

"With you inside?" Cerise didn't move.

"Just for a minute."

Cerise shrugged, walked outside, and pressed something on the door. The same whir buzzed through the room again.

No one moved.

"Handy device." Goebel walked to the door and slapped the seemingly empty doorway with a flat palm. It thumped, stopping short. He looked back across the room. "Type of shield. Fuses the air together. You're familiar, Signore Tash." He hit the shield again as if for added emphasis.

Palmer didn't answer.

"Signorina, if you would." Goebel motioned toward the doorway.

Brier just stared at him, unwilling to get too close.

"I'm unarmed." He held his hands out. Wearing just a button-down shirt and dark pants, he didn't seem to have many places to hide a weapon.

She touched her own robe, wishing for something useful under it, something more than a thin nightgown. Glancing at Palmer, she moved forward, stopping out of arm's reach.

Goebel placed both hands on the shield, leaning all his weight against it. "If you please, signorina."

Brier moved forward, one tiny step at a time. Slowly, she reached out, feeling for the shield. Again, her hand passed straight through the doorframe. She stretched out her fingers then pulled her hand back sharply.

Goebel hit the shield again, letting her hear the reverberation. He looked at her. "Go ahead. Step through."

Brier glanced at the woman outside and shifted uncomfortably. She really was frighteningly beautiful.

Goebel followed her gaze to look at the woman. "Cerise, back up."

Cerise cocked an eyebrow but took an exaggeratedly large step back.

He looked back at Brier. "Signorina?"

Brier took a step forward, rocking back and forth through the doorway, not even a tug telling her something might be there.

She stepped back into the room and moved away from Goebel, never taking her eyes off him.

He took his hands off the shield. "You can turn it off now, Cerise."

"I don't know," she said. "You've been so rude to me, maybe I should leave you in there with them for a few hours."

Goebel released a breath. "No one finds you amusing, Cerise."

After another pause, the whir came again, and Cerise moved back into the room. Goebel looked at Brier. "It's the strongest thing we've managed to make. If that can't contain you, we have no hope to force you to remain here."

"Who are you?" Brier ran her eyes over him.

"The more important question is, who are *you*, signorina."

"I told you." Her voice sounded petulant even to her own ears.

"And I told you," Goebel said. "You are *Nothing*, signorina—the very embodiment of Nothing. Chaos."

She didn't respond.

"It's why we can't hold you against your wishes," Goebel said. "It's possible to keep something in a room. You can't keep Nothing."

Brier looked among the people around her, from Palmer to Goebel to Cerise and then back at Palmer.

The young man walked closer to her, his energy radiating strength and support.

"As that is the case," Goebel continued, grasping his hands behind his back. "We respectfully request you choose to stay with us, at least for the time being."

Brier still didn't answer.

He looked at Palmer. "You, signore, we could keep you, but we likewise request you stay."

"You think I'm 'Nothing' too?" Palmer asked sarcastically.

"You are Everything. Kosmos." Goebel looked between the two of them. "Kosmos and Chaos, two parts of the same whole. Order and Mayhem. Everything and Nothing."

Palmer and Brier shared a look. Palmer's raised eyebrows clearly said he was questioning Goebel's and Cerise's sanity.

"Your hearing, Signore Tash," Goebel said, "it is better here?"

Palmer looked at him, the look on his face wavering for just a second.

"Your sense of smell, signorina?"

Brier frowned herself, unsure how to answer.

"Ruhegipfel is special," Goebel said. "Everything should feel better for you here, both of you." When neither answered, he looked back at Palmer. "Your shoulder, for example, signore. Even untrained, I'm sure that would heal for you."

Palmer frowned.

"Indulge me?"

Palmer just continued to glare.

"Well," Goebel still managed to smile, "if you get the time. Just focus on that healing. We'll see where you stand on that." When neither of them responded for a final time, Goebel turned to Cerise. "I think we're done here for now."

The woman nodded.

He looked back at Brier and Palmer. "All I ask is for you to think about what I've said."

Without another word, the two swept out of the room, shutting the door behind them. Brier listened but heard no whir that time, no click. Their captors—or hosts?—hadn't bothered to lock them in.

Neither spoke for a long moment.

"They're mad," Palmer finally said, moving to the window and pushing it up.

A cold wind blew in. Brier wrapped the robe more tightly around herself, her mind turning as she tried to make sense of the entire situation. "What did he mean about your hearing?"

Palmer didn't look at her. "We wouldn't be able to get down this way. It's a sheer drop, at least ten stories with that cliff."

"Are you ignoring me?" She frowned.

He glanced at her and went back to studying the landscape. "It isn't important."

"Answering me?"

"My hearing," he said.

She watched him for another moment and decided she still needed to know. "Tell me."

Palmer sighed, shutting the window again with a click. The chill lingered behind. He looked at Brier. "My hearing is wrong. I only hear one thing at a time, whatever my mind believes is the most important in the room. Like, say a Seer is giving a lecture and there's a bird chirping outside the window. Most people would hear both. I only get one or the other."

"Annoying," she said.

"Can be," he said. "Depends on how boring the lecture is."

Brier managed a weak smile. "But not here?"

Palmer pressed his lips together and shook his head quickly.

"My problem's always been smell," Brier said, letting him get back to searching the room. "Every summer, the smell is awful. The physicians could never find a reason for it."

"I never told anyone about mine."

"Oh, I never would have if I had known it wasn't normal." Brier crossed her arms. "To me, everyone was smelling rot every summer. But no, just me." She paused. "Maybe it really *was* me."

Palmer looked up from tracing one of the seams between the stone blocks making the wall. "What?"

"I always sort of worried that I was smelling myself rotting. If he's right, if we died, maybe I was right."

"We aren't dead." Palmer frowned. "They're obviously deranged—one more reason we need to get out of here."

Brier looked across the room. "The door isn't locked."

"They'll be watching that, no doubt."

Brier watched him go back to examining each of the other windows in the room. "So, you plan to climb out a window, down a sheer rock face—all with a broken shoulder—into a mountain pass with no food, no water, no other supplies, no clue where you *are*, and... what, exactly? Start walking until you find a town? Or die?"

Palmer didn't answer but stopped studying the mountains.

"*Do* you know where we are?" Brier asked, motioning out the window. "Nothing out there looks like Latysia to me, not by a long shot."

Palmer didn't move for a long moment but then finally released a breath and sat heavily on the bed. "We can't stay here. Who knows what they're planning on doing with us."

"Build a temple to honor us, from the sound of things." Brier looked toward the doorway.

Palmer managed a weak laugh.

Brier moved toward him. "Signore Tash—"

"Palmer, please." He didn't look at her. "I'm not really a *signore*, anyway. Just Tash, if you prefer."

Brier studied the side of his face as she sat next to him. "Palmer, then. Easier than you calling me Chastain-Bochard, at least, if we were to go by last name."

"I could call you *signorina* if you prefer," he said.

"We've both been kidnapped and are being held the gods know where by people who seem to think we are the physical embodiments of some… metaphysical concept." Brier crossed her arms. "I think we're past the point of strict formalities."

Palmer gave a nodding shrug. "You want me to just call you Brier, then?"

"It is my name." She looked at the door again. "Allegedly."

"I'm sure it is," Palmer said.

The room went silent.

"Palmer," Brier said.

"Yeah?"

"Your name is Palmer."

He frowned. "Is that odd?"

"You are *Innato*, then?" She looked at him. "It's not a *Savrio* name."

He paused then nodded. "Born in Latysia. Lived in town until my mother died. Entered the Augarian after the Reclamation."

"Ward of the Church?"

He nod-shrugged again.

"And then you stayed on."

"As an acolyte," he supplied.

"You must be very talented."

"So they tell me."

Brier studied him, trying to decipher his tone. For the first time, she realized he was shirtless under the wrap and sling. "Aren't you cold?"

"No, actually." He shook his head, paused. "Is it making you uncomfortable? There's a robe—"

"It's fine," Brier cut him off. "I can't imagine it would be easy to get anything on with your arm right now."

Palmer nodded.

Shifting on the bed, Brier pulled her feet up under herself, her entire body buried under her robe. "So what are we going to do?"

Palmer raised a questioning eyebrow.

"I'm assuming we aren't planning that daring window escape, so we need to plan something."

Palmer took a breath. "Let's look at what we have. We're here, in the mountains. We don't know exactly where we are or how far we are from Latysia. I'm hurt. We don't have any supplies." He looked at her, pursing his lips slightly. "I'm going to assume you don't have a lot of experience camping?"

Brier didn't deny it, shaking her head.

"So, heading out the door and walking is out," he said.

"Unless we have a death wish."

Palmer made a face that said he didn't disagree. "Though sitting around here could possibly not be much better."

Brier frowned. "You think they're going to kill us?"

"They're clearly insane," Palmer said. "It's certainly possible. Who says releasing Chaos and What-Not doesn't eventually involve cutting us open?"

Brier winced.

"Sorry."

Brier pressed her lips together into a thin line, looking back at the door cautiously. "But..."

Palmer waited for her to continue.

"But." Brier looked back at him. "What if they're right?"

"And we're dead children holding the essence of... whatever?"

Put that way, it did sound rather insane. Brier shrugged. "I've always felt odd. It would explain a lot."

"I think everyone feels odd," Palmer said. "It's called being human."

Brier hummed, tapping her fingers on the mattress by her thigh. "I've always been an extra level of odd. I don't know about you, but me..."

Palmer shook his head but didn't debate it.

"Well," Brier continued, "we can't walk out of here. I doubt anyone knows where we are, to send rescue. We're at least here until we can find a map somewhere. We might as well hear them out, don't you think?"

"Strange things can happen when you're being held in a room being told things as though they're true," Palmer said. "I've seen it happen in classes. You can start believing things when you know you shouldn't. Words can just... work their way into your head like the truth."

"Well..." Brier played with the edge of her robe in her lap. "We'll just have to be careful."

CHAPTER EIGHT

BRIER HAD TO ADMIT IT: she liked the cold. Whereas Palmer didn't seem to feel it, Brier reveled in it. Starting high on the side of the mountain, the snow line sat not much farther up than Ruhegipfel, leaving something Brier had never before seen in her lifetime gleaming just outside her window every morning. After over a week of living and training there, she still couldn't take her eyes off it.

Everything about Ruhegipfel left her feeling light and invigorated. That sensation was almost worth having been kidnapped.

"Signorina, *please* pay attention."

Brier forced herself to stop staring out the window.

Goebel looked back, exasperated. "Have you been listening?"

"Is there always snow?" Brier asked. "All through summer?"

"Signorina." Goebel crossed his arms.

"Just answer her question, and we can move on." Palmer glanced up from the book in his lap solely with his eyes, on his face the same entirely displeased look that had been there since Brier had convinced him to attempt "training." Well, he'd also been partially convinced by seeing tall, blond Cerise turn into a little dark-haired boy before walking—phasing, Goebel had called it—through a table. As much of a skeptic as Palmer seemed to be, seeing a woman transform, multiple times, in the middle of a dining hall left little room for argument.

Goebel sighed. "Yes. It rarely gets warm enough this high up to melt it."

A raven flapped into the room and landed on a rafter. Brier frowned at it, getting a better look. Just Rocco. They seemed to have escaped eavesdropping shapeshifters for the moment. She turned back to Goebel. "I'm about to wring that bird's neck if it keeps following me around."

"I'd sincerely advise against it." Goebel took a seat across the room from her. "Now, would you care to try, signorina?"

Brier blinked. "Try what?"

"Dissolving something, I imagine," Palmer said.

Brier looked at him then back at Goebel.

Goebel pinched the bridge of his nose. "Please, signorina, you need to *pay attention*."

Brier straightened, mockingly intent. "Go ahead, signore. You have my *undivided* attention."

"We need to see to what extent we can control your powers." Goebel pushed a lit candlestick forward. "Signorina?"

Brier released a breath and focused on the flame. Nothing happened.

"Stop focusing on the light," Goebel said. "Focus on the nothing around it."

Brier glanced up at him then looked back down, trying to wrap her mind around what he meant. She looked around the flame, at nothing, at the air around it, shimmering with heat. Slowly, she imagined pushing the air back in on itself, closer and closer to the flame. A resistance started to build in her head, something tight and springy. The fire pushed back, but she continued constricting it, tighter and tighter. Slowly, the flame began to flicker and dance, desperate against its new confines. It finally lost its fight, disappearing into nothing. Brier continued to look at the now-dead candle, the smoke disappearing as soon as it touched her confines. Nothing pushed down further. A little at first, and then more and more, the stick began disappearing as though the top of it had never been.

"Let go," Goebel instructed.

Brier's focus broke. She snapped her eyes back up to him and started, finding him directly in front of her, seemingly out of nowhere.

He smiled at her, his face warm, and touched her shoulder lightly. "Very good, *Schatzi*."

Brier frowned, feeling Palmer's tension more than seeing it. She glanced at him—still entranced with his book—before looking back at Goebel. "*Schatzi*. What language is that?"

Goebel seemed to snap out of his thoughts and moved to a chair across the room. "Hmm?"

"It isn't Latysian," Brier said.

"No," he said. "I speak a few languages."

"What language is *that*, though?"

Goebel hesitated, just for a second. "Almanian, signorina. We've had many visitors here through the years. I've learned quite a bit from them."

Palmer's head finally rose, and an awkward silence took the room. Brier could only wonder if the information meant more to Palmer than it did to her, for the language did nothing to help her narrow down where they might be on a map.

Goebel cleared his throat. "You have both done well today. Why don't we finish early? Perhaps Cerise will show you the way up to the snow to see it for yourself, signorina."

"I think she'd be just as likely to dump it on top of us as let us look," Brier said, doing her best to hide the contempt in her voice and barely managing.

Goebel laughed. "If you're lucky, that's all she'd do, I would think. I'm glad you have learned Cerise quickly."

"Nankil," Palmer finally said. "She's the Raven."

Goebel raised an eyebrow.

"From these myths," Palmer clarified, tapping the cover of his book, using his good arm. "If we are what you say we are, we are the dawn of creation. Chaos, the void from which everything came. Kosmos, order from nothing, everything. The gods embodying creation and destruction, the alpha and the omega.

"But in these stories, they aren't alone for long. The trickster, the Raven, he, she, it is the spark that starts what we know as life and is the messenger between it all, who connects the gods to life." Palmer lifted his eyes to the raven on the rafters.

It remained still but cocked its head to one side as if it understood it was being discussed.

Palmer looked back at Goebel. "A being necessary but damaging all in one. Its own duality. Its own importance. Cerise."

Goebel smiled. "You have been studying."

"I don't sleep well, nights," Palmer said.

"Well, I imagine you won't need to much at all, soon." Goebel moved to the bookshelf on one wall, running his fingers over the spines. He found what he was looking for, pulled the book out, and turned back to Palmer. "You are the creator and the protector. What good is a protector while he sleeps?"

Palmer shook his head. "I'm still human."

"The more you learn to control your powers, the more your body will accept them. You'll be able to choose what you hear, for example, even multiple things at once, rather than blocking out everything simply because your mind can't handle the onslaught. Your body will heal if you let it." Goebel handed Palmer the book. "Look at 'Healing' if you're up tonight. 'Thought Reading and Omniscience' after that while you're at it."

Palmer took the book silently.

"He's omniscient?" Brier pointed.

"He is Everything," Goebel said. "He knows what he wants to know. Or at least, he will once he is able to filter through everything to get to what he wants to know. It's more a matter of control than ability."

Brier looked at the book, at Palmer's face, at Goebel. "Am I?"

Goebel smiled at her. "Not as far as I am aware, signorina. You will just have to settle yourself with all that you *can* do instead. And in all honesty, from what I have seen, those things will appear much more impressive."

Brier met his eyes and frowned, trying to discern what she was seeing behind them.

He turned away too quickly.

"What is it that I can do?" she asked his back.

"Some good things... and more than a few bad," Goebel said.

Her eyebrows furrowed. "Bad things?"

"Well, signorina." He turned around to face her. "He's the protector. From what do you think he is protecting?"

Brier's heart rate spiked, her nerves lighting up all at once. She didn't answer.

"Both of you are absolutely essential to the world," Goebel said, "essential to each other. But where there is creation, there must be destruction. It's why we're pushing Signore Tash harder than you, in all honesty, signorina. If we push you too far too quickly, there could be catastrophic results. It would have been preferable if we could have trained you from a much younger age, but we will do the best with what we are given."

"What sort of catastrophic events?" Palmer asked.

"Well, the last time something went wrong with Chaos, we lost the East Wing."

"Last time?" Brier frowned.

Goebel hesitated, a vague look of pain crossing his face before he managed another smile for her. "You are as old as time itself, signorina. You can't imagine this has been your only incarnation."

"You've trained people before, then?" Brier asked.

"Not just 'people.' My family has trained *you* before, signorina—several times throughout the ages, at this point. It is your memory that is gone, not your past."

A million questions raced through Brier's mind, but she couldn't figure out how to ask one.

Palmer just nodded, the same look of confusion on his face.

Goebel looked between both of them. "Have a good afternoon. I'll see you both at dinner."

Brier watched Goebel make a quick retreat, letting himself out of the library without another word. She looked at Palmer. "What was that about?"

Palmer shrugged, his bad shoulder seeming to move more than it had the past few days. "I have no idea."

A squall howled against the windows, shaking the glass. Brier lay awake, listening to the havoc.

Hail. The ice began to ping off the glass, growing louder and louder as the wind caught it, driving it toward the building. She finally sat up. Taking a deep breath, Brier looked at the window. With the moon blocked out, her room was pitch black, with not even a fire in the distance suggesting anything existed beyond her own body.

Fumbling for a match, Brier lit the candle on her nightstand, the small flame not reaching the far corners of the room. She slid out of bed all the same, pulling on her robe and finding her cloth slippers before picking up the candle and moving toward the door.

Part of Brier had become used to Ruhegipfel's emptiness—it was something she should like, she supposed, all things considered—but still, their light occupancy seemed... wrong. So far, Brier had counted at least sixty rooms in the old castle. Who knew how many more were out past those.

She had never realized how used to the bustle of the Augarian Palace she had become. With so many living and working inside it, she knew of only two, maybe three, rooms that consistently lacked occupants.

A wave of homesickness shot through her. Were people looking for them? Probably for her, at least. Palmer couldn't have been the first acolyte to disappear into the night, not with the decadence of Latysia beckoning no more than a few hundred yards outside their dormitories. The Church couldn't look for all of them.

But her... Her father would be worried sick. He or Nico or another Adessi might even send search parties out into Latysia, looking for her, wondering if news of her sudden engagement had sent her out looking for adventure, something more—the arms of a lover, perhaps.

But no. Nico would know better.

Her chest twinged.

Nico. He would likely be more worried than even her father. And Brier didn't trust him not to do something stupid because of it. She closed her eyes, doing her best to will some sense into him from however many hundreds of miles away they were.

Her feet seemed to stop in front of Palmer's bedroom of their own accord. She stared at his door for a moment, trying to see if any light shone out from beneath it. Finally, she decided just to take the chance. She lifted her fist.

"Come in," his voice called before she had the chance to swing it forward.

She hesitated.

"Brier?" he asked.

She placed her hand on the latch, pushed the door open, and stepped inside. She didn't speak until it shut fully behind her. "You knew I was there?"

Palmer shrugged, a book in his lap as always seemed to be the case those days. "I used to be able to do it as a kid, too. Made myself forget when I found out it wasn't normal. All of this is bringing it back, knowing people are coming before they arrive."

Brier nodded.

Palmer motioned her forward. "Come sit. I can barely see you over there."

"Shouldn't you be able to see everything?"

"Not how it works, it seems." He gathered up the papers around him and shoved them haphazardly on top of his nightstand.

Brier moved to the opposite side of the bed, setting her candle on the matching stand. She glanced at him as she sat and did a double take. "Your sling is gone."

He sighed, seeming unwilling to admit it. "Yeah."

"Are you... healed?" she asked.

He made a face, seemingly unable to acknowledge the truth again.

Brier started to ask another question but cut herself off, getting the distinct impression he didn't care to discuss it. She settled herself on the bed. Finally turning toward him, she propped her chin in one hand. "Are you scared, Palmer?"

He frowned. "Scared of what?"

"I don't know," she said. "I just keep feeling like I should be. Like, all of this is so easy. There has to be something else... out there or in here. Something. We're lost up in the mountains, for gods' sakes."

"Well," Palmer said, "if something does happen, you can always rain destruction down on everyone."

Brier snorted. "Allegedly."

The corners of Palmer's mouth turned up in a half smile.

Brier rolled her eyes at him before continuing, "Almanian. Where do they speak that?"

"Almania, I'd imagine," Palmer said.

"Thank you." Brier gave him a dry look. "Do you think we're in Almania, then?"

"Too many mountains." Palmer shook his head, seemingly glad

for the change of topic. "I'd say we're in the Cimas. Sviza or Osteran, maybe."

Brier pursed her lips. "How far away are those from home?"

"They're north of Latysia some, oh, five hundred miles, give or take."

Brier's mouth opened, though nothing came out. The distance was unfathomable. She sputtered. "How could we possibly have traveled five hundred miles?"

"Dosed us with something, I'd imagine. And Cerise likely moves more quickly when she's not stuck walking."

Brier furrowed her eyebrows, waiting for more explanation.

"She can fly when she changes into a bird," he said. "It's faster than walking." Brier supposed she should have thought of that. Obviously, the absurdity of the woman flying to and from places had just been muted under everything else she had suddenly found to be true the past week. She let the idea pass as she looked at the stacks of books on the nightstands. "Do you think the temple would give you credit for all the reading you've been doing? Make up for your missed classes?"

"I don't think any of that is canon that the Masters would approve." Palmer shook his head. "The university, maybe. Could at least make an argument for it."

Her eyebrows rose. "You take classes there, too?"

"Some Seers are politicians as well, you know. We can't spend all our time in the temple."

"So you want to be a politician?"

He seemed to mull the thought over while he studied her. He finally asked, "You want the honest answer?"

"I wouldn't have asked otherwise."

He took a breath, his jaw hardening. "I was getting as much of an education as they would let me so I would have it when I left."

Brier's forehead creased. "Left?"

Palmer nodded. "I became a Ward of the Church because my father died being an honor-driven fool named a hero. They kept me on because I'm possibly the only one who was ever able to truly predict things whether I meant to or not. With any sort of ambition, I could have gone far with that. But why would I want to spend my life sucking up to charlatans who finance their opulence by leading the uneducated to believe they can speak to gods and predict the future? No, I was planning to finish my course at university and then set off one night. Sneak out into Latysia and walk until I found somewhere I could make an honest living. As a scholar somewhere, maybe. There are supposed to be great schools in the east."

Brier waited until she was sure he had finished. "For an acolyte, you seem to have a very dire view of religion."

"I've yet to see one piece of evidence that it is anything but lies made to placate the masses."

Brier tilted her head to the side. "You don't believe in the gods?"

"Not especially," he said.

"Even if you are one?"

Palmer laughed. "We, you and me, obviously we're special. Gods, though? I find that rather hard to believe."

Brier nodded slowly. "Then what are we?"

Palmer paused and seemed to come up with a blank. "I don't know."

The wind changed, sending the hail into the windows once again. The entire side of the building seemed to shudder under the attack.

Palmer watched the window for a moment then looked back at Brier. "Don't think that's you, do you?"

Brier looked at him.

His eyes crinkled at the corners. He was actually teasing her.

She smiled, leaning against the headboard. "Not as far as I know. I've never shaken down a building before."

"Doesn't mean you couldn't." He looked at the dark window, only their weak reflections shining back at them. "If the great Signore Goebel is to be believed, you could end all life as we know it."

"I'll try not to let it go to my head." Brier stretched out her legs, crossing them at the ankles. "Anyway, I'm not a 'roughing it' kind of girl. I quite like things existing."

He allowed a smile, looking at her for a long moment before finally glancing away again.

"What?" Brier asked.

"Nothing." Palmer shook his head, focusing on his book.

"No, you were thinking something."

He didn't answer right away, and Brier began to wonder if he was going to at all.

"How did you end up in the Augarian?" he finally asked.

Brier narrowed her eyes slightly, strongly suspecting he was changing the topic. She answered anyway, "I was born there."

He looked up again sharply. "You aren't *Innato*?"

"Of course I am," Brier said. "How else would I have been there when the library burned? My father isn't a soldier. And even if he were, do you really think he would have brought a five-year-old girl with him into battle?"

Something flashed over Palmer's face. "The *library* burned?"

"The Augarian Library," she said. "During the Reclamation. I went looking for my father when the fighting started and ended up trapped inside. That's the fire Goebel was talking about, from when I almost died. Or... did die."

Palmer just looked at her, some sort of horrified shock lingering in his eyes.

"What?" She shifted uncomfortably.

Palmer blinked, dropping his eyes as he shook his head. "Nothing. Sorry. I suppose I just assumed you were *Savrio*."

"The hair?" Brier let the odd moment pass, pointing at her own fair head, markedly different from his dark complexion.

He shrugged.

"Inherited from my mother, apparently," Brier explained, whether or not he cared. "Who knows where she got it? Maybe she had some northern roots from before the *Savrio* came and saved us all."

"Or claimed they saved us."

Brier hesitated. "We never would have displaced the *Bugiardi* without their troops."

"Latysia has been sacked three times in as many decades," Palmer argued. "Every other city-state within a hundred miles wants the wealth the Church has collected there. I don't think the *Savrio* were our only chance at retaking the city, no matter what they would like us to believe."

Brier felt her face react before she could stop it, half expecting Orris Adessi-Guillroy to somehow storm in from five hundred miles away at Palmer's near blasphemies.

"Sorry," Palmer said before she could recover. "You probably have more *Savrio* friends than I do."

Brier managed to wipe away her stunned expression, offering a smile. If the continued existence of the world relied on their cooperation, starting an argument over politics she barely knew as more than children's stories likely wasn't the best plan.

He smiled back, twisting to grab one of the books off his nightstand as the conversation died, not seeming to know what else to do with himself. He held another toward her. "Do you read?"

That actually made her laugh. "You realize I am the librarian's daughter? My father tried to get me reading before I could properly walk."

"Just was... asking." Palmer motioned with the book limply. "Would you like one?"

She took the book, letting him retreat behind his own once again. A smart, sometimes awkward, skeptical religious man, Palmer only seemed to become more contradictory as Brier got to know him. For the time, she let him bury himself in his book. With the way things were going, she would have plenty of time to figure out the conundrum that was Palmer Tash.

CHAPTER NINE

BRIER WINCED AS SUNLIGHT STRUCK her face. How Palmer slept with the curtains pulled open in an east-facing room was anyone's guess.

She supposed that was a moot point, though. Likely, he didn't sleep.

Prying one eye open, Brier looked at the rest of the empty mattress. She lifted her head.

Palmer sat at the desk, hunched over something.

Outside the window, the day shone brightly, a clear blue sky stretching out over the peaks and valleys as if the storm had never been. Brier slid her eyes back to Palmer, forcing herself to sit up. "Did you sleep at all last night?"

Palmer lifted his head and looked at her. "A couple of hours."

Brier nodded and stretched. "When did I fall asleep?"

"I wasn't keeping track."

She pursed her lips, unsure if she should feel uncomfortable or not. "You could have told me to go back to my room."

Palmer's brow furrowed slightly, but he recovered. "It didn't bother me at all. The bed alone is about the size of my cell under the temple, anyway. I'm used to much, much tighter quarters than this."

Brier nodded, a sudden shiver running up her spine. She looked at Palmer but couldn't find a way to ask the question, whether he had felt something... odd.

Palmer stiffened anyway, holding still for a long moment before finally looking back at her. "Someone's coming."

"Goebel?" Brier asked.

"No. Someone from down the mountain. A group of some sort."

Brier blinked, the information refusing to click, make sense. "Someone's coming to Ruhegipfel?"

"I'm pretty sure." Palmer nodded once to himself and quickly ran his eyes over her. "Why don't you go get dressed? I'll meet you at your room."

Brier didn't argue, less than keen to be caught leaving Palmer's room in her nightgown. She slipped out of bed and down the hall, as silent as a shadow.

The difference was immediate. Even before Brier could see them, before she could hear them, Ruhegipfel felt fuller, livelier.

Palmer's face remained stony, suspicious, as he leaned back against the wall, waiting for some sign of the visitors.

Brier shifted her weight between her feet awkwardly, listening to the snatches of conversation echoing through the maze of halls now and again—too distant, too garbled to make out words. She finally sighed and looked at Palmer. "They aren't attacking. I'd think they're friendly."

"We'll wait," Palmer said.

Brier frowned but didn't argue. She tapped her fingers on her thigh. "You don't know who they are?"

Palmer shook his head.

"How many there are?"

"I'm not getting anything about them," Palmer said. "There's a lot of... interference."

Brier looked at him questioningly.

"I get bits of things here and there, but most of it's garbled, like too many people are yelling for my attention at once when I try to focus. I'm stuck letting things come to me."

"That's not much use now, is it?" Brier released a breath, leaning back against the wall next to him. Crossing her arms, she forced herself to stop tapping. "I don't like waiting."

"Patience is a virtue."

"Thank you, Sage."

Palmer made a face but remained silent.

Brier studied him. "You know, for the supposed protector of the universe, you aren't exactly the most proactive person in the world."

Palmer just pressed his lips together.

Brier started tapping her fingers again, that time on her upper arm, then finally jerked herself away from the wall. "Well, you can wait. I'm going to see who's here."

"Brier..." Palmer began.

She marched away, not bothering to look back.

After a few seconds, his footsteps followed her. "Brier, wait up."

"We've yet to hear any sort of commotion. I think it's safe if we want to go see."

"It's looking for trouble, in my opinion," Palmer said.

"Well, Cerise is down there, I'm sure," Brier returned.

"I wasn't making a joke."

"No, I was, I believe." Brier turned a corner and started down the stairs. "You don't have to come if you'd rather wait."

"I'm not letting you go down there alone." His voice was not more than a step behind her.

Smiling, Brier slowed before turning to face him. She cocked her head back. Perhaps two or three inches taller than her normally, he suddenly towered over her, standing on a higher step.

His eyebrows furrowed. "Did I actually convince you?"

She half laughed. "No, I just thought that was cute."

"What was?"

"You didn't know me a couple weeks ago," Brier said. "It's cute you're so... protective."

More footsteps made her turn again before he could answer.

Goebel looked almost surprised to find them there, his eyebrows rising for a split second before he recovered. "Signorina, signore. We were just coming to find you."

See? Brier could nearly feel Palmer's response in her head. She ignored it. Offering Goebel a quick smile, she slid her eyes toward another man at the bottom of the stairwell.

Not more than a year or two older than Goebel, the man bore him a striking resemblance, his face only slightly longer, his eyes closer set.

His smile-smirk said he found something amusing. The man quickly ran his eyes over her and then turned to Goebel. "She and Marina are about the same size, I take it. Little things."

Goebel shot the man a dark look, his normal control visibly shaken. The expression made him look younger, nearly petulant. He looked back at them, glancing at Brier before resting his eyes on Palmer. "My brother, Reinhald."

A little head peeked out from behind the corner. Reinhald looked back, and it disappeared again. Brier leaned forward slightly, trying to see without losing her balance on the smooth step, its surface dipped with age.

"Let's leave the stairwell, shall we?" Reinhald smiled, motioning back to the hall behind him.

Goebel nodded, motioning for Brier and Palmer to follow.

Near the bottom of the stairs, a group of half a dozen stood clumped in the hallway, four men, a woman, and a little girl no older than six.

Brier looked at all of them.

They all looked back.

"*Dea,*" one of the men toward the back murmured.

Another glanced at the speaker, his sneer weakly concealed.

"This is Signorina Brier Chastain—" Goebel started.

"Chastain-Bochard," Brier corrected without thinking.

"And Signore Palmer Tash," Goebel finished, as though he hadn't heard. "They are two permanent residents of Ruhegipfel."

"For now, at least," Reinhald said, looking at the group and then back at Goebel. "Ruhegipfel is the home of travelers, after all."

Goebel didn't answer him.

"Have you been traveling, then, Signore Reinhald?" Brier asked in the lull.

He smiled. "Always."

Wings flapped and settled in the next room.

Reinhald turned toward the sound. "Ah, we were wondering when Mademoiselle Cerise would join us."

Brier barely managed to hide her grimace as the blond woman strolled out of the next room.

"I've been around, darling." She smiled. "Saw you coming up the hill."

"I wouldn't have assumed elsewise," Reinhald answered.

"Reinhald." Cerise moved forward to kiss both of his cheeks. "Where have you been this time?"

"Here and there," Reinhald said. "Wherever the road takes me. Wherever they allow me."

"Wherever lacks proper security?" Cerise teased, her words nearly flirty.

"That as well." Reinhald held out his arms as if accepting a blow. "It is always such a treat to see you, Cerise."

Brier couldn't determine if Reinhald meant to be sarcastic or not.

"And you." Cerise seemed downright sincere, her eyes flicking to the rest of the group. "Who have you brought us this time?"

"Ah, where are my manners?" Reinhald turned back to the group. "*Damen und Herren, Mesdames et Messieurs, Signore e Signori*, may I present Herr Amand Dunst and Herr Wigmund Gehring, Madame Roxana Blanc, Monsignor Noé Tailler, Signore Lonzo Abatescianni, and Mademoiselle Rosette."

The little girl continued to stare silently at Brier.

Brier chose to ignore her and opened her mouth.

"They will be staying with us at least a night or two," Goebel cut in before Brier could speak. "Some for longer."

Brier snapped her mouth shut again and instead nodded as she looked over the newcomers. The two herrs seemed more interested in the old castle than in any of them—other than perhaps Cerise, at whom the shorter of the two tall men continued to glance out of the corner of his eye. Both were tall and undoubtedly well fed, and their rich—if odd— clothing screamed wealth.

The monsignor, on the other hand, was a short, thin man, looking even shorter than he truly was between the tall herrs and the curvy madame—looking wealthy in her own right. All the same, he didn't seem poor in his simple but well-fitting clothes—a tradesman perhaps.

That left the little girl and the signore, both watching her and Palmer. The little girl seemed confused, the signore scared as he ran a thin strand of wooden beads through his fingers, just visible outside the gaping sleeves of his robe.

Brier watched the beads for another moment before meeting his wide eyes. "Are you a Seer, signore?"

The man's eyebrows rose farther into his dark hairline.

"A Bugiardi one," Palmer said, studying the man.

"Come now," Reinhald said, even though Palmer hadn't sounded particularly belligerent to Brier. "We are all friends here. There are no old politics at Ruhegipfel."

"Will we be shown to our rooms soon?" Madame Roxana asked, her words heavily accented. "I would quite like to rest a bit. I was not aware it was such a climb to get here."

"Of course, madame," Reinhald spoke gallantly. "We will send your bags up after you. Cerise?"

Cerise cocked an eyebrow but surprisingly didn't argue, leading the small group down another hall toward the far staircase.

Brier watched them go and then addressed the three remaining men. "I've never seen Cerise so well behaved."

"She knows those travelers are what put clothes on her back these days," Reinhald said then looked at his brother. "Should we retreat? I'd love a chance to speak with our 'permanent guests.'"

Goebel just motioned down the hall, letting Reinhald lead them to the small library. They filed in, and no one spoke until the door had clicked shut. Flopping into a chair, Reinhald studied them. "So, Brier and Palmer, was it?"

"Yes," Palmer said, crossing his arms across his chest.

Reinhald smiled, looking at Goebel. "Truly a protector, I see."

"He is not the most trusting of men, I admit." Goebel moved across the room toward the remaining chairs. "Who did you bring us this time?"

Reinhald sat back, tenting his fingers. "The herren and Madame Roxana are simply tourists. Nearly killed the lot of them coming up the hill, I think." Reinhald held his hands out as if resting them on a large stomach. "More money than sense, from what I can tell. Always good for us."

"And the other three?" Goebel asked without pause.

Reinhald smirked. "Noé is a tailor. Out of work. Offered to trade him a roof for a few weeks in return for payment in kind. Been a while since we've had anything made new." He motioned to Brier's dress. "Case in point."

"It's a perfectly nice dress." Brier placed her hands on the red bodice.

"Yes, but at least a decade old," Reinhald answered.

"The Seer?" Goebel cut in. "Abatescianni?"

"Found him in a small country parish." Reinhald looked back over at his brother. "He managed to find himself persona non grata with his church after one too many disruptive visions."

"Predictions?" Goebel asked.

"Maybe. More, he can see what others miss," Reinhald said, motioning toward Brier and Palmer. "He had their number right away."

Goebel paused and finally nodded once. "And the girl?"

"Street rat. Found her in the markets of Tetii."

"Picked her up from a vendor, then?" Goebel cocked an eyebrow. "Is there a going price for street urchins these days?"

"Picked her up pickpocketing our good Madame Roxana. Not too poor at it either." Reinhald either missed or ignored his brother's sarcasm. "Madame Roxana was busy enough yelling at some poor peddler I still don't know if she realizes she's missing a purse."

"You aren't much in the practice of picking up urchins," Goebel said.

"I am when they have special abilities," Reinhald said. "Exactly what, I'm not sure. But Rosette, no doubt, is no common urchin. And she's small. She won't take up much space. Some training, and who knows what she'll be able to do?"

Goebel frowned. "You expect me to train her, then, I take it?"

"You already have two pupils. I assumed a third wouldn't be overly taxing." Reinhald smiled in return. "If you find her too much to handle, hand her off to Cerise. Woman could use some other distraction that doesn't involve spying on us."

"More likely than not, she would just enlist the girl as another spy around here," Brier said.

"Fair enough, fair enough." Reinhald laughed, looking her over. "Tell me, Brier, do you like that dress?"

Brier looked down at the simple kirtle, laced up the front over a white smock. It certainly wasn't anything fancy—no woman in the Augarian of any sort of rank would be caught dead in it—but it was nice and undoubtedly functional.

"I do." She looked back up. "Should I not?"

"I believe it was Marina's favorite," Reinhald said. "I'm trying to discern just how similar you are."

"Who's Marina?" Brier asked, frowning.

Goebel's eyes flashed. "Stop it."

Brier looked between the two brothers then at Palmer, who shrugged, apparently just as lost.

"Calm down, little brother." Reinhald held up his hands innocently, looking back at Brier and Palmer. "How long have you two been here?"

The lingering look on Goebel's face—angry, sad, pained—was such that Brier let the topic drop. "A few weeks."

Reinhald clicked his tongue. "Not much time for training."

"Are you on a deadline?" Palmer asked sharply.

Reinhald glanced at him, looked back at Brier, and then finally looked at the door. "We just tend to have bad luck with untrained... personalities, around here."

Brier nodded, studying him as he seemed to gaze at something in the distance beyond their sight. "Are you?"

Reinhald looked back at her. "Am I what, dear?"

Brier thought of the best way to phrase it. "Special?"

"Yes and no," Reinhald said. "Dominik hasn't filled you in?"

"Dominik?" Brier asked.

Reinhald motioned toward his brother.

"Goebel?" she said.

"Goebel is our family name," Reinhald said.

Brier glanced at Goebel, unable to hide her smile as something about the name sounded far too young for the seemingly timeless man across from her. "Your given name is Dominik?"

Goebel gave a vague motion of confirmation.

"No, he hasn't," Palmer said.

Brier blinked, confused, but slowly her mind snapped back to Reinhald's question. She shook her head. "Oh, no."

"We are Watchers." Reinhald motioned between his brother and himself. "As was our father and his father. It is the gift of Ruhegipfel."

"Like... Seers?" Brier asked.

"Lord, no." Reinhald snorted. "Watchers, *Veritants,* those who can see what others cannot and control what others dare not."

"Like us, you mean," Palmer said, face still as stony as ever. "The uncontrollable."

"Exactly." Reinhald settled back in the chair, apparently unfazed by Palmer's snark. "We may not be quite as magnificent in our abilities as either of you, but our gift is to help control yours. And it has the rather pleasant side effect of extending our lives, at least longer than others would find average."

Brier looked at Palmer, trying to judge his reaction. If he had any opinion on Reinhald's revelation, Palmer didn't show it.

"But now, I believe we were going to speak about you, not us." Reinhald smiled.

"What about us?" Palmer asked, his words clipped.

"Are you able to work without coaching at this point?"

Palmer seemed to measure his words. "What do you mean?"

"Are you able to control your powers without someone else being there?"

"From what we've tried," Palmer said.

"Do you think you could handle an attack?"

"An attack?" Brier's eyebrows rose. "You think we're going to be attacked?"

Reinhald's smile disappeared, but his face was still kind. "Ruhegipfel is a stronghold and far enough into the mountains to dissuade most with a mind toward conquest. But you are a very desirable being for someone hoping to do the world wrong. I, for one, am always a strong proponent of preparing you in case of an attempted attack and kidnapping."

"You mean like you did?" Palmer said. It didn't truly seem to be a question.

"Yes." Reinhald's smile returned. "But by someone with far less gallant intentions." He looked at Brier. "I don't believe you left without some share of suspicion, especially after your little fainting spell during that eclipse. And you would be something to hold if someone had malevolent intent. A woman who can level cities at will? Quite the weapon."

"She isn't a weapon." Palmer's entire body stiffened, nearly buzzing with tension.

"Isn't *just* a weapon," Reinhald answered. "She is a woman, no doubt—a beautiful one at that—but used incorrectly, she could change warfare as we know it."

"I have no desire to be a weapon, signore," Brier said.

"Which is why you must learn to protect yourself. Tomorrow morning, we'll redouble our efforts."

Your little fainting spell during that eclipse.

Palmer sat at the desk in his room, resting his head in his hands as the words bounced around his mind.

When the darkness descends...

Releasing a frustrated grunt, Palmer pushed back, the chair scraping the floor as he stood. Rubbing his temples, he paced along the far wall, a knot in his stomach, which he'd felt since Brier had fallen asleep the night before, pulling tighter. He scoffed, but the sound came out weak. *Visions and prophecies.* He had spent nineteen years scoffing at the idea, at the drivel "Seers" passed off as truth. *Now...*

And the library fire. That stupid daydream.

"I went looking for my father when the fighting started and ended up trapped inside."

He had seen that. As much as he didn't truly want to admit it, he had. He'd seen Brier's death—near death—had seen the darkness descend on her as well. And if he could bring himself to believe what the Goebels said was true about her, she could certainly crack a city open—destroy Latysia. At least if they ever returned there. He looked out the window, the mountain peaks just visible in the last moments of twilight.

He turned the prophecy over in his mind, stanzas rising and falling as he flitted over them before he forced it away. Prophecy or not, Brier didn't seem the type to mete out doom. She certainly didn't seem vengeful. And the idea of old gods was just patently absurd.

Sitting once again, he forced it all out: the words, Brier, any lingering "visions" around the edges of his mind. Even if he was less than wholeheartedly going after whatever psychic ability his training was supposed to enhance, he was certainly getting better at blocking things out.

Perhaps that alone was worth the entire exercise.

After three days of Reinhald's new training, Brier's head felt as though it were going to explode. She flopped down on her bed, squeezing her eyes shut and fighting off the building migraine. If only she had something to drink.

Releasing a breath, she looked up at the ceiling, studying the wooden rafters. At least she could take some comfort in knowing that Palmer didn't seem to be progressing any better than she was. She at least had managed to send a tremor through the library large enough to make the shelves shake. Palmer continued to muddle on with some vague sense of precognition that seemed neither here nor there.

Someone knocked.

Brier winced, pinching the bridge of her nose for a moment before she answered, "Come in."

The door slid open, and Palmer came into view. "Hi."

"Hi," she returned, watching him stand awkwardly just beyond the doorway. She smiled. "You may come in if you like."

"Thank you." He stepped inside, shutting the door behind him. Still, he stood stiffly, not moving any closer.

Brier shook her head, teasing, "We've spent a night in bed together, Palmer. You're perfectly welcome to make yourself at home."

"I didn't want to be presumptuous." A flush started low on his neck. "We haven't talked much the past few days."

"Truly." She continued smiling. "I was beginning to wonder if you were avoiding me."

Palmer's eyebrows rose as he blanched slightly. "What? Why would I do that?"

Brier nearly laughed. "I was just teasing you. I promise. I take it humor isn't your strong suit?"

"Oh." Palmer dropped eye contact. "I suppose not."

She watched him for another moment before motioning to the chair at her little desk. "Really, you don't have to stand there."

"I'm fine," he said. "Thank you."

As he wasn't looking at her anyway, Brier finally rolled her eyes. She could barely imagine Palmer sharing a classroom with Nico, Leone, and that lot. As similar as all the students she knew seemed, Palmer was just too... different. She tried a different tactic. "Does Goebel *look* like a Dominik to you?"

Palmer finally met her gaze again, his eyebrows knotted. "What?"

"Goebel? Dominik?"

"Oh..." Still looking confused, Palmer answered, "I hadn't thought about it."

"It just sounds so young, to me. Don't you think?"

"Again," Palmer said as he shook his head, "hadn't thought about it."

"And Goebel..." Brier kept the thought going, at least on her side. "Well, I don't know. How old do you think he is?"

Palmer paused, managing his own smile. "Again—"

"You haven't thought about it," Brier finished with a sigh. "I got it."

Palmer just continued to smile. That was a nice change, at least.

She glanced around the room before speaking again. "What do you think of Reinhald?"

"Do you think he's listening?" Palmer scanned the room himself before looking back at her.

"The ravens have me paranoid," Brier said. "Damned things always seem to be there when you least want them."

Palmer searched the ceiling and looked back at her. "Would you like me to check out the window?"

"You're making fun of me." Brier gave him a look.

"No, I agree," he said. "Cerise knows more than she ever should."

Brier hummed in agreement. "But Reinhald... What do you think?"

"He's..." Palmer took a moment. "He's interesting, at least."

"Certainly." Brier glanced down at her borrowed skirt before studying Palmer for a long moment through her eyelashes. "Do you know anything more about Marina?"

Palmer shook his head. "Haven't found her in any of the ledgers I have in my room. She was never mentioned and didn't live here, or at least hasn't lived here in over a decade. I can keep looking if you like."

"And you don't... know?"

Palmer's jaw tightened, but he answered, "No."

"Work on that omniscient thing, won't you? You never have it when it would actually be helpful."

"I'm not working on that one too hard, in all honesty," Palmer admitted.

Brier paused. "No?"

"I'm not sleeping at all now," he said. "Do you know how boring night is? Everyone else is asleep. There's really nothing to do but read. I've gotten through at least a fourth of the library here as it is. If I knew everything already, what would I do with my time?"

"You could pick up a hobby," Brier said.

"Like what?"

"I don't know, but with an extra eight hours to practice it every day, I imagine you'd pick it up like that." She snapped her fingers.

He looked at her, silent for a long moment, a strange look on his face, but shook his head before she could ask about it. "How have you been doing with everything? We still had the entire castle, last I checked."

"I admit *I* haven't been practicing as much as I could be, either. At least, not any more than Reinhald's been forcing me."

"No?" Palmer asked, no judgment in his tone.

She shook her head. "Omniscience at least sounds like it could be fun. I just... obliterate things."

"Still probably best you practice." Palmer pressed his lips together, something churning behind his eyes. "You don't want it to get away from you."

Brier tried to read him. Whatever was bothering him, she couldn't tell. She cocked her head slightly to one side. "I will if you're there."

"All right," Palmer said.

She hesitated at his quick answer, fully expecting more awkward hedging from the man. "Come by tonight?"

Palmer's eyebrows rose. "What?"

There it was.

"You don't sleep anyway," she said. "It's as good a time as any, don't you think?"

Palmer swallowed, pausing, and finally nodded. "Right, sure, sounds good."

Something pressed into the back of Brier's mind as she lay in her room. She pushed herself up to rest on her elbows and moved to sit on the edge of the bed. Something moved around outside the room, not Palmer returning—or coming absurdly early for their night practice session—but something. Forcing herself up and across the room, Brier pulled the door open slowly, leaning out. She looked down the hall one way, then the other. A flash of blond hair disappeared around the far corner, a second too late to be unseen.

"Rosette?" Brier called, the name sounding vaguely correct in her mind.

The blond head reappeared, the little girl's large blue eyes studying Brier carefully.

Brier shook her head, attempting to think of something to say. "Are you lost?"

Rosette hesitated, finally nodded.

"I know the feeling around here," Brier said, more to herself than the child.

The little girl remained silent.

"Well," Brier addressed Rosette again, "where were you trying to go? Maybe I can point you in the right direction."

"You're different." The little girl finally stepped around the corner into full view though she didn't move any closer.

Brier hesitated. "Different?"

"Like the man and bird-lady," Rosette said. "Different."

Brier studied Rosette—the pretty blond curls surrounding a thin face with too-large blue eyes, the scrawny, seemingly underfed body. Brier finally asked, "Are you different?"

Rosette paused then nodded.

"What is it that you do?"

Rosette shifted, looking down at the ragged shoes on her feet. Brier supposed they didn't have a handy supply of those in the castle.

"I hurt people," Rosette said softly.

Brier couldn't stop her eyebrows from rising.

"I don't mean to." Rosette glanced up, looked away again. "Not most of the time. Bad things just happen when I get mad."

"Like what?" Brier asked.

"People get sick. Or angry. One mean man went crazy. They sent him to the fool's tower." Rosette raised her eyes as if she could see the tower off in the distance. "I think he's dead now."

A shiver moved over Brier's skin, but she held her ground. "You made him crazy?"

"He tried to attack me," Rosette said. "One night when I was looking for a place to sleep. He grabbed me, started trying to tear everything off me. I got so scared and so angry... his mind broke. The lawmen came and took him to the fool's tower when they found him the next day. Then one of the angry lunatics already up there attacked him. So he's dead now."

"You..." Brier started. She looked both ways down the hall and then held her door open wider. "Here, why don't you come in so we can talk?"

Rosette shifted on her feet, seeming to consider ducking back behind her corner again.

"I won't hurt you," Brier said.

Rosette hesitated another moment and finally nodded, following Brier into the room.

"Go ahead and have a seat if you like." Brier motioned to the end of the bed before taking the seat at the desk herself.

Rosette planted herself with a bounce, smoothing her too-big dress and placing her hands in her lap as though impersonating what she believed to be a proper lady.

Brier smiled weakly, took a breath. "So... you hurt people."

Rosette nodded, her satirically proper posture slouching as she dropped her eyes.

"You make them sick?"

"Or fight," Rosette said quietly.

Brier nodded. "Does Reinhald know what you can do?"

Rosette shook her head.

"Do you not want him to know?"

"He knows I'm different," Rosette said. "But I didn't want him to not take me. People don't like people who hurt people."

"Some people do." Brier leaned forward, ignoring the stiffness in her muscles. "Oh, *cara*, I really don't think you have to worry. I can hurt people too. If they didn't want dangerous women at Ruhegipfel, I wouldn't be here. Debatable if Cerise would be."

"The bird-lady?" Rosette asked.

"That's her." Brier sighed, scanning the rafters.

Rosette shifted on the bed. "Can you make people sick?"

"Well, no," Brier said. Then she amended, "Not that I know of. But, do you want to see something?"

Rosette nodded.

Brier picked up a scrap of paper from her desk and held it up. "You see this?"

Rosette nodded again.

Brier studied it, forcing through an unwelcome tingling radiating through her. Slowly, the paper began to dissolve, pieces flaking off and disappearing until nothing was left. Brier rubbed her fingers together, showing Rosette her palm as though she were a magician presenting a successful trick. "I destroy things."

Rosette stared, a mixture of shock and delight on her thin face. She leaned forward. "Can you do it again?"

Brier couldn't help but smile at her enthusiasm. "Do you have something for me to destroy? I don't have much paper to spare."

Rosette stuck her hands into the pockets of the dress but came up with only lint. She frowned at it before holding it out to Brier. "Does that work?"

Brier picked it out of Rosette's hand gently and placed it in her palm. "Let's see."

The tingling came more easily that time as the nothing surrounded the lint and peeled it apart bit by bit, working slowly until it seemed to have never existed.

Rosette clapped, scooting forward until she was barely on the bed. "Can you teach me to do that?"

"I don't think so. Sorry." Brier shook her head. "I wouldn't know how to even if I could."

The excitement dropped out of Rosette's face, but she nodded.

"I might be able to help you with your powers, though, if you'd like me to try," Brier offered. "I'm not very good at anything yet, but that doesn't mean we can't get control of ourselves. With any luck, we'll only be as dangerous as we want to be."

Brier yawned, her candle flickering dangerously low. Perhaps Palmer didn't need sleep, but she wasn't quite so gifted. The time late and growing later, she half wondered if Palmer had forgotten or changed his mind.

After a few more minutes, she fished out another taper and lit it with the dying candle before replacing it in the holder. She wrapped herself in a robe, slid her feet into her slippers, picked up the candle, and headed for the door.

Even with the new additions, Ruhegipfel was still silent at night, seeming to gape with emptiness. Within view of Palmer's door, Brier heard another set of footsteps. She froze, listening. Carefully, she approached the corner. Another candle moved away from her toward the stairs. Sending one last glance at Palmer's door, Brier turned the corner to follow the other footsteps.

Goebel spun as she stepped into the library, releasing a breath when he saw her. "Signorina. I see you have mastered moving silently. I'm glad you've been practicing your abilities."

Brier just nodded, hiding her confusion. "What are you doing up?"

"Oh." Goebel looked around and motioned with the book in his hand. "Reading. I couldn't sleep."

Brier studied his face in the weak light, the shadows catching the bags under his eyes, the faint wrinkles making him look decades older. "Have you not been sleeping either? You look exhausted."

"It's nothing for you to worry yourself about, signorina." Goebel turned his back to her.

She hesitated and set her candle down on a table. "Goebel?"

"Yes, signorina?" His voice sounded weary.

"Who's Marina?"

The candle in his hand shook slightly. He set it down, remaining silent.

She didn't let it go that time. "Goebel?"

He released a breath and finally turned to face Brier. "She's you, signorina. The last you."

Brier furrowed her eyebrows.

He forced a pained smile, opened the book in his hand, and pulled out a worn portrait miniature. "Here."

Brier moved forward, taking the small painting and tilting it toward the candlelight. A pretty, dark-complexioned woman looked back at her, the corner of her mouth turned slightly up as if trying not to smile. Brier held it back toward Goebel. "She's very pretty."

Goebel nodded, glancing at the picture before tucking it away again. He avoided Brier's eyes as he moved things on the shelf, an inch forward or back. "Marina."

Brier watched him. "What do you mean 'the last me'?"

He finally stopped shuffling things and looked at her. "I mean the last Chaos, signorina."

Brier looked where he had stuck the miniature out of view, a sinking feeling growing in her stomach. "What happened to her?"

Goebel cleared his throat and swallowed. "She died."

Brier's body stiffened. "How?"

Goebel shook his head, sitting heavily in a chair. "I don't think we need to talk about it."

"*How?*" Brier insisted.

Goebel released another long breath and met her eyes. "It wasn't pleasant, signorina. It would probably be best to leave it at that."

"Because..." Brier pressed her lips together. "Was it—"

"Signorina, *please.*" Goebel rubbed his face with his hands.

A realization hit her. "You were in love with her."

"She was a... remarkable woman," Goebel said weakly.

Brier sat in the largest chair in the library, pulling her feet up under her. "When did she die?"

Goebel settled on rubbing his temples. "Fifteen years or so, now."

"I wasn't in the fire until thirteen years ago," Brier said.

Goebel looked at her. "You're an ancient deity, signorina. You don't think you could wait a couple of years before once again reincarnating?"

"Brier," she said. "You may call me Brier, you know, if you like. Your brother does."

"Reinhald and I are quite different, if you haven't gathered," Goebel said, nearly bitter.

Brier smiled. "Really, though. Signorina is quite the mouthful when you say it all the time. I won't even insist on calling you Dominik."

Goebel dropped his hands and shook his head. "Reinhald is always interesting to have back."

"He makes Cerise behave better."

"They have a history," Goebel said.

"Lovers?" Brier asked.

"Now and again." Goebel stood. "Why are you up? I thought everyone would be long abed at this point."

Brier shrugged. "Couldn't sleep."

Goebel nodded, letting them both fall into their own thoughts for a few moments.

"Goebel?"

He looked up.

"If I'm a reincarnation, is that what happens after we die? We're reincarnated?"

Goebel shook his head. "I've never died, signorina. I couldn't tell you for sure."

"But you said I'm a reincarnation," she insisted.

"Of Chaos. Chaos can't die like a human can."

Brier shifted in her seat, attempting to digest his words. She continued carefully, "Then what happens to humans?"

He sighed. "As far as my studies have taught me?"

Brier looked at him and shrugged. "If that's all you can give."

"We die," he said.

Brier thought through her words. "And that's it?"

"That's it."

"No afterlife?"

"I don't believe so."

Brier looked down at her hands. "That's rather depressing."

"Then believe in one if you like," Goebel said. "It isn't as though I'll be able to gloat if I die and it proves I'm right. There's no reason to distress yourself if you need to believe in something. If you're right, you'll find out you were right. If you're wrong, you won't be around to know the difference."

Brier nodded, still looking at her lap. She pulled her hands into the sleeves of her robe, retreating against the cold.

"But you don't have to worry yourself with that, signorina. Chaos can't die."

"Brier can." She met his eyes. "And I am Brier."

He didn't answer right away but gave her a sad smile. "You do remind me a good deal of her, you know."

"Of Marina?"

He nodded once.

"Fifteen years," Brier said after a pause. "You must have been young when you knew her."

"How old do you think I am?" Goebel asked.

Brier shrugged. "Thirty-two, thirty-three?"

"Not bad," Goebel said. "Most people guess older."

"The gray, I would think." Brier tapped her temple. "You don't look *old*, though."

He nodded. "Thirty-four, for the record. Physically, at least. As Reinhald said, all of this does wreak havoc with our aging."

"How old are you otherwise?" Brier asked.

"We tend to lose track around here." He looked into the distance. "I'd known Marina since I was much younger, though, however many years it's been. She spent most of her childhood here."

Brier frowned. "Did she die here?"

Goebel's head snapped back to face her.

"Sorry," Brier said, "I was just wondering, if she was from here, how did I end up—"

"A mistake," he said. His jaw worked as though he were trying to force more words out with his tongue. "Mistakes, actually. A few of them. She never should have ended up where she was."

Brier nodded, a million more questions racing around her mind.

Because of the deeply pained look on his face, she refrained from asking any of them, unsure whether he was in any state to give an answer she'd understand. She pressed her lips together. "I'm sorry."

"For what, signorina?"

"For your loss," Brier said. "She was obviously very special to you."

He sighed, standing and moving to the window. In the moonlight, the snowy peaks shone all around them, blue and eerie. "What's done is done, signorina. There is nowhere for us to go but forward."

Brier hesitated but finally stood and moved toward him at the window. Reaching out, she laid a hand on his shoulder, squeezing it lightly. "She's very lucky to have someone to remember her so strongly."

His body shuddered, and a choked-back sob sounded loudly throughout the silent room.

Brier pulled her hand back smoothly. "Would you like me to go?"

"No." He shook his head and took a deep breath as he slowly pulled himself together. "It's fine. Old wounds can just feel newer alone at night."

Brier nodded even though he wouldn't see her. "I understand. I'm more homesick at night."

Goebel wiped a hand over his face and finally turned away from the window, still not looking at her.

She watched him for a moment before speaking again. "Do they know I'm alive?"

He slowly lifted his eyes. "I'm sorry?"

"My father. My friends there. Do they know I'm alive?"

Goebel released a shaky breath. "I don't believe they have any evidence to the contrary, signorina."

She hesitated. "Will I ever see them again, Goebel?"

He didn't answer her right away, taking a moment to look out the window at something invisible in the distance before looking back. "I imagine you will, signorina. I just can't say how."

CHAPTER TEN

IT WAS DAYLIGHT BEFORE PALMER managed to steel his resolve, the mixture of thoughts spinning through his mind locking him in place through the night, thoughts of Ruhegipfel and premonitions and Brier being... He couldn't think of the way to end that thought even then, as many different ways as it could go. Brier being... Brier. He released a breath as he walked down the hall toward her room.

Empty.

He knew it before he even touched the knob. Still, he pulled the door open and looked around as if trying to see if he had missed her.

Library. The thought came to his mind, unbidden.

He knew it was right.

Moving quickly, he pulled the door shut and moved to the stairs.

"Up already?" Reinhald's voice echoed through the halls. Palmer stopped at the bottom of the staircase, listening to the voices around the corner.

Someone speaking much more softly hushed Reinhald, the words indistinguishable.

"She who?" Reinhald asked, his voice just as loud as before.

Palmer moved forward as quietly as possible.

"Brier," Goebel's voice was audible now. "She fell asleep in the old wingback."

"Truly have a thing for our Chaos, don't you?"

Whether or not Goebel rolled his eyes, his voice made it sound very much so. "She's half my age."

"Doesn't stop many."

"Just because *you* have eyes for every woman you see doesn't make everything lewd."

"Just, with your history…"

Footsteps started away quickly.

"Oh, lighten up, Dom," Reinhald's voice followed the steps away from the stairwell.

Palmer stepped out from around the corner, watching as Reinhald disappeared down the hall.

Images came to Palmer easily, controllable. A young girl ran down a hall, tight black curls bouncing along with her, two boys following close at her heels. A young Goebel; fifteen perhaps; with the girl, older that time; his hands at her hips; smiling.

Marina. The name appeared in his head as though it had always been there. Palmer blinked, looking at the library as the visions slipped away. Pushing the door open quietly, he stepped inside.

Brier was barely visible, wrapped up in her robe, curled into the seat of a large chair, her hair loose, covering her face.

Palmer shifted uncomfortably in the doorway and finally cleared his throat.

Brier stirred, pushing her hair back and groaning. "Oh, that is *not* a good position to sleep in."

"Why did you sleep here, then?" Palmer asked.

She blinked, focused on his face, and rolled her eyes, continuing to untangle herself. "So you are alive."

"Sorry." He shifted. "I got… distracted."

She hummed, stretching and wincing. "I really need to stop falling asleep in random places."

"Why were you down here?"

"I was *trying* to stay awake." Brier fixed him with a look that made him flush.

He turned away to hide the color rising in his cheeks. "So you were talking to Goebel?"

Brier hummed again.

The heat slowly receded as Palmer gained control of himself, and he dared to turn back around. "I know who Marina is."

"The last me. Yeah."

"Oh." Palmer hesitated. "I was going to say Goebel's old girlfriend."

"Who was also, apparently, my last incarnation." Brier stood. "A little late to the party this time, Signore Omniscience."

Palmer shifted, feeling as though he were six years old again and had been caught stealing cookies out of the kitchen. The words all came out in a rush. "I'm sorry, all right? I froze up."

Brier studied him, tilting her head slightly to the side.

"Can you not do that?" He frowned, forcing himself to hold his ground and act like a man.

"Do what?" she asked.

"Stare at me like that."

She continued to study him. "I'm just trying to understand what you meant by 'froze up.'"

"Then just ask," he said, his voice stronger than he would have thought he'd be able to manage.

One eyebrow arched perfectly. "All right, then. What do you mean by—"

"Damn it, Brier, don't be snarky."

Brier sat with a thump. "*You* weren't the one who was stood up last night."

"I really meant to come," he said, the strength in his voice deserting him in an instant so that he sounded sheepish.

"Then why didn't you?"

"Just..."

She continued to watch him, waiting.

His stomach twisted. "Just, you scare me a little, all right?"

Both eyebrows rose. "I *scare* you?"

"That came out wrong." He held up his hands. "I just... I don't have much experience with women."

She frowned. "Did you think I was propositioning you?"

"No—"

"Because I'd like to think you'd know it if I were propositioning you."

"Brier, will you shut up and let me finish for once?" Palmer threw up his hands.

Brier snapped her mouth shut but continued to look at him in a way that seemed far too intimidating for her size.

Palmer swallowed and thought his words through. The honest ones came out. "I didn't mean you *scare* me. I just meant... I trip myself up around you sometimes. I didn't want to look like an idiot."

The look on her face melted into something kinder, even offering a hint of a smile. "Is this women in general, or just me?"

"Can't say I have much experience to know." Palmer crossed his arms, cursing himself as he shifted his weight between his feet again.

"You've seemed perfectly fine with me before." She seemed to be nearly teasing him, though he didn't understand why or how.

He frowned. "Well, I wasn't coming over..."

She finally laughed. "Palmer, I *promise* I wasn't propositioning you yesterday."

"I didn't say that you were."

She raised an eyebrow, disbelieving, but didn't argue.

Palmer ran his hand through his hair, a bit surprised at how long it felt after years of being kept short because he'd been an acolyte. He forced himself to focus. "Did Goebel sleep in here too?"

"I don't know." Brier let him change the topic. "He was awake, last I knew."

"He and Reinhald were out in the hallway before I came in. I think Reinhald was accusing him of making a move on you. You know, because of the whole Marina thing."

Brier shrugged.

Palmer's eyebrows knitted. "Did he?"

All he got was another shrug.

"Brier," Palmer said, voice a little sharp.

"Oh, it was nothing sordid, Palmer, I assure you." Brier waved it away. "He was talking about his dead girlfriend, nearly crying. I think he confused me for her for a second. He apologized immediately after. Wouldn't come within three yards of me the rest of the time we were talking."

"Immediately after *what*?" Palmer asked.

"Kissing me," Brier said, as though it were obvious. "Chastely, if it matters."

"He's old enough to be your father."

"I suppose. If he had had kids young." She pursed her lips as she thought, her face slowly turning into a knowing smile as she continued to look at him. "It really was nothing, Palmer. He's really worked up about this whole Marina thing—and sleep deprived, I'd bet. As far as I know, he could have been hallucinating."

Palmer tried to think of something to say but didn't trust himself enough to find anything that didn't sound... wrong.

"Now, what's that stormy look?" Brier smirked. "Not jealous, are we?"

"Why would I be?" Palmer asked.

"I don't know," she said. "Why are you?"

"I'm not."

"Good." She continued to smirk.

Silence fell over them for a long moment.

"He's not a bad kisser."

"Brier!" Palmer exclaimed.

She shrugged. "Just saying."

He shook his head, looking away.

CHAPTER ELEVEN

THE SKY WAS CLEAR, THE night silent. Everything seemed to have properly gone to sleep, yet Brier couldn't. As tired as she was, she just couldn't close her eyes and drift off.

Perhaps Palmer had rubbed off on her.

She certainly hoped not. She liked sleep far too much.

Turning onto her side, Brier stared out the window at the dark mountains. Something glided past in the moonlight and disappeared into the darkness. An owl, possibly. Or Cerise, looking to stir up more trouble.

Maybe no one truly slept in Ruhegipfel after a while. The place was special, no doubt, but also unsettling in a way Brier couldn't quite explain. Perhaps unease was keeping her awake. She'd been ignoring it for days, but the sensation was there, hiding in a corner of her mind, something wrong that she couldn't quite place.

She sighed and rolled onto her back, letting her head land heavily on the pillow.

Brier.

The voice in her head made her shoulders tense.

Open the door.

She shook her head slightly as if she could shake Palmer's voice loose.

Open the door, it repeated.

Cautiously, Brier stood and moved across the room. She waited next to the door, listening.

"Brier?"

His voice made her jump. She jerked the door open. "*How* are you in my *head*?"

"I remembered how to?" Palmer shrugged sheepishly. "I thought it was better than waking up the entire castle, shouting."

Brier pressed her lips together but didn't berate him.

"We need to go," he said, his body straightening into something surely meant to look determined.

She frowned. "Go? Go where?"

"Home, out, somewhere not here." He glanced down the hallway then looked back at her. "Can I come in?"

Brier stepped back just enough to let him slide through. "What are you talking about?"

He closed the door behind him with a click. "We need to leave."

"Why?"

"We…" He glanced at the door, shifting on his feet. "There isn't a lot of time to explain, all right? We need to go."

"You better believe there's time to explain before running off into the night on a frozen mountain because you got spooked."

He swallowed, finally leaning forward and speaking in barely a whisper, "Do you know what happened to Marina?"

"She died." Brier didn't bother to drop her voice to match his.

"How?" He met her eyes in the dim room.

Brier paused and finally shook her head. "I don't know. Somehow bad."

"I was trying to remember more about her for you," Palmer said, glancing back at the closed door once again. "Reinhald killed her."

Brier opened her mouth but didn't speak.

"Correct me if I'm wrong, but I was thinking you'd prefer not to wait around for that to happen to you," Palmer continued.

Brier's mouth worked as she tried to force out something that made sense. "Reinhald?"

Palmer released a breath. "Do you trust me, Brier?"

She hesitated before saying the first words that came to mind. "Should I?"

"Brier, please," he said, his eyes earnest.

Finally, she gave up trying to talk and simply nodded once.

"Then come on," Palmer said, moving toward a bag in the room. "Pack your things. We need to leave."

His flurry of activity finally snapped Brier out of her haze. "Could you be mistaken?"

"You wanted omniscient." He grabbed some things out of her dresser and stuffed them in the bag. "I remembered. Bad things happen here to people with powers—especially dangerous powers."

"We should take Rosette, then," Brier said.

Palmer slowed, shoving yet another robe into the already bulging pack. "Rosette?"

"She has powers. Dangerous ones. They don't know yet, but..."

Palmer hesitated and finally nodded. "Go grab her, then. I think she trusts you more than me."

Brier nodded. "What will you do?"

"Finish packing what we can carry."

Brier shifted the little girl on her hip, trying not to disturb her more than necessary as they hurried down toward the valley. Though Brier and Palmer couldn't sleep, at least Rosette deserved to get some.

Palmer led the way, glancing furtively back at the castle, which grew ever smaller behind them, high on the hill. Only when Ruhegipfel had shrunk to nothing more than a vague shadow off in the darkness did he ease off, settling into a more humane pace.

He motioned toward the girl in Brier's arms. "Do you need me to carry her?"

"Don't bother her." She shook her head, speaking softly. "Anyway, I think the bags weigh more. She's nothing but bones."

He glanced at the castle-shadow and the rest of the land around them. *All right.*

"And stay out of my head," Brier hissed. "I don't like it."

He nodded, looking down the hill. "There's a town not too far away, down in the valley. We can rest for a bit when we get there."

Brier didn't respond but just continued placing one foot in front of the other as they walked in silence. Finally, she cleared her throat. "Are you ever actually going to tell me the entire story?"

"What?"

"I took Reinhald as a murderer on your word. You don't think I deserve a little more of an explanation?"

Palmer seemed to be working something out even as he spoke. "*Murderer* is a little harsh, I suppose."

Brier frowned, slowing to a stop. "What?"

"Keep moving, or your legs are going to stiffen up."

"Did he kill her or not?" Brier remained in place, shifting Rosette higher up on her hip before going still again.

"He did," Palmer said. "He did. Can we talk about this once we get to town?"

"I think I deserve to know," Brier said.

Palmer sighed, turning to face her straight on. "She died as his weapon, all right? Died because he pushed her into battle."

Brier furrowed her eyebrows and shook her head slightly. "Goebel loved her."

Palmer paused, swallowing as he looked back up the mountain. "They're not good people, Brier."

She didn't answer.

"Come on." Palmer turned and walked away. "We need to get as far away as possible before morning."

"Why would he even need her for a battle?" Brier followed, forcing her legs forward again. "I can't imagine Ruhegipfel's been in many wars. Who are they really going to fight?"

"Whoever pays the best," Palmer said.

"Palmer," Brier hissed, her voice rising as much as she dared with Rosette still in her arms. "You need to tell me what the hell you're talking about."

He released a breath and slowed, just enough to end up next to her. "They're mercenaries. Or were. Reinhald and Goebel are only able to control our powers. They can't attack anyone on their own. And who's going to pay for a magical mercenary who can't actually use their magic to fight? They *need* you."

Brier pressed her lips together, trying to take everything he said in, trying to determine if she could believe it. "They know you're omniscient. Why would they even attempt to lie?"

"Hoping it would take a while for that to come up?" Palmer suggested. "I don't know. Honestly, I don't think they fully know what I can do." Palmer's pace quickened again. "Please trust me. I'm trying…"

Brier waited for him to finish the thought.

"I'm trying to… *protect* us."

Brier let the statement hang over them for a long moment. Finally, she forced herself to speak again. "Do you at least know where we're going?"

"Enough so," he said.

Brier released a breath through her nose, unanswering.

CHAPTER TWELVE

*"*W*HAT DO YOU MEAN 'THEY'RE gone'?" Reinhald paced.
"Exactly that," Goebel answered, rubbing his hands over his face, dark circles plainly visible under his eyes. "They're gone. Not here. Somewhere else."*

"Both of them?"

"The girl too." Cerise strolled into the room, her quick stride betraying her apparent calm. "The little one."

"Rosette?" Reinhald stopped moving and looked at her.

Cerise shrugged, crossing her arms.

"Did we even know what she is?" Reinhald turned to Goebel.

"You're the one who brought her here." Goebel sighed, looking out the window.

Reinhald was already back to Cerise. "Get out there. Look wherever you need to. Just bring them back here."

Cerise gave a half salute, and a raven replaced the woman in an instant. Rocco flapped after her.

Palmer opened his eyes, and the Ruhegipfel library dissolved into a small attic room as his eyes focused, a little unwillingly. Obviously, he would need more actual practice if he was going to make a habit of doing that, calling up *real* visions. Scanning the windows, the rafters, even the hatch that led to the ladder down, his eyes landed on the two blondes lying on a pallet in the corner. It wasn't as nice as the bed at Ruhegipfel or the one Brier must have had in the Augarian Palace, but Brier had still been dead asleep from the second she lay down. Rosette had never stirred at all.

As if Rosette could feel his eyes upon her, her eyes fluttered open, meeting Palmer's in the gray morning light. He pressed a finger to his lips, glancing at Brier. Rosette followed his gaze, moving only her eyes, then nodded as if she understood, allowing Brier to continue cradling her.

Palmer released a breath, looking at the small window on the far wall once again. Wherever Cerise and Rocco were, they weren't there yet.

"Are they looking for us?" Rosette finally asked, her tiny voice carrying remarkably well across the room.

Palmer nodded.

"Are we running?"

He took his time answering and finally just released another long breath. "I don't know yet."

Brier seemed to wince in her sleep, and her eyes opened gradually. She looked slowly around the room. Finally, she groaned. "I was half hoping last night was a dream."

Palmer gave her a small smile. "They know we're gone. Cerise is out looking for us... with the bird."

Brier sat up, wincing again. "Please don't say we have to go. I don't think I could walk more right now."

He sat forward, resting his elbows on his knees. "I was just trying to figure out if it would be safer to go or to attempt to wait it out here."

"They'll be flying." Brier didn't look at him, focused on rubbing her right calf. "They're more likely to spot us if we're out on the road."

"More people could pinpoint us here," Palmer argued.

"Just the innkeeper."

Rosette popped up to her feet. "I can help! I can keep him from telling."

Palmer frowned. "How?"

"I'll make him sick. Lose his voice."

"No." Palmer shook his head.

"That's not a bad idea." Brier leaned forward over her legs, grimacing as she stretched. "Cerise undoubtedly knows all the paths out of the mountains, and she'll be moving faster than we ever could." Brier sat up straight again, turning her head to Palmer. "And she's proven she can best you."

Palmer made a face. "She wasn't a woman when that happened."

"Now, now," Brier said, cocking an eyebrow and jutting out her jaw in some mixture of mockery and challenge. "No shame in getting your ass handed to you by a girl."

He just met her eyes, not rising to the bait.

"I have no doubt she's the one they're sending for a reason." Brier looked away, backing down. "She can beat us in a fight. And she can track us if we're on the move."

"We've been trained now," Palmer argued. "And we're together. We'd at least have a better chance now."

"Why did we have to leave?" Rosette's question hung in the air between them all awkwardly.

Brier raised her eyebrows and motioned for Palmer to answer.

Palmer pressed his lips together, considering what to say. He saw images of Marina's battle, which he'd been too young to remember, flickering into other images of the Augarian crumbling entirely if another battle—one with Brier—happened. The prophecy he'd refused to give credence to seemed more and more real the longer it plagued the back of his mind. He finally spoke, cautiously, looking only at Rosette. "They were lying to us. A long time ago, some people took over our home— Brier's and my home—and promised to pay Reinhald a lot of money if he helped them. He did, and a lot of people got killed because of it."

"Would we be killed?" Rosette's face worked through the information.

"Very possibly," Palmer said.

"And *that's* her connection to the Augarian," Brier murmured, her jaw clenched. *Why I reincarnated there.*

Palmer caught her ending thought like a whisper but didn't acknowledge it. Letting her know he could speak into her head had gone so well already.

Brier pressed her lips together tightly, unhappily, but gave him a single nod. "If we're going to be hiding out here, we're going to need food. Water—"

"I have some." Palmer grabbed his bag. "Not much, but enough for a few days."

"I'm good at finding food," Rosette said.

"We shouldn't go out." Palmer frowned.

"No one will see me." Rosette smiled. "They never do."

The small space didn't do anything for Brier's mood. Small and light on her feet, Rosette, at least, was allowed out to get supplies—something she was unquestionably good at. Bigger and more noticeable, Brier was restricted to the room with Palmer, waiting for whatever he was waiting for. She watched him out of the corner of her eye, certain she was still missing something, but whatever it was, he seemed less than willing to share. She stood sharply, unsure what she could even ask at that point.

Pulling the musty curtain back, Brier scanned the road below their little hideout, watching the townspeople stroll by in their odd, plain outfits.

"You should get back." Palmer watched her.

"Maybe you can spend all day staring at a wall. I can't." She didn't move. "Not without going mad, at least."

She could feel the unease coming off him, but he didn't chide her, thankfully. In her mood, he likely would have found her leftover apple core hitting him upside the head.

She finally let the fabric drop back into place and sat heavily on the pallet serving as the only bed in the small, dusty room, its floor rough and its low ceiling slanted. It had to be nearly as bad as actually being imprisoned, back home. "We can't stay here forever, I hope you realize."

"Rosette will be back soon," Palmer said. "You shouldn't worry."

Brier frowned. "I wasn't talking about Rosette."

"You always get tetchy when you're worried about Rosette being gone." He glanced at the window again.

"I get 'tetchy' sitting around here doing nothing day after day." She narrowed her eyes at him. "How long are you expecting us to go on playing ghosts in the attic? We'll have to go eventually, if only because Rosette won't be able to keep the innkeeper sick much longer without accidentally killing him. She's only six, you realize."

Palmer ran a hand through his hair, slid it back around, and covered his mouth with his palm. "Where would we go, Brier?"

Her eyebrows furrowed. "What?"

He shrugged, dropped his hand. "Where do we go? We can't go back to Ruhegipfel. We can't go back to the Augarian. Do you have a plan?"

"Why can't we go back home?"

Something flashed over his face as though the question had thrown him for some reason. The look disappeared before she could fully understand it. "People know who you are there, too. I imagine it's why the elder Adessi-Guillroy was interested in you marrying his son. I can't imagine it's just because you're pretty." He paused. "Or for extended reading hours."

Her shoulders stiffened. "I take back what I said about working on the omniscience thing. It's creepy."

He shrugged. "I wasn't trying. You were just dreaming about it last night."

She stood again and paced in the short area where the beams were high enough to stand upright. "What did I tell you about staying out of my head?"

"It's not my fault," he said. "Your thoughts leach into mine sometimes."

Maybe I should just try stealing all of your thoughts, then. Brier made a face as she mocked him in her head.

Maybe you should, his voice responded.

"Stop it!" She turned on him.

"Stop thinking so loudly, then," he snapped back. "Your voice is in my head just as much as mine is in yours."

The thought made her pause.

"You're harder to keep out than the rest of it," he mumbled in conclusion, looking down at his hands.

Brier hesitated another moment and finally attempted to direct her thoughts forward. *Does it feel as weird to you as it does to me?*

He lifted his eyes. *It feels pretty damned weird.*

Brier finally sighed, looking out the window again before leaning against the wall and looking back at him. "Then what are we doing?"

"About what?" he asked.

"We can't go back. We can't go home. We can't live up here the rest of our lives. We have to do something."

Palmer looked down, back up, and down again. "I suppose the only answer is 'go somewhere else.'"

"Go where?"

He shrugged. "Etrusa, maybe? We'd speak the language. Maybe I could take up as a county Seer. I could support us like that."

"You don't want to be a Seer." She shook her head.

"No, but I'm trained to be. And I think you'd prefer that to us trying to live as farmers on some barren plot somewhere."

"I'm not sure how a county parish would take to their Seer supporting a young woman and little girl on their tithing. You'd think tongues would wag." Brier released a breath. "Anyway, it wouldn't be fair to ask you to support us. You aren't my husband. You aren't her father."

"And what would you do, Brier?" he asked. "You aren't trained in anything, not even pickpocketing like Rosette. You aren't qualified for a career, and I don't think you're very well suited to a life on the street. I'm not going to leave you to be a beggar or prostitute."

Brier frowned. "I'd like to think I would find some other choice than those two."

"All the same," Palmer said.

Brier released a long breath. "I'd think you'd make a better scholar than Seer. What about one of those great universities you were talking about in the east?"

"I'm too young. Not qualified. I haven't finished my course at university."

"Not qualified?" Brier raised an eyebrow. "You know everything. Quite literally. I'd think they would be hard pressed to find someone more qualified to teach."

"I don't think 'omniscient being' would work on my curriculum vitae."

"You could always fake something there," she argued.

"They wouldn't look into a nineteen-year-old claiming the background I'd need to teach? Last thing we need is them sending a letter to Latysia."

Brier pursed her lips, looking down at her feet as she considered their quickly dwindling options. "So, what do we do?"

"Either wait here or head south, I suppose," Palmer said, offering an apologetic smile. "We can't trust that people will speak Latysian much farther north. And I'm not sure we'd want to find out with autumn coming. I'd personally prefer not freezing to death in the mountains."

"People will be expecting us to go south," she said.

"Hopefully, they've already checked and are looking elsewhere."

Brier released a tense breath through her nose but didn't argue. She looked back out the window.

Even in the valley, the night air chilled Brier enough to make her shiver. After nearly a week locked inside an attic, the world outside seemed too big, too cold, and too sharp. The smell of dry leaves and dirt freshly turned up from the harvest replaced the dust and dank she had grown used to in the small room. It assaulted her, making her nervous.

Pulling the hood farther over her face, Brier burrowed into the thick robe, feeling entirely the shadow in the night, running away from some unseen foe, from daybreak.

Rosette didn't seem nearly so perturbed, running out ahead, stopping to look at something interesting at the side of the road, then running back to them just to start all over again. She was a little girl out past her bedtime, enjoying her refound freedom, having the time of her life.

Palmer let her go but watched closely, ever cautious, always ready to call her back at the first sign of... anything, Brier supposed.

Brier came up beside him, watching Rosette duck behind a boulder and reappear on the other side. "You aren't worried about her being so far ahead?"

"I'm keeping an eye on her," Palmer said. "She seems to know what she's doing so far."

Brier's shoulders tensed. She frowned at the feeling.

"What?" Palmer asked, studying the side of her face for a moment before looking back at Rosette and scanning the path.

Something clicked. Brier forced herself to relax, trying to sound as nonchalant as possible. "You trust a six-year-old to take care of herself more than me."

"No." He shook his head.

She sent him a look.

He didn't bother to attempt a better defense, continuing to scan the area.

She remained silent, disappearing farther into her robe.

"Quiet night," Palmer finally said.

"Yeah," Brier didn't fight the change in topic, unsure she wanted to continue with hers.

"I don't like it," he continued.

"No?"

"Easier for someone to hear us coming."

Brier shrugged. "Easier for us to hear them."

"Not if they're sleeping."

Brier looked around, her world framed by the hood of her robe, boxing her in. "It's freezing out. I don't think this is camping weather."

"Unless there's a reason for it to be," Palmer said.

She frowned at him. "Like what?"

"Looking for someone," he said. "Or for trouble, for that matter. Any night is a night for camping, to a criminal."

"We may not have *much* training, but I think the three of us could take your average robber. Not as though we have much to steal, anyway." She paused. "It would be Cerise finding us I'd be more worried about."

Palmer nodded.

"You don't know where she is?"

"No." He sighed and jumped slightly as a twig snapped under his foot. He scanned the area. "Since they realized we were gone, I haven't been able to see any of them. It's like there's something in the way, something blocking them."

Your powers are only ever nearly infuriating, huh?

He gave her a weak smile.

Rosette rebounded, coming to a halt directly ahead of them. "Why are you going so slow?"

Palmer's smile grew, suddenly looking more genuine. "We don't want to waste all our energy now. We have a long few days ahead of us."

"We'll be fine." Rosette nodded, her body language determined.

"I'm sure we will be," he agreed.

CHAPTER THIRTEEN

"WE WON'T BE ABLE TO *keep these shields up much longer without Brier sensing it.*"

The voices, more inside his head than out, jolted Palmer out of his daze. He straightened his back and looked at the two sleeping women then around the little circle they had found hidden in some rocks. Nobody was around, not that he knew. He closed his eyes, trying to focus.

"It isn't her we have to worry about. Palmer's further along with his abilities. He'll sense us coming before the girl."

"We don't even know if we're going the right way."

Goebel's voice hit Palmer louder, clearer than the others.

"Did you see them?" Reinhald asked.

"No," Cerise's voice joined. *"But where else would they be going? There's only one road south through the mountains."*

"Unless they're going southeast," Goebel said.

Reinhald snorted unhappily. *"They wouldn't know those roads."*

"Palmer arguably would," Goebel said, his voice almost teasing.

The speaking paused for a long moment.

"Cerise," Reinhald started again, *"fly a circle east in the morning. See if you find any sign of them."*

The voices shut off, as if a door had shut in Palmer's face. He looked up at the sky, off to the east.

"What was that?" Brier's whisper made him jump. It was somehow more intrusive than the other voices.

"What?"

"Shh." Brier glanced back at Rosette.

However, he honestly wasn't worried about Rosette, who slept more soundly than any child Palmer had ever met. He dropped his voice. "What are you doing up?"

"I don't know." Brier sat next to him, pulling her knees up to her chest. "Something woke me. Nothing's happened?"

"Not around here," Palmer said.

She frowned, tilting her head as she studied him in that way of hers.

He sighed. "They're still looking."

"Cerise?" She pulled her robe down more tightly, forming a little tent around herself.

"And the Goebels," Palmer said.

"You saw it?"

He nodded. "Popped into my head all of a sudden, but they're blocking me somehow. Heard that much. Goebel is worried you'll sense them if they keep it up, though."

"Me?"

"It's what he said." Palmer looked around again. "I couldn't see them. Just heard it, and then they shut me back out. Maybe that's what woke you?"

"Maybe," she said softly. "You don't know where they are?"

He hesitated and saw no reason to worry her. "No."

"I suppose I should keep an eye out." Brier yawned. "If I'm the one they're worried about."

"In the morning, maybe," Palmer said. "You should try to get back to sleep. We have another long day ahead of us."

"What else is new at this point?" Brier sighed. "I stopped being able to feel my legs two days ago."

"I don't think that's a good thing." He looked at the lump that was her knees under her cloak.

"I'm tougher than you think, Signore Tash." She added under her breath, an afterthought, "Tougher than I would think."

Palmer tried to think of something to say but came up empty.

"You know," she continued in the silence, "if you're going to try to pass yourself off as a village Seer, you should probably add something to Tash as your name."

"Sage Tash-Parrino?" Palmer raised an eyebrow.

"No." She apparently missed his sarcasm. "No reason a Parrino would be out in the country. Tash-Paro, perhaps. Tash-Conus if you aspire to greatness."

"I'm not sure how the Church would feel about me taking either of those."

"So we find somewhere too small for them to take notice," Brier said simply, pursing her lips as a thought came to her. "Tash, though. It's not a very common name, is it?"

"Not as far as I know," he said.

"We should probably change that as well, then. Be entirely new people."

"You don't want to be Brier anymore?"

"Brier Chastain-Bochard," she said. "If you think a village Seer traveling with a woman and a little girl—*supporting* a woman and little girl—would raise eyebrows, do you think it would help if that woman's called *Bochard*? Wouldn't exactly go without notice, I would think."

"Fair point," he answered.

Brier smiled. "I thought so."

Palmer sat in silence for a long moment. "Who do you think we should be then, Signorina not–Brier Chastain-Bochard?"

Her smile slid off her face slowly as she considered the question. "I don't know... What's your middle name?"

"Don't have one." Palmer shook his head.

Her frown deepened. "Your father's name?"

"Not one I care to use."

She sighed dramatically. "You're not being very helpful."

"I'm just saying." Palmer looked away, scanning the area as he tried to ignore the thoughts bubbling up. If he started to think about his father, he'd start to think about his father leaving—chasing some dream of gold and glory—and then he'd think about what that had done to his mother— his mother and him.

Brier released another long breath, pursing her lips. "What's your mother's name, then?"

He furrowed his eyebrows, forcing himself back to the present. "You want to give me my mother's name?"

"Just use it for inspiration."

He hesitated and finally spoke softly. "Iris."

Brier nodded contemplatively. "Pretty."

He didn't answer.

She tried out the sounds. "Is. Ir. Ris. Rhys? I knew a boy named Rhys once."

Palmer just looked at her.

"Rhys Ceresei, I think it was."

"I don't think I should steal the man's entire identity if it was," Palmer said.

"Perhaps not," she agreed. "Cersetto, then?"

"Is that even a name?" Palmer asked.

"I don't know." Brier rolled her eyes. "It sounds like one, doesn't it?"

He shrugged, studying her. "Are you going to be Clover, then?"

Brier's head snapped toward him, then her face set as something dawned on her.

"Sorry," he said before she could speak, tapping the side of his head. "But, your mother's name, yes?"

Brier rolled her eyes, and she looked away again. "I don't know if I'm much of a 'Clover.' My father always joked that they named me Brier because—"

"You're like your mother, only pricklier."

That time, he was rewarded with a proper glare.

"Sorry. I really wasn't trying."

She kept her eyes narrowed for another moment before finally speaking again. "I can see how you lost that young."

"What?" he asked.

"Your..." She tapped the side of her head, nearly mocking. "It could be hard for some people to be around."

"People like you?"

"More than me," she said, not giving him time to linger on the thought. "People have their secrets. The more you have, the less likely you are to care for having a child around who knows them all. Would be hard on a small boy, hard enough that he might forget he can."

He studied her. "What are your secrets, then?"

"Don't you go thinking about *that* too much, Palmer-Rhys. I don't like you in my head as it is."

He managed a smile. "I really do try to stay out of your head as much as possible, you know."

"So you tell me." She yawned.

You can poke around in mine if it makes you feel better.

She released a sigh-groan. "Why would I want to do that?"

I don't know. If you don't want to feel like it's all me in yours. He looked away. *I don't have anything to hide.*

"Oh, I sincerely doubt that," she answered.

He let the topic drop. "What do you want to be called, then?"

Brier pressed her lips together, staring off for a long moment before finally speaking again. "Portia."

"Portia?" He frowned.

"It was the name of a girl my father had watch me when I was little." Brier shrugged, her body language turning defensive. "A maid's daughter, I think. She was sent away not long after Nico arrived. I don't know where she is now."

"Why was she sent away?"

Brier smiled. "No one would tell me at the time, but I found out years later that, word was, five months after she'd gone, she had had a child and a Parrino was paying for her household."

"She had a Seer's child?"

"So it would seem," Brier said. "Fitting name, isn't it?"

"Fitting?"

"You support us, and there's no way people aren't going to whisper that the little blond girl living with us isn't ours."

"She's too old to be ours."

"She's small for her age," Brier argued. "And since when has logic found a place in town gossip?"

"About as often as it has in religion." Palmer glanced upward then around them, down the valley pass below them and at the mountain trail behind them.

Brier laughed lightly, glancing at Rosette. "How did you manage to become an acolyte with that attitude?"

"Natural talent and not giving a damn, mostly," he said.

Brier smiled, but the expression slowly slid off.

"What?" Palmer asked, doing his best to not slip into her mind as he tried to read the look.

"Oh." The smile came back, a little more forced. "I was just thinking that I'm relatively sure that's Nico's entire approach to life." She paused. "Did you know Nico? You might have been in some of the same classes."

"Adessi-Guillroy?" Palmer asked. When she nodded, he continued, "Not well. We didn't exactly run in the same circles."

"I think you would have gotten along."

Palmer snorted before he could stop himself.

"You don't think so?"

Palmer pulled at the sparse grass covering the clearing, not sure how to even begin answering. "I think we're very different people."

"You might be surprised," Brier said, adding, "He isn't as much of an ass when he isn't trying to be."

Palmer didn't answer, continuing to pluck at the grass. The silence stretched on awkwardly. Flicking his eyes back to her, he prepared some sort of an apology, but Brier wasn't even looking at him.

"It's hard to care sometimes, isn't it?" Brier stared up at the clear, cool sky.

"I... uh..." The half-formed apology tried to stumble out of his mouth. He stopped it and recovered. "What?"

She made a face, as if trying to think of the correct words. Finally she just shook her head. "What do you think happens after we die, Palmer?"

He hesitated then repeated, "What?"

"With your views on religion, I doubt you believe we travel to the gods' plane to live there after we die."

He thought about it. "I suppose not."

"Did you ever?" She frowned.

"I never spent much time thinking about it, I guess." He shrugged. "What about you?"

"I always sort of believed it, I suppose." Brier sighed. "Never thought of anything else that might happen. Though more and more, I've been thinking about this being all there is."

Palmer furrowed his eyebrows. "Yeah?"

She nodded, an odd look crossing her face.

He felt himself sliding into her mind and did his best to pull back out.

She finally just sighed again. "I try not to. It's unsettling, thinking we all just... disappear. But then, would it really be so bad? You're gone. You can't care if there's someplace to go to after or not. It only matters while we're here. And really, there being nothing, that little weird something in me loves that. Craves it, in a way. Perhaps that's just as unsettling in itself."

Palmer took a moment and finally said, "I don't want to die."

"Oh, neither do I," she assured him quickly. "Really. I've never thought that. I just..." She closed her eyes and opened them again. "You're something, everything. You struggle with your body sensing too much. Whatever is in you wants to know everything, experience everything. Mine wants nothing, and that's a problem in a living body. I sense things. I feel things. And, honestly, it feels like part of me is still coming to terms with that."

Palmer nodded.

She finally looked at him. "I probably sound mad."

"I don't think I, of all people, can call you mad."

She nodded, studying her interlaced hands. "It wouldn't be all bad though, really, don't you think?"

"Dying?" Palmer asked.

"There not being anything after we die."

He didn't have an answer, so he simply waited for her to continue.

"You'd at least think people would live better if they knew they wouldn't get a second chance."

As they traveled, the mountains slowly began to level out, turning into rolling farmland. All at once, Brier felt as though she could breathe again. The silent tension Palmer had been carrying with him through the mountains evaporated as they moved through the golden-brown fields.

"It really is fall, isn't it?" Palmer touched a haystack as they passed.

Brier looked at it then looked forward again. "So it seems. How far do we want to go... want to *keep* going? I'd think we'd try to get settled somewhere before it turns too cold."

Palmer slowed to a stop, looking at the farmhouse in the distance, at the rolling hills stretching out before them in every direction. "There's a city southwest of us. Rentia. Probably three or four days away. A small town, village really, is straight ahead. We'd be there by nightfall. And another small town is a day's walk east." He looked at Brier. "What's your poison?"

"We shouldn't go toward the water." Rosette appeared from between the stalks of an unharvested field, seeming to materialize out of nowhere. "The people there are sick."

Brier raised an eyebrow.

"Not from *me*." Rosette pouted.

Brier glanced at Palmer then back at Rosette. "How do you know that?"

"There's a lot of them." Rosette shrugged. "I can feel it. Sort of."

Palmer looked back to the southwest, peering into the distance for a long moment before wincing.

Brier watched his face and felt something flare. A vision flashed through her mind—of people coughing, vomiting, locked under quarantine as they wasted away—as vivid as reality. As it faded, she found herself still standing in the field with Palmer staring at her, an expectant look on his face.

"Yeah," she said, coming back out of Palmer's mind. "Not southwest."

He nodded, looking around. "East, maybe, then."

"Why east?" Brier asked.

He shrugged good-naturedly. "I have a good feeling about it."

By nightfall, the lights of the small town could just be seen in the distance, candlelight flickering in unshuttered windows, all gathered in a clump near the top of a little hill. It seemed warm, quaint, inviting—and just a little too far to reach before darkness would make walking too dangerous. They made camp with what few blankets they had in their packs.

"Do you think they'll like us there?" Rosette laid her head in Brier's lap, facing the town.

"We're likable people." Brier smiled, petting Rosette's hair lightly, smoothing out the knots that had formed. "If not, we'll just go on to the next one. No harm done."

"Will we have a house?"

Brier hesitated but finally nodded, the motion slowly growing in conviction. "Yes. Yes, of course. Hopefully, there will be one. If not, we'll just have to ask Palmer to build us one. There's plenty of land around."

"He knows how?" Rosette looked up at her.

"Well, he's supposed to know everything." Brier glanced over her shoulder, offering Palmer a quick smile where he sat a little ways away, giving them some sort of bedtime privacy. "Building a house has to be in there somewhere."

He smiled back.

"I've never lived in a house before." Rosette yawned.

Brier was at a loss for what to say, but it didn't matter. Rosette drifted off. Brier let the girl sleep in her lap a moment longer, watching the lights in the distance.

You should probably try to sleep too.

Brier looked back over her shoulder. *I'm fine.*

Palmer nodded, looking down at the brown grass.

Brier watched him for another moment. *Was that your vision?*

He raised his eyes again, questioning her.

The sickness, she specified. *In that town.*

He nodded.

Did you send it to me?

He shook his head.

She frowned. *Then how did I see it?*

Were you wondering what I was thinking? he asked. *I get pulled into your head sometimes when I'm wondering that.*

Brier lifted Rosette's head gently, laying it back down once she freed herself. She moved toward Palmer. *Could I even do that?*

We have a connection. Palmer watched her, some tension making his jaw go hard. *I don't see why you couldn't.*

She knelt in front of him, meeting his eyes for a long moment before reaching out and touching the side of his face.

"What—" he started.

She just shook her head, shutting her eyes and easing her way into his head. The slip was less jarring that time, a smooth passage, not a falling jerk into another place.

A ring of acolytes in their brown robes sat around a fire as someone, a Master, circled.

"Um... a bird?" One of the acolytes suggested.

"What kind of bird?" The Master stopped behind the speaker.

"A black one?"

"I think it's the city burning," another acolyte volunteered.

The image flickered unhappily. It was too recent a memory anyway. Brier pushed her way further back.

A small cell, nothing in it. Palmer unpacked his even smaller trunk, alone. So strangely alone.

An acolyte's first day in his own cell.

Further back.

A dormitory filled with young boys—Wards of the Church. Most argued loudly, tugging at some new toy while the caretakers fought to maintain order. Palmer sat on his own, shifting on an uncomfortable, squeaky bed, staring out a window.

The memory flickered unhappily but didn't die. Brier hesitated, curiosity getting the best of her. She pushed back even further.

Screaming. Panic. Fear—the kind that hit deep in the stomach, scrambling any logical thought. People hurtled down the streets of Latysia, heading for the last slums, heading for the river as fires jumped from roof to roof, out of the Augarian, over the mansions, down to the close-packed houses of Latysia's average citizens, inching ever closer to the wood tinderboxes of the poor.

Brier shivered involuntarily. The Reclamation.

"Palmer!" a woman, his mother, called out, grabbing the six-year-old's hand and pulling him close as they forced their way through the panicked crowd.

He clung to her, his lifeline, the only thing still protecting him from the madness.

They reached the river, by choice or by being swept along with the masses he didn't know.

His mother stopped them just outside the banks of the snaking, stinking water, grabbing both of his shoulders even as the crowd continued to jostle them. The fires swept ever closer, faster and faster as wooden house after wooden house went up.

She shook him slightly, forcing him to look at her. "Palmer. We need to swim. Do you remember when Hollis taught you how?"

Palmer nodded, his head barely moving.

"Stay by me." She tightened her hold on him. "But if you can't, if we get separated, keep going. We'll meet each other on the other side, where it's safe. Do you understand?"

How anything could be safe here, in all of the pandemonium, he didn't know.

"Palmer, say you understand me."

"I understand," Palmer barely whispered, his small voice getting lost in the cacophony.

His mother bent to kiss his forehead softly before jerking up and pulling him toward the river. "We do this together, manari. *"*

He gave another small nod, and they splashed into the river, lost among the countless others.

Seemingly wide and lazy, the speed under the Rumano's surface was swift. It pulled at Palmer's pants, threatening to take him off his feet altogether. Still, he followed at his mother's heels, struggling to keep up as she pushed her way forward in the water.

A man rushed forward, knocking Palmer loose. The current caught him, dragging him down and spinning him until he didn't know which way was up. Palmer fought to swim, holding his breath until he simply couldn't any longer. When he gasped, water filled his lungs, burning as it forced its way inside of him. He tried to cough and felt himself gagging, only taking in more water.

Slowly, his movements became sluggish. He stopped kicking, his hands went limp, his panic died as his vision blurred, and his mind went cloudy.

And then... light. The glow sank through him, filled him, and colored the world around him.

And it felt... right.

Palmer jerked back, looking at Brier as he breathed heavily. He finally turned away. "Sorry."

"You drowned," she said.

"I know, thanks."

She hesitated at the bite in his words but then continued all the same, "You said you didn't have anything to hide."

"I'm not hiding it," he said. "I just don't like thinking about it."

Brier nodded, releasing a breath. "I remember thinking, 'Is dying really this peaceful?'"

He looked back at her. "What?"

"That calm that comes right before you pass out. It was so… peaceful. Though I don't know if you passed out like me. I didn't get the light."

He just looked at her, his forehead creased.

"You aren't the only one who died, you know." Brier sat back.

He didn't speak but managed a strained smile.

Brier pressed her lips together, not pushing him as the full weight of the memory dissipated between them. She moved to take a seat beside him and found she finally needed to ask, "What happened to your mother?"

Palmer took a moment long enough that Brier began to wonder if he was going to answer at all. He released a breath. "She found me downriver when I finally washed up."

Brier's eyebrows rose. She fought her surprise away, clearing her throat. "So she survived?"

"Long enough to find me," he said, voice muffled.

Brier kept herself from asking more, just watching Palmer play with the grass.

He finally looked up again. "There had been that illness in Latysia that year, especially bad down near the river. More people were dying than they knew what to do with, so they had just been throwing the poor in, letting them wash away. The water was contaminated." He released a shaky breath. "More than a few managed to make it across, just to catch the illness on the other side."

"Like your mother."

He nodded, not meeting her eyes.

Brier pressed her lips together, sighing through her nose as she leaned back on her elbows in the grass. "Sometimes I think I'm lucky my mother died when I was so young."

"Yeah?" Palmer still kept his eyes down.

Brier nodded. "She was rather sickly, by all accounts, in and out of bed for the better part of her life. It's why I don't think anyone especially wondered when I had to take to bed every summer. Just taking after her, you know? It sounds likely she would have died anyway. At least this way, I can't miss her. You can't miss someone you can't remember."

Palmer ripped out a blade of grass with fervor.

"Though yours seemed very nice," Brier tried softly.

"She was wonderful," Palmer said. "Didn't deserve to die like that."

Brier tried to think of something else to say but couldn't find anything that wouldn't sound like a false platitude. She just nodded, slipping her hand into his.

CHAPTER FOURTEEN

P ALMER SAT SILENTLY ON A bench with both girls, watching a man move slowly back and forth across the small rectory. Sage Visentin, the village Seer, had to be over ninety. A bent little old man, he shuffled around, his feet dragging noisily on the floor. He took a kettle off the fire and poured the tea into a cup, seemingly drop by drop—however that was possible—before replacing it. He paused, finally looking toward the bench. "Would you care for a cup?"

Palmer, Brier, and Rosette looked at each other, shaking their heads in unison.

His hand trembling, the Seer shuffled back across the room with his tea, heading for the desk chair in the opposite corner.

Rosette watched him, her head cocked to the side. "Are you going to die?"

"Shh!" Brier looked back at the old Seer. "I'm sorry, Sage—"

Sage Visentin merely smiled, seemed to find the question amusing. "All of us are going to die someday, child." He sat, his bones creaking as he lowered himself into the chair with a groan. "Some of us just sooner than others." He looked among the three of them. "What did you say brought you to Lantello?"

"I don't think we did." Palmer sat forward, arms on his knees. "In all honesty, Sage, we are looking for a place to stay."

"And why Lantello?" Sage Visentin's face remained kind, his brown eyes seeming remarkably alert in his weathered old face.

"Well." Palmer took a moment, the story they had planned going muddy in his mind. Short lies he could do. Lies of omission he could do as easily as breathing. Actually relating an entire story like that, though... He really should have thought the plan through a little more. "We don't have anywhere else to go."

Slightly worried, Brier flicked her eyes toward him, but she didn't contradict him.

The Seer looked at them all, his eyes settling on Rosette before looking back at Palmer questioningly.

"Oh." Palmer's eyes widened as he recognized the silent question. "No, no. I'm Rhys, and this is Portia and her sister, Pandora."

Sage Visentin nodded slowly, his head moving an inch at a time. "And what are you three running from?"

Palmer frowned, the question a little more perceptive than he liked. "Sage?"

"Your accents, they're Latysian, no?" Sage Visentin studied them. "Though your clothes most certainly are not. You look as though you have been walking for weeks. You are certainly running from *something*."

"Kidnappers, Sage," Brier spoke when Palmer came up at a loss for words. She took over, delivering their story much more smoothly than Palmer had been managing, even as she adapted it last minute. "We're orphans, Wards of the Church. Rhys and I aged out a few years ago, so we decided there was truly nothing for us in Latysia. Pandora didn't want to be left alone, so we took her and headed out. We didn't get far, though... before we were taken off the road. We managed to escape, I'm not quite sure how long ago now, but have been wandering ever since. We just found our way out of the mountains a few days ago, and now we need a place to stay."

Sage Visentin's eyes didn't show any kind of accusation, just curiosity. After a long moment, he nodded again. "Well then, we are a simple country parish here, but it cannot be said that we turn away those in need. It isn't large, but we have a room for travelers you may stay in until we might find a place for you."

Palmer finally cut back in. "Thank you, Sage."

Sage Visentin waved the thanks away, taking a long sip of his tea. "Do you have occupations?"

Palmer looked at Brier and Rosette and then back at the Seer. "No, Sage."

He looked between them. "Wards of the Church?"

"Yes, Sage," Palmer said.

"You have been educated, then?"

"Yes, Sage," Brier said. Then she backtracked. "Not Pandora, much—she was too young—but Rhys, quite thoroughly."

He looked at Palmer. "You can read?"

"Yes, Sage."

"I might have some use for you, then." The Seer set his cup down with a shaking clatter. "My eyes have gotten quite bad with time. I have repeatedly been promised a replacement, but it seems the Church forgets about our little outpost more often than not. You have been trained in the religion, I take it?"

Palmer's cheek twitched.

"Of course," Brier supplied. "We both were."

"Then I can certainly find some use for you." The Seer smiled at Palmer then looked back at Brier. "And what can you do, child?"

Brier hesitated, apparently at a loss.

"She can read as well," Palmer supplied.

Sage Visentin nodded, keeping his eyes on Brier. "Can you cook?"

She hesitated. "I've... never tried, Sage."

"Gardening?" he asked. "Signora Terzi keeps quite an impressive herb garden. I'm sure she could use the help."

Brier floundered. "I can sew, embroider..."

"Sage, with all due respect," Palmer interjected, "I was intending to care for them. If you have any work I may secure for the long term—"

"This is not a town for idleness," Sage Visentin cut him off, eyes still on Brier. "I'm sure we will find something suitable that needs to be done."

Brier wiped sweat from her forehead, resting back on her heels. Her back hurt, her shoulders hurt, and her knees hurt from being on all fours. Her body might have adapted to hours of walking out in the wilderness, eating what Rosette found or Palmer had brought, but scrubbing floors was an entirely different brand of torture. She was quickly developing a new respect for the girls rarely seen around the palace who scrubbed the dirt off the marble floors and disappeared before the sight of them could bother a resident. Brier didn't know what they were paid for their work, but it certainly wasn't enough.

"You haven't finished?"

The voice made Brier jump.

"You're even slower than that sister of yours." Signora Terzi shook her head but still smiled, striding across the room more quickly than her stout frame would have seemed to allow.

"Pandora is a quicker study than I, I suppose." Brier went back to scrubbing, doing her best to keep the sarcasm out of her voice.

"You've never scrubbed a floor before?"

"Never found its way to being one of my chores, honestly, signora." Brier didn't look at the older woman.

Signora Terzi clicked her tongue, circling Brier. "You and your sister... tiny little things, aren't you?"

"Signora?" Brier lifted her eyes.

"We need to get some good food in you, by my estimation. Two girls, and there can't be a hundred pounds between the pair of you."

"I believe I have lost some weight recently, signora," Brier said, flexing her hand, unsure if the stiff fingers or raw skin hurt worse. "We've been walking for quite some time without much food."

"I heard, poor souls." Signora Terzi clucked again. "Sage Visentin should have sent you here straight away for a proper meal before anything. Well, finish up that floor and then come get something from the kitchen. We just took some fresh bread from the oven."

Brier tried to ignore the growl in her stomach at the mention of food. "Thank you, signora."

By the time Brier finished and forced her body upright again— apparently against its wishes—Rosette was already happily chomping away at the half-eaten loaf of coarse bread sitting on a wooden plank in the center of a modest kitchen table.

Signora Terzi laughed, bringing in a thick wedge of cheese. "Slow down, *piccola*. It's not going anywhere."

"It's *good*," Rosette said, crumbs spraying out from the corners of her mouth.

"Don't speak with your mouth full." Brier sent Rosette a chastising look before wiping her raw hands on her skirts and tearing off her own chunk of bread.

"Sorry," Rosette mumbled, grabbing a slice of cheese as soon as Signora Terzi had cut it, her hand no more than a blur between the block and her mouth.

"Pandora!" Brier snapped.

"Oh, let the child eat." Signora Terzi waved the admonishment away, handing Brier her own thick slice of cheese. "You too."

Hard and pungent, the wedge was exactly what Brier would have avoided on a dinner table a few months before. Weeks of stale crackers and hours of scrubbing, however, made any food impossible to turn away. She took a large bite, quickly following it with a chunk of bread. The grains in the bread, half-milled and making the bread rough and dark, crunched between her teeth. It was simple fare for a simple people.

"Where will you be staying?" Signora Terzi looked between them, not eating.

Rosette began to open her mouth, looked at Brier guiltily, and continued chewing.

"In a room at the rectory," Brier answered. "Sage Visentin has given Pandora and me the beds in the travelers' room, and Rhys is sleeping on a pallet in Sage Visentin's cell."

"Oh, the sweet young man I saw at the church earlier?"

"Yes, signora," Brier said. "Rhys. Sage Visentin's having him help there."

"Handsome young man," Signora Terzi said. "Too thin as well, but that's the lot of you. But still, the good Sage should have known better. Could have sent you girls straight over here. My dear Sofia's room has been sitting empty ever since she got married last year."

"Oh." Brier paused, food momentarily forgotten. "Thank you very much, signora, for your generosity, but we'd really prefer to be kept together."

Signora Terzi studied Brier. "The boy is special to you, I take it?"

"They're in love," Rosette said. She ducked behind her piece of bread with a smirk when Brier sent her a dark look.

Brier looked back at Signora Terzi. "He's a very dear friend, of both my sister and me. I've known him since we were both children. Even before our parents died."

Signora Terzi shook her head. "So young to be alone in the world. But I understand. Even an old woman like me can remember being young and in love."

"We're not in love," Brier said, filling her mouth with another large bite of cheese and bread.

"Of course, *cara*." Signora Terzi gave Brier a knowing smile that Brier wasn't sure she appreciated.

Palmer dipped an old pen into an ink well, copying the charts without thinking and making corrections as he went along.

"How are you doing?"

Sage Visentin's voice made Palmer jump. He looked over his shoulder, meeting the Seer's eyes, which were poking out over the top of thick reading glasses.

"Do you need help with any of the symbols?" Sage Visentin asked at Palmer's hesitation.

Palmer looked down at his chart, comparing it quickly to the Seer's. He shook his head, quickly adding a mistake or two before looking back across the room. "No, Sage. I think I'm doing well."

The Seer forced himself out of his chair—the chair, his body, or both creaking unhappily. He tottered over, pulling the glasses up to see clearly over Palmer's shoulder. He squinted, taking the chart in and nodding. "Better than well. I'm surprised they didn't keep you on to study. I've seen some newly trained Seers come out this way who don't chart half so well."

Palmer cleared his throat. "Thank you, Sage, but I didn't much care to be a Seer."

"No?" Sage Visentin asked.

"No. I wouldn't have been able to care for Portia and Pandora, that way."

Sage Visentin smiled. "You would have been able to care for them, I am sure. As a member of the Church, it would be your duty to. It would be other relationships that would not be allowed."

Palmer felt his face beginning to flush and forced the blush away. "That wasn't what I meant, Sage."

"There is no shame in wishing for marriage and family." The Seer's eyes twinkled kindly.

"No disrespect, Sage." Palmer felt the words coming more quickly than he could stop them. "But it would seem that the Church finds only shame in it."

The increasingly common amused smile turned up the corners of the old Seer's face. "Well, I suppose, then, we do things here a little differently than the Augarian might prefer. I'll trust you not to report us."

Palmer wasn't sure how to respond and decided staying silent was the smartest choice.

"In fact, the last replacement they sent for me is now quite happily married. Seems he was never much one for that part of the Church, either. We offered to allow him to stay on all the same, but it seems he finds farming much more agreeable to his temperament."

"You would have had a married Seer?" Palmer frowned.

"Well, I can't very well go on forever." Sage Visentin smiled. "And they leave us to our own devices here more often than not. I doubt the Augur is going to rally his forces to take on a small country village outside the borders of Latysia."

Palmer once again came up at a loss and just nodded.

"I'll let you work." Sage Visentin patted Palmer's arm lightly before picking up his own book and settling back into his chair. "You seem to be doing a better job than even I would."

Brier's body ached. She did her best to forget about it, leaning back against the stucco wall of the church's small garden. The sun long gone, a chill had saturated the air, but she didn't care, just enjoying being outside and doing nothing after hours of cleaning. Brier closed her eyes and took a deep breath, letting her mind wander, stretching out and sensing what was beyond it. Her mind crept along, following the shadows, weaving its way wider and wider around her.

Something flickered behind her eyes, a face, gone in less than a second. She frowned and focused. The face slid back into place then disappeared just as quickly, but not before she felt the recognition hit her, deep in the stomach.

Nico. His face was serious as he talked to someone.

She tried to get the image back but came up with nothing, just the shadows and the cold autumn night.

"What are you doing out here?"

She jumped, her body jarring painfully.

"Sorry." Palmer offered an apologetic smile.

"It's all right," she said. "Were you having a vision?"

He frowned, shaking his head. "No. Why?"

She released a breath, dropping her head against the wall. "Nothing. It… it's been a long, long day."

"Things didn't go well with Signora Terzi?"

She sent him as dark a look as she could muster.

His eyes widened. "What?"

Pulling her hands out from under her cloak, she held them up for him to see. Even in the pale moonlight, the red chafing was plainly evident, angry, nearly glowing. "She had me scrub the floor in her front room. I can barely curl my fingers now."

"Oh, Bri." He took her arm at the wrist and looked at her left hand. "Did you tell her?"

She shrugged, studying him as the pain seemed to lessen at his touch. "Since when have you called me 'Bri'?"

He hesitated. "It's just what came out. Sorry."

"Nothing to apologize for," she said, taking her hand back. "I have bruises on my knees, too, from kneeling all day. I don't think I'm cut out for this."

"We'll find you something else to do," Palmer said authoritatively. "This isn't acceptable."

"Like what?" She pulled her lips to the side, staring out at the garden, blue and barely visible in the dark. "Not like I'm much good for anything else."

"Sure you are." He looked surprised by the vehemence in his own voice and lowered it slightly. "What did you used to do back home?"

"Drink," she said, not sure if she was being humorous or not.

He actually rolled his eyes at her. "What else? You didn't spend all of your time drinking."

"A fair bit of it," she said. "Not as though there was anything else to do."

"You said you sewed," Palmer argued.

"Sometimes." She pushed a loose piece of hair away from her face with the back of her hand. "Embroidery more than anything."

"There has to be a seamstress around. Or a tailor. Maybe you could work with them."

Brier shook her head, pulling her cloak away to look at the simple linen blouse and homespun skirt she had been given. "The people around here don't seem much for embroidery. There don't seem to be many wealthy ladies demanding it. I wouldn't be surprised if most around here sew their own clothes, in general."

Palmer released a breath. "We'll find you something, all right? I'm not going to let you rub your hands down to the bone day after day."

Brier actually managed a smile for him, nudging him lightly with her elbow. "You're very sweet. You know that?"

He offered an embarrassed smile, looking down and away. "I'm just trying to make sure we're all right."

"You're good like that." She sighed. "It's just hard realizing you're really just not much use to anybody."

"Brier." He turned to her and caught her chin to turn her face toward him. "Don't *ever* say that. You are a brilliant, strong woman. You're part of what has kept me going."

She just looked into his eyes questioningly.

He suddenly seemed to realize their closeness. Clearing his throat, he dropped his hand from her chin and pulled back to a respectable distance.

She still watched him, cocking her head slightly to the side. "Are you in love with me, Palmer?"

"What?" His head snapped back to face her, his voice too loud again.

She smiled. "Rosette has been telling people we're in love."

A sound escaped that seemed lost halfway between a scoff and a laugh. "Where did she get that from?"

"She's six." Brier shrugged. "I'm pretty sure I still had an imaginary friend at six. Who knows where children come up with things?"

He nodded, a faraway look in his eyes.

She kept herself from sliding into his head, instead pushing herself upright with a grimace. "We should get inside. Our darling Pandora doesn't like being left alone too long."

Palmer sighed, standing himself. "I still don't know why you insisted on 'Pandora.'"

"She makes people sick," Brier said. "I thought it was fitting."

CHAPTER FIFTEEN

THE FOLLOWING WEEKS TURNED EASIER for Brier. Whether Palmer had said something or Signora Terzi had figured it out on her own, she pulled Brier off what seemed to be hard labor, setting her instead to sweeping, dusting, and straightening more often than not. Though that wasn't her first choice for a vocation, Brier could at least manage it. Rosette, on the other hand, took to the work with a cheerful fervor, cleaning every small crevice of the house, lovingly polishing anything she saw as precious. As long as Signora Terzi allowed her to play with Sofia's old dolls and kept bread on the table for lunch, Rosette seemed happier than Brier could ever remember being.

Still, Rosette refused to put on weight. The hollow that Brier's stomach had developed after days of walking started to fill back out. She began to feel a little sturdier in a way she hadn't noticed had been missing, but Rosette remained the same little wisp of a girl she had always been.

"*Sottile come un pezzo di paglia,*" as Signora Terzi put it, *thin as a piece of straw.*

Brier observed Rosette carefully, alert for any signs of illness, but the little girl still seemed to be happy and healthy, even as a wisp.

Things could have been worse. Even living at the church was proving unobtrusive. For someone so seemingly close to meeting his makers, someone who had spent his entire life dedicated to their service, Sage Visentin seemed rather uninterested in religion. Beyond his weekly sermons for the town, the Seer focused on charity and education, something even Palmer seemed able to support.

One day, Brier was watching Palmer from her place on the floor of the small library Sage Visentin had collected over his long life, studying the concentration on his face. She glanced around and saw Sage Visentin with Rosette in the chapel, letting her put out the candles. Brier looked back at Palmer. "Careful. Someone's going to mistake you for a devoted religious scholar if you keep this up."

Palmer glanced at her, looked back at the book, and rubbed one hand over his once-again-short hair. "It's not a religious text."

"Then what is it?" She stood and moved behind him.

"Just an atlas." He pushed the book over so she could see it.

She looked at the beautiful, illuminated maps stretched out over the parchment, which appeared at least a century old. "Why so concerned, then?"

"Concerned?" Palmer asked.

"Serious, at least," she amended. "You were very focused."

"Just looking at where they're…" He searched for a word and settled on "wrong."

She leaned in a little, speaking lightly into his ear. "Well, not everyone can be omniscient… like some people."

He rolled his eyes, leaning slightly away from her before looking back. "Looking at mistakes helps me remember what's right. All right?"

She nodded. At Rosette's giggle, she turned to look back toward the chapel. "He's really good with her."

"What?" Palmer asked.

"Sage Visentin and Rosette. Pandora. She seems happy here."

"She likes having a family, I think," Palmer said.

"A family?"

He looked at her. "A sister." He motioned to Sage Visentin. "A grandfather. She's pieced together something she's been missing since her mother died."

"Been in her head too?" Brier rested against the desk.

"Briefly. I try not to be."

"Like you try not to be in mine?" She raised an eyebrow.

"No," he said. "I end up in your head without meaning to, half the time. I have to work at hers. And I don't especially care for it."

"For the work?"

"No, how it feels."

Brier looked at him questioningly.

"It's... odd in there. Dark."

Her eyebrows furrowed.

"Not 'she's going to kill us in our sleep' dark, just... literally dark. Like there's nothing where something should be, and everything is hidden in the corners, out of sight. Perhaps you'd be more comfortable in there than me."

She considered it, trying to work out what differences might exist between Rosette and her. She finally just shrugged. "I haven't been able to get into anyone else's head. Just yours."

"You do... something to me. My abilities." Palmer turned to look behind them. Rosette was speaking in Sage Visentin's ear, giggling now and again, amused by whatever secrets she was telling.

"What do you mean?" Brier asked.

He shook his head as if he couldn't explain it to himself, let alone her. "They work better with you, but I can't control it as well either. It's..."

"Odd?" she suggested.

He offered a quick smile.

Brier looked back at Rosette and the old Seer as the girl giggled again. "Anything we should be worried about?"

Palmer studied them for a moment and turned back around. "No. She's talking about Signora Terzi."

Brier nodded, watching him move to a new book. "You realize you're being groomed to take over, don't you?"

"Hmm?" He didn't look up.

"Sage Visentin has found a protégé." She glanced back toward the chapel. The other two had moved out of view—quickly for the nonagenarian. "Signora Terzi let slip that she wouldn't be surprised if you started giving sermons soon."

"I wouldn't be allowed."

"Allowed by whom?"

"The Church."

"I don't think they much care about that," she said, smiling. "There's no one else here. And he likes you."

Palmer didn't answer.

"It's what you were thinking, isn't it? To be a Seer in some remote village where we would be left alone? This seems to be the place for that."

He paused, sighed. "I suppose."

"That sounds enthusiastic." Brier moved to the tallest bookshelf on the far wall, running her finger along the spines.

"Do you know what happened to the replacement that was originally sent for Sage Visentin?" Palmer turned to watch her.

"Something bad?" she asked.

"He's married," Palmer said. "Signore Oren Arbore. Just had his fourth child, based on the church records."

"Not a bad fate." Brier lost interest in the old books and turned to face him. "I take it he no longer is interested in a life with the Church."

"Not at all," Palmer said. "Though Sage Visentin said they wouldn't have been against it."

"Against what?"

"Against him being married and being their Seer."

Brier's eyebrows rose.

"They are not the most conservative lot here," Palmer said.

"Downright reformists." Brier pursed her lips. "Sounds like the perfect church for you."

"Maybe," Palmer answered.

Brier checked behind them then moved closer as she dropped her voice. "Well, you're basically a god. If you can't be trusted to reform a church, who can be?"

Palmer gave her a less-than-amused look, rolling his eyes before turning back to his book. "I'm not sure major reform is the way to go if we're trying to keep our heads down."

"It doesn't have to be major." Brier finally allowed herself to smile. "As long as you keep letting us live here, I'm happy."

"Should we get married, then?" he asked sarcastically.

"Signora Terzi would be all for it," Brier teased, pushing it further. "And I think I'd make a very good wife, don't you?"

Palmer didn't answer, a visible flush working its way up his neck.

Brier smiled to herself, letting the thought of what the rest of their lives could be, living in the town, settle over them for a moment. A flash of home passed through her mind: her father, Nico, the library, the entire life she'd left behind. She glanced at Palmer to see if he had felt her thoughts, but he seemed intent on the book in front of him. She could be happy in Lantello. Life would no doubt be simpler. However, she couldn't fight the knot in her stomach, which was forming at the thought of never going back.

Faces haunted her: nonsensical, angry, scared, all vaguely familiar but oddly morphed. They didn't jerk her awake, like the nightmares she had had as a child, but left her uneasy, waking her with a weight in her chest.

Deep in the country, the nights were quiet, stretching on without fanfare as the townspeople all turned in, waiting for daylight to restart their days. But the darkness felt too quiet when Brier woke up alone. And she had more often than not, the past few nights. Releasing a breath, she took her eyes off the ceiling and scanned the rest of the little room. Even Rosette slept silently. No tossing, no snoring, a lump barely visible across the room.

Brier let her mind reach out, touched on Sage Visentin, and shivered. Even if he didn't seem outwardly different, as the autumn went, so did his strength. The Nothing was closing in on him.

She kept her mind moving, refusing to linger on the thought, and found Palmer, awake as always, in the garden.

Isn't it cold out there?

I don't feel it, he answered almost immediately, as if he had been expecting her to speak.

I'm sure your body does.

She could almost feel him shrug half-heartedly. *What are you doing up?*

She chose not to share the nonsense dream or the odd drive to return home, as dangerous as that might be. *Sage Visentin is dying.*

He paused. *Are you sure?*

I think so. It's getting closer.

Can you stop it?

Would you really want me to if I could?

Another pause. *I don't know.*

Brier waited but got nothing else. *What are you doing?*

Meditating, he answered. *It's nearly as good as sleeping.*

She nodded even though it was just to herself. *Can I come sit with you? I can't sleep.*

If you like. I'm up against the church wall.

Brier slid out of bed and fumbled with finding her robe and shoes in the dark. She slipped them on, looking around for a hat. Then she paused and shrugged to herself. She was bundled up enough, she supposed.

Palmer didn't even wait for her to fully leave the church. His voice slipped through her mind at the threshold. *When is he going to die?*

Brier stepped out into the cold night air, latching the door as quietly as she could behind her before answering. *How would I know?*

Death. Palmer opened his eyes as she approached, watching as she found a dry patch on the ground and settled herself next to him. *It's sort of your area, isn't it?*

"He's still living for now," Brier said, the whisper jarring in the silence. *I feel it close, though, waiting for him. But it's patient, not pressing down on him, just waiting nearby for when he's ready to go.*

Palmer didn't answer.

I mean, it's understandable, Brier argued. *The man must be nearing a hundred, honestly. There's only so long people can live.*

Palmer nodded, not looking at her, staring out across the garden.

She felt the slide into his mind and placed a hand on the ground as though it would help anchor her there. *What are you thinking?*

He looked at her, sad eyes shining in the weak moonlight. *What happens to us after he dies?*

Brier frowned but could only shrug. *You're the omniscient one. You tell me.*

Palmer studied her for another moment then shook his head, looking away again. *There are too many ways it could go. I don't know which is right. I can't sort through it.*

Brier looked at the side of his face and reached out to touch his temple.

He leaned away from her. "Please don't."

The whisper hit her as strongly as if he had yelled. She jerked her hand back and rested it in her lap for a long moment.

Sorry.

She nearly smiled, even through the haze of melancholia Palmer was giving off. He wasn't a man who couldn't apologize. Still, the smile died before it could reach her lips. *That bad?*

Some of them are. Others not as much.

Brier pulled her legs up to her chest, wrapping her arms around her knees. *Tell me one of the good ones?*

Palmer released a long breath, looking at her and offering a weak smile. *We stay here. You get married. As does Rosette, eventually. Both happily.*

You don't?

He shrugged.

Do you not want to get married?

I'd never thought about it, Brier. He shook his head. *By the time I was old enough to understand, I was already in line for the Church. I never figured I'd be able to get married, so there was no reason to think about if I wanted to.*

Brier nodded, thinking. *I wonder if Sage Visentin ever wanted to get married.*

Palmer stood, brushing off the seat of his pants. *Don't see why he wouldn't have if he did. We should get you back inside. It's cold.*

I'm fine. Brier looked up at him.

He frowned. *Are you sure?*

I'm not a child, Palmer. You don't need to send someone in to fetch me a coat. I'm fine.

He hesitated and finally sat again. *Sorry.*

You really don't need to treat me like a child all the time.

I don't.

"You really do," she snapped.

Palmer looked down and away.

She sighed at the hurt, confused expression on his face. *Sorry.*

I don't mean to.

I know. A cloud moved over the moon, turning the night pitch black until it passed. Brier looked up into the sky. *Have they given up looking?*

He didn't need to ask who. *Goebel has.*

But not the other two?

She took his lack of answer as a yes. *Should we be worried?*

No reason for them to look here.

Doesn't mean we shouldn't be worried.

Better things to worry about if we're going to start measuring every possible outcome.

Brier frowned, trying to discern what he meant under those words. Something tried to flash through her mind—a large crack opening up under tile. The image was snatched back before she could make sense of it. Still, Brier shifted uncomfortably. *What do you mean?*

He shook his head.

What do you see, Palmer?

Nothing that's going to happen, he answered, still not looking at her.

She considered forcing the topic but couldn't bring herself to go through with it. She wasn't sure she wanted to know. Releasing a breath, she dropped her head back against the stucco wall as they kept each other company.

CHAPTER SIXTEEN

THE CHURCH, PERFECTLY FINE THROUGH the fall, became a cold place come winter. Even keeping the fires burning, Palmer was able to see his breath mornings. It was probably for the best that Sage Visentin had taken to bed most days. Between Palmer's nights awake and Brier's and Rosette's help in the mornings before they left for Signora Terzi's, he was able to keep the church running without much help from the old man.

The sound of the front doors opening was clear even from deep in the little library. Palmer stood, quickly allowing his mind to land on the still-sleeping Seer in the far room before he entered the simple chapel.

A brown-haired girl, probably a little younger than Brier, stood at the end of the pews, carrying a basket and looking around. She smiled when she saw him, moving up the aisle with quick, short steps.

"Sage Cersetto, isn't it?" She held out a hand with her approach and shook his warmly. "Sage Visentin's helper?"

Palmer didn't object to the misplaced honorific but simply nodded. "May I help you?"

"I'm Vivi Terzi." She pulled her hand back. "Eudocia Terzi's niece."

"Good to meet you," Palmer said.

"Oh, we've met before." She paused and backtracked. "Well, not technically, I suppose, but I've seen you at services, helping Sage Visentin. We heard he was feeling poorly."

Palmer nodded, keeping his voice low. "The cold is making it hard for him to move around much."

"Oh, I hope he feels better soon." Vivi looked truly distressed. She held her basket out toward Palmer. "My mother sent me with some goods for Sage Visentin, to help him feel better. You as well. We've been meaning to properly welcome you forever. Just, everyone was so busy with the harvest, and then… Everyone is so glad Sage Visentin finally has help around here. Especially Signore Arbore. He's been worried he was going to be pulled back in if Sage Visentin got too old before they sent someone else, I think."

Palmer just took the basket silently.

Vivi looked at him expectantly then finally continued with a good-natured shrug. "But you're here now. Is Sage Visentin around?"

"He's in bed," Palmer said. "Resting seems to be the best remedy for him for the time being."

"Oh, of course." She finally dropped her voice to a whisper. "Sorry. Do you know when he might be up?"

"I'm not sure." He added, "I'm sorry."

"Oh, it's fine." She waved her hand much like her aunt. "We'll just come back over later. We don't live far."

"I'm glad." Palmer couldn't think of anything else to say.

A shriek made Vivi jump and nearly made Palmer drop the basket, a single, high-pitched wail, prolonged and growing louder. Vivi rushed to the door, Palmer a second behind her.

Brier ran up the street, Rosette on her hip, trying to shush the shrieking child.

"Wha—" Palmer started.

"Take her." Brier shuffled Rosette into his arms and sped off across the chapel toward Sage Visentin's cell, skirts flying behind her.

Palmer watched her, frozen, still holding the screaming Rosette. Signora Terzi lumbered up the church steps, out of breath.

"Aunt Eudocia." Vivi stepped forward. "What—"

The door to the cell opened, and Rosette stopped, the silence settling around them ominously.

"*Piccola*." Signora Terzi petted Rosette's hair lightly. "Whatever has gotten into you?"

Rosette began squirming, forcing Palmer to put her down. As soon as her feet were on the stone floor, she took off, following Brier back into the rectory.

The women followed closely, Palmer making a slow procession after them, his dread growing steadily.

He found Rosette in front of Brier at Sage Visentin's bedside, whimpering, "You have to stop it. Make it stop. Make it stop."

"Shh, *piccola*." Brier pulled her into a hug. "Shh, it will be all right."

"Eudocia," Sage Visentin said, his voice barely a whisper.

Signora Terzi moved across the room in two steps and dropped next to the bed, speaking with the Seer in hushed whispers.

Palmer didn't move from his spot by the door. He looked at the pair at the bed; at Vivi standing, face sad, a little ways in front of him; and finally at Brier and Rosette. *He's dying?*

Brier looked up from murmuring to Rosette to meet his eyes, still rocking the crying girl against herself. *Yes.*

How soon?

Brier glanced at the old Seer, murmured something else as Rosette let out a sob, and looked back at Palmer. *Now. You don't see it?*

Palmer felt the sadness in the cold room, seeing it as well in the faces in front of him, but he had a feeling that wasn't what Brier was talking about. *See what?*

The darkness.

Palmer just shook his head slightly. He definitely didn't see that.

Sage Visentin laid his shaking hand on Signora Terzi's forehead, leaving it there for a long moment, as though in benediction, before pulling it back and letting it drop on the bed.

Signora Terzi let out a gut-wrenching sob, and Vivi comforted her as the Seer looked at Palmer. The corners of his mouth turned up in what seemed to be the start of a smile, his eyes still twinkling even as they seemed to be dimming. He gave a shallow nod—in acknowledgement perhaps, or thanks, Palmer wasn't sure which.

Palmer started to speak, but the Seer's eyes were already on Brier.

"Thank you," he whispered, just loud enough for Palmer to hear across the room. "I'm ready."

Brier met his eyes for a long moment, still rocking Rosette, before giving her own shallow nod. She held Rosette more tightly, muffling the little girl's shouts as Sage Visentin closed his eyes. The old man's chest rose and fell, growing shallower and shallower until it simply stopped altogether.

A shiver went through him.

Brier inhaled.

Rosette and Signora Terzi sobbed.

The bed was full of Nothing.

Palmer sat in the silence of the chapel, barely moving. With all of the candles extinguished, and only the fireplace lit to one side, the small room suddenly felt gaping. Fading into darkness, the pulpit caught the light now and again, simple wood symbols appearing out of the shadows only when a log crackled or the fire flared. The body having been moved and the first wave of shocked—or just curious—mourners gone, the church felt empty.

The wooden floorboards creaked under Brier's feet, her cloth slippers brushing lightly as she approached. Palmer didn't move, staring at the pulpit, still as a statue.

After a quick pause, Brier continued forward, sitting next to him with a sigh.

Silence retook them.

"Is she all right?" Palmer finally asked.

Brier nodded, eyes still forward. "Finally wore herself out crying, I think. She's asleep."

Palmer nodded himself, listening to the fire crackle behind them. "She knew?"

"Sensed it, I think," Brier said. "She was sweeping in the kitchen, and then next thing we knew, she started screaming. Wouldn't stop. I had to figure it out myself."

"How?"

Brier hesitated. "How which part?"

"Either," he said. "How she knew. How you knew."

Brier released a breath through her nose. "You said it yourself: death is my area. Once I tried to figure it out, I sensed it. How she knew, I don't know. Sensed it too, I guess." Brier finally turned to face him. "It's hit her hard, Palmer. Poor girl has seen too much death in her life."

He couldn't find the words to speak. He unlaced his hands and sat back before going still again.

Without a word, Brier faced forward again, reaching over to lay one hand over his.

He didn't fight it, turning his hand so they met, palm to palm, curling around one another. And suddenly he didn't feel so alone.

"What did you see?" he asked.

She looked at him.

"You asked if I saw it. The darkness?"

"Oh." She looked straight. "It was Nothing, I suppose—Nothing closing in on him. I... stopped it. For a little while, at least. Enough for everyone to say goodbye."

"You stopped him from dying?"

"I..." She paused, struggling for words. "It's going to sound strange."

"I think strange has long since passed, Bri."

She smiled slightly, but it slid off her face as soon as it appeared. "I... well, I asked it to wait. And it did. Slowed down, at least."

Palmer nodded, sliding his hand so their fingers interlaced. She allowed it. Palmer held still for a long moment, finally looking down at their hands, his fingers coming up over the back of her thin, pale hand—still soft even under the calluses.

Carefully, he freed his hand, turning hers over. He touched the rough patches along the mounds of her palm. "Those from cleaning?"

Brier nodded, pulling her hand back.

He felt the loss immediately but had to let it go, watching her study her own palm.

"A true working woman's hands," Brier said before looking back at him. "Everyone back home would be scandalized."

Palmer looked away again, the word *home* sitting poorly with him. He leaned forward, elbows on his knees. "They want me to perform his funeral."

Brier didn't bother to look surprised.

"I don't know how to be a Seer, Bri."

"You've been training for a decade," she said, "and have been all but running the church the past month."

"The last funeral I went to was my mother's," he said quietly.

Her hand found his again, silently.

"Do you want to stay here?" he asked, fighting off the mix of visions that had been pushing down on him more and more consistently. An inevitable bad end was chasing them no matter where they settled.

Brier pursed her lips slightly. "We can't move Rosette right now."

He nodded.

"And where would we go?"

"I don't know." He shook his head. "I don't know."

The day of the funeral dawned gray and dreary. The wind bit at Brier's cheeks where she stood toward the back of the congregation, nearly at the graveyard gates, listening for any sound of Rosette coming from the church, from the bed she had refused to leave for days. Pulling her thin coat tighter around herself, Brier watched the two men from the town fight their way through the last few inches of frozen ground to make a proper grave. Palmer waited at the head of them all, looking as dazedly stoic as ever. Only the dark circles under his eyes hinted at any sort of true sadness.

Fleetingly, Brier remembered the funeral mass she had attended however many years before for a member of the Augur's college—Sage Something-Parrino. She could almost feel the black silk under her fingers, the thickness of the skirts, the embroidered bodice she had gotten just for the occasion, something eleven-year-old her would no doubt grow out of within a couple of years, if not sooner. The sea of black-veiled women at the church made it seem more an excuse to dress up and affect sadness than a truly somber event. The wailing had seemed theatrical, false, even to a child.

No one in Lantello wore black that day. With no time, money, or ability to get anything other than normal church-best clothing, the crowd was as colorful as ever. The sorrow, however, was genuine—no theatrics, just proper grief for the loss of a loved man, a dear friend. Brier felt the tears well up in her eyes and had to turn away.

After a few words, short, sweet, and hardly religious, and a few shovels of dirt, it was over. A fresh grave sat in the middle of a bare graveyard under a gray sky.

Brier remained where she was, letting the rest of the mourners filter out, not meeting any eyes.

Someone touched her arm, and she looked up just in time to see Signora Terzi shuffle out, dabbing her eyes behind the only proper mourning veil in sight. Brier's eyes slid down to a tiny, older woman peering up at her.

She patted Brier's elbow—perhaps the easiest thing for her to reach—before speaking. "We're glad to have you, but if you plan to live at the church, you might do well to at least get married."

Brier tried to respond but came up blank as the woman continued away. Shutting her mouth wordlessly, Brier looked back at Palmer, still standing by the grave, seemingly lost in his own world. She placed a hand over her stomach, finally registering the pull somewhere behind her navel, a desire to at least be near him if nothing more. Or was there something more? She forced the thought away, turning back to check on Rosette. Palmer seemed to want to be alone, and she had a six-year-old to care for.

CHAPTER SEVENTEEN

THE FACES WERE WORSE. STRESS, the lack of sleep, or something else—whatever the cause, Brier could barely close her eyes anymore without the odd visions fighting their way into her mind. Many nights, she barely managed to fall asleep—some nights, not at all.

At least she was never the only one.

Nothing if not a creature of habit, Palmer had taken up residence most nights in the back corner of the chapel, nearly hidden in his little nook. The first night after the funeral, she had missed him entirely, and the next, he had slipped away before she could say a word. And so she had been reduced to sneaking around, purposefully hiding herself from his powers long enough to come upon him before he noticed.

Moving silently once again, she made her way through the chapel, keeping her energy muted until she was next to him. She sat with a thump.

Palmer started. "Gods! Stop doing that."

"It's the only way you don't run away from me." She stirred the fire, just reachable with a poker, giving them a little more light before settling back against the wall next to him and pulling her knees up to her chest.

He shook his head. "I haven't been running away from you."

"Could have fooled me." She sent him a look.

He didn't answer.

"I don't think Rosette has seen you in days."

"Rosette hasn't left your room," Palmer said.

"Doesn't mean you couldn't come see her."

Palmer stared into the fire.

Brier pursed her lips and fidgeted, working out words in her head. "You aren't the only one who's hurting, you know."

"I'm not hurting."

"Don't lie to me, Palmer Tash." Brier frowned. "I know you better than that."

"I've just been…" He released a breath. "Thinking."

"About leaving?" she asked.

"About…" He paused. "It doesn't matter."

Brier closed her eyes, releasing a long breath. Between the sobbing Rosette, the sullen Palmer, the faces, and everything else, she couldn't bring herself to ask him about what might happen in the morning, let alone what he might be seeing for the rest of their lives. She was too exhausted to care. "I'm so tired."

"Then go to sleep."

"I would if I could." She looked at him again, not lifting her head.

Palmer seemed to debate saying something in his head but finally just reached out a hand to pat her clumsily on the back.

Brier snorted. "You aren't very good at the whole 'comforting someone' thing, hmm?"

He pulled his hand back sharply. "I've never had to before."

Brier rolled her eyes. "It's really not that hard, I promise. It's just being there for someone. *Not* disappearing any time they may possibly need you. Offering some *support* when they have a sobbing little girl who won't get out of bed. I'm surprised she's not wasting away, honestly. Gods know I've barely been able to get her to eat lately."

"She's grieving in her way," Palmer said. "She'll get over it."

"How can you just say that?"

"I lost my mother, who I had known a whole hell of a lot longer than this, when I was her age," he said, "and I got over it. She'll manage."

Brier frowned. "You obviously didn't."

He sighed, looking away from her. "Didn't what?"

"Get over it." Brier stood and moved back through the chapel. "You wouldn't be being such a jackass if you had, I'd bet."

"Hey." He scrambled up after her. "You have *no* right to judge me."

"And why not?" She spun back around.

"I lost my mother when I was six. My father, for all intents and purposes, when I was even younger. I grew up *alone* in a dorm with a hundred other little boys without their families, being pushed into a vocation I had no interest in but having no other choices."

"I didn't exactly have nothing but rainbows and sweets in my childhood."

"Oh, poor little rich girl," he nearly spat. "Lost her mother and then got to spend the rest of her life being taken care of while doing whatever she wanted. Yes, I think our lives are nearly identical."

Brier stiffened, her anger nearly crackling over her skin. "You hated your life, I got that, but don't you *dare* discount mine just because you're pitying yourself."

"Ask anyone, Bri, who had it worse off. I don't think they'd say you."

"I think they'd say Rosette," Brier snapped.

Palmer finally fell quiet.

"Did *you* ever live on the streets, Palmer Tash? Did you forget to tell me about that part in your little pity party? Yes, things were awful—I get it—but you don't have a monopoly on crappy childhoods."

Palmer remained silent.

Brier scoffed. "For someone who apologizes for everything, you really don't when it matters, huh?"

He didn't move.

Brier spun on her heel and walked away, ignoring her pounding heart.

Without Sage Visentin, all of Lantello seemed to go dead. Perhaps winter had caused the eerie silence, but Brier couldn't help but believe that losing the Seer had turned the already quiet village into something that seemed filled with more spirits than people.

Poor Signora Terzi seemed hit the worst. Always warm and smiling before, she became silent and withdrawn. Even without Rosette's help, Brier found her work dwindling. The only guests became family, happy to take care of the kitchen and the dirt themselves, and Signora Terzi removed herself to two or three rooms, asking only in single-word directions for those to be kept up. Most days, under Sofia or Vivi Terzi's tutelage, Brier made food, swept, and then had the rest of her day left to her own designs.

She wasn't sure if she was avoiding Palmer or if Palmer was avoiding her, but the church also felt emptier than ever.

Setting a tray down on the small desk in her and Rosette's room, Brier looked at the small lump buried under the blanket on the cot. "Rosette, *piccola*, it's been over a week. You need to eat."

"I don't wanna," the girl's voice came, muffled, weak.

Brier released a breath through her nose and placed her hands on her hips. "Rosette, if you don't eat now, I am going to force-feed you. You can't bring someone back to life by starving yourself to death."

Rosette gave a shaky breath and barely whispered, "I killed him."

Brier frowned, moving across the room slowly and sitting on the cot. "What do you mean?"

"He got sick."

Brier peeled the blanket back slightly. Beyond the sadness etched into the little girl's face, she looked exactly the same. Brier hesitated then stroked Rosette's matted hair. "He wasn't sick, *piccola*. He was old."

Rosette hiccupped a sob. "But I make everyone sick. They all die!"

"Oh, Rosie." Brier turned Rosette over and met her eyes. "People die. It's just what happens. Sage Visentin was very, very old. He wasn't sick. He was always going to die. Do you remember what you asked him the first night we got here?"

Rosette nodded slightly, looking away.

"He didn't die because of you, I promise." Brier tilted Rosette's chin up, the little girl's blue eyes rimmed with red. "Do you trust me?"

Rosette nodded slightly, bottom lip jutted out in a way that made her look even younger than she was.

"Then trust me now. You did *not* have anything to do with Sage Visentin's death. Don't you think I would know?"

Rosette gave the same small nod.

"Now, please eat, Rosie. For me?"

Rosette sat up slowly, her body seeming as stiff as Sage Visentin's always had.

Brier got up, brought the tray to the cot, and watched to make sure Rosette ate properly.

After a few bites, Rosette turned to Brier, and her eyes finally seemed to focus a little. "Why are you and Palmer fighting?"

Brier frowned. "What makes you think we're fighting?"

"You're angry."

"Doesn't mean we're fighting."

Rosette took another small bite, her eyes dropping to her lap. "Palmer's the only one who makes you angry like that."

Brier snorted lightly, shaking her head. "You just haven't seen me around many other people, Rosie."

Rosette gave her a disbelieving look then dropped her eyes back to the food. "You promise I didn't kill him?"

"I promise." Brier touched Rosette's thin shoulder, gripping it lightly. "I really do."

Palmer rubbed his hands over his face. His body felt... off. Maybe he was tired. Was that what *tired* felt like? He had been awake long enough he wasn't sure anymore. Whatever the feeling was, he didn't like it. He crossed his arms over his desk, rested his forehead on top of them, and closed his eyes.

"Are you actually sleeping?"

He jerked back upright, nearly toppling out of his chair.

Brier stood in the doorway with a candle, her head tilted as she studied him. "Sorry. I didn't know you'd be... asleep."

"I wasn't." He rubbed his face again, looking at her. "Did you need something?"

"Are we ready to apologize and start being friends again?" Brier set the candle on a shelf.

"I wasn't aware we weren't," he said. "Or were, I guess, for that matter."

She raised an eyebrow, the flickering light catching her features softly.

He swallowed. "We would have had to have been friends to not be friends, wouldn't we?"

She frowned, the question seeming to hit her harder than he would have expected. "What were we if not friends, Palmer?"

"I don't know." He looked away. "I never thought about it."

She released a breath, crossing her arms as she looked around the room. "Well, I considered you my friend, at least. You can think of me however you so choose."

He yawned, freezing for a long moment after he finished before sliding his eyes back up to hers. He repeated, "Did you need something?"

"I'm sorry," she said.

He gaped, unable to think of how to respond with his head still in a fog.

She paused then continued when he didn't speak, "I shouldn't have said what I did. I know that you had a very hard childhood, and I respect that. Whether or not you are going to say it back, whether or not you want to be friends, I wanted to clear the air. For Rosette's sake if nothing else."

He tried to get his mouth to work, to think of something to say.

"She finally ate today... if you care," Brier said. "She was blaming herself for him dying. I at least got her to stop feeling guilty enough to eat. It would probably help if you wanted to speak with her as well. As long as you can be congenial."

He swallowed. "Why was she blaming herself?"

"She thought she made him sick."

"But he wasn't ill."

"That's what I told her. But she's seen sickness. And been around a lot of death. I can at least understand where she's coming from."

Palmer nodded. "I'll talk to her."

Brier nodded back, standing silently in the doorway for another moment before picking up her candle. "Well, I'll leave you to... whatever you were doing. I didn't mean to interrupt."

He finally found his voice. "Brier?"

Her face came into greater focus, with the candle so close.

"I'm sorry, too."

Brier offered a weak smile. "It's been hard on all of us."

He nodded. "We'll talk in the morning?"

"All right," she said. "I'm going to try to get Rosette up first, though. The girl has been in bed too long. It can't be good for her health."

"I'll come and help," he said.

The smile grew a little stronger. "Truly?"

"I'll be there," he agreed, stopping her once again as she turned to go. "And Brier?"

She looked at him over her shoulder.

"I think we should stay here." Of all the bad outcomes he'd been plagued with, he hoped they could at least avoid the worst of them by staying put.

If she had any questions, she kept them to herself. Offering a weak smile, she said good night, leaving Palmer alone with the heaviness that seemed to be hanging in the air lately.

CHAPTER EIGHTEEN

Brier sat at the window, watching the flakes coming down and glowing in the firelight every now and then. She sliced a piece of bread off a charred loaf, taking a bite before looking behind her at Palmer. "How long do you think it will keep snowing?"

"How would I know?" Palmer took his own bite of bread. She watched him make a face at the burnt edge—she'd misjudged the temperature in the oven again—but he didn't comment.

"How do you know anything?" she returned.

He shook his head. "I've been fighting to filter things out lately. I'm not going to let it all rush back just to attempt aeromancy."

Brier pressed her lips together, debating asking what he had resorted to blocking out, but she let it go. She felt no need to ruin the fragile peace they'd managed to rebuild over the past few days. "Do you think it's odd?"

"What?" he asked. "The snow?"

"That nobody has come since Sage Visentin's funeral," Brier specified. "It's like the entire town has vanished."

"They didn't come too often when he was alive, either. Everyone seems rather self-sufficient."

"It just seems... odd," she repeated.

He shrugged.

She sighed, sitting in silence with him for another long moment. "Did I ever tell you what one of the women said to me at the funeral?"

He shook his head, eyes on the burnt bread.

"Well," Brier started, trying to keep her voice light, "one of the women stopped me, just as everyone was leaving, and said, 'We're glad to have you, but if you plan to live at the church, you might do well to at least get married.'"

Palmer frowned, studying her. "She meant us?"

Brier half laughed. "I can only assume."

Palmer shook his head slightly. "Why?"

Brier shrugged. "I would suppose the idea of an unmarried young man and woman living together in the church rectory is scandalous in her mind."

"More so than having their Seer married."

"They already told you that was fine by them."

"Sage Visentin told me." He glanced at the window toward the graveyard. "Not the town."

"The town followed his word. You have to admit that."

Palmer didn't answer.

"Anyway." She took another bite, wishing she were a better baker. "You aren't truly a Seer, not technically and certainly not as far as they know. If you are their spiritual leader, they've basically accepted a complete break with the Augarian. The Church wouldn't sanctify anything you performed."

Palmer nodded. "Wouldn't sanctify a marriage I performed, either."

Brier smiled. "You couldn't perform a marriage you yourself were a part of, anyway."

"Not without starting our own religion." Palmer picked at his food.

Brier pursed her lips slightly, considering it. "Signore Arbore is a Seer. He isn't practicing, obviously, but if we needed someone, I'm sure that's whom they would ask."

Palmer finally brought his eyes back up to study her. "Did you want to get married?"

Brier hesitated, the gravity of her words hitting her all at once. "Just thinking out loud."

He nodded, looking back at his food. He picked at the unburnt places. "I thought you were already engaged."

The thought hit her, hard, in the stomach. She sucked in a breath a little too quickly. Something flickered in the back of her mind but pulled back with a jolt.

Palmer stood and moved toward the doorway.

Standing after him, she frowned. "Palmer?"

He froze in the doorway, not looking at her.

"What was that?"

"Nothing."

The discomfort around him nearly made her let it go, but she refused to do so again. "Look at me."

Slowly, nearly unwillingly, Palmer turned back around.

She narrowed her eyes slightly, letting herself slide into his head before he could object. Faces flew at her, a whirl inside his head, before the images settled on the one she had never quite been able to grasp. Nico. Standing there. Wherever *there* was. Not a room she knew. Silent. But something was wrong. Even after so long and so far away, she could still tell when something was off with him. Trouble. Danger. Warning bells began going off in her head. Or Palmer's head—she couldn't tell which. But they were there. They made her heart race and her stomach try to jump into her throat. Panic—hers, Palmer's, Nico's, it all jumbled into one unreadable mess.

Something forced her out of the vision so strongly she nearly fell over.

Brier's hands flew out, landing on the table behind her as she steadied herself. Panting for breath, she studied Palmer as the quiet rectory with its warm fire came back into focus.

Palmer moved toward the door once again.

"What was that?" Her voice came before she could think the words, her voice sounding unnaturally high as panic worked its way through her.

He swallowed and replied weakly, "I don't know."

"Was it a vision? A thought? A memory? What?"

He released a breath and turned to face her. "I don't know, Bri. Everything I've been seeing is like that lately. I can't make any sense of it."

Her entire body vibrated, from her fingertips through her core and down to her feet. She tried to take a deep breath but couldn't quite manage. "But you knew who that was. Why didn't you tell me?"

"Because I knew it would upset you, and there's nothing we can do about it."

"Is he in trouble?"

"Brier—"

"Is he in trouble?" she repeated, her voice stronger.

"I don't know." He shook his head. "I really don't know, Brier. I'd tell you if I did."

"Why would you? You don't like him."

"But I do you," he said. The statement hung in the air between them, tainting the silence. He swallowed again before continuing unsurely, "If I thought there really was something wrong, I would tell you, Bri. I know you care about him. But I don't even know what that vision is. For all I know, someone's planted it, trying to get us to go back there."

"Who would do that?" Brier frowned. "Who *could* do that?"

"I don't know," Palmer said. "I just don't trust it."

"Why not?"

"It's…" he started, shook his head. "It's nothing, Bri."

"Don't you do that, Palmer Tash." Brier set her jaw. "We're in this together. You don't get to keep things from me."

He started to say something but obviously thought better of it. Finally, he nodded. "All right."

She swallowed. "So?"

Palmer released a breath. "One of the visions, about if we go back, is… bad. I'd prefer to keep that one from happening if at all possible."

"How bad?"

He took a moment, seeming to measure his words. "People die."

Brier's stomach squirmed. "How many people?"

"A lot," he said.

She let the thought sink in but managed to offer him a weak smile. "And that's why you wanted to stay here?"

"Why I don't especially trust anyone who might be trying to get us back to Latysia." He scratched the back of his neck.

Brier nodded, forcing herself to unclench her teeth. "We'll stay here, then."

Palmer nodded back, the stress easing at least slightly from his shoulders.

"But you can't keep things from me." She pointed, taking a step forward. "We work better when we're working together, anyway. Don't you think?"

"We seem to." The corner of his mouth turned up into something like a half smile.

Brier held his eyes for another moment, feeling the tension rising between them, growing tight as a bowstring—tension... and something else, that odd pull she'd felt at the funeral: wanting to be close to him, needing that comfort, needing that something.

Oh, hell. She gave in, earning a confused look from Palmer for the last second before she leaned in and kissed him.

Palmer froze, his breath seeming to catch in his chest for too long before he could recover. He moved his hand slightly; pulled it back, unsure; and began to move it forward again, but before he could fully react, Brier had pulled back, looking at him nearly apologetically.

"Wha...?" he started but couldn't think of how to finish.

Brier flushed slightly, a pretty pink color rising in her cheeks, just visible in the candlelight. "Sorry, I shouldn't have—"

"No, it..." Palmer started over, "I just... Wow."

She released a soft laugh. "Is that a good 'wow'?"

He opened his mouth but just found himself nodding.

She smiled. "Friends again?"

"I, uh..." He lost the rest of the sentence and nodded again.

"Good." She looked at him for another long moment before leaning forward and kissing him again.

He recovered more quickly that time, moving slightly closer, resting his hand lightly on her hip, unable to think of what else to do.

If she took issue with it, she didn't let on. A quick smile, and she said her good night, leaving him, still half in a daze, standing in the middle of the rectory.

Another moment, standing there like an idiot, and Palmer finally recovered, releasing a long breath he hadn't noticed he'd been holding, feeling the tension in his body lessen, if not disappear. How he'd lost his breath, how his body had reacted, he didn't know if that was normal or not. If it was just normal for a first kiss—gods, he would never let her know it was a first kiss, one last thing to keep from her—or something about her. Or something about them. Opposites connected. The buzzing tingle in his body, however… Whatever it was, he couldn't bring himself to hate it. Planting himself, he forced himself not to follow her. She needed sleep. Rosette was sleeping. Talking would have to wait until morning.

Morning. He moved to the window and pulled the curtain back slightly, unable to see anything but the odd flash of snow, falling more heavily in the slowly dying firelight. He didn't know how he'd wait—the exhaustion he'd been dragging along after himself was entirely gone.

CHAPTER NINETEEN

THE NEXT MORNING ARRIVED, COATED in gray and white. Fine white powder sparkled thickly on every branch and wall, pure and untouched around the church. And Palmer couldn't see it stopping anytime soon. The falling snow turned Brier into Rosette, it seemed, wide-eyed and enthusiastic, practically vibrating with excitement. Rosette, alternatively, turned uncharacteristically dire, eyeing the snow out the window with a caution Palmer was more used to seeing in his own reflection. But if Brier had become Rosette, and Rosette him, he supposed that left only Brier for him to embody in turn. He tried to consider what that might mean for his personality, but the only thought that would willingly come to mind was the memory of her kiss.

A tickle in his head snapped him out of his thoughts. Brier's light, knowing smile made his cheeks grow hot. He looked away.

"Can we go out?" Brier had already abandoned that train of thought.

Palmer did his best to join her, sure his embarrassment was still completely apparent. He looked out the window. "I'd wait. You don't want to get lost if it really starts coming down."

"I hate snow." Rosette pouted from her place in the corner, huddled in a pile of blankets.

"Why's that?" Palmer asked before Brier could.

"It's too cold," she said. "People go to sleep in it and never wake back up."

A flash of a snowy street fluttered past Palmer's mind, the same soft snow turning dingy in the soot of a city. Street children ran around, doing their best to find a warm place for the night. He blinked to clear it, glancing at Brier to see if she had seen. Her apparent confusion said she hadn't.

Palmer looked back at Rosette. "Well, we have a fire here and a sturdy roof over our heads. We won't have to sleep in it."

"Other people will," Rosette mumbled, disappearing entirely into her pile.

Palmer couldn't deny that.

"I think it's pretty." Brier turned back to stare out the window, blissfully unaware.

"First the good Sage's death, and then this?" the voice broke through the block in Palmer's mind, barely a whisper. *"Something's not right, if you ask me."*

"What do you mean?"

"That little girl... There's something not right about her. They say she started screaming the day Sage Visentin passed all the way over at Eudocia Terzi's. Like she knew."

"How could she?"

"I don't know, but I don't like it."

"Palmer?" Brier frowned. "Palmer?"

He blinked multiple times in quick succession, trying to focus on her.

She looked at him, eyebrows furrowed. "Is everything all right?"

Palmer glanced at the pile of blankets that was Rosette and looked back at Brier. "We can talk about it later."

Her voice slipped into his head. *You look like you've seen a ghost.*

We'll talk later.

She continued to frown but didn't push him. "Do you think we have enough food? I don't know if we'll get any more with this weather."

"We've got enough," Palmer said. "And I saw preserves downstairs if we run low."

Brier nodded.

"She's been working in Signora Terzi's house. Nothing has happened there."

"Are you sure? We haven't seen Eudocia in over a week. Maybe she's dead as well."

"Don't say that." The voice sounded legitimately scared.

"I'm just saying... we don't know that she's fine."

"So what do we do?"

"What you do with any witch, in my opinion."

"Palmer," Brier said sharply.

He looked at her.

She frowned deeply, searching his face. *What is it?*

Palmer looked at the Rosette bundle again. "Do you need anything to eat, Rosie?"

"No." Her mumble was barely audible.

He looked back at Brier. *Chapel?*

Brier continued to frown but nodded, looking at the bundle herself. "We'll be right back, Rosie."

Brier didn't get a response at all.

Palmer moved through the doorway and found a spot out of sight from the rectory's small main room.

Not waiting for him to stop moving, Brier spoke in a sharp whisper. "What is it?"

"Someone's talking about us."

She shook her head slightly. "Who?"

"I don't know. Two men. Someone in the village."

"Bad things." It wasn't a question.

"They..." He glanced over his shoulder at the rectory then looked at Brier. "They think Rosette's a witch."

Her eyebrows rose, furrowed, and ended up somewhere confused in the middle of her forehead. "A witch?"

"She knew Sage Visentin was dying. That's not something a normal little girl would know."

"What...?" She closed her eyes and took a second to gather herself before looking back at him. "What are they planning to do? They wouldn't strangle her at the crossroads, would they?"

"It's just whispers," Palmer said. "But whispers in winter have a way of spreading. Especially with this weather. There's nothing else to do."

"What about us?"

Palmer looked at her questioningly.

"They don't know us separately from her. If she is under suspicion, we can't be far behind."

Palmer pressed his lips together tightly and studied the pulpit before speaking. "We'll have to give them something else to talk about."

"Like what?" she asked.

"Maybe, once the snow stops, it's time to get married."

Brier and Palmer let Rosette sleep in Palmer's old place, next to the fire, as the cold seemed to seep in the windows. They set themselves up in the corner closest to the chapel. Brier turned onto her side, looking at the back of Palmer's head as she let everything mull about in her mind. He sat, resting against a leg of her cot. Though he was sitting, his breathing came slow and even. If she hadn't known any better, she would have thought him asleep.

She reached out and touched his shoulder.

Palmer started, twisting his head to look at her.

Sorry. She offered a smile, though it was probably lost in the dark. *Didn't mean to startle you.*

I thought you were asleep. He slid his body around to properly face her.

I was. Just woke up.

He hesitated. *Bad dreams?*

No. She tried to make out his face in the darkness. *Should I have had one?*

Not from me.

She squinted, trying to make out each of his features, one by one. Finally, she just shifted back on the cot. *Come sit with me.*

He didn't move, seemingly uncomprehending.

She scooted back farther, nodding at the free space. *No reason for you to sit on the floor.*

She could almost feel him frowning.

Didn't I tell you you'd know it if I were propositioning you, Palmer Tash? She smiled. *There is a child in the room.*

I... His answer died off, and Palmer pushed himself off the floor and sat on the edge of the cot. *Maybe it's just being inside all of the time.*

What is? Brier asked, tilting her head to look up at his shadow of a shape.

Why you're having trouble sleeping. We haven't been able to do anything.

Maybe. But that's all right. I've just been thinking.

Thinking about what?

Everything. She smiled to herself. *Nothing.*

He snorted but caught himself, glancing at Rosette before pulling his legs up. *Fitting.*

I thought so.

The conversation dropped off.

Did you ever have to share a bed, Palmer? Brier finally found herself asking.

He shook his head then paused. *Well, I did with my mother for a little while when I was a child. Not other than that. We each got a cot in the dormitories.*

Brier nodded.

You didn't, of course.

She looked at him.

Didn't have to? The words sounded less than sure following her pause.

Brier thought her words through before continuing. *I didn't like sleeping alone as a child. Portia, the real Portia, would spend the night with me sometimes when I was really little. Then Nico, of course, after she left, relatively often.*

Your father let a boy sleep in your room?

You assume my father knew a thing about it. Brier smiled, propping herself up on her elbow. *Nico and I grew up in that palace. We could get from one end to the other without a soul knowing.*

He didn't answer.

We were just children for most of it. She felt a sudden urge to defend herself. *Entirely innocent.*

He just nodded.

She adjusted on the small cot. *Do you want to lie down? It's putting a crick in my neck lying like this.*

He studied her for a long moment. *Are you* sure *I'll know it when you start propositioning me? I'm rather dense, I admit.*

She smiled, rolling her eyes, confident he wouldn't be able to tell. *Oh, lie down, Palmer. I still don't like sleeping alone.*

Touching him while she was sleeping made the visions stronger. Brier didn't know if Palmer could tell—if he could, he likely wouldn't have continued sharing her cot, she supposed, when she thought about it—but she saw them all now, whenever he relaxed his guard enough to have them slip through: some happy, some sad—staying there, going home, finding a new home, even their wedding, kneeling across from each other, though the temple they knelt in looked strange. As real as some seemed, however, she couldn't shake the odd graininess that seemed to saturate them, leaving her feeling off balance and uncomfortable in her own mind.

That one image, of course, always came back—the one tangled in a distorted, grotesque Augarian. Nico. Always Nico. Somewhere. Trapped in some unnatural darkness as the rest of the world seemed to come down around him.

Brier did her best to ignore it, but every time it slipped its way into her dreams, it jerked her awake, heart pounding. Still, she did her best to hide it, forcing her breathing back to normal—or normal enough to feign sleep.

You saw that. His voice made her start. He touched her arm, rubbing it lightly in the silence.

How long have you known?

He shrugged. *I don't sleep, you know.*

Brier pressed her lips together, trying to rid herself of the last, lingering panic the vision had shot through her. It was getting harder and harder to ignore.

Are we going?

She took a moment, the question not fully making sense. *Going where?*

There. He apparently didn't feel the need to name the place.

Brier let the single word sink in before trying to answer. *You said we couldn't.*

We can't stay here much longer. The whispers are getting worse.

Against Rosette?

He nodded.

I thought that was why we were getting married.

He took a long pause. *I'm not sure we'll be able to stop it even then.*

Brier tried to wade through their options, her entire life slowly starting to feel as if it was built on sand, the ground sliding away right from under her every time it seemed they had made some lasting decision. *And your vision about going back?*

Palmer sighed, deeply enough that she could feel his chest rise and fall. *I don't know what my visions are at this point. We could go back and not have the world end. We could go somewhere else and have them burn us all for witchcraft. I'm not much use right now other than making you worry about him.*

She didn't need to ask which "him" Palmer meant. *Do you know anything else? What's happening to him?*

I'd tell you if I knew.

Do you think we could just stop to check without people dying? Brier asked. *There are enough passageways through the palace that we could likely find him without anyone knowing we were there. Then we could keep going south before anything happened.*

The silence dragged out, not doing a thing to help the tension in the air. Finally, Palmer answered, *If we go back, we aren't leaving again.*

You're sure about that?

Sure enough. The uncertainty of it all washed over her. People dying, them dying, could she take either on her conscience and still remain sane? Part of her wished she could just go back to being the librarian's daughter, wandering around the palace doing stupid things because she had nothing better to do. Part of her even wished she could have just married Nico and gone out to the country as plenty of the Augarian wives did, living in some villa and never having to consider anything more difficult than if she wanted to redecorate with red or blue silk. But after everything they had gone through... all of those wishes had been lost the minute she'd come to in that strange little room in Ruhegipfel. She ran her thumb over the calluses on her palm, turning to face Palmer on the cot. *Kiss me?*

Palmer's head turned toward her, his confusion at the sudden change in topic nearly palpable.

You haven't, you know, she continued.

Haven't what?

Kissed me. She felt him frown more than saw it. *I kissed you. You haven't kissed me.*

He took another moment and finally leaned forward. His lips met hers lightly, hesitantly.

Brier slipped her hand into his hair, holding him more tightly to her, feeling his body react to hers—a spark between them, some energy, opposites drawing one to the other.

She pushed farther forward. He drew back.

What?

She heard him swallow. *We can't do this, Bri.*

Can't do what?

You know what.

Brier released a shaky breath. *What if I wanted to?*

You don't.

You don't know that.

I don't?

With another pained breath, she lay on her back, staring at the dark ceiling. *You're really not like a lot of men, are you, Palmer?*

What do you mean?

She didn't answer. *Probably for the best.*

He repeated, *What do you mean?*

She just shook her head. *How soon do you think we'd be able to go? Not until after winter?*

He took a long moment. She felt his mind slipping away and tried to stay out of it, not wanting to know. He closed his eyes, looked at her again, and turned his head toward where Rosette slept. *I'm not sure we'll last that long. It might have to be now.*

Brier didn't trust herself to answer.

CHAPTER TWENTY

P ALMER WAVERED BETWEEN RELIEF AND apprehension as Latysia came into view, stretching out in front of them. Snow had made travel slow, difficult work. The rain it turned into farther south wasn't much better. What dirt roads they found had long since turned to mud, and the barren fields had provided little, if any, food.

The first sun they had seen in days illuminated the city that had once been home. More and more buildings, all packed up against one another, appeared as they approached, climbing the sharp hill before reaching the high stone walls of the Augarian. The sight nearly stopped Palmer in his tracks.

"Oh," Brier murmured, coming up beside him.

He turned to look at her. If she had anything else to say after that, it died in her throat. Still, the fear in her eyes made him tense. "Are you all right?"

She started, glancing at him before looking back up the hill. "I'll be fine."

"Is that it?" Rosette asked, her small voice nearly nonexistent.

Brier snapped her head toward the little girl, her face melting into worry from fear. "That's it. Where Palmer and I grew up."

"It looks a lot like Tetii," Rosette said in the same small voice, leaning against Brier's leg as though it were the only thing holding her up.

Brier gathered the girl up, settling Rosette on her hip before looking at Palmer.

He looked back.

Now what do we do?

Palmer looked up the hill and released a short breath. *I don't know.*

Brier didn't know if Latysia had always felt so gritty or if that was a recent change. Nico might have gone out beyond the walls regularly enough to get into some trouble or another, but she never had. Her world had consisted of the hundred or so acres encased by the Augarian Walls—the palace, the library, the temple, the university, and the four or five hundred people who moved around inside them. Sure, she'd known about the world outside of it, but her life had never stretched out so far. For some reason, because they were back, down in the town, in the little inn Palmer had found for them, the world suddenly seemed so much larger than it had miles and miles before. Ruhegipfel, Lantello, the distance between, they had all been part of some greater adventure thrust upon them. That had been part of an entirely different life, a life that had made them different. The juxtaposition left her dizzy.

The door opened and closed softly behind her. "Is she all right?"

Brier looked at Palmer and then over at Rosette, the little lump on the bed. "I don't think she's sick. She doesn't have a fever or anything, at least. She just seems exhausted."

Palmer nodded, sitting down on the small window seat next to Brier. "I had a look around. We're out of the way enough down here I don't think we'd have any problem staying a few days while we figure out a plan. Maybe even longer."

Brier hummed.

"What?" He frowned.

"I was just thinking..." Brier paused and started again, "It's not a very nice part of town, is it?"

"It's where my mother and I stayed for a while when we had nowhere else to go," Palmer said. "After my father was chased out in the Occupation."

She blinked, at a loss for words. "Sorry, I really didn't mean... It isn't that bad of a—"

"Yeah, it is," he cut her off. "But it's out of the way and not a place we're likely to be recognized. Least of all you, I imagine."

"Just me?"

"Some of the other wards who aged out may live around here." Palmer glanced out the window before looking back at her. "I doubt any of your friends do."

"Unless there's a brothel nearby," Brier said, managing a weak smile.

"Not one I think any of them would frequent."

Brier slid her hand into Palmer's, looking back at Rosette. "We need to get her a place to live, permanently. She's just a little girl."

"We're doing our best, Bri."

Brier nodded. "I know we are. I know you are."

"And you."

She didn't respond, looking out the window. With the buildings so closely packed together and clothing stretched out on lines between high windows, it was impossible to see very far down the street, let alone up to the Augarian. They were secluded, down in the slums where no one she had ever met would have agreed to go to for anything more than an expedition.

She looked back at him. "Once we're inside the palace, I can get us around. It's getting through the gate that will be a problem. If we just try to go through, they're going to recognize us. And after being gone so long, there's no way the entire place wouldn't know we're back within the hour."

"Know you're back, at least," Palmer said. "Two-to-one odds they just assumed I ran off. You're the one they'd look for."

She didn't let on she'd had the same thought. "Then they'd think we ran off together, showing up like this."

Palmer paused, pressing his lips tightly together as he thought.

"What's that look?" Brier frowned, eyeing him cautiously.

"What if you didn't run away with me?" he started slowly, his eyes still far away as he worked it out. He finally met her gaze. "What if I took you with me?"

"What? Like kidnapped me?"

He nodded.

"Why the hell would you do that?"

He shrugged. "I needed you for something. It doesn't matter."

"Of course it matters." Brier shook her head. "Why would anyone believe that you were going to kidnap me on your way out of town? It makes no logical sense. And it doesn't exactly help with us getting in without people noticing."

"Unless you know a way in that isn't through one of the gates, I think someone is going to notice us."

Brier clenched her jaw. Though she knew many paths for getting around the palace, she didn't actually know any ways out of the Augarian. She'd have to find Nico to ask him if he did, for anything like that, and that would rather defeat the purpose. "So you're willing to not only have everyone know we're back—I'm back—and get yourself arrested for kidnapping me?"

"I can't see another way in, so we need them to believe you still don't know what you are." He leaned forward over his knees toward her. "With any luck, they'll put you back in your room, and we can find… everyone we need to before figuring out what to do next."

"And they'll put you in gaol," she said.

"You know where the cells are, don't you?"

"Yes," she said. "Though if you're admitting to kidnapping a woman, kidnapping *me*, I doubt you'll be kept there long. Sounds like the perfect way for you to end up with your neck in a noose."

"Ideally, you'd get me out before that happened."

She continued to frown. "Me?"

"You told me you could get around the palace without a soul seeing you. We'd at least be in the palace then."

"I never went to the gaol," she said. "And I wouldn't have the ability to get you out of a cell even if I got there."

"Doors can't hold you, remember?"

"Doesn't mean they can't hold *you*," Brier said.

"There's a reason Goebel didn't just lock me in that room to start with, Bri. You opened the locked door just fine. Once the membrane came down, he could walk right in. It wasn't as though you walked *through* the door itself. You opened it. I could have walked right out."

Brier still frowned. "It sounds like doing a lot of hoping we're lucky for that to work."

"Do you have a better plan?"

She released a breath through her nose, rubbing her temples before looking at him again. "Not at the moment."

He held his hands out wide.

"That doesn't mean you have a good plan, though," Brier continued. "What would we do with Rosette?"

He frowned, his eyes slipping away from her as he thought again.

Brier looked back out the window before sighing again. "Well, we might want to figure out what we're trying to accomplish first, I suppose."

Palmer's eyes flicked back to her. "Finding the Guillroy, isn't it?"

She shook her head. "If our only plan is to possibly end up with you on the wrong end of a noose, I think we need more of a reason than that to go back in there rather than staying right here until the weather's better before going south."

"Can you honestly say you could be this close and leave again?" Palmer watched her, his eyes seeming to bore through her. After the past months, the man knew her a little too well.

Also, she had to admit the other part of what had brought them back to Latysia—why he had said they wouldn't leave if they came. "We want to stop running."

He gave a small smile. "And you want to stop running here."

"So we don't only need to find Nico. We need to find a way to get settled with certain people knowing what we are."

He nodded.

"Is that even possible?"

"You could always blast a hole in the wall and walk in," Palmer said. "I don't think many people would bother you after that."

She actually found herself smiling. "I think we might be better off trying to figure out *who* knows before we tell the entire world. Orris Adessi-Guillroy, possibly some of the Seers..." The smile slid away as the momentousness of what they were attempting to do sank in. "Perhaps we just need to get in long enough to find Nico, my father, any of your friends... Then we could set up our own household somewhere nearby, with just them knowing where we are."

"You don't want to live in the Augarian?" He frowned.

"*You* don't want to live in the Augarian," she argued. "You don't want to be a Seer. You were planning on leaving anyway."

Palmer didn't respond, waiting for her to continue.

"If we can, I'd want to be here, be where I could see Nico and my father—even if I'd likely still have to go to the library to ever find him—but I don't have to live in the palace. We could let them know we're here, then set up in Latysia. Us and Rosette."

A smile broke out on Palmer's face before he seemed to catch himself. "But that still leaves us with how we want to explain your disappearance, assuming we don't want to tell them the truth."

"You're not getting yourself hanged for me." Brier rolled her eyes.

"I'm open to suggestions."

Brier pursed her lips. A thought hit her. "What if you aren't the kidnapper but the rescuer?"

He lifted an eyebrow.

"Maybe I *was* kidnapped. Someone snuck in, or I even did something stupid like try to sneak out one night—anyone would believe that—and they grabbed me. Simply as a coincidence, you were out in Latysia that night. You saw them with me and tried to help. Eventually, you were able to save both Rosette and me and endeavored to bring us home. Some months later... you're a hero."

Palmer looked skeptical. "You really think people would buy that?"

"You have both of us with you. Witnesses, if you will." She glanced at Rosette then looked back at Palmer. "And this way, you won't be locked up. I need you, Palmer. I... I don't think I can do this alone."

He dropped his eyes. "I'm sure you could."

"You *can't* leave me, Palmer. Promise."

He swallowed but took her hand. "I will do everything in my power to be there, Bri. To protect you and Rosette."

"Promise me." She squeezed his hand gently.

"I promise."

CHAPTER TWENTY-ONE

B RIER STRAIGHTENED ROSETTE'S SKIRTS, TYING them securely around Rosette's small waist. She turned the little girl to face her and bent closer to her face. "Too tight?"

Rosette just shook her head.

Brier released a breath. "And you know what we tell people when we get up to the guards?"

Rosette's eyes didn't leave her feet. She mumbled, "Palmer saved us."

"From whom?"

"Kidnappers."

Brier studied Rosette for a long moment. She couldn't bring herself to drill the poor girl further. Brier laid her hand on Rosette's forehead then on her cheeks, making sure for the hundredth time that Rosette's paleness wasn't a fever. The girl didn't feel too warm or too cold. She just looked pale—pale and exhausted, as if the last stretch south had somehow broken her spirit.

"Do you think we should find other clothes?" Palmer looked down at his jacket. Not too worn from the journey from Lantello, it was still undoubtedly foreign, out of the ordinary for anyone but a traveler to Latysia.

Brier shook her head, looking at her own simple dress. "We've been gone for months. I think it would look more suspicious for us to have new Latysian clothes than to be in these." She looked back at Rosette. "We'll be there with you the entire time, I promise. Just stay quiet as much as you can and out of the way. All right?"

Rosette nodded.

Some image flickered in the back of Brier's mind, too quickly to leave anything but colors, falling crimson. She looked back at Palmer, raising an eyebrow.

He just shrugged, concern still visible on his face.

She watched him for another long moment.

I really don't know, Bri.

She nodded once, finally straightening and brushing herself off. She touched the top of Rosette's head lightly before turning to Palmer. "Well?"

He frowned. "Well what?"

"I think we're as ready as we'll ever be." She motioned between Rosette and herself. "Are you ready to give it a go?"

Palmer took a moment and finally nodded. "I suppose it's now or never."

"That's the spirit." Brier placed a hand on Rosette's back, just between the shoulder blades, half comforting, half shepherding her toward the door.

"Always," Palmer mumbled, letting them pass before picking up his pack and closing the door behind them.

Brier's sense of unease grew the closer they got to the Walls. The mostly empty streets could be ignored. People near the Walls were no doubt locked in their grand villas, staying warm in the sunny but biting winter day. The silence made sense, but it still seemed forced, unnatural.

As the gates came into view, Palmer slowed, with Brier following suit. *What the hell happened?* he asked.

Brier frowned, glancing at Palmer before searching for what he found wrong. The answer slowly came to her. Two bright-colored guards stood at their posts as always, watching the empty streets in front of them, but several others—these men in the dreary colors of soldiers, not guards—milled around, in and out of view, just beyond the gates, around the perimeters, and even along the top of the Walls. Brier frowned, craning her head backward, trying to spot the men keeping watch over the surrounding landscape.

She looked at Palmer. *Are we under attack?*

Not that I can tell. His brow furrowed, scanning the area as they continued slowly forward. *I don't like it.*

"Halt!" The left guard recognized their approach, leaning his pike out slightly to obstruct the gates.

All three of them did as ordered, unthinkingly, still out of distance of the menacing pikes. They were not the colorful ceremonial spears Brier was used to seeing in the palace.

The right guard followed suit, fully blocking the gate. Brier looked at them both, narrowing her eyes slightly. As if they would be stupid enough to rush the gate, unarmed, with such a presence in full view.

"Identify yourselves." The left guard eyed their clothes suspiciously.

Brier felt her old self flooding back, unbidden. Pulling her shoulders back, she took a few steps forward, and the guard hesitated to point that pike of his. Perhaps he wasn't completely used to it yet.

Her voice was loud, assured, entitled. "I am Brier Chastain-Bochard. And it has been quite a long excursion getting back here for both my companions and myself. I would appreciate it if we were allowed inside."

"Chastain-Bochard?" An older man in a smart gray uniform strode forward, knocking the right guard's pike harmlessly out of the way, nearly throwing the poor boy off balance.

Brier straightened even more, her chest puffing out slightly. "Yes, signore. And you are?"

"Do you have identification?"

Brier frowned and hesitated. "No, signore. Does it look as though we have much with us?"

His brown eyes continued to scan her suspiciously.

"I assure you that you could find someone to vouch for my identity, signore, if you're so worried," Brier snapped. "Go find my father and ask."

"Citron Chastain-Bochard?" the man asked.

"Yes, signore." She gave him a tight, sarcastic smile. "My father."

"Citron Chastain-Bochard died two weeks ago."

Brier's mouth dropped open wordlessly as the wind was knocked out of her.

Palmer took a step closer to her but stopped when the left guard swung his pike out slightly.

"He... " Brier swallowed and finally found words again. "He's dead?"

The man gave a curt nod. "Winter illness."

Brier opened her mouth and closed it again, surely looking like a fish gasping for breath on land, unable to find words quickly enough.

"What is happening out...?" The familiar voice died off as Nico appeared around a corner before he stopped dead in his tracks. His own shock matched hers. "Bri?"

The man looked at Nico with a frown. "You know her?"

"Signore." Nico seemed to snap out of his thoughts, straightening. "She's Brier Chastain-Bochard."

Brier just blinked, trying to meet Nico's eyes. "My father's dead?"

Nico seemed to start moving forward, stopped, and held his ground. He looked back at the man in gray. "Permission to allow them inside, signore?"

The man nodded, still eyeing the three outside the gates suspiciously.

Nico jerked forward, taking Brier's arm and all but pulling her through the Augarian gates. Palmer followed quickly with Rosette.

The changes were even sharper inside. The once-calm piazza had turned into a buzz of activity. Men of all ages stood around haphazard tents, some talking, some pacing, some drilling. The sense that they had somehow entered an army barracks made Brier's head spin. She let Nico lead.

A little ways past the line of gray-clad men, in the shadow of the palace, Nico finally stopped. Turning, he grasped both of Brier's shoulders, searching her face. "Dear gods, it is you, isn't it?"

"I'm not sure who else I'd be," she said, still half in a daze. He pulled her into a tight hug, his wool jacket scratching her arms. She squirmed away, looking down. The gray coat with its gold buttons stared back up at her, fancier than the others but still undoubtedly matching. "What are you wearing?"

He shook his head. "It's a long story. We should get you inside."

"What's going on?" she asked, her voice nearly sounding like a whine.

"Bri, come on." He started moving her forward again.

She glanced back. Palmer still followed closely, bless him, leading Rosette by the hand while Rosette kept her eyes on her shoes.

Nico slowed, glancing back before looking at Brier questioningly. "They're with you?"

She nodded.

He glanced back again, looking Palmer and Rosette over once before giving a quick nod. "You'd better come, too."

The palace showed even more changes. The lavish artwork and priceless artifacts had been removed—stuck somewhere for safekeeping, no doubt—and replaced with the same walking sentries, keeping watch as serious-looking politicians dashed across the hall, like mice scared to be out in the open.

We're preparing for war.

Brier only straightened slightly, not turning to look at Palmer and trying not to give any outward sign of the voice in her head. *War with whom?*

I don't know.

Brier found her voice again and asked Nico, "Are we at war?"

Nico sighed, slowing to a stop near an alcove. He turned to face her, giving a nod of acknowledgment to two of the men in gray walking past before speaking again. "You have to understand, Bri, they've been telling everybody you're dead."

"Dead?" she repeated.

He nodded, glancing around, his eyes falling on Palmer for a long moment before moving back to Brier. "Dead, and the Bugiardi were the ones to do it. They've been preparing for war since."

"Is that why you're dressed like a soldier?" Brier asked.

Nico made a face. "That, and my father's doing. What...?" He trailed off as a few more men in gray circled back around.

He released a breath, nodding down the hall. "Let's go. There are eyes everywhere. We shouldn't take too long."

Brier just nodded, letting him continue to lead them down the hallway.

Maybe not quite as gaudy as the ballroom had been a lifetime ago at Brier's birthday, the rest of the palace still reeked of opulence. Palmer kept a tight hold on Rosette's hand, staying close on Brier's heels. He could understand why many of the Parrinos endeavored to live in the palace rather than the temple. Power and wealth were much more appealing than religion and self-denial. But the halls, the soldiers, indeed the whole place also smelled of corruption.

The Guillroy seemed to know exactly where they were headed, turning corners without thought. Brier did too if her growing hesitation was any indication. Palmer could see her shoulders growing tenser, could *feel* her growing tenser. It put him on edge.

Finally dropping his hold on Brier's arm, Nico pushed open a pair of large double doors, the hinges creaking as if purposefully trying to announce their presence. The men speaking at the end of the room fell silent, looking up at their approach. Scanning them quickly, Palmer saw confusion on a few faces, annoyance on others, and complete shock on the rest. He focused on the shock, sizing up those faces.

"What is the meaning of this?" One of the oldest of the annoyed group pushed himself to his feet.

"Beg your pardon, signore." Nico gave a lame excuse for a bow, barely bending, before looking at another man who was already moving across the room. "You remember Brier, Father."

Orris Adessi-Guillroy apparently heard the bite in his son's voice, pausing midstep for just a split second before continuing forward. "Brier, child…"

"I hear tell that there have been greatly exaggerated rumors of my death, signore," Brier said, her body language nearly confident but for her rapid blinking. Palmer wasn't sure anyone else noticed.

Orris paused for another long moment, glancing at the table of men behind him before continuing, his words sounding sickeningly false. "We had to assume the worse, *dolcezza*, what with your disappearance. Where have you been?"

Brier swallowed but otherwise managed to maintain her calm appearance. "I was kidnapped, signore."

"By the Bugiardi," another man interjected from the table.

Brier hesitated only slightly. "I don't know, signore. All I know is I woke up one morning, and strangers had me." She looked at Palmer, offering a small smile before continuing in the same tone. "If it weren't for Signore Tash, they might very well still have me."

"Signore Tash?" Orris asked, sliding his eyes back to Palmer.

"Palmer Tash," Palmer answered, not elaborating.

"Signore Tash," Brier said, "saw that I was in trouble the night I was taken and followed. Once I woke up from whatever had knocked me out, he helped me escape. And Rosette, too."

"The little girl." Orris looked at Brier, not quite looking as though he believed what she was saying.

Brier nodded. "She had been taken as well, a good while before me—an orphan they had working for them. Signore Tash, at great risk to himself, helped us, and we've been trying to get back ever since."

"Long time to walk back," Orris said.

"It was a long walk," Brier answered, "believe me."

"The boy is a hero, then." Another man from the table moved forward. "Saved the girl, both girls, from a most certain death at the hands of the Bugiardi, I am sure!"

Orris nodded, mostly to keep the man from continuing, it seemed. He looked at Brier. "You must be exhausted, *dolcezza*. Why don't you go lie down?"

"I'm fine, thank you," Brier said. "Though we could all likely use new clothes, I'm sure."

"Of course." Orris turned. "Your room has been left as it was, as far as I am aware."

"It has," Nico said, his voice a little hard.

Brier looked between them, trying to read their faces. "Thank you."

"If you'll allow us to finish our meeting..." Orris motioned toward the door before turning to move back to his seat.

Brier frowned suspiciously for a moment before she recovered, putting her stoicism back in place. "Signore Adessi-Guillroy?"

He turned back toward her.

"They tell me my father died."

"Ah." Orris cleared his throat awkwardly. "Yes. An unfortunate turn, that. They gave him a very fitting funeral, I assure you."

"Did he suffer?"

Orris looked at her for a long moment and offered an uncomfortable smile. "We shall talk after the meeting, *dolcezza*."

"I should like to visit his grave," she said, "if you have already had the funeral."

"Of course," Orris said. "Once you have changed, I'm sure Nicodemo would be happy to take you."

"I will," Nico assured her.

She nodded, face still hard. "Thank you."

Orris motioned toward the door again, offering nothing short of a dismissal.

They shuffled out of the room. Motioning to the guard outside in the hall, Nico led them away, letting the other man close the doors behind them.

Nico glanced back at Palmer and Rosette. He caught his hands behind his back, letting his eyes linger on Palmer. "Thank you very much for your help in recovering my fiancée. I can handle things from here."

"They're coming with us." Brier started forward, a new determination in her quick gait.

Nico turned and took two running steps to catch up to her before speaking again. "Why?"

"Because they are." Brier didn't stop moving or even look at him. "When did your father become *that* much of an ass?"

Nico glanced back again before addressing Brier. "I'd rather not talk about this right now."

She turned into a stairwell and ran up the steps. "Anything you can say to me you can say to them."

"But perhaps not say to everyone." Nico followed, taking the steps two at a time. "The walls have ears around here lately."

Palmer lagged behind as Rosette's short legs could not move quickly enough. He finally lifted her into his arms and attempted to climb faster.

Brier glanced at Nico, meeting his eyes for a moment before continuing on in silence. "He's in the catacombs?"

"Yes," Nico answered.

Brier just nodded, continuing her circuitous route through the palace.

Palmer reached the top of the stairs, panting but doing his best to pretend he wasn't. He shifted Rosette in his arms and did his best to keep up. "Wouldn't the catacombs be down?"

Nico looked back, glaring.

Brier simply said, "Eventually."

Brier could feel Palmer struggling with Rosette behind them and knew she should slow but couldn't bring herself to. With anger, sadness, confusion all coursing through her at once, she felt as though by moving—maybe, just maybe—she'd be able to outrun them all. They rounded the last corner and finally headed down the long flights of steps into the catacombs that spread out under the city.

Nico caught her arm and stepped in front of her as they reached the end of the hallway.

A man—more a boy, really—in gray straightened at the sound of footsteps.

Nico placed his hand to his temple halfheartedly. The boy answered with a full salute, allowing them to pass.

Brier frowned, stepping through after Nico into the dark cavernous tunnels.

What is it?

She looked at Palmer. *They've never guarded down here before. It's all wrong.* Her eyes went to Rosette. "Are you all right, Rosie?"

Rosette nodded slightly, burying her face into Palmer's shoulder.

"It isn't really a place for a child," Nico said.

Brier looked back at Nico, not acknowledging the statement. "Where is he?"

Nico frowned but motioned for her to follow.

As they walked deeper into the tunnels, something just behind Brier's eyes began to tingle. Fresh death was everywhere—too much to be natural. She looked around. New dirt filled more than its share of the graves. "How many people have died?"

"What?" Nico asked.

"All of these." She motioned to at least four new graves down the row, carved into the wall, just the ones in sight. "They're new."

Nico looked around. "Winter illness. It was bad this year."

A vision pressed into her head—tea, a vial.

Poison, Palmer supplied.

Brier spun around, looking at each grave. "Something's very wrong here, Nic."

Nico just nodded, turning a corner and motioning toward yet another fresh grave.

Brier hesitated and finally stepped forward, running her fingers over the name, newly carved into the soft stone shelf under the grave, still rough, even: 'Citron Chastain-Bochard.' The library's crest bookended the name, carved into each end of the platform. The space was a simple place of honor for a moderately important man. A vision tickled the back of her mind but was pulled away again.

Do you want to see?

Brier just shook her head slightly, trying to keep her hand steady. *No. Please, no.*

"Bri." Nico touched the small of her back. "We don't have to stay—"

"Could I just—" She paused. "Have a moment to myself?"

Nico hesitated but finally nodded. "I... we'll be just down the hall."

Their footsteps retreated from her, going just far enough to leave a vague sense of privacy. Still, Brier didn't cry, feeling as though she couldn't cry. Instead, something hard formed deep in her chest, tempering her. Everything was wrong. Everything had gone wrong, somewhere along the way. Their entire plan crumbled in front of her eyes. They couldn't leave the Augarian. Not now.

She reached out and found Nico, feeling his tension, anger, and confusion; then Rosette, scared and drained. Finally, she found Palmer and slid into his mind as she traced her father's name again. *Was he poisoned?*

He didn't speak right away but answered honestly. *Yes.*

Why?

Palmer paused a long time. *I don't know.*

Brier released a shaky breath. *Who?* It didn't seem like a true question, even to herself, the word too weak, sliding up in tone noncommittally.

Again, he answered, *I don't know.*

Brier touched the *n* of her father's name as she let the Nothing in her slip through the dirt. It found the matching Nothing inside it, bit by bit slipping away, wiggling its way out of the dirt, through the air, and into some greater mass beyond it, beyond her, beyond anything. And it found the poison, something thick and vile, dripping away, left behind as the Nothing dissipated. She shivered, feeling any sadness in her turning to anger.

We can't let this happen.

What?

She didn't answer, unsure if she had even meant to send him the thought. She turned to Nico sharply. "Is there somewhere we can talk?"

Nico looked at her, some unclear emotion passing through his eyes, though his face remained stoic. He nodded. "Come with me."

Brier moved to Palmer and took Rosette in her arms, feeling the need to comfort someone, something, anything, before looking back at Nico. "Lead the way."

CHAPTER TWENTY-TWO

RIER KNEW WHERE THEY WERE headed before they were even halfway there. She let her attention wander, keeping a tight hold on Rosette.

Palmer kept a close tail, careful never to put himself between her and Nico. If not for the circumstances, she might have smiled at having two protectors, watching and waiting. As things stood, she was glad to have them.

After a final turn, they arrived in a small cupboard of a room, empty save for a cot on one side and a washbasin on the other.

Brier moved to the cot and set Rosette down. "You can lie here for a little while, all right, *piccola*? Sleep if you can."

Rosette just watched her with wide, reticent eyes.

Brier did her best to hide her frown as she turned toward Nico. "Been a while."

"Still no one ever comes in here, from what I can tell." Nico looked around the small room, his large frame seeming too big for it now, his eyes tracing the seams of the wall before glancing out the small, round window on one side. He looked back at her. "It's as safe a place as any."

"Not much how I imagined rooms in here would be," Palmer finally said.

"It's overflow for the servant's quarters," Brier said before Nico could jump in with something biting. "Nico and I used to duck in here now and again when we didn't want others to find us." She looked back at Nico. "Though not for years, now. How long has it been?"

Nico shrugged, looking at Palmer again, his face dark.

"You don't need to worry about them, Nic." Brier leaned back against the wall. "Really."

"You need to worry about everyone right now, Bri." Nico looked back at her, crossing his arms. "It's what this city has become."

Brier shook her head, looking down and away for a long moment before meeting Nico's eyes again. "What happened to this place while I was gone?"

"We're a city preparing for war," Nico said. "The morning they found you gone... I don't even really know—they wouldn't let me get into your room—but they said you had been kidnapped—killed, more than likely—and there was evidence that pointed to it being the Bugiardis' doing. I... they..." The words seemed to catch in Nico's throat. He took a shaky breath, waited for his stoic façade to regain its shape before speaking again. "What really happened to you?"

"I told you," Brier said. "I was kidnapped."

"Really, Bri." He met her eyes, and something hard yet unstable lay behind his, though he was trying intensely to hide it.

"Really," she said. "I was kidnapped. Brought north. Palmer helped me escape."

Nico just frowned. "You weren't just blowing smoke up their asses?"

"Mad as it sounds, no." She avoided the rest of the story. "Is your father in charge, now?"

"Trying to be." Nico's cheek twitched. "You saw, yourself. Masses died this winter, including the Augur. They haven't replaced him. The council all but took over. They haven't even let the Seers *talk* about a conclave. They claimed there needed to be a strong, secular body in charge of a war. And he who controls the army..."

"The army"—Brier ran her eyes over his gray uniform and brought them back up to Nico's face—"including you?"

He made a face, motioning vaguely to the jacket. "My father's doing, I assure you. You want to seem invested in war with no experience yourself, what do you do?"

"Offer up your only son?"

Nico offered a tight smile and then motioned to the window. "The boys out there have been drilling nonstop. They aren't bad at this point."

He dropped his voice. "If you ask me, what's left of the council has taken over one country, and they're preparing to try for a second."

"Winter illness," Palmer said. "How many died?"

Nico narrowed his eyes. "Does it matter?"

"Answer the question," Brier prompted.

Nico hesitated but did so all the same. "A couple dozen, maybe more."

"Just in the Augarian?" Palmer asked.

Nico seemed loath to answer but settled on nodding.

"It isn't generally that bad," Palmer said, glancing at Brier before looking back at Nico. "Are we sure those were all natural?"

"What are you suggesting?" Nico asked, head cocked to the side, eyes narrowed in challenge.

"There are always two or three every winter," Palmer said. "The old, young, and sickly, mostly. But a bad strain... It would be the perfect excuse to," he paused, "help nature along?"

Nico opened his mouth, but Brier cut him off. "It does seem rather convenient. The Augur. Multiple deaths in the council. My father. Enough to redistribute power."

Nico closed his mouth again and finally gave some mix of a shrug and a nod. "I can't say I haven't had similar thoughts at times. But they have all the normal signs of winter illness before they die. If it's something else, they're targeting people who are already sick."

"Or they found something that provides the same symptoms," Palmer said.

Nico took a deep breath and addressed Brier. "All right, I know he saved you or whatnot, but who is he?"

"Palmer Tash," Brier said. "He's an acolyte. Was until recently, I suppose." She looked at Palmer for confirmation.

"I don't intend to go back," he said.

"Are things as bad at the temple?" Brier looked back to Nico.

"Things are bad everywhere," Nico said, studying Palmer. "What was an acolyte doing chasing down kidnappers?"

"Can we please focus, Nico?" Brier frowned.

"I'm trying to, Bri, but up until thirty minutes ago, I thought you were dead," he snapped, "so forgive me for still trying to get my head wrapped around… things."

Her face softened as she saw the struggle he was trying to hide from them all, perhaps even from himself. Finally, she moved forward, fingers going to the top buttons on his coat. "I don't think I've ever seen you with a coat properly buttoned, Nic."

"Regulation," he said.

She worked her fingers down Nico's chest, ignoring the waves of discomfort coming from Palmer. Undoing each gold button slowly, she exposed a thin white shirt under the heavy coat. Nico didn't stop her. Carefully, she slid the coat off his shoulders, holding its heavy weight in her hands for a moment before folding it once and laying it over the washbasin.

"Amazing you can breathe in that thing." She turned back to appraise him, studying the gray pants and white shirt before nodding. "Feel better now?"

Nico looked at her for another moment before moving closer. He swept her up to him. The kiss caught her off guard, strong, intense, as if he were trying to prove something. Finally pulling back, he rested his forehead against hers. "Don't *ever* do that to me again."

"Get kidnapped in the middle of the night?" She leaned back just enough to meet his eyes. "I promise I will do my very best to avoid it."

He snorted a laugh and kissed her again until she finally pulled back.

Brier cast a glance across the room. Palmer seemed to have found something remarkably interesting on the wall closest to him. She looked back at Nico and touched his face lightly before stepping away. "Now, what are we going to do?"

"Going to do about what?" Nico asked.

"You're really going to let the council—your father—start a war? I may have been kidnapped, but it certainly wasn't anyone Bugiardi."

"It's too late to stop it at this point." Nico shook his head.

"First blows haven't been struck." Palmer finally looked back toward them.

"And there is something very, very rotten here," Brier agreed. "We can't just ignore it."

"Try to stop it, Bri, and you're going to find yourself locked up as a traitor." Nico locked his jaw then looked at Palmer. "And *you're* going to end up dead."

Palmer's fists clenched and relaxed. "Is that a threat?"

"It's a fact," Nico said. "There are more than a few people freshly in gaol right now, more than a few killed—mostly those without any sort of contacts higher up." Nico arched an eyebrow imperially, his body stiff as he looked Palmer over as though critiquing him. "Forgive the assumption, but you aren't from some greatly important family, are you, Tash?"

Palmer met Nico's eyes for a long moment before shifting to Brier. "And you wonder why I didn't much care for him in school?"

Brier changed the topic before the tension could escalate. "So what do you suggest then, Nic?"

Nico continued to frown, directing it toward her. "Since when have you been an activist, Bri?"

Brier hesitated and motioned toward the window. "Since I saw this." He didn't answer.

"This isn't right, Nico," Brier said softly.

"Well, what's 'right' is what's getting people killed, Bri," Nico nearly hissed. "You've been gone. You won't be beyond suspicion." He sighed, seeming to try to force the tension out of his body. "Don't do something stupid. I'm not going to lose you again."

She'd lost weight. Brier supposed there was really no surprise in that, but staring at the full wardrobe of her dresses, all still hanging in their proper places and waiting for her, she truly faced it for the first time. Being alone, even just to change, unnerved her. The beautiful silk dresses seemed unnecessarily opulent, nearly gaudy, and too big for her gaunt frame.

She reached out and found Palmer farther from her than she liked. *Where are you?*

With some soldier getting clothes. Floor down, I think.

She remained still, staring into the wardrobe. *And Rosette?*

Next door.

A shiver moved through her. *I don't like this.*

It'll be all right.

The door opened, making Brier spin. She released a breath. "You scared me."

"Sorry," Nico said, closing the door behind him. "I figured you'd rather have me up here than some random guard."

"They think I need a guard?" Brier frowned.

"I told you." He crossed his arms. "You've been gone. Council isn't sure if it can trust you. I just relieved the guard they had outside the door."

She didn't answer.

He moved farther into the room. "Why haven't you changed?"

"I think all of these will be big on me now." Brier pulled out a gray dress. "We didn't have much food out on the road."

Nico looked at her for a long moment and finally moved forward. "You really want to wear gray?"

"It seems fitting, doesn't it?" She laid the dress out, hands going to the tie of her skirt.

Nico shook his head, pulling out another dress. "Here, wear the green one. Last thing we need around here is more gray."

"I can dress myself just fine, Nico." She slid her skirt off, ignoring him as he studied her in just the short shift.

"You are thin," he said, a frown evident in his voice.

"As I said." Brier picked up the gray dress.

Nico didn't answer right away. "I'm trying to help you, you realize?"

Brier paused, halfway through working her arms into the bodice, the weight of the silk dragging her down. She finally nodded, sliding it over her head and wiggling to make the skirts fall into place. "I forgot how much fabric we wear around here. It's so heavy. You could make three dresses just out of this one, I'd bet."

"It suits you better than whatever they had you in." Nico crossed his arms.

Brier didn't answer, lacing the dress up as tightly as it would go, feeling the silk brush over her feet as she turned this way and that. Nobody would be able to scrub floors done up as such. "Where are the others?"

"You mean the acolyte and the child?"

Brier nodded.

Nico released a slow breath, moving closer to her. "I don't know what happened to you while you were gone, Bri, but it's all right now. I can take care of you. I'm sure they'll both be fine."

"No. You don't understand, Nico."

"Then explain it to me."

She looked at him, searching his face for a long moment before shaking her head. "There are things so much bigger than this, Nic. So much bigger than either of us. It's just... important."

Nico frowned, searching her face right back. "Did he touch you?"

"What?" Her eyebrows rose.

"Did *they* touch you?"

"No." She shuddered. "Nobody 'touched' me."

"Hurt you, then?"

"I'm *fine*, Nico." She shook her head, looking away from him.

"No, you aren't," he said. "I know you, Bri. There's something seriously wrong. Something you aren't telling me."

She released a breath, looked around. "I don't know, Nico. If the walls have ears, we really shouldn't talk about it."

"I'm worried about you, Bri."

She smiled weakly. "I'm worried about me, too."

He didn't seem to have an answer to that.

"Just," she continued, "please trust me? I need to be with them. It really might be a matter of life and death."

He frowned, searching her face. "I can stay with you, you know. No one's going to hurt you while I'm here."

"I would love that," she assured him. "But I need them too."

"We could bring a cot for the child in here."

"Nico, please." She looked into his eyes, pleading with him silently.

He released a long breath, slowly, between his teeth. "I'll see what I can do, all right?"

"Thank you." She relaxed slightly.

He cupped her face in his hand, running his thumb along her cheek. "You know I'd never let anything happen to you, Bri."

"I know," she said. "Neither would he."

CHAPTER TWENTY-THREE

PALMER SAT IN A DARK corner of the room, eyes closed, not sleeping. He felt Brier and Rosette one room over, both asleep, no one else around but the guard outside his door. He vaguely longed for the ability to phase like Cerise. He was a prisoner, kept in a gilded cage for the moment, but a prisoner no less. And even just the wall between him and the girls made him uneasy, made him feel ineffective.

He released a breath, trying to ease the tension in his shoulders, searching farther into the building. The vast majority of its inhabitants seemed to be asleep, including a few other guards no doubt meant to keep watch of the halls. Finally, down on the first floor, he found movement. A picture filtered in, still slightly murky but clearer than his visions.

Nico walked into a darkened room, not much different than all the other visions of it, save for the men on the other side.

"I was summoned?" Nico asked, the word 'summoned' sounding like something vile. He glanced back as the door closed behind him before looking at the men.

Palmer felt the slight tug of Brier's subconscious as she stirred. He let the vision filter into her as well.

One of the men from before studied Nico. "You've been watching the girl?"

"Yes, signore." Nico clasped his hands behind his back, truly looking the part of the good soldier.

"And?" the man asked when Nico didn't continue.

"And, signore?" Nico asked, feigning ignorance.

"And has she said anything, Nicodemo?" His father glowered at him.

"She's said a great many things, Father," Nico said. "Are you looking for anything in particular?"

"That smart mouth of yours is going to get you into trouble someday."

"I'm not attempting to be smart," Nico said, just as stoic as he had been the entire day. "I'm simply asking. Would you prefer me to outline every conversation we've had the entire afternoon?"

Orris Adessi-Guillroy narrowed his eyes.

"Has she said anything more about her story?" yet another man asked.

"Her story, signore?"

"About the supposed kidnapping. Did she tell you anything of it?"

Nico shook his head. "She maintains that she was kidnapped, as she said, signore. She hasn't talked much about it otherwise."

"Do you believe her?"

Nico pressed his lips together but nodded. "I do."

"Why the pause?" Orris kept his eyes on his son, looking nearly predatory.

"I was simply thinking, Father," Nico said, visibly tensing, though his face didn't change. "If anything, I'm worried about her."

"Why is that?" the first man asked.

Nico shifted his gaze. "I believe she has been traumatized, signore. She claims she was not mistreated, but she seems strongly overdependent on this Palmer Tash."

The last man at the end of the table finally spoke. "That is not uncommon. I know many stories of women who cling to someone they see as a protector after a traumatic experience." He looked at his peers and back at Nico. "She is in a weakened state, no doubt."

Orris nodded, thinking. "Stay close to her. See if she says anything."

"What are you expecting her to say, Father?" Nico asked, his body still tense.

"Anything of interest," Orris answered.

The connection with Brier strained, tugging strongly before breaking. Palmer opened his eyes, blinking in the darkness. *Are you all right?*

She didn't answer.

Brier? Panic was building in his chest, but he tried to keep it out of his voice.

I'm all right, she finally answered.

He released a breath and the tension that flowed out with it.

You're all right over there? she asked.

Fine.

Everything went silent.

I'm going to try to go back to sleep, Brier finally said. *I don't want Nico to know I know he was gone.*

Probably smart, Palmer agreed.

Another long pause.

I wish you were over here, she sent him.

I wish I were too.

He waited for an answer, but that time the silence stretched on so long he began to check if she had fallen back asleep.

I love you. Her words filtered through, so light he could barely hear them, as if they came out of a dream. Still, they made him freeze.

I... he started, but she was certainly asleep. He poked around her head a moment, looking for any lingering thoughts or feelings, but he found little—nothing that would help him understand whether she had really meant to say it—but enough to ruin any chance of more rest.

Brier awoke as first light filtered through her window. The silk sheets under her felt wonderful. And the soft mattress... She had forgotten how nice it was not to wake with something hard digging into her hip. She leaned back into the warm body behind her and froze. Realization came a second later. *Nico.* Whereas Palmer was only slightly taller than her, Nico's body outstretched hers, engulfing her. His arm lay over her waist loosely, harder than she remembered but still familiar.

But it felt... wrong. She felt invaded. Watched.

She wanted a drink.

Sliding her gaze across the room, she met Rosette's, wide awake and sad. Brier slowly pushed Nico's arm off her—managing to move without waking him—and crossed the room in a few strides to sit next to the little girl. "Did you sleep well?"

Rosette shrugged.

"You're going to forget how to talk if you keep shrugging like that."

She shrugged again.

Brier gave Rosette a quick smile, not sure if it quite reached her eyes, before standing to grab a brush off the corner of her desk. "Turn around. I'm going to try to get some of those knots out of your hair."

Rosette eyed Nico, still asleep in the bed, but did as she was told. *You're awake?*

Brier glanced at the wall separating them from the next room then set to brushing Rosette's long hair, the blond looking dark with dirt. Brier's, more than likely, wasn't much better. *Rosette and I are.*

How is she?

No worse than she has been, I suppose.

Rosette shifted, almost as though she had heard something, but remained silent.

The Guillroy's back, Palmer continued.

It wasn't a question. *Still asleep.*

What are you going to do? Palmer asked.

You tell me.

You know my visions are barely working.

Sadly. She sighed. *I suppose we should just be careful about what we say around him, hmm?*

I doubt he and I will be spending much quality time together.

Brier actually smiled. *True.*

"Are we going to leave?" Rosette finally spoke, her voice not more than a breath.

Brier glanced at Nico then at the wall hiding Palmer. "We'll see."

"I could make the guard sick."

"Shh," Brier hushed her. "Be careful what you say out loud."

Rosette nodded.

Palmer's voice returned. *Someone's coming.*

Who?

A long pause. *I don't know.*

"What are you doing?"

Brier started, her eyes wide, before she recovered. She forced a smile. "Since when have you ever gotten up before ten, Nico?"

"Since people actually started requiring me to arrive on time." He sat up, watching her. "What are you doing?"

"Rosette's hair is knotted." Brier returned to working out the worst of the kinks with her fingers. "I imagine we could both do well with a bath. I figured you wouldn't be up for a while."

"We could get someone else to deal with that."

"I don't mind it." Brier tugged at another knot as gently as possible. Rosette didn't complain, didn't so much as whimper.

"Did you sleep well?" Brier asked.

Nico didn't hesitate. "Well enough."

"I thought I felt you get up at some point." Brier kept watching him through her eyelashes. "Couldn't sleep?"

"I was fine." He moved to get out of bed. "Do you want me to get us all breakfast? You could use a good meal, I'm sure. Both of you."

Brier finally looked at him straight on. "And Palmer, too?"

Nico's jaw tightened, but he nodded. "I'll see what I can do."

"Thank you."

Nico picked up his uniform, slid the jacket back on over the shirt, and buttoned it silently.

Brier finally stopped brushing. "Are you upset with me, Nic?"

He raised his eyes to hers, frowning questioningly. "What?"

"You seem like you're upset."

Nico released a long breath, finishing the last two buttons on his jacket before answering, "Not at you."

"Then at whom?"

"At what, more." He glanced at his face in the mirror before heading for the door.

"At what, then?" she persisted.

He sighed, his hand on the latch, and glanced back at her before opening the door. "Life."

The door clicked shut behind him before she had a chance to think of an answer.

Palmer didn't move from his spot in the corner, waiting, listening to the steps growing closer and closer. Four, maybe five people, rounded the corner, walked down the hall, and passed Brier's room. He released a breath, glad they were coming for him rather than the girls. Voices spoke softly for a moment, and finally the door unlocked.

A man in gray opened the door. As he looked around the room, his eyebrows knotted, confused for a split second before his eyes fell on Palmer. He straightened, trying to look commanding, no doubt. "Signore Tash, if you would come with me."

"Come where?" Palmer didn't move, simply regarding the soldier with cool disinterest.

"You have been summoned."

Palmer raised an eyebrow. "Last I was told, I was to stay here."

"Well, now you've been told to move." Another man, surly looking, strode into the room and motioned at Palmer with his chin while addressing the first soldier, "Get him up."

The first soldier saluted, moving toward Palmer less than confidently.

"I can stand myself." Palmer shook his head, checking the room next door. He could feel growing alarm, but both girls were still there. He stood, brushing off the pants he had been given and looking between the two men. "Where are we going?"

"Just get moving." The surly soldier motioned with his chin again, that time toward the door.

The other man behind Palmer pushed him forward.

Palmer didn't attempt to fight it, biding his time.

What's going on? Panic colored Brier's voice.

Everything's fine.

Crossing the threshold, Palmer looked at the men filling the hallway. Four stood just outside the door with another two down the hall, all watching him cautiously. Wherever they had been told to take him, they certainly weren't going to risk his escaping.

Palmer studied each of them in turn, finally settling back on the surly one. "Is there something I can help you with?"

The surly one grabbed Palmer by the shoulder, pushing him forward. "Come on."

Brier stood at the door, trying to hear the voices in the hall. Feet shuffled. Her hand went to the handle. She hesitated. "Rosie?"

Rosette looked up from the cot.

"Try the handle. Just lightly."

Dutifully, Rosette moved across the room and pressed lightly on the metal handle. It stopped short.

Nico had locked them in.

Brier pursed her lips. "Can you go sit on the bed for me?"

Rosette cocked her head to one side.

"I don't want you caught up in anything."

Rosette moved, more slowly that time but obediently nonetheless.

Brier replaced her fingers on the handle and slid her hand forward, feeling it turn easily under her palm. She pushed the door open, just a crack, pressing her face against it to see.

A wall of gray jackets was retreating down the hall, their backs toward her, with Palmer lost somewhere in the middle.

"May I inquire as to what is happening, signori?" Her voice beat her down the hallway as she stepped out of the room.

The soldiers turned, surprise on most of their faces.

The largest, who looked at least vaguely familiar, recovered first. "Please return to your room, signorina. This is official business."

"Official business doing *what*, pray tell?" Brier crossed her arms and tilted her head back, attempting to appear imposing even at a head shorter than him and in just her robe.

"Brier, it's fine," Palmer said. "Go back inside."

The big guard smirked, moving back toward her. "Yes, why don't you be a good girl and leave this to us."

"And what if I don't?" She tilted her head back even farther to keep eye contact as he approached.

The man narrowed his eyes. "Then, if I were you, I would be very glad that Adessi-Guillroy hasn't woken up and still wants his little whore when she's obviously spoilt goods. Tell me, how many different men had you while you were gone? Just lover boy over there, or did those 'kidnappers' of yours start a line?"

The slap resounded in the hallway, and Brier's hand was smarting before she had the chance to reconsider it.

"You little bitch." The man grabbed her and lifted Brier off her feet by the fabric of her dressing gown.

"Hey!" Palmer shouted down the hall.

Brier heard a scuffle to the right, the soldiers struggling to hold Palmer. She brought her hands up to the soldier's as she tried to free herself, but it seemed no use. He had her, his face twisted with rage.

Power tingled in her body, snaking toward her attacker. She fought it back, unwilling to expose herself in front of such a large audience. She swung her feet out and connected, hard, with the man's shin.

He bent, nearly dropping her. As he recovered, his face curled into a sneer. He threw her to the floor.

Her body jerked as her left arm took the brunt of the impact. She let out a soft grunt, trying to recover before he could reach her.

The man was already over her again, one foot pulled back.

With a blur, the man slammed into the wall, Nico's elbow pinning him under the chin.

"What the *hell* is going on?" Nico asked.

The scuffle down the hall went quiet. Everything seemed to freeze outside the man squirming against the wall. After one last shove, the soldier managed to get some space from Nico, if not much. "The bitch slapped me."

"He deserved it, I assure you." Brier pushed herself up to sitting, babying her left arm, still shaking from adrenaline. "Tell me, signore, were you implying that I had been repeatedly raped? Or that I was simply waiting for the chance to be kidnapped so I'd have the *excuse* to spread my legs to anyone who asked?"

The man took a step toward her. Nico slammed him back into the wall. The guard grimaced, pushed Nico back, and took a few steps—that time away from Brier—before turning back to Nico. "I'd watch that slut of yours, Adessi. She sticks her nose in the wrong place, and you won't always be there to save her."

"How is Sara, Matos?" Nico ran his eyes over the man. "Last I heard, she was having a *very* good time down on the piazza, yes?"

The soldier narrowed his eyes but motioned to the others at the end of the hall. The wall of gray began shepherding Palmer away once again.

"Hey!" Brier scrambled to get up.

Nico hushed her sharply, grabbing her good arm and all but shoving her back into her room.

"Watch it." She stumbled slightly as he shut and locked the door behind him. "I've been manhandled enough for one day, thank you very much."

"Are you *trying* to get yourself killed, Brier?" Nico snapped.

"I was *trying* to find out what was happening," she returned.

"I thought I had locked you in here." Nico looked at the door accusingly before turning back to Brier. "Looking for answers around here *will* get you killed. I told you to keep your head down."

"Where are they taking him?"

"I don't know."

Brier frowned darkly.

He sighed. "If you *promise* to stay put, I'll go find out, all right? I need to grab your breakfast anyway. I had to drop the tray to stop Matos from knocking out your teeth."

"I don't think he was aiming for my face," Brier mumbled.

Nico gave her a hard stare.

She looked away, rubbing her left arm. "Matos? He was your classmate, wasn't he?"

Nico nodded, looking her over carefully. "Are you hurt?"

"Just a bruised arm, I think," Brier said. "And ego, perhaps."

Nico walked over to her and slid the robe slowly off her shoulder to get a better look at her arm. He frowned at the wine-colored mark already forming along her upper arm.

"I didn't say a small one." She made a face and pulled away, holding the fabric in place over her chest. "I'm fine though, Nico. It's not broken."

He pulled her back into place, brushing his fingers along the mark. Her arm involuntarily jerked away from him.

He released her. "Sorry."

She didn't answer.

He sighed. "Can I trust you to stay out of trouble if I run down the hall?"

She pressed her lips together and finally nodded. "You'll try to find out what's going on?"

He sighed again, softer that time. "I'll do my best, Bri. Why don't you get dressed?" His eyes dropped to her left arm. "Long sleeves, maybe. I wouldn't want to give Matos the satisfaction."

Brier couldn't find it in herself to disagree.

CHAPTER TWENTY-FOUR

P ALMER LOOKED FROM ONE MAN to the next, an odd sense of déjà vu hitting him. The Seers from months ago. The board deciding whether or not to take him as an acolyte. Everything important in his life so far seemed to end with a panel of men, seated at a table, judging him.

However, the current group was joined by a wall of gray-attired soldiers lining any and all escape routes, which made the gathering feel more like a tribunal than a panel.

None of the men spoke, so neither did Palmer. He simply stood in the middle of the room, looking from one serious face to the other. He could wait as long as they could. Something flashed in his head, but he pushed it away, unwilling to indulge a murky vision.

At last, the far door opened, and a Seer in his red robes strode into the room. "I apologize, signori. You caught me in the middle of morning prayer."

The voice clicked with Palmer, and his meeting with the headmaster however many months before slid into place—Sage Lee-Parrino.

"Good that you could join us, Sage." The man at the end of the table looked at the Seer, pulling out the last empty chair. "We have been alerted that Signore Tash was one of yours?"

"Tash?" Sage Lee-Parrino peered into the dark room, recognition and confusion mixing on his face. "Yes, yes. He was one of our acolytes. Disappeared a few months ago. A very promising boy."

"Can you think of any reason why he would have disappeared?"

"You could feel free to ask me that, signore," Palmer finally spoke. "I'm standing right here."

"We will speak with you in a moment." Another of the men down the table glared.

Palmer just clasped his hands behind his back—a rather good imitation of Nico last night, if he did say so himself—and waited.

"Please answer the question, Sage. Can you think of anything that would have led to Signore Tash's rash departure?"

Sage Lee-Parrino looked at Palmer for a long moment then at the man at the table. "Nothing comes to mind. He had just been apprenticed to one of our top astrologists, in fact."

"How would you describe his personality?"

Palmer frowned at both of them but didn't comment.

"Quiet," Sage Lee-Parrino said. "In the top quarter of all his classes, but not *the* top. A few friends, but not overwhelmingly popular. Nothing tremendously remarkable."

"Did you ever notice any suspicious activities?"

"Suspicious how, signore?"

Palmer's frown deepened. Never had he heard Sage Lee-Parrino call anyone "signore." Palmer could nearly feel the power of the Church disintegrating in the room with the one word.

"Odd friends? Unaccounted nights? Conversations that seemed... off?"

Sage Lee-Parrino looked at Palmer then back at the man. "Not that I can recall, but I was not the keeper of the boys. I mostly saw those in trouble or those falling behind in their programs, which Tash was not."

"As far as you are aware, Signore Tash did not get into trouble often?" the man clarified.

"Not that I am aware," Sage Lee-Parrino said.

The man turned his eyes to Palmer. "Signore Tash, would you agree with the good Sage?"

"About not being in trouble?" Palmer asked. "I didn't tend to be."

"You weren't one to sneak out at night, then?"

Palmer took a moment, sensing a trap, and proceeded cautiously. "I didn't often find reason to, signore."

"So what, then, were you doing out the night Signorina Chastain was captured?" The man held his hands out, a smirk forming at the corners of his mouth. "Seems like quite the coincidence that you would come across a kidnapping the one night you chose to sneak out."

Palmer met the man's eyes as he thought through his words. "Yes, it was."

"Tell me, Signore Tash." The man leaned forward over the table toward him. "Have you ever had any contact with people outside of the Augarian?"

He refused to trip up. "I lived outside the Augarian until I was six, signore, so yes."

"While you were an acolyte?"

Palmer shifted then made himself hold still. "I'm sure there have been some in passing. None that I remember specifically."

"No Bugiardi?"

"No, signore. Not that I am aware of." Palmer finally narrowed his own eyes slightly. "Am I being accused of something?"

"Signore Tash." The man leaned back again, tenting his fingers. "Do you truly expect us to believe that the one night you just happened to sneak out—which you rarely, if ever, did—you just happened to stumble upon a kidnapping, and that you, who have no military training, decided the best course of action was to intercede?"

"Wouldn't you have, signore?" Palmer asked. "I saw someone in trouble. I didn't think. I tried to help."

"And you didn't think that finding a guard or someone better trained might have been a smarter course of action?"

"I just said I didn't think, signore. I just acted."

The man sat back, looking up and down the table.

Palmer stood motionless, waiting. Speaking seemed dangerous at the moment.

Orris finally shifted in his large chair toward the center of the table, regarding Palmer as though he were some sort of dangerous bug, something to squash at the first possible moment. "Tell me, Tash, had you ever met Signorina Chastain before?"

No *signore* from Orris Adessi-Guillroy. Palmer weighed his options quickly and could see the man knew at least part of the answer, so he didn't dare lie. "Yes, signore."

Orris raised an eyebrow, maybe actually surprised by Palmer's answer. "Was this at the temple?"

Palmer took another moment. "No, signore."

"Well, then, where might you have met her, Tash? She didn't often spend her time bothering acolytes, as far as I am aware."

"She did not," Palmer agreed. "I had seen her a few times around the university, generally waiting for your son, I believe."

"Did you see her or meet her, Tash?"

"Saw her on those instances," Palmer said. "I then briefly had the chance to meet her on her last birthday."

Orris continued to study him with the same cautious disgust. "When on her birthday was that?"

"Well." Palmer paused. "A friend of mine did convince me to sneak out one night previously, the night of Signorina Chastain-Bochard's birthday. He was quite enamored with another girl he believed was going to be in attendance."

"Does this 'friend' have a name?" Orris asked.

"I'd rather not get him in trouble, signore." Palmer continued before Orris could demand an answer, "While my friend was talking to this girl, I came across Signorina Chastain-Bochard, and we shared a few words. I had no other contact with her after that night until she was kidnapped."

"Curious," Orris said.

Palmer didn't rise to the bait.

"Curious," Orris continued even without Palmer's prompting, "that for an acolyte who didn't often sneak out, both times you have recounted led you straight to Signorina Chastain."

Palmer waited and spoke only when it seemed Orris wouldn't continue without it. "I suppose it is, signore."

"You still wish for us to consider it a coincidence, Tash?"

"I'm not sure what else I would call it."

Orris studied Palmer, glanced at the other men at the table, and then addressed Palmer again. "Do you wish to hear what I think happened, Tash?"

"If you so like, signore. I already told you what did happen."

"I think," Orris continued, undeterred, "you have long planned to kidnap Signorina Chastain."

Palmer furrowed his eyebrows. "Oh? To what purpose?"

"You have familial ties to the Bugiardi, do you not, Tash?"

"My father was widely renowned as one of the most heroic soldiers in the Reclamation," Palmer said.

"But your mother's sister, with whom you lived during the Occupation..." Orris gave a sly smile. "It has been widely reported she had a Bugiardi lover while you were under her roof."

Palmer bristled but did his best to suppress it. Anger would only condemn him. "If she did, I was much too young to recognize it. I wasn't yet five when we left my aunt's house."

"A little boy without his father," Orris said, leaning back in his chair. "I don't think anyone would be surprised at you looking for a surrogate father."

"Sadly, I had to get by without one," Palmer said, his words clipped short.

"Or," Orris leaned forward again, "you found one and have long been plotting to bring him back."

"I assure you I have not." Palmer released a tense breath through his teeth, doing his best to remain collected. "And even if I had, I am not sure how Signorina Chastain-Bochard's kidnapping would help to do so."

"You were there the night she was betrothed to my son if you were at her birthday." Orris narrowed his eyes into a true glare. "If you were looking for someone you could use to start a war, you had found her."

"*I* did not," Palmer insisted. "And further, if I had, why would I then bring her back?"

"A change of heart? Father dearest betraying you? A growing affection for Signorina Chastain? I am not a mind reader, Tash."

"But you are not a bad storyteller." The scathing remark escaped before Palmer could stop it.

Orris motioned with his hand, and the soldiers began to encroach. Looking from side to side, the rest of the men at the table nodded—save Sage Lee-Parrino—and Orris looked back at Palmer. "Tash, your loyalty to the Augarian and to Latysia has been called into question, and we do not find sufficient evidence to refute it. It is my duty to declare you a traitor to the state. You shall be held until further notice, until such a time when your sentence can be reached."

Palmer's eyes widened, but he didn't attempt a fight. The soldiers' hands clamped down, and they led him away.

Brier paced, the damned green dress scraping the tile as she moved. Her sense of dread wouldn't leave, but every time she tried to calm her nerves and find Palmer, the signal came back muddied, unclear, too far away. He was alive—she was all but sure on that—but something was happening, getting in the way. She just wished she knew what.

Flexing her hand, she fought the urge to walk out the door and look for him. Nico had double, perhaps triple-checked the lock before leaving. There would be no way to hide that she had gotten out illegally somehow—lock picking or magic. Either possibility would bring even more scrutiny down upon her.

"You don't sense any death, do you, Rosie?" Brier glanced across the room.

Rosette shook her head from her place in the corner. "People are scared, though. And mad."

"They truly are," Brier agreed.

The lock clicked in the door. Brier stopped moving and turned slightly toward the sound.

Nico stepped inside then frowned. "Have you been standing there since I left?"

"Pacing, actually," Brier said. "Not as though there is much left to do here. All my books are gone."

"Sent back to the library," Nico said. "New librarian's orders."

"New librarian," she repeated.

"The new Bochard." He avoided her eyes.

Brier frowned. "They take my name, too?"

"I don't believe it has been discussed, whether or not you will remain Chastain-Bochard. There's not much precedent for it." Nico locked the door again and checked the handle before turning around.

"So just Brier Chastain, then?"

"I don't know, Bri." He sighed. "Does it matter?"

"Just wondering where I stand." Brier started to pace again. "I mean, they've let me keep my room, so far, but if they seem eager to clean house..."

"You can simply enough switch to Brier Adessi-Guillroy if it bothers you." He moved across the room to sit at the desk.

She paused, frowning at him. "What?"

"We were still engaged, last I checked." Nico rested his elbows on his knees.

She looked at him for another moment and finally just shook her head as she moved to the bed. She sat with a thump, her skirts puffing out around her. "Why would your father want you to marry me now?"

"Why would he have wanted me to marry you before?"

The memory of Palmer's voice tickled the back of her head. She pushed it away, shrugging.

He released a breath, searching her face before speaking. "I'd still be happy to marry you, Bri, you know. Things are horrible right now, but us together... We've always been able to get through things better when we're together. You know that."

Brier's mind was searching for Palmer once again, and she tried to focus on the conversation. "I'm not sure your father would let us get married even if we wanted to right now."

"He's the one who announced we were engaged."

"What feels like three lifetimes ago," Brier said.

Nico looked at Rosette, who seemed completely enthralled with one of Brier's old dolls in her lap, touching the dark hair and porcelain face. He moved next to Brier on the bed, taking her hand in his. "I know something happened out there to you, Bri, but it's all right. You're back. It's all fine now."

She gave him a sad smile. "You know better than that, Nic. It really isn't."

At nightfall, the room next door was still empty. Though that left her unsettled, Brier didn't dare ask Nico about it. She lay awake as the hours passed, watching Nico asleep in bed next to her and the small lump that was Rosette across the room. Being separated felt wrong. She felt vulnerable. Unbalanced. Dangerous.

What sleep she did get was fitful, never more than a few minutes at a time, plagued with muddy images. Men. Chairs. The dark room. Something trying to reach her but not quite succeeding.

Finally she heard words filtering in, far away, as though through water: *"Tash, your loyalty to the Augarian and to Latysia has been called into question, and we do not find sufficient evidence to refute it. It is my duty to declare you a traitor to the state. You shall be held until further notice, until such a time when your sentence can be reached."*

CHAPTER TWENTY-FIVE

NOT FAR UNDERNEATH THE PALACE, the cells of the gaol seemed a world away from the gilded rooms upstairs. Able to touch each wall with his arms outstretched and with barely enough room to stretch out his legs, Palmer studied the rough stone walls encasing him. The bars forming the far wall offered the only source of air or light. Distant torches made the shadows morph and the stones of the hallway appear oddly orange. Day or night, one wouldn't know locked away there.

And the water... He grimaced as another drip hit a puddle growing somewhere in the distance. All the walls seemed to drip, glistening as water trickled in every crack, as if the very ground were trying to wash the cells away.

Palmer sat with his back against the far wall, feet pointing toward the bars, doing his best to calm his breathing, focusing on finding Brier. Sporadically, he sent out visions of the trial, such as it was. He hoped that it was still night and that, asleep, Brier would get them.

Footsteps made his eyes snap open. Boots pounded the rough stone floors, coming down the stairs somewhere to his left but stopping before they reached his cell. A gate clanged open. Someone tried speaking, a man's voice growing louder and louder until he was shouting, the panic resounding in the enclosed space. The boots trudged off, and the screaming man was dragged away with them.

Palmer shuddered internally, the fear, paranoia, and panic down in the gaol settling into his bones. With all of that in the air, perhaps Rosette would find him.

Brier moved as silently as possible, sliding out of her robe and into the least bulky of the dresses in her closet. Adding a cloak with a hood, she glanced at Nico and froze as he turned over in his sleep. She waited, stepping back to be out of sight should he wake, but no, his breathing remained low and steady. He still slept.

Hood securely over her face, Brier moved toward the cot in the corner. She placed a hand on Rosette's shoulder, shushing the girl when Rosette stirred.

Rosette just looked up, her large blue eyes catching the moonlight as she waited.

"Palmer's in trouble," Brier whispered, glancing at Nico, who didn't even turn. She looked back at Rosette. "We're going to save him."

Rosette just nodded, sliding out of bed as quietly as a mouse.

With one last glance at Nico, Brier moved to the door. After a quick mental apology to her friend, fiancé, and captor, Brier pushed, the locked door opening with nothing more than a quiet brush along the marble floor.

Brier stuck her head out into the dark hall and found herself alone. Rosette's hand slid up into hers, and they started forward, Brier closing the door behind them. The darkness seemed to work with her rather than against her, letting her hide in every shadow instead of hiding the world from her. Their bare feet silent against the smooth floor, Brier's heart pounding in her ears was the only sound following them down the twisting halls toward the only place she could think of a traitor being put—Deadman's Row.

Her childhood came back to her in flashes: ducking out of sight at the first sound of footsteps; cutting through old forgotten rooms and passageways, long before abandoned, forgotten by everyone but their designer. It had been a game a decade before, a way to beat Nico in races, but it became entirely serious, a path that might be her only escape— their only escape.

The words found her again, stronger but still distorted: *"Tash, your loyalty to the Augarian and to Latysia has been called into question..."*

They made her falter, slowing her for a split second before she headed forward with even greater urgency. As she moved lower and lower through the building, Rosette's footsteps beside her became stronger as the girl no longer followed but seemed to know the way. Brier glanced at her in the dark.

"I can feel them," Rosette whispered, moving out in front. "This way."

Brier hesitated but didn't argue, picking up her long skirts slightly in order to keep up as Rosette broke into a run.

Ducking through passageways, under staircases, and around corners, Rosette seemed to grow stronger and stronger. They found a door even Brier didn't know existed, which brought them into the storage under the palace and then even lower.

Moving down a steep set of stairs, they finally slowed again, unable to keep their balance on the slick, thin steps at anything faster than a steady walk. Brier vaguely registered the roughness of the floor under her still-calloused feet, feeling the cold water splash up into her skirts every time she hit a puddle—the hem no doubt becoming soiled from dragging over the dirty ground—but that all seemed unimportant and far away. She listened carefully for voices, footsteps, or any other sound indicating someone was out in front of them, but she heard nothing. She placed her hand on a ledge as they rounded a corner and felt wet dust and grime stick to her fingers. It hadn't been touched, let alone cleaned, in ages. However they brought people into the gaol, that path wasn't it.

They reached the bottom of the stairs, and Rosette took Brier's hand again as they moved slowly down the long hallway. The already stale air turned putrid, the smell of waste and rot filling the air. Brier gagged, fought the reflex down, and tried not to breathe. She certainly had not missed that smell of decay. They passed the first gate, where a prone body lay out, unmoving.

"He's sick," Rosette whispered.

"I know, Rosie. I know," Brier answered, moving by the row of cells, each offset to keep their inhabitants from being able to see any others. Some were empty. Some contained sleeping men. One man was awake but curled up in the corner, talking to himself, seemingly unaware of their presence.

Rosette looked up, mouth open, but Brier shushed her, continuing forward silently, checking each cell as she went. Palmer's vision again hit her, full on, too loud, blurring her sight: Palmer in front of a table, a Seer walking in. She brought her hands up to her ears as though that would help as she tried to push it out of her head. It wavered and pushed back, shooting pain behind her eyes.

Stop it!

The vision died all at once, and the tunnel came back into view.

Brier?

Down here, somewhere... she answered, looking farther down the shadowy hallway. *Where are you?*

Here. A hand appeared between some bars farther down the row, waving.

Brier headed forward, running past the last few cells, letting Rosette work her way more slowly. Brier skidded to a stop in front of Palmer's cell, water on the ground making even the rough stones slick. She released a breath of relief, whispering, "That hurt, I'll have you know, yelling in my head like that."

"Sorry." Palmer rested his hands on the bars. "I've been trying to get something to you all night."

"I finally got it." Brier looked at the bars, pulling her hood back. "Where's the lock?"

Palmer stepped back slightly, motioning to one side of the bars. "Are you all right?"

"Fine." Brier placed her hand over the lock and pulled lightly. The barred door swung open with a loud squeak. Brier winced, glancing down the hallway before looking back at Palmer. "Why?"

"That soldier threw you, hard."

"Just a bruise, I promise." Brier stepped back, glancing at Rosette.

Rosette stood at another cell, studying whomever it held.

"Rosie," Brier hissed. "Come here."

Rosette looked at her, unmoving.

A hand reached out for her.

"Rosette!" Brier's voice came out too loud, echoing off the walls. She slapped her hand over her mouth.

Rosette jumped back, out of reach, but it was too late. The sound of men stirring filled the hallway. Voices echoed from the far end. Boots clattered down stairs.

Palmer stepped out of the cell. "Run?"

"Run," Brier agreed, grabbing Rosette's hand as they shot down the hall toward their staircase.

Brier suddenly became glad she didn't have her slippers on. Barefoot, she wasn't slowed down, her rough feet catching the slick steps better than any shoes she owned. Palmer, on the other hand, was lagging behind. Brier glanced back. "All right?"

"Fine," he panted, beginning to take the short steps two at a time.

The sound of shouting prisoners, sane and mad, echoed after them, and the stomping of boots grew ever closer as they sprinted.

Brier slipped, caught herself with her hands, and continued forward, the long staircase seeming even longer as they headed for the surface.

They burst through the doorway at the top, Rosette first, then Brier, then Palmer. Rosette hesitated, looking at the packed basement, lost. Brier took over, grabbing Rosette off her feet before heading straight for the doorway through which they'd entered. The extra weight slowed her, kept her from hiking up her skirt, and made running difficult.

"Give me." Palmer easily caught them and grabbed Rosette into his arms. "You lead."

Brier ducked into a hallway, cutting one way then another. She wound her way toward the piazza, then the back of the building, then the piazza again. Indecisive, she tried to lose anyone in pursuit. The rough stone turned to marble again, and she slid, her wet feet losing all traction. Mentally, she thanked Palmer for taking Rosette as she balanced herself and kept going.

After another turn, they reached the main entrance of the palace, the tight passageways opening up to the gaping hall. Second thoughts passed through Brier's mind. The hall left them exposed and unprotected, but it was too late to turn around. She continued forward.

Guards appeared through the far doors. Brier turned toward the staircase, but more stood there, and they turned toward the fugitives. More soldiers trickled in the far door, surrounding them, cutting them off from the passageway. They skidded to a halt, caught in the middle, hearts pounding, out of breath.

Someone clapped, slowly, sarcastically as he came down the stairs through the gray coats. "I had a feeling we might have to watch you, *dolcezza*. You always did have a way of popping up out of nowhere around here. Plenty of passageways I'm sure even we haven't found."

Brier watched Orris Adessi-Guillroy make his way to the main floor as Palmer put Rosette down beside her.

Take Rosette. Head for the passageway. I'll try to lead them the other way.

There are too many, Brier answered, chest still rising and falling quickly. *They'd get us both.* "I didn't know you would be up, signore."

"A commotion of this size tends to draw attention, *dolcezza*."

The nickname, sickeningly sweet over some dark malice, made her stomach twist. She glanced at Palmer. *Anyway, I'm not leaving you.*

"Why keep her?" Palmer spoke up. "Them. If you want me, I'll come quietly."

Orris gave a slow smile. "Oh, I think you know exactly why we want her, Tash. You are the one of no consequence."

"Nico will never forgive you if you hurt me," Brier said, her voice sounding more certain than she felt.

"My son will do as I tell him." Orris broke through the last of the soldiers, standing opposite them in the circle. He motioned to the men around them. "Just as they will do as I tell them."

"You always did love the idea of being a despot, didn't you?" Brier snapped, her voice filled with more venom than she had ever heard in herself.

Orris actually smirked, sliding his eyes to Palmer. "This kidnapping of yours has turned her rather feisty, hasn't it?"

"*I* didn't kidnap her," Palmer said, his jaw clenched.

"So you insist," Orris said. "Sadly, I doubt anyone will believe you."

"I'm not sure why it would matter if they believed me," Palmer answered. "You intend to execute me, I'm sure, before any sort of proper trial."

"Not as dumb as I took you for." Orris's smirk grew. He looked to the soldier closest to him. "Take her. The others are disposable."

The soldiers started forward.

The hall rumbled, the very walls flexing.

The soldiers halted, looking around.

The smirk slowly left Orris' face. "Are you not so clueless, *dolcezza*?"

Brier just looked back, lifting her eyebrows, a challenge.

"I'd be careful, if I were you." Orris took a few steps closer.

"I was about to say the same to you," Brier answered.

The hall rumbled again, that time more violently. An empty frame came off a wall, and the wood splintered on the floor. An unlit chandelier shook dangerously above them.

Palmer moved a little closer to her, keeping Rosette safely between them, nearly pressed into Brier's skirts.

Orris narrowed his eyes and motioned to the guards on one side of the room. "Grab her."

The soldiers didn't manage more than a step forward. The ground shuddered violently, knocking them off their feet. The other soldiers began to move. Pillars fell, blocking any advancement, nearly crushing many. The roof cracked. Orris took a step back. The chandelier came loose and fell with a clatter as the metal bent and crystal shattered.

One soldier broke free and grabbed for Rosette. He doubled over, vomiting blood before he could touch her. Confusion and panic slunk through the ranks of soldiers. Some retreated to the safety of doorways while others still tried to move forward.

Another pillar collapsed, and a chunk of ceiling fell between them and Orris. Dust stirred up. More marble fell, growing closer and closer to the three in the middle of the room.

"Brier!" Palmer took her wrist and pulled her toward the quickly weakening line behind them.

The destruction was growing too great as anger, power, and freedom all coursed through her, bringing the building down, demolishing everything around her.

"Brier! Go!" Palmer jerked her toward the passageway.

His energy met hers, clearing her head. She blinked, looking around at the building still falling, the men who dared to get too close to Rosette writhing on the floor, others still trying to clear a way through the debris, helping others caught under pillars or tiles from the ceiling.

"Go!" Palmer repeated, pushing her roughly.

She looked across the room, and her eyes met Nico's for a split second as he arrived through a doorway and froze in shock.

She turned, grabbing Rosette, and let Palmer push her forward, running from the destruction.

In a daze, Brier led them deeper through the passageway, and they finally reemerged in another gaping hall, seemingly abandoned. Brier stepped out, looking around at the green-streaked marble, the bright paintings in archways, and the gold inlay in the woodwork.

"Where are we?" Palmer asked.

Brier shook her head. "I don't know. I've never been here before."

Palmer just looked at her.

"Is there anyone around?" She looked back at him.

Palmer scanned the area. "No one."

Brier took Rosette's hand, moving forward slowly. "We're still in the palace. I think."

"I thought you'd been everywhere in the palace."

"I thought I had," she said. "I'm not sure how to get out from here."

Palmer offered her a weak smile. "That's all right. We come to a dead end, you can just blast us through the wall."

Brier frowned. "Not funny."

"Did I kill them?" Rosette asked, her soft voice cutting.

Brier looked down at her. "What?"

"The sick men," Rosette said. "I gave them what the man in the cell had."

Brier released a breath, couldn't bring herself to lie. "I don't know, Rosie. I don't know."

Rosette squeezed Brier's hand but just looked down.

"We did what we had to do, *piccola*."

"I mean really, Rosie, Brier nearly brought the place down," Palmer said.

Brier shot Palmer a look.

He offered another weak smile, sliding a hand around her waist and holding her on one side as she held Rosette's hand on the other.

Her arm flinched away slightly as his body came too close, the bruise smarting. "Careful. That's the side I landed on."

Palmer slid away from her, looking around before stopping them entirely. "Let me see it."

"I think we have more important things to worry about right now," Brier said.

"I think we're as alone as we're going to be."

Brier studied his face for a moment and finally nodded, moving them into an open room. "Rosie, keep a look out, will you?"

Rosette nodded, moving to the doorway to wait.

After pushing her cloak back, Brier reached behind herself to undo the laces of her dress, loosening it just enough to slide the long left sleeve down.

Palmer looked at the bruise, frowning deeply as he touched it. "I'm sorry I couldn't stop him."

"You had more than a few people to stop you," she said, wincing. "I didn't handle myself too poorly, I don't think."

"I think that slap nearly knocked him over," Palmer agreed, laying his hand flat over the worst of the bruise.

She hissed as a warm, golden light spread out from his hand, reaching out to the edges of the bruise before slowly fading again, taking the color and pain with it. Within a few moments, it was gone, the lingering ache dissipating with the light.

Brier pulled back, twisting her arm to study the once-again pale, smooth skin.

"I've been working on that." Palmer smiled softly.

One arm still crossed over to the other, Brier looked up. "Thank you."

He continued to smile, staring into her eyes for a long moment before he leaned forward. He met her lips with his, kissing her softly, lingering. She responded, bringing her hand up to his face, kissing him back, not caring that they were trapped, not caring that her sleeve slid down farther, not caring that they were all possibly dead.

Something pushed against Brier's mind, something foreign, encroaching. She pulled back.

"What?" Palmer asked.

"Brier," Rosette called, turning toward them. "There's a little girl."

Stepping out of Palmer's arms, Brier moved to the doorway.

A dark-haired girl, smaller than Rosette, sniffled across the hall from them, standing in the opposite doorway. Brier hesitated, the increasingly invading feeling making her pause.

The little girl looked up. "Can you help me?"

Palmer started forward, Rosette following a step behind him.

The little girl's eyes slid over to Brier, and they were black, too old for the little girl's face.

Grabbing Rosette's arm, Brier jerked her back, protecting Rosette behind her skirts.

Palmer froze, glancing at Brier, at the little girl, then back.

"I've brought down one hall so far tonight, Cerise," Brier said. "I am perfectly willing to do it again."

The little girl looked at Brier for another moment, wide-eyed, but finally sighed, rolling her eyes when Brier kept glaring. "You were so much more fun when you weren't paranoid."

"I think I have the right to be at this point," Brier answered.

The little girl crossed her arms, slowly morphing back into the familiar tall blonde. "Ruin all my fun, why don't you?"

"What are you doing here?" Palmer backed up, standing slightly ahead of Brier, completely blocking Rosette from view.

"Waiting for you, of course," Cerise said. "We figured you'd end up back 'home' sooner or later."

"We?" Brier frowned.

The weight pressing on Brier's mind retreated in a rush, and she felt Palmer tense.

Reinhald stepped out of the darkness. "You are both very hard people to track down."

Palmer kept his eyes on the two across the hall, turning his head only slightly toward Brier. *You don't know a way out of here?*

I told you, I'm not even sure of where "here" is, she answered.

"There's no need to run." Reinhald looked between the two of them. "We have no desire to hurt you. And this hall is far too beautiful to risk destruction, anyway."

"Why should we trust you?" Palmer's hand curled into a fist.

"Well, for one, I think we are the less likely to hurt you, of those looking for you in this building right now. Two, I still have use for both of you. And I imagine it would be easier for all involved if you chose to help willingly rather than by force."

None of them moved.

Reinhald sighed. "I have an army staging not far from the city, better trained than any of the boys they have drilling outside right now, I'd wager. If it is your desire to reclaim your home, we can help you do that."

Palmer's body grew so tense Brier was worried he might snap. "We're not helping you fight a war."

"Do you really have any better options right now?" Reinhald cocked an eyebrow. "War is brewing whether you come with us or remain here."

He's right. Brier frowned. *They're just going to capture all of us if we stay.*

Palmer didn't seem to have any argument for that.

"Where's Goebel?" Brier finally asked and then clarified, "Dominik."

"Out with the army. He doesn't much care for it in here." Cerise looked Brier over with a smirk. "Have you no shame? There was a child in the room."

Brier looked down at her half-undone dress and scrambled to right herself. "I hurt my arm."

"Right." Cerise continued to smirk. "I saw you two in there. Goebel will be crushed, I'm sure."

"Not the time, Cerise," Reinhald hissed.

"The last time someone worked with you, she ended up dead." Palmer kept his eyes on Reinhald.

"Marina was... unfortunate," Reinhald said, "but she knew the risks."

"Do you?" Palmer returned. "If you bring her into your fight, there may very well not be a city for you to conquer at the end of it."

Brier glanced at Palmer, trying to get a read on what he saw. All she could hear echoing through her head were his old words: *One of the visions, about if we go back, is... bad. I'd prefer to keep that one from happening if at all possible.*

"That isn't your choice to make," Reinhald answered. "Destruction is her birthright. It will find her one way or the other. We will at least allow her to find it as herself. I wouldn't expect quite so generous an offer from the men chasing you after your demonstration out there. To them, you will be nothing more than a weapon."

They looked down the hallway at a pair of large double doors, latched from the inside. Palmer didn't speak.

Brier looked at Cerise then Reinhald. "You can get us out of here?"

"Of course," he said.

She looked at Palmer. *We don't have much of a choice.*

"You could *choose* to level everything and be done with it," Palmer mumbled.

She squeezed his hand lightly then released it. She looked back at Reinhald. "Time is wasting, then."

Reinhald smiled, stepping out into the hallway. "Follow us."

CHAPTER TWENTY-SIX

THE PASSAGEWAY OUT OF THE Augarian seemed newer, more roughly made than those inside the building, leaving Brier with the distinct impression that it had been formed by someone tunneling in, not built by the designers themselves.

They worked their way farther and farther down a slope, slowly curving away to the left before they began to climb again.

Palmer seemed torn, sometimes walking behind them, checking that no one was coming, sometimes separating her and Rosette from Reinhald and Cerise. He vaguely reminded Brier of a guard dog. She finally stopped him as he once again moved forward, taking his hand with her left and Rosette's with her right, making the center link going forward through the tight passageway.

Just when Palmer feared they might never make it out of the rough tunnel, Reinhald stopped at a wall, climbed up a small series of grooves serving as a ladder, and pushed a stone loose above them. He disappeared into the light with Cerise flying up after him.

Palmer dropped back, letting Brier go first, then Rosette, and finally him.

Brier blinked, trying to let her eyes adjust to the light outside the tunnels, the sun low on the horizon. Brier looked behind them and saw the river and some distant houses but not Latysia itself. They had settled themselves perfectly, protected from view in the small dip of a valley, just deep enough to swallow up the rows of tents stretching out before them.

"How did we miss this?" Palmer murmured, looking around.

"We were too far west, I think," Brier answered, whether he meant the question to be rhetorical or not.

A well-groomed soldier in red stepped forward and saluted Reinhald. "They didn't tell us you'd be back this morning, sir."

"Dropping off someone we should all be very grateful to see." Reinhald smiled. "Is my brother awake?"

"I believe so, sir." The soldier saluted again, speaking with an oddly rough accent.

Reinhald motioned the rest of them forward. Brier walked after them, watching the soldier watching Cerise and then her for a moment before he moved back to the tunnel to replace the covering.

Walking through the aisles of tents, Brier could see discipline in every line and knot. Each tent lined up perfectly with the tent on either side and the one across from it, forming a perfect grid. The knots tying the flaps down looked likewise identical, perfect in each twist and turn. This was a practiced army, drilled into perfection, trained for duty.

The tents sitting outside the Augarian, the former students and young boys drilling in the piazza, flashed through Brier's mind. If these soldiers were half as trained in battle as discipline, the gray coats didn't stand a chance.

Who are they? Brier asked.

The soldiers?

Brier didn't bother to confirm the obvious.

Palmer took a moment. *Gaitian.*

She wracked her memory, but the name didn't sound familiar. *Why are they here?*

Same reason Reinhald is. Money.

Reinhald made a sharp turn, bringing their party up to a row of larger tents, those having walls that rose off the ground before reaching a point—unlike the little triangles of the other rows—culminating in the largest tent at the center of the line.

Reinhald stopped them a few tents down from the largest and bent to poke his head through the flap.

Brier heard murmurs then a rustling. Reinhald pulled his head back out. Goebel quickly followed, still in the process of throwing a thick coat on over nightclothes.

Goebel looked from Reinhald to Palmer, to Brier, and back to Reinhald. "You actually found them."

"You sound as though you doubted me, little brother." Reinhald smiled.

Goebel frowned, already studying Palmer and Brier. He looked them over before meeting their eyes. "You look thin."

"So we keep being told," Brier said.

"They should be cooking breakfast." Goebel buttoned his coat properly, glancing at Reinhald. "I take it none of you have eaten."

Reinhald waved it away. "Have you seen Gully?"

"Plotting away in his tent, last I saw him."

Reinhald nodded once, looking at the rest of the people standing beside him and then back at his brother. "Why don't you get them fed? I'm sure they'll plan better on a full stomach. Meet me at Gully's after you're through."

Goebel gave a sarcastic half-salute, letting Reinhald wander off before looking back at Palmer and Brier. "I hope neither of you are here under duress."

"So little faith in us, Goebel darling." Cerise crossed her arms.

Goebel cocked an eyebrow at her.

"We don't have anywhere else to go," Brier said, bringing Goebel's eyes back to her. "We're here as it is the best option we seem to have out of them all."

Goebel's face twitched with some inscrutable emotion. "I know the feeling."

General Gully was a large, heavy man, filling up the bulk of the largest tent on the field just by standing at full height. Standing in front of the giant of a man, Palmer barely reached General Gully's shoulders. Still, the man smiled widely under his thick beard, arms akimbo, as they entered, his gruff face welcoming.

"The long-awaited Chaos, I take it." General Gully looked at Brier, his words barely understandable under his rough, grumbling accent. "And Kosmos."

"I prefer Palmer, if it's all the same to you." Palmer crossed his arms, taking a small step back so that he didn't have to crane his neck to meet the general's eyes. "And this is Brier."

General Gully nodded, looking between them. "Little things, aren't you?"

"Pardon me for saying, signore," Brier finally said, "but, though we may be little things, you are quite a large thing yourself. It might throw off your perspective."

The general laughed loudly, his belly shaking with it. Palmer barely refrained from wincing, half expecting it to be heard all the way back in the Augarian.

"I like her, Reinhald." The general clapped Reinhald on the back, nearly throwing the shorter man off his feet.

Reinhald gave a less genuine smile, planting his feet more firmly on the ground. "I'm glad, General. I apologize it took so long."

"We were beginning to wonder if we would have you come at all." General Gully looked between Palmer and Brier. "At least before all the men became too restless to sit still any longer. Only so long you can keep a soldier far from home, sitting still."

Brier and Palmer just nodded.

"Now." General Gully turned around, picking a pewter cup off a table and taking a large drink from it before setting it back down and looking at a map there. "Now that we have everyone, let's plan."

Reinhald strode across the room to look at the map, leaving Palmer and Brier back with Goebel.

"We're attacking right away?" Brier looked at Goebel.

"We've been waiting here a long time," Goebel said softly, keeping his eyes on his brother. "They were about ready to go in without you, I think. I doubt it will be a long wait now."

When the darkness descends, the end shall begin. The damn prophecy tried to play through Palmer's head. He forced it out before speaking to Brier. *You're sure you want to help them?*

We don't have another choice if we want a chance to stop what they're doing to the city.

You know who we'll be fighting. Palmer couldn't imagine Egidio was still in the city at that point. His friends weren't likely in much danger.

But Brier's... Nico Adessi-Guillroy flashed through his mind so quickly Palmer wasn't sure if it was his thought or hers.

Brier's jaw locked, but she took a few steps closer to the men at the table. "How many men do you have?"

General Gully turned around. "What was that?"

"How many men do you have?" she repeated, voice not quite as strong. "They have guards and soldiers all over the Augarian. I'd like to know what we will be bringing to the fight."

We. So Brier had made her choice.

General Gully smiled at her. "For one thing, we will be bringing you."

"Thank you." Brier crossed her arms, affecting what Palmer was quickly beginning to recognize as false confidence. "But I can't fight an entire army by myself, General. I would not be here with you if I could."

The old gods awaken to mete out our doom.

"She does have spirit." General Gully glanced at Reinhald and then looked back at Brier. "We have just fewer than thirteen hundred men— most of them here, a few others on either side of the city, opposite the river."

Brier nodded, but Palmer could see the number meant little to her.

Uncontrolled, uncontrollable, their vengeance will know no bounds...

"It's not a bad size," Goebel supplied from the back of the tent. "It's likely more than they have guarding the Augarian. If not, they have no more than that."

"And with you, we no doubt will have the upper hand," General Gully said, gesturing at her with the pointer.

"I worry you overestimate my abilities too greatly, signore." Brier frowned, stepping back to stand with Palmer.

"You just brought down the main hall of the palace," Reinhald said. "I don't think we are."

Until the land cracks open and the vessel succumbs...

"I was angry," Brier said. "I wasn't thinking."

"Then don't think," Reinhald said. "Anyway, Dominik will be with you. He can help direct your abilities if need be."

...inside the walls of the city.

"Why does she need to go back in there at all?" Palmer broke in, fighting the path that seemed less and less possible to avoid. "If you need something brought down, she could do that as well out here—"

"Only if we wanted to wipe the city from the earth entirely," Reinhald cut him off.

"We can't assume she'll be able to control her powers even with her targets in sight," Goebel supplied, voice resigned if displeased. "We leave her out here, and we'd only be able to ask her to bring the city down as a whole."

Brier's lips pressed into a thin line, but she nodded. "I'll go."

Uncontrolled...

"Then I'm going, too," Palmer said, and all the eyes in the room turned toward him. He attempted to sound as self-assured as Brier. "If she goes, I do."

Reinhald and General Gully frowned, but Goebel spoke first. "I agree. Brier might be the most suited toward war, but she could still use a protector. Someone better than me." Goebel fixed his eyes on his brother. "Perhaps past exploits would have gone better if there had been one for Marina."

Reinhald caved first, nodding. "All right. So the three of them will move together. What about the little girl?"

Brier frowned, her chest swelling some. "Rosette?"

Reinhald nodded. "What can she do? You took her for a reason, I'm sure."

"She wanted to come with us, is why I took her," Brier said, voice curt. "Anyway, even if she could do something, you aren't truly considering sending a six-year-old into battle."

"It would depend on what she could do," Reinhald said. "Believe me, if you had been properly trained, I would have sent you."

Brier's shoulders tightened, and Palmer felt energy flicker in the air. He did his best to dissipate it, to *control* it, before things started shaking again.

"Rosette will wait here," Brier said in a commanding tone. "You try to do any differently with her, and I will walk off right now."

Reinhald narrowed his eyes, but Goebel jumped in once again. "If she has no relevant powers, none that she knows how to use, at least, there's no reason to get the girl killed. Leave her here."

Reinhald continued to stare Brier down. To her credit, she stared right back, the same regal, entitled body language taking over as in the Augarian. Palmer suddenly felt a little more content with her upbringing.

"I don't need a little girl getting in the way on a battlefield." General Gully shook his head. "She should be sent home to her mother, if anything."

"She's an orphan," Brier said.

"An orphanage, then," he said.

Brier switched her glare to the general, and Palmer felt a new sort of respect for her, managing to look as intimidating as she did against a man twice her size.

The general just smiled again, holding up a hand. "Duly noted." He looked back at Reinhald. "How many do you think we could get through the tunnels into the capital without being noticed?"

"You can only walk two abreast through most of the tunnels." Reinhald sent a last warning glance at Brier before returning to the map. "Still, you could stage a fair enough number in the hall on the other side, assuming no one was there, though I wouldn't risk trapping too many people at once, especially not until after they stop looking for them." He motioned toward Brier and Palmer vaguely, not meeting either's eyes.

General Gully nodded. "We'll give it a few more days to plan and let things cool. Then we attack."

In order to protect the camp's position, the only fires allowed were small and inside the tents, meant to keep out the cold night air.

In their own small tent, Brier tucked Rosette into one of the low cots that seemed specially made to fit inside the little triangles. She murmured platitudes, stroking Rosette's hair, all the while feeling Palmer's eyes on them from across the tent in the low light. He would have it no other way, of course, but to be there with them. She couldn't say she wasn't grateful.

"We could still run," Palmer finally spoke, the first time since they'd settled in the tent.

Brier pressed her lips together, squeezing Rosette's shoulder a final time before she moved to sit next to Palmer. "If we leave, what's left of the council is going to destroy Latysia themselves."

Is there anything left for us here, anyway?

Her father's grave, Nico's face as the great hall had come down, and everything else from the past few days flitted through her mind. Everything that should have driven her away somehow only increased her resolve to remain. "We can't run."

"Why not?" he asked.

The tent flap opened slightly, letting in a blast of cold air and saving Brier from having to try to explain a drive she couldn't even explain to herself. She looked up into Goebel's face.

"Signorina, could I speak with you for a moment?"

The words took a second to register, but Brier nodded, standing. Palmer stood as well. Squeezing his arm lightly, Brier eased him back down. "Stay with Rosette. I'll be right outside."

Palmer frowned but let her go without argument.

No longer chased away by a fire, the cold wind pricked at Brier's cheeks, but the bite of it she had experienced in Lantello seemed to be gone. Like everything else in the past few months, reality seemed to be melting away, changing too quickly to seem substantive. Pulling her coat more tightly around her, she looked at Goebel expectantly, not offering to speak first.

He cleared his throat, taking another moment before finally starting. "I, well, I just wanted to apologize."

Brier furrowed her eyebrows. "Apologize for what?"

"For..." He hesitated once again before finishing the thought, "making you run."

She shook her head. "You didn't make us run."

"No?" He looked genuinely shocked, his eyebrows rising then furrowing, just barely visible in the weak glow emanating through the canvas tent.

"If anyone did, it was your brother," Brier said. "Palmer saw what happened to Marina. He didn't want it to happen to me."

Goebel looked away, nodding sadly. After a few more moments, he dared to look back up at her. "You were very impressive today, signorina."

"Impressive?" Brier asked.

"I'm not sure Reinhald has ever had someone stand up to him the way you did earlier. You've grown quite the backbone."

"I've had to," Brier said. "We had one child with us. Palmer didn't need to take care of two."

Goebel studied her face, nodding slightly before speaking again. "Do you know why I didn't want Marina involved in any of this, signorina?"

"Because you were in love with her?"

He gave a soft laugh. "That too. But more than that, she was a brilliant, powerful woman but rash, hotheaded. I think the idea of power and a battle excited her too much to say no when Reinhald first brought up the idea. Fighting solely because you want to fight never can lead to good.

"You, on the other hand..." He took a breath. "I was scared of making you fight for the exact opposite reason. When I first met you, you seemed so meek, young. I was worried you would be forced into a fight you had no stomach for."

Brier opened her mouth.

"But now," he continued before she could speak, "you've truly grown. You have something to fight for. And maybe that's what Chaos really needs. Some..."

"Order?" she suggested.

He smiled. "If there is anyone who could do good with only the power to destroy, I would believe it of you, signorina. You are truly something special. I will be honored to fight beside you."

Brier smiled.

After another moment, Goebel simply nodded, turning to head back into the grid of tents.

"Goebel?" Brier called after him.

He turned to look back.

She took a few steps closer to him. "Could you answer a question for me?"

He frowned slightly but nodded. "I will do my best."

She studied his face, almost completely hidden in the shadows between the tents. "Tell me... how much of this fight is yours, and how much of it is your brother's."

Goebel remained silent.

"Correct me if I'm wrong," she said, "but you don't much seem like a man who would care to take over a country."

He offered her another weak smile. "I agree. I am not."

"Then why are you here?" she asked. "Palmer said you gave up looking before Reinhald and Cerise did. I would expect you to be back at Ruhegipfel."

Goebel took a moment and then finally moved back toward her. He reached out and took one of Brier's hands between both of his. "Signorina, I would not wish for anyone in your position to face my brother alone. I am not here to take a country. I'm here to find some peace."

"Peace?" she asked.

"I didn't help Marina," he said quietly. "She died while I was sitting home, stewing. I believe I'm looking for a chance to rewrite the past. "

Brier's heart beat in her throat. She swallowed noisily, looking out across the expanse of tents as soldiers packed up, some even laughing.

Palmer squeezed her hand lightly before dropping it again. "Are you all right?"

"Been better," she admitted.

He nodded, swinging his arms back and forth around himself. "We'll be all right."

She looked at him. "You're getting to be a better liar, Palmer Tash."

"I'm not lying," he said.

She just raised an eyebrow at him.

"You'll be all right, at least," he said, looking away from her, watching men suit up and get into formation. "I won't let anything happen to you."

She managed a smile, trying not to argue away his bravado after he'd spent all night trying to push away images of destruction—at least she could hope they were simply images rather than visions. "I know you won't."

Palmer finally turned toward her. "Brier?"

She lifted her eyebrows slightly, waiting for him to continue.

"If... if something happens to me..."

"It won't," Brier said.

"If it does, though…" He hesitated. "If it does, I just…" He struggled with the end of the sentence.

Brier saved him the work, leaning forward and pressing her lips to his lightly. Palmer hesitated but finally let whatever it was go and returned the kiss, wrapping his arms around her waist and holding her tightly to himself. She felt the familiar spark between them, felt her body tingle with his passion, his desperation, his fear. Brave words or no, he was no surer of himself than she was.

"Oy. Break it up." Cerise came up behind them, holding out two swords. "Reinhald said to give you these."

Brier eyed the metal weapons cautiously, leaving one hand on Palmer's waist. "Why?"

"In case someone breaks the line—or you do something stupid and let yourselves get separated—I'd think you'd want at least something to block a sword coming at your heads." Cerise shoved one at each of them, looking at Palmer. "Especially you, Kos. At least your girl could blast them through a wall."

"You think I know how to use this?" Brier frowned, testing the grip uncertainly.

"Hold the gold end, fight with the pointy end." She turned back to where Reinhald was staging with some other soldiers.

Brier looked back at Palmer. "I really don't like her."

"Whyever might that be?" Palmer examined the sword in his hands before clasping the scabbard around his hips. He told Brier, "We'll try to keep you from needing a sword."

"Or from destroying the city?"

Even though she'd meant to lighten the mood, Palmer's jaw went hard as he looked toward the city. Releasing a breath, she slipped her hand into his, praying to whatever gods existed, for them to get through the fight.

Goebel appeared. "We're getting ready to move out. You two ready?"

"I think we're as ready as we'll ever be." Brier gave a tight smile.

Palmer just nodded.

Goebel looked toward the city and then back at the two of them. "Stay close. We'll all do our best to get out of this alive."

CHAPTER TWENTY-SEVEN

WITH THE CRUSH OF SOLDIERS coming up behind them, the tunnel under Latysia suddenly seemed even smaller than it had before. The rock seemed too close, the air too warm and stale. Brier felt her chest tighten but did her best to ignore it.

Are you all right?

She glanced over at Palmer. *Do I look that bad?*

You look pale. Hard to tell in the torchlight, though.

Just nervous, I suppose.

Despite how many were marching through it, the tunnel seemed oddly quiet. Brier wondered if that was a trick of the rock or something the soldiers had been trained in as well. She wouldn't have been surprised at the latter. With their grid tents and near-mechanical movements, being trained in silent walking didn't seem out of the question.

The line slowed all at once, as though the men shared a brain.

Do you think they're all actually the same person? Brier glanced at Palmer.

He actually smiled.

Just saying. She waited to see what would happen.

Toward the front, one of the men signaled, his arm movements catching the torchlight awkwardly, nearly seeming to make him dance.

"We're at the door," Goebel interpreted quietly, even his quiet whisper earning a glare from the closest soldiers. "They're going to go in and clear the way. Then we go and try to make it to our position."

Brier nodded as Palmer did the same in the corner of her eye.

The door creaked open, and a blast of fresh air shot through the tunnel. Soldiers flooded out two at a time. Brier let them move, her feet suddenly feeling heavy, something in her stomach churning unhappily.

The dancing soldier at the end of the tunnel gestured sharply, looking straight at them with a scowl.

"Time to go, *Schatzi*." Goebel seemed barely able to get the words out. He placed a hand at the small of Brier's back, pushing forward slightly. He looked at Palmer and back at her. "Just do what comes naturally."

Palmer stepped through the end of the tunnel, keeping Brier close, keeping her left flank to Goebel's right. The red-coated soldiers swarmed from pillar to pillar in the otherwise empty hallway, still oddly silent, red ghosts haunting the wing.

Goebel held up a hand, stopping the three of them farther back. Palmer didn't argue, waiting out of the way for something to happen. The tension grew, pressing down on them. Palmer's vision blurred. He tried getting a clearer picture. An energy around the room swooped in, a vision trying to black out his sight altogether. Forcing it back out, he put up a block. If he had to decide between no visions or being blind from too much bombarding him at once, he would have to choose no visions. He only hoped the block would keep his hearing from devolving as well.

The soldiers jumping from pillar to pillar gathered around the large set of doors on the far end of the hallway with amazing precision. Everything seemed to freeze for just a second, then at a sharp arm wave from one of the soldiers, the doors burst open.

Someone shouted, then another. The soldiers rushed out, the first sounds of metal on metal following closely.

Palmer, Brier, and Goebel didn't move, watching the soldiers pour out to join the fighting clearly audible from the emptying hallway.

Goebel finally nodded. "Keep close to me."

They began their slow trek forward, Palmer feeling Brier tense beside him. He resisted the impulse to touch her by keeping his fingers wrapped around the hilt of his sword.

"This way!" Goebel called, heading up a staircase to their right, keeping behind the line of soldiers.

The mayhem through the doors left Brier dizzy, a heady buzz of power saturating the air. The screams, clashes, and falling men—all of it fed something in her, making her feel more powerful than she had ever experienced. She nearly forgot to move, finding a place at the top of the staircase and just looking at the fighting below them.

"Brier." Palmer looked at her expectantly.

His voice snapped her out of her daze, at least enough to move. She blinked, following him forward.

A gray-coated soldier rushed forward, the first up the staircase facing them. His sword connected with Goebel's, the sound lost in the general cacophony. Brier froze again and couldn't help but watch.

"Brier!" Palmer repeated, shouting that time and pulling his own sword free of its scabbard. "Do something!"

She started, touched her sword, and felt a power growing within her even before she had a chance to wrap her hand around it. A dark light, a contradiction in itself, grew around her core and shot out in front of her. It caught a gray soldier dead on. His torso disappeared, head and legs tumbling to the ground, useless. No blood, no anything came from the wound, his torso simply having ceased to exist.

The ray of darkness swung wildly, both red and gray soldiers diving out of its way, flooring disappearing in its path.

Goebel pushed his opponent toward the beam. The light caught the man in his fall, dissolving him. Throwing his hands up before the beam could move toward him, Goebel sent some kind of energy toward it. The light wavered, constricted, but continued forward, his abilities not strong enough to outweigh hers. "Control, Brier. Control!"

Brier gasped as the light shot back into her, nearly making her tumble back.

Goebel swung at another soldier brave enough to approach, calling back to Brier, "You'll kill us all that way. Use it—don't be controlled by it." He swung again and grunted as the soldier's sword caught his. He pushed the man back.

Catching his foot in a crack, the gray soldier tumbled through the newly formed gap along the platform and tumbled down into the mayhem below.

Goebel looked at Palmer. "Help her."

"How?" Palmer grabbed Brier's arm, pulling her back toward a corner.

"Protect her," Goebel shouted, sending another wave of constriction as the dark light tried to build again. "There's too much chaos down there. It's overwhelming her."

"Thanks—clear as mud," Palmer mumbled, hacking at a soldier who came too close but lacking any sort of finesse.

Still, a warm, calming energy hit Brier, shielding her from the mesmerizing mayhem below. It cleared her head and made her feel human.

Palmer glanced at her questioningly for a second.

"Thanks." She pulled her sword, still unsure what to do with it.

"Just try not to hit me with that, all right?" Palmer shook his head, moving sideways with her, using Goebel as a shield.

Brier didn't respond, watching a line of enemy soldiers coming up the stairs behind them. She gathered herself and sent a controlled push. The air compressed, expanded, and compressed again, the wave growing as it moved ever closer to the staircases. It hit, tumbling the men back down.

"*Großartig!*" Goebel exclaimed, earning only a confused look from Brier. He glanced back at her with a quick smile. "Good, *Schatzi*, keep it up."

Brier offered a smile back and moved closer to Palmer, placing a hand on his back—more for her comfort than his—before letting her mind stretch out. Under Palmer's net, the mayhem fed her without overwhelming her. She took the fighting in, and the light built again.

"Brier..." Palmer sent her a cautious glance.

"I've got it." She glanced around and focused on the beams holding the stairs. Releasing a breath, she let the darkness shoot out again. The beams dissolved, and the stairs crumbled. Men shouted, falling and pushing, trying to get back to solid ground. Marble hit the floor, littering the lower level with debris. The dark light snapped back, Brier absorbing it more easily. She swung to look at Goebel. "No one's coming up this way."

His blade connected with a soldier, sending him to the ground with blood pulsing out of his neck. Goebel just nodded, ignoring the dying man. "This way."

The red soldiers cleared the stairs ahead of the trio, letting them move quickly to the lower level. After a few well-timed slices, they slid through a door, taking them away from the worst of the fighting.

The power in the air dissipated, leaving Brier deflated. She nudged at the net over her, which suddenly felt too heavy.

Palmer glanced at her.

"I'm good."

He hesitated but finally nodded once, and the net fell away.

Brier followed Goebel closely, letting him and the handful of soldiers lead the way. The sounds of screaming and fighting echoed from other hallways. Brier shivered. A second Reclamation. She prayed to never see a third.

They turned a corner. Palmer's hiss said even he recognized their new destination.

Brier took two jogging steps, coming up beside Goebel. "We're heading for the council?"

Goebel nodded.

"Shouldn't we focus on all the soldiers out there?"

Goebel sighed. "There's been a change of plans."

Palmer touched Brier's arm, bringing her back toward him. *Just stay alert, Bri.*

Brier pressed her lips together, focused on her surroundings.

Palmer kept a strong hold on the hilt of his sword. If only he had had it the last time he had been brought to those doors. His fervor faltered slightly. Sure, he might have found himself dead because of it, but at least it would have been a satisfying death if only he had been able to rid the world of Orris Adessi-Guillroy.

Brier's hesitation, however, was palpable. She nearly wavered, her energy making her skin shimmer. He did his best to calm her, sending out as much energy as he dared without draining himself—or weakening his mental block.

The soldiers moved up to the door at the end of the hall, flapping their arms in their odd, silent language.

"Wait," Brier said, quietly at first then growing in conviction. "Wait."

"We need to do this, Brier." Goebel glanced at her.

"No." She shook her head, the shimmering energy dancing across her skin as she stopped halfway to the door. "There are no guards."

Goebel frowned. "What?"

"If they're in there, why aren't there guards here?"

Goebel hesitated only a few steps ahead of her, but it was too late. The soldiers rammed the door, storming in in waves.

Someone shouted as the room exploded. Flames began to crackle beyond the door, thick, black smoke permeating the air.

"Back, back, back, back!" a red soldier shouted, motioning everyone away from the room.

Palmer grabbed Brier by the hand, pulling her down the hall, afraid of losing her in the confusion. They ran, turning one corner then another. Gray soldiers blocked their retreat. Swords once again clanged in the halls. Palmer lifted his out of instinct. It caught a soldier's blade with not more than an inch clearance from Palmer's head. Pain radiated out from Palmer's arm, the poor hold on his blade making it slip, twisting his wrists.

A blast of energy shot out, and the man flew back. Brier glanced at Palmer as she tossed her sword to a red soldier just in time for him to rejoin the attack. She managed to smile. "I've got you."

"Might want to hold onto that sword." Palmer blocked another hit.

"I think he could use it more." Brier sent another blast out, and some soldiers slid back, some losing their footing altogether.

Goebel shoved his way to the front, knocking Palmer to one side and Brier to the back. "Palmer, there. Brier, stop the fire."

"What?" Brier stumbled backward, still somehow able to push Palmer's next attacker away.

"Stop the fire!" Goebel shouted.

"How?" she asked.

"Like the candle!"

Brier hesitated.

"Go!"

Palmer moved to follow her but got caught up with another soldier and began hacking at the man. Not more than sixteen, the boy didn't seem much more trained than him. Each swing was clunky, not landing correctly. Palmer finally managed to sidestep, and the boy stumbled forward with the momentum of his own swing. A red-coated soldier spun, bringing his sword down the boy's spine.

Palmer felt his stomach turn but didn't have the time to linger. He spun, finding Brier no longer behind him. He ran back down the hall, pushing his way through the back line of red soldiers, all ready for their fight.

Smoke filled the hall, thin at first but growing into a wall caught behind some invisible line. A red soldier guarded her, fighting what gray soldiers broke through as Brier fought the smoke, sweat beading on her brow.

The library. A little girl trapped in a book chest. The memories flickered, lost and confused, forcing their way past the mental block and throwing Palmer off balance.

He blinked, trying to regain his bearings. He saw the hallway, the library, the hallway again. Lost between realities, Palmer watched a free gray soldier seeming to move in slow motion. The pike in his hand reached out, glancing off the red soldier's sword. Palmer heard himself call out but couldn't recover. The pike found its mark, low in Brier's side, and threw her forward, unmoving.

Palmer shouted, screaming something even he couldn't understand. The wall of smoke released, washing forward, obscuring everyone and everything in its path. Still, Palmer started forward, coughing, trying to find her somewhere in front of him. His vision blurred, whether Brier's doing or just the smoke, he could no longer tell. He coughed and stumbled. Seeing the flames in the distance, he slowed.

Someone grabbed his collar and pulled him back. He fell with the person, his mind lost and his world as black as the smoke.

Brier... His mind flickered, trying to find something but coming up with nothing.

CHAPTER TWENTY-EIGHT

BRIER'S EYELIDS FLUTTERED, TRYING TO open, feeling heavy and drugged. Her breath came labored, a stabbing pain shooting through her left side. She gasped shallowly as her sight finally returned. Eyes darting from side to side, she tried to take in the room. She stood, tied upright, encased in some sort of glass tube. The room around her was too bright to be comfortable. Mirrors on the ceiling reflected the light coming in through high windows. Joining with torches burning and gold glinting on the walls, the glare hurt her eyes. Her hands went to the rope around her waist. Her side panged again. Pressing her hand to it, she felt dried blood on the cloth crack under her hand. She hissed as her fingers touched the wound. What she wouldn't give to have Palmer with her. Destruction wouldn't help her heal any. She brought her hand back to the ropes, working on the knot.

Slowly, it loosened. After a few more pulls, it fell, landing on the floor of the tube with a thud. She finally looked down, shifting on the oddly perforated floor, metal crosshatched into a grid. The entire setup left her with an odd sense of dread in the pit of her stomach. She reached out, feeling the glass for any sort of seam, some door that would let her out.

Just as she began to contemplate breaking her way through, the doors on the far side of the room opened.

She paused, resting one hand on the tube and placing the other just to the side of her wound, her body already feeling weak from her search. Blasting her way out and running was out of the question, at least until she regained some strength.

A man, an alchemist she vaguely recognized, shuffled into the room, looking at her furtively as he brought various arcane objects in, setting up the shining instruments in the corner.

Her dread continued to grow. Still, Brier watched him silently.

A few more men filtered in, speaking in hushed tones. None of them met her eyes.

Finally, Orris Adessi-Guillroy strode in, not moving any more quickly than if he were walking into a party fashionably late. He moved to the other men and spoke with them at length before finally turning his eyes to Brier. They nearly seemed to twinkle with some perverse pleasure.

"I hope you aren't planning on dissecting me," Brier finally said into the silence, not sure if she was being sarcastic or not. She bunched her loose dress slightly, trying to push the fabric to the wound.

"Nothing quite so barbaric, I assure you." Orris glanced back at the other men. "No, they are working on solving a little problem we've had."

Brier set her face. Even if she felt clammy and pale, she refused to seem weak. "And what is that?"

"As it seems you are well aware, we haven't had a way to contain you, not in that body." Orris looked her over. "We have had some success containing just... your essence, shall we say, but there doesn't seem to be a way for us to actually use that *without* a physical host. You see our conundrum."

"You can't kill me without not being able to use me?"

"Exactly," Orris said with his smooth smile. "I'm glad you understand."

"Well, anything that *doesn't* end up with my being killed, I have to say I'm more in favor of."

Orris nodded slowly, running his eyes over her as though critiquing a prized mare he was considering purchasing. "Well, we had a few suggestions that we should just force a new reincarnation, leave it with a host we could more easily control. The problem there, you see, is we have yet to find a way to force it to reincarnate. It will just wait until it finds someone it likes. And even if we did, that... thing in you tends to bring with it a bit of an independent streak, which can be very troublesome. We at least had some hope that you would be possible to control. But alas, it seems not so. So we are stuck with a body we can't contain or a power we can't use. Whatever should we do?"

"You could always let me go," Brier said, wincing as she pushed the fabric more tightly against her wound.

Orris laughed. "I'm beginning to see why my son likes you. I admit I always just thought it was his weakness for a pretty face."

"I'm sure the face didn't hurt, knowing Nico." Brier took as deep a breath as she could manage, fighting off the vertigo still threatening the edges of her vision.

Orris just smiled, moving toward the men at the corner of the room. "Luckily for us, it hasn't quite come to that. Releasing you." He picked up something small and walked up to the tube. He held the item up for Brier to see. "Have you ever seen this before?"

Brier looked at the hazy blue lump and nodded slowly. "Frozen smoke."

Orris actually looked surprised, his eyebrows rising. "Very good, *dolcezza*. Can you tell me exactly what it does?"

Brier hesitated but finally just had to shake her head.

"It's something quite interesting our alchemists invented." Orris pulled his hand back, studying the haze between his fingers as he spoke. "You see, what is so interesting about this little ball is that it is nearly entirely made of nothing."

Brier frowned but didn't speak.

"You can see it, you can touch it, but it is really more what isn't there than what it is. The little, little parts of something catch enough nothing in it that it is something that shouldn't be. Frozen smoke. Nothing you can hold."

Brier continued to stare. As her heart rate spiked, her wound pounded with each pulse.

"Of course we haven't yet had too much ability to test it, but from all we can figure, it should be possible to... encase you, shall we say, and hold you at least long enough to figure out just how to use you. With any luck, it won't kill you."

Brier tried to think of something to say, only managed, "Here's hoping."

Orris rapped the glass with his knuckles before moving back toward the men in the corner. "Good luck."

Brier released an incredulous breath. "Thanks."

After a few more quiet words with the men in the corner, Orris nodded. "Come get me when you're done."

"Aren't even going to stick around to watch your handiwork?" Brier called after his retreating form.

"Time is precious, *dolcezza*." He sent a last glance her way.

Brier watched the door close behind him, and she was alone with the men in the corner.

The holes at the bottom of the tube started to rumble. Her skirt fluttered around her feet as a breeze stirred beneath them. Hair whipped around her face.

Adrenaline lessened her pain. Brier tried to gather energy to blast her way out, but doing so only left her breathless. Slowly, blue began to fill the tube, starting at the bottom of her feet and slowly rising farther and farther, flooding around her.

She gave up on her powers and pounded on the glass, trying to crack it. It was too thick. She was too weak. Panic clouded her thoughts.

The alchemists wouldn't look at her, refusing to see their doing. They left her in the quickly filling tube, trying in vain to break free.

Her mind turned as hazy as the air around her. Her limbs began to freeze up, unable to keep moving as the blue grew thicker and thicker around her. Finally, she was encased, frozen, alone.

Palmer groaned, bringing his hand to the back of his head as he opened his eyes. Slowly, he looked around, taking in the dark stone walls pressed close together in thin arches. He paused, trying to place himself, his mind feeling deprived and sluggish.

"I was starting to think you were dead," a man said.

Palmer twisted, doing his best to see through the darkness.

Nico continued to sharpen his blade, seeming entirely focused on the stone against the edge of the sword.

Palmer pushed himself up to a seated position, trying to remember what had happened. "Where are we?"

"One of the hidden passageways," Nico said, finally sliding the sword back into its scabbard before he hooked a crossbow back over his shoulder. Palmer watched the weapons carefully. Standing, Nico moved toward him. "How's your head? It looked like you took a pretty bad hit after you passed out."

Palmer searched his scalp with his fingers and felt a lump that was already healing. At least he had that going for him. "I'm fine. Where's Brier?"

"You think I'd be here with you if I knew that?" Nico squatted in front of him, looking at both of Palmer's eyes. "What's your name?"

Palmer frowned as scenes of the battle started to come back, making his stomach clench.

Nico lifted an eyebrow, waiting.

"Palmer," he finally said.

"How old are you?"

"Is that important?"

"I'm checking if you know." Nico rested his hands on his knees, pulling back slightly to see Palmer's entire face.

"Nineteen," Palmer said. Then a thought hit him. "Twenty, depending what month it is."

Nico nodded, looking as though he was half paying attention to the answer, at best. "You don't seem to have sustained any serious damage. Impressive for the amount of time you were out."

"Thank you?" Palmer watched him.

"Not sure that was meant to be a compliment." Nico stood again, looking each way down the hallway before looking back at Palmer. "If you think you can walk, we should probably keep moving. I don't think they know about this passage yet, but I don't much relish the thought of being cornered back here if they do."

Palmer shifted, pushing himself to his feet with a grunt. Healing or not, his body still wasn't happy with him at the moment. He looked back at Nico. "Why are you helping me?"

"I couldn't get to Brier in time." Nico pulled a torch off the wall. "I figured you were my best shot at finding her again."

"So you're using me," Palmer said.

Nico shrugged, starting forward.

Palmer couldn't blame him under the current circumstances. "Where are we going?"

"You tell me." Nico looked at him. "You did something to stop her from bringing the place down last time. I take it you have some hocus-pocus, or whatever it is, yourself."

Palmer released a breath, closing his eyes. Slowly he took down the block, and his dull headache turned sharp all at once. He grimaced, feeling his other senses trying to black out as the mayhem outside the passageway assaulted him. He still pushed forward, trying to find Brier through all the chaos that had nothing to do with her.

"Well, do you?" Nico asked.

"Give me a second," Palmer hissed, eyes still closed. He could feel Nico's eyes on him, but the man remained silent. Palmer continued searching, only able to go foot by foot as his head continued to feel as though it were about to burst.

"Nothing?" Nico pushed.

"There's a lot happening out there right now," Palmer snapped. "It's not some magic tracker for just her."

"If you don't find anything..." Nico hesitated. "Does that mean she's...?"

Palmer didn't answer, not letting himself think of the possibility. Then he found a slight trickle emanating from somewhere, Nothing leaking out into a distant room, contaminating it, seeping through the air, moving through the dirt, working ever closer to the surface.

"She's alive." Palmer put the block back up, meeting Nico's eyes as his own vision came back. "But I think she's dying."

CHAPTER TWENTY-NINE

ROSETTE FELT A TINGLE RUN through her body, growing stronger and stronger as she headed for the surface. The tunnel seemed to grow tighter around her, as if her small body had suddenly decided to expand.

Pushing her way through the last doorway, she climbed out into the middle of a piazza. People ran, their clothes ripped and dirty, as the sky above them slowly turned red.

The ground trembled under Rosette's feet. She looked down. Thick black tendrils wound their way around her ankles, the vine-like energy pushing out of the tile below her feet. They climbed her legs, cold yet invigorating. She had to admit she liked it.

The ground cracked open, and a running soldier tumbled in headfirst with his momentum. Even at a distance, Rosette heard his neck snap. One of the black tendrils stretched out from her, following him down into the crevice.

Something deep inside of her continued to expand, something long forgotten gorging itself, reveling in the panic and anger around her. Rosette took a deep breath, sweat and blood filling her senses, only adding to the heady sense of power.

A soft tugging made her look down again. The tendrils, entirely wrapped around her ankles like ivy, gently urged her feet forward. With a wide wave of her hand, the piazza shifted, seeming to tilt. People flew off their feet, skidding across the marble, thrown into pillars, lost in the crevice.

Rosette just smiled, walking slowly, one foot in front of the other, toward the temple.

Nico and Palmer rounded a corner, arriving at a gaping space that had once been a wall. Parts of splintered wood and stone still hung precariously over the void, falling at random.

"What the...?" Nico looked up.

Palmer followed his gaze and saw the roof hanging out at an unnatural angle, clinging to the walls that still stood, a blood-red sky behind it, stretching cloudless toward the Augarian Wall. Palmer shivered. "What you get for killing Chaos, I guess."

"What?" Nico frowned at him.

"I'll explain as we go." Palmer stepped over what was left of a wall, watching the roof for any sign of movement. A piece of loose tile wavered slightly but didn't fall.

"Come on." Nico joined him, moving farther from the building. "We don't want to be here when that comes down."

Palmer nodded, moving carefully and keeping a wary eye on the sky even as scores of people panicked around them.

Nico led, moving with quick, practiced steps. Lacking Brier, Palmer supposed Nico didn't make for a bad guide.

The ground rumbled under their feet. They slowed, waiting for it to pass.

"Killing chaos." Nico looked back at him. "Is that a saying?"

"What?" Palmer frowned.

"That's what you get for killing chaos," Nico quoted, starting forward again as the tremor passed. "I don't know the saying."

"Oh." Palmer followed close behind. "I meant it literally."

"Literally killing chaos," Nico repeated, moving them closer to the piazza.

"It's why your father's interested in her," Palmer said, his jaw clenching at the thought. "That fiancée of yours is the physical incarnation of Chaos."

Nico threw Palmer a questioning look.

"You saw the hall come down just as well I as did," Palmer said.

Nico made a face but didn't argue. "And that makes you what, then? The physical incarnation of order?"

Palmer opened his mouth, trying to think of what to say, but finally shrugged. "Basically."

"I was being sarcastic," Nico said.

"I wasn't," Palmer answered.

Nico looked up at the sky and around at the cracking buildings. "So you're saying she's doing this."

"I think it's a fair enough assumption."

Something rumbled, exploded, and crashed. Nico and Palmer rushed forward, looking around a corner to the piazza just in time to see part of the temple come down in a cloud of dust.

Nico looked at Palmer, wide-eyed.

"Why don't we start there?" Palmer offered a tight smile.

Shapes moved through Brier's mind, soft and white, like bright clouds passing over. She watched them, unthinking, too dazed to care.

"Hey…" The voice echoed in her head, distant, removed. "Hey." It moved closer, unwilling to be ignored. "Hey there."

Brier shifted her eyes over to the dark-complexioned girl, floating in the middle of the clouds, dressed entirely in white that shone just as brightly as the rest of the hazy world.

"About time." The girl floated back a few inches.

Brier looked around her new world, moving only her eyes, unable or perhaps just unwilling to shift her entire head.

The girl rolled her eyes. "Oh, you can do better than that."

Brier blinked slowly. "Am I dead?"

"No," the girl said. "Not yet, at least."

"Then where am I… are we?"

"Nowhere, I suppose." The girl looked around. "Seems to be the way it goes."

Brier finally turned her head, a vague recognition trying to awaken in the back of her mind. "Do I know you?"

"Yes and no," she said.

The name formed on her lips, unbidden. "Marina?"

The dark girl furrowed her eyebrows slightly, looking slightly intrigued. "How did you get that?"

"Goebel had a miniature of you." Brier shut her heavy eyes again.

"She's up?" Another voice, light and airy, came from Brier's other side.

Brier forced her eyes open, frowning. A woman looking remarkably like Brier moved forward, likewise glowing white but somehow seeming bogged down as she moved through the haze. Brier frowned as she registered the woman was soaked through. Droplets of water made their way out of her long blond hair, falling down before they disappeared somewhere below her small feet.

The woman hung in the ether, studying Brier carefully. "Oh, you've grown so."

"There truly is a family resemblance, isn't there?" Marina looked between them.

Brier looked back at the woman, studying her face. "Are you my mother?"

Clover Chastain offered a sad smile. "Hello, *cara*."

"You're dead," Brier said then looked at Marina. "So are you."

"I noticed," Marina returned, giving a snide smile. Clover didn't answer.

"If I'm not dead," Brier continued, "then what am I doing here?"

Clover reached out as though to stroke Brier's hair. Her hand couldn't quite touch. "We're here to help you."

"Help me do what?" Brier asked.

"Survive."

Rosette looked around what was left of the sanctuary. Lacking its far wall—and many of the pews farthest from the altar—the sanctuary sat open to the sky, bathed in the deep-red glow that had stretched out over the city and was spreading toward the countryside.

Something dripped on her. Rosette lifted her hand up to study it.

A thick, crimson droplet worked its way down her hand. Another fell through the missing ceiling and then another, the liquid spreading out across the piazza.

The people still outside screamed yet again, running from the rain, covering their heads with their arms, trying to find a building that was still standing with some integrity. The black tendrils branched out, retracted, and shook the ground. Rosette watched the palace shudder, and the roof came crashing down on one side as she rubbed the thick liquid between her fingers absentmindedly.

Someone ran into the temple.

Arm outstretched, Rosette flung him away easily. He landed with a sickening *crack*, sliding across the marble, the floor quickly growing slick with the liquid.

Another body came into view.

Rosette swung her arm again, but that time the power rebounded, lifted her off her feet, and swung her into the steps leading up to the altar. She grunted as she landed, hard.

Palmer dropped his arms from in front of his face, looking across the sanctuary. "Rosette?"

Rosette looked at him, blinking.

"What...?" Palmer looked at her then started forward. "Are you all right?"

She nodded, the sting from the fall already dissipated.

He took another step, still seeming like he didn't fully believe her, but then he paused, looking at the rubble around him and the liquid falling from the sky. "Did you do this?"

"No." Rosette shifted, with the tendrils tugging her up until she was sitting. She lifted a foot, showing the black wrapped around her ankles and feet, hanging down, anchoring her to the ground. "They did."

Palmer moved closer to her, a soldier behind him following closely.

Rosette lifted her hand.

"No!" Palmer held up his hands again. "He's helping. You met Nico."

Rosette dropped her hand again, but she still glared at the soldier suspiciously, even though she could place his face upon looking harder.

"He's Brier's friend," Palmer continued.

The tendrils tightened around Rosette's legs at the name. "She's dying."

Palmer paused. "Brier?"

Rosette nodded, looking down at her feet again. "They want me to help her."

Palmer continued forward, watching the tendrils carefully. "What are 'they'?"

Rosette shrugged, looking at the broken wall before looking back to him.

Standing in front of her, Palmer carefully brought his hand closer to the black vines. They squirmed, pushing back. The more he fought it, the more they pushed, keeping him from touching them.

"What is it?" Nico asked quietly, glancing over his shoulder every few seconds as he held his crossbow with a bolt cranked into place.

"Nothing, I think," Palmer said. "Without Brier, it's found Rosette."

"I'm helping." Rosette smiled. "They want everyone to go away so you can help Brier."

Palmer glanced over his shoulder at the piazza before looking at Rosette. "You need to stop that, all right, Rosie? Hurting those people isn't helping."

"Yes, it is," Rosette insisted. "She needs them gone so you can save her. They're giving you more help."

Palmer frowned. "More help?"

The ground tremored again, but that time the buildings didn't fall. Rosette just grinned, watching as the previously still man outside began to rise. Other dead began to follow him, covered in the blood rain, climbing out of crevices, untangling themselves from fallen debris.

"Tash..." Nico watched, eyes wide.

Palmer turned, his eyes catching the movement. He watched, seemingly frozen before he turned back to her. "Rosette, stop that."

Rosette shook her head. "It's not me. It's them."

The ground under the sanctuary began to shake and crack open. Half-decayed hands broke the surface, trying to claw their way up.

Nico jumped back as a gaping crevice opened beside him. "The catacombs. They're all under the city."

Palmer turned back to Rosette. "Do you know where Brier is?"

Rosette looked back at him.

"Rosette," he snapped, an edge to his voice. "Do you know where Brier is?"

Rosette looked at the bodies crawling up, the first beginning to move toward the palace. She looked back at Palmer and moved the tendrils. "They do."

"Tash!" Nico leveled his bow, his body strung just as tight as more and more bodies appeared.

"They won't hurt you," Rosette said. "I won't tell them to."

Nico didn't lower the bow.

"Can you lead us there?" Palmer took Rosette's shoulders.

"You can't?" Rosette tilted her head.

His face went grim. "Not with everything else happening."

It made sense, she supposed, looking down at the black around her ankles. Rosette finally nodded, hopping up. "Follow me."

CHAPTER THIRTY

"**P**ERSONALLY, I THINK YOU'VE GOT the better end of the deal so far." Marina floated, cross-legged, as though sitting in the air. "They just straight out killed me. Tried to stuff me in a box."

Brier didn't know how to react. The haze still trapped her, making it harder and harder to breathe. She addressed the other woman, her mother, not much older than she was. "She's me. A past incarnation. I still don't understand why *you're* here."

Clover looked at Brier for a moment, then her eyes finally slid off to one side. "Did your father ever tell you how I died?"

"You were sick," Brier answered.

Clover released a breath, seemingly unable to meet Brier's eyes. "I had something inside me. Like you. Not Chaos, but something I didn't understand. After you were born, I did get sick, but it was in my head. I kept having visions. Visions of you older. You burning. You suffering from having something inside of you. Like me. And then I had a vision of you escaping. My something buried under the water, never reaching you. And so I left one night. One cold, cold night..."

Clover released a pained breath but met Brier's eyes and continued, "I want you to understand, Brier, that I'm not proud of what I did. But I didn't know what I had, what I'd been seeing. I truly thought I was doing what was best."

"So she threw herself off a bridge," Marina supplied.

Clover sent Marina a dark look. "Thank you, Marina."

"Trapped her with me, for whatever reason," Marina continued, unperturbed. "Been stuck together for I don't even know how long. Where I go, she does, dripping water the whole way." Marina sighed. "All I can say is that I'm glad *I* didn't end up looking like how I died." She shivered. "I don't think the charred look is one I'd like to have for all eternity."

"Charred?" Brier looked at her. "I thought you said they locked you in a box."

"And then tried to burn me." Marina made a face. "Like I said, I think you've gotten the better end of the deal."

Brier's insides squirmed at the idea of fire... more fire. She tried to put the thought out of her mind and turned back to her mother. "You drowned yourself?"

Clover nodded, looking down. "I never should have, I know."

"Nobody ever told me."

"Not something you want to tell a little girl," Clover said. "Especially not about her own mother. Anyway, I don't believe it was widely discussed. It would have ruined your father's career."

"I still had a right to know," Brier said.

The hazy world phased in and out.

"What do you mean you can't stop it?" The voice filtered in through the mist. Orris.

Anger flared inside Brier's chest, nearly seeming to shake her world.

"We have her contained, signore. She can't move. But we can't stop... it... from draining."

"The entire city is coming down!"

"All we could do right now is break her out."

"That's not an option."

"Then you have to wait, signore."

"Sounds like you might be getting out of here soon." Marina looked at Brier, resting her chin in one hand.

Brier didn't answer, looking between the women on either side of her. "Both of you are dead."

"I thought we established that." Marina rolled her eyes.

"We are." Clover gave another sad smile.

"Does that mean there *is* an afterlife?"

Clover continued smiling sadly.

Marina shrugged. "At least for us. Take that as you will."

"I don't care how you do it. Just do it! This is not acceptable!"

Brier shivered with anger, looking from one woman to the other. "You're sure you can't get me out of here?"

"I'm all ears if you can think of a way." Marina studied her nails. "Best we can do is keep you awake."

Brier clenched her teeth, listening to what she could, hoping her anger would do something, anything. But there she stayed as the world grew hazier around her.

Cerise swung to one side, her blade connecting with a soldier's. The boy watched her, eyes wide, terrified, more a child than a soldier. She pulled back and swung again, an easy lob he just barely managed to block.

His eyes slid past her. She phased as another blade moved straight through her, connecting with the boy soldier. Then she spun, her own blade connecting with the soldier behind her. He fell, surprise stuck to his face as he crumpled.

"Drama queens, all of them," Cerise mumbled, phasing through another blade that swung at her and then dispatching the wielder handily.

Footsteps ran up behind her. She spun, her blade connecting with another.

"Careful with that." Goebel parried. "Someone could get hurt."

Cerise smiled, swinging at another soldier without looking. He fell with a shout. "That's sort of the point, Goebel darling."

Goebel nodded, swinging at a soldier coming up to their right. Their swords clashed, two among hundreds. After a few more swings, Goebel made a direct hit, the blade cutting into the man's leg, stopping with a jerk at the bone.

Goebel pulled back as Cerise finished that man off with her backswing and caught another on the swing forward.

She looked back at Goebel. "Obviously, I missed my calling."

"Obviously." Goebel moved, covering her back as Cerise continued to dispatch attackers effortlessly.

"Where are the kids?" Cerise glanced at him for just a second, catching a blade without looking and throwing the soldier back with a shove.

"Lost them in the mess." Goebel grimaced. "Been trying to find them."

The ground rumbled angrily under them.

"Well, I take it Mademoiselle Chaos is still around here somewhere." Cerise planted her feet more firmly into the ground, ready to phase again should anything fall.

Goebel nodded. "Her doing, I'd..." The rest of whatever Goebel had intended to say died off.

Cerise glanced back at him, her eyes quickly sliding to the bodies around them. One by one, the dead began to twitch, some missing limbs or chunks of flesh. One with a head barely attached to his neck jerked, and all of them struggled their way up to standing. The sound of the battle quieted as more and more people stopped to watch the dead return to walking.

The ground rumbled again.

"Do we also think that's her?" Cerise asked quietly.

"I don't know." Goebel's eyes moved from one corpse to the next, caught as much as everyone else, frozen in the moment, waiting to see what the dead soldiers would do.

A cry went out, a low roaring that moved from one corpse to the next, shaking the building. Swords flew into their hands.

Cerise looked at Goebel. "I think it's time to run."

"Agreed." Goebel nodded.

Palmer heard the roar of the dead echoing through the half-demolished buildings and rising through the ground as more and more bodies fought to free themselves from graves long forgotten under the city.

Palmer moved quickly after Rosette, the little girl looking almost painfully serene as they hurried through the mayhem. Nico kept his bow ready, struggling to choose between it and his sword, ready for an onslaught. However, they were ignored, even the blood rain dripping off them as though they were waterproof, dead warriors focusing on moving slowly toward each of the buildings circling the piazza.

Rosette glanced at Nico. "You can stop that." The vines expanded and retracted as they searched the ground, opening up wide crevices wherever they chose. "You can't hurt someone who's already dead."

"Then what are we supposed to do?" Nico hissed.

"Nothing." Rosette looked forward again. "If you're going to help, they won't hurt you. They're helping her."

"Her, Brier?" Palmer watched the dead warriors meet the first wave of living soldiers, losing limbs and weapons but still moving forward, resorting to ripping apart any man trying to stand against them, using their hands if they needed to. He grimaced, looking away and trying to focus on Rosette.

Rosette tilted her head slightly, seeming to consider the question, and finally nodded. "Her, Chaos."

A corpse pushed its way past, nearly knocking Nico off his feet. He spun, the bow shaking slightly as Nico froze.

"He isn't attacking you," Palmer said.

"No." Nico looked back then took a few hurried steps to catch up with Rosette, still watching the corpse warrior continue forward. "That's Brier's father."

The middle-aged corpse threw himself on a guard in front of a building, pulling him apart.

Palmer swallowed and could only manage, "Oh."

"This way." Rosette turned them down an alleyway between two still-standing buildings.

The roaring and screaming faded as they moved around to a side door and descended into a small building on the outskirts of the university complex.

"You're sure she's not leading us into a trap?" Nico murmured, keeping no more than a few inches from Palmer's side.

Palmer took a moment, watching the back of Rosette's head. She seemed taller, more solid. His eyes dropped to the blackness around her ankles, barely visible in the dim light inside. Whatever Brier had unleashed upon the world was feeding Rosette better than all the meals she had ever been given in Lantello. He glanced back at Nico. "I don't know why she'd have a reason to."

"That isn't a 'no,'" Nico mumbled, looking behind them.

Palmer couldn't answer.

Nico sighed. "Great."

"If you have a better plan, I'd be happy to hear it," Palmer whispered.

"What?" Rosette turned to look at him.

"Nothing." Palmer shook his head. "How far are we going?"

"I don't know," Rosette said.

Nico met Palmer's eyes, giving him a dark look, but they continued forward.

Another rumble went through the hallway, but that time, it didn't dissipate. A steady roar grew closer and closer to them. Nico jerked around, Palmer turned, and even Rosette looked over her shoulder.

A wall of water advanced toward them, sweeping up the wall-mounted torches in its wake, one by one.

"Run!" Palmer yelled.

All three turned and sprinted down the hall, trying to outrun the river, which surged faster and faster as the tunnel narrowed.

The torrent was too quick. Palmer's feet lifted off the ground as the current swept him along, under the water, tumbling, to the surface again, then back under. He did his best to fight it, losing his bearings but still fighting.

He had almost drowned once. He wouldn't again. Closing his eyes, he pushed energy out, unsure it would do anything, but he had to try, at least. The water rippled, shifting enough to show a set of stairs to their right. He looked back, trying to at least find Rosette, and had to dodge her as the tendrils seemed to shoot her forward. Her body broke the surface and disappeared entirely. Unthinking, he followed, grasping the slippery platform at the top of the stairs. He gasped for air, pulling himself upward as Nico found the surface next to him.

Rosette rested against the far edge of the platform, her wide eyes blinking repeatedly. "That wasn't fun."

A strange sound started, and Palmer realized he was laughing. He did his best to gain control of himself. "No..." Another laugh broke through.

He managed to dampen it enough to at least get the words out. "No, it wasn't."

"I don't see what's so funny." Nico grunted as he pulled himself out of the water, his woolen uniform soaked through.

"It's just... absurd." Palmer continued laughing, the sound dying down to a chuckle. "We're... here. I just wanted to finish school and then leave... and I'm... here."

"That's all well and good"—Nico narrowed his eyes—"but we have some things that need to get done 'here' if you don't mind."

Palmer nodded, the last of his laughter finally dying away. Taking another breath, he chanced lowering the block, forcing his mind away from the Nothing around Rosette as he searched down through the water. The water rippled again in response, seeming to dip out of the way as his energy met the rest of the Nothing flowing under it. The headache began again. Then he felt her. Somewhere down the hall, Brier flickered, disappearing for a second as the Nothing continued to flow toward them, before coming back, pulsing lightly. Palmer's stomach twisted, and he moved toward the edge.

"What are you doing?" Nico watched him.

Palmer didn't answer, forcing as much energy as he could toward the Nothing below the surface. The water wavered again as a shimmer of gold dove into it, pulling it apart.

"That feels funny." Rosette squirmed unhappily.

Palmer looked back, letting up just an inch. "Does it hurt you?"

"It's just... press-y." She made a face.

Palmer looked at the dent in the water, the weak flicker in the distance driving him forward. He glanced at Rosette. "Can you pull back? Ask *them* to pull back?"

Rosette frowned but nodded. The Nothing retreating toward the wall, and Palmer pressed the water out farther, leaving a thin, dry pathway down the hall.

He looked at Rosette. "Can you hold that?"

"I think so." She nodded.

"Think?" Nico frowned.

Palmer felt a last flicker before he put the blocks up as far as he dared. "We'll have to take it, at least if we want to reach Brier while she's still alive."

Rosette stood. Nico met Palmer's eyes.

"It's up to you." Palmer shrugged, working his way down onto the path between the barrier-held water. "I'm going."

Palmer helped Rosette down after him and didn't otherwise look back as he moved forward. After another moment, Nico's footsteps followed him into the hall.

CHAPTER THIRTY-ONE

THE RUMBLING RECURRED MORE QUICKLY, more persistently, registering somewhere in the back of Brier's mind.

Brier tried to breathe but felt her chest becoming too heavy.

"I don't care. Burn it if you have to!"

The voices filtered into the cloudy world, barely understandable as Brier's eyes tried to drift shut.

"We're under half the library," the other voice responded, just as exasperated. *"We set a fire down here, and the entire place is going to come down! The books... it would be a holocaust."*

"We have to stop her. Screw the bloody books."

"Looks like I spoke too soon." Marina floated past, making Brier's eyes flutter back open. "Cure it with fire. Always seems to be their plan."

Brier didn't respond, couldn't respond.

"Oh well, looks like you might suffocate before you have a chance to burn, anyway," Marina continued. "Lucky there, if you ask me."

"Brier." Clover's voice, soft and soothing, surrounded her and warmed her. "Stay strong, *cara*. You're stronger than this."

Brier took another shallow breath and let her eyelids flutter shut, the warmth soothing her aching body.

"Something's burning." Rosette pointed forward.

Palmer's stomach dropped. White smoke drifted out of a doorway at the end of the hall, slowly growing stronger and stronger. Palmer ran up the last few steps out of the tunnel, out of the water, sprinting down the hallway toward it.

One of the wood pillars in the room had already caught, the fire working its way up slowly, spreading out to a table beside it. Glass instruments cracked in the heat. On the far side of the blaze, he saw Brier. Something blue and ethereal encased her, her face looking grimly determined, hands outstretched as if pounding in an attempt at freedom.

Nico caught up and started toward the blue cube encasing her.

"Put that out!" Palmer shouted at Nico while pointing at the fire and moving closer to Brier.

Somewhere in the background, Palmer heard the sound of cloth being beaten against flames. He heard Rosette's footsteps, oddly heavy for a little girl, joining them. Then he focused on Brier.

When he touched the blue, it tremored under his palm. He pulled back and tried forcing energy into it. It swelled but didn't break. He looked around and caught Nico beating the fire with his wet shirt as well as the black vines around Rosette containing it in its corner. A long, metal pipe caught Palmer's eye. Grabbing it, he moved to the blue. He pulled the pipe back and vaguely prayed Brier wouldn't splinter with it.

"Hang in there," he barely whispered.

He swung hard, and the blue chipped, quivering with momentum.

Palmer pumped more energy into it and swung again.

It splintered that time, hairline fractures branching out around Brier in the center.

Panic set in. Palmer swung and swung and swung again. Slowly, the blue fell away, a chip here, a slab there, until it released the woman in the center.

Unsupported, Brier crumpled, her body limp. Palmer dropped the pipe and caught Brier's head just before it hit the tile floor. He ended up on his knees, holding her. "Brier. Come on. Come on, wake up."

Something cracked. Palmer looked up and saw the burning pillar starting to splinter.

"We need to get out of here!" Nico called over, coughing as smoke swirled up around him.

Palmer didn't argue. Lifting Brier, he threw her over his shoulder, feeling as though she barely weighed a thing. "Go!" he called, running toward the door and holding onto Brier as though his life depended on it. Perhaps it did.

Cerise ran, not stopping, not looking back. Scrambling over debris, dodging stones as they fell, she heard Goebel's footsteps behind her, hoping they'd be able to find a way out.

They skidded to a halt at the top of a staircase that no doubt had seen better days. Made of wood—unlike the stone that comprised the bulk of the staircases they had passed—some of the steps already had splintered beyond repair.

Goebel came up beside her and looked down the staircase. "Think we can get down?"

"I know I can." Cerise tossed him a weak smile. "What about you?"

Goebel gave a shaky breath, offering his own forced smile. "See you at the bottom?"

"See you at the bottom." Cerise started on the first step, jumped as it cracked, and caught the next step that seemed to have any integrity. She glanced back at Goebel, feathers already sprouting along her shoulders. "I think I'll leave the stairs for you."

"Oh, thank you." Goebel groaned.

Cerise's skin tingled, and all at once she was in the air, coasting toward the floor. With a flap, she circled, then legs grew out of her claws as she landed lightly on the ground.

Goebel hurried down the vibrating steps. One broke, nearly throwing him forward. He jumped the last three or four, his feet trying to go out from under him. He crouched, panting for breath as he looked at her. "Thanks for that."

The staircase came crashing down.

"Was just letting you get down without me wrecking them, darling." Cerise turned, heading for the nearest doorway. The ground was slick, coated entirely in red from the doorway to the wall twenty or so yards away.

Goebel looked up, watching more red drip down the small awning over the door. "Is that... blood?"

"This *so* did not happen when Marina died." Cerise looked behind them.

The ground shook, a crack appearing in the tile. Fingers began to push their way through, white bone pressing dirt out of the way.

"Out we go," Cerise said, starting away from the building. The blood rain drenched her, sliding over her skin and soaking into her hair. Her feet skidded across the wet ground. "Whose bright idea was it to make every damn thing around here marble?"

Goebel just grunted.

A crack opened in front of them. They turned and found rubble blocking the alleyway before them. After one more turn, they ran headfirst into a group of soldiers.

With every soldier covered in blood, Cerise couldn't tell whose side they were on. She wasn't sure they even cared right then as they brandished their swords, prepared for the dead warriors.

At the end of the world, the only fight was trying to stay alive.

"Mr. Goebel!" one of the soldiers called.

Gully's men, Cerise supposed. Or at least one of Gully's men amongst many.

"Here!" the soldier tossed a sword in their direction.

Cerise caught it out of the air, smirking at Goebel as she found a place in the ring of soldiers. "Get your own."

Another soldier handed Goebel one, and the small band of the living watched as cracks continued to open up, more and more dead joining the fight as those already walking drew closer.

"Goebel?" Cerise said.

"Yeah?"

"Try not to die?"

He snorted. "I'll do my very best."

"Good." She rolled her shoulders. "I don't want to have to put you down for good."

The sound of metal hitting metal restarted, metal hitting bone, soldiers trying to hack down the dead as best they could, taking off legs, arms, anything that would keep them from fighting on.

None of the hits helped. Too many dead continued to advance. They poured out of cracks, slowly walking toward the living. And every man that fell added one more animated corpse to the battle.

Cerise found Goebel behind her. Placing her hand in his, she squeezed, still slashing at dead warriors who came too close. "Been good knowing you, Goebel darling."

"Fly away," he shouted over the noise. "I'll be all right."

"You're a bad liar, darling." She swung wide, taking off a dead warrior's head. Its body flailed wildly, still moving hands that searched for its skull. "Can't anyway. Not with this sticking to me. It's too thick."

Goebel squeezed her hand back. "It has been a pleasure to have been annoyed by you, Cerise Filou."

Cerise smiled to herself, taking another wide swing.

It swiped air. The corpses still stood but no longer advanced, frozen as though waiting for something.

The living among them looked from side to side, too scared to lower their weapons yet too frightened to be hopeful.

Slowly, the heavy rain stopped, the falling drops slowing then seeming to pull back up into the red sky, leaving the battlefield below coated in a thick red.

The first dead warrior dropped, then the next and the next. Corpses fell, once again truly dead.

One soldier let out a cheer, and the others, maybe twenty in all, joined him, watching the bodies fall around them, piles of corpses covering the ground as far as the eye could see, but dead, a threat no more.

Cerise, still cautious, dropped into a squat, using her sword to poke at a body nearby. It didn't move.

"What happened?" Goebel looked around, his chest still rising and falling quickly.

"I think we won." Cerise straightened, staring at the carnage surrounding them, taking it all in.

"How?"

She looked at him, his entire body coated in red, barely recognizable. She couldn't look much better. "Maybe they rescued her."

"Or..."

The thought died off, neither of them willing to finish it.

Palmer didn't stop until they reached daylight. Already, the blood rain had stopped. Even the sky was lightening. However, death still filled the air. Rot and blood and poison lifted like a fine mist off the piazza, contaminating the air.

He gently slid Brier off his shoulder and laid her down in a protected alcove a half-destroyed wall had formed, doing his best to keep her out of the pools of blood.

Nico came up beside Palmer, dropping to his knees. "Is she...?"

Palmer couldn't bring himself to look away from Brier's pale face, still so set in determination. He smoothed a piece of hair out of her face and felt a zap as he touched her skin. He pulled his hand back sharply, watching a gold spark run down her face to her side.

"Gods." He turned her slightly and saw the gaping wound through her ripped dress. The gold light gathered then dissipated just as quickly.

"Let me see." Nico pushed closer, ripping the hole in the dress wider, pulling the blood-caked fabric out of the way. He frowned. "I can't tell how deep it is."

Palmer swallowed, motioned Nico away. "Let me try."

Nico leaned back but didn't move from his spot near her body.

Gently, Palmer laid his hand over the wound. Gold light once again gathered, a stabbing pain shooting through his palm. Still, he didn't pull back. If anything, he pushed tighter, letting the wound suck him dry. He grew lightheaded, fighting to keep his eyesight from going dark, worried he'd have to stop.

His hand burned, shooting pain into his body. He couldn't take it anymore. He pulled back, panting for air.

Nico watched him, looking surprised but not shocked. After another moment, Nico leaned forward, searching Brier's side before looking back up. "You healed that, at least."

Palmer cradled his hand to his side, the pain still emanating, but he looked. The gaping wound was no more, just a long, pink scar marring her smooth skin. He released a pained breath and turned Brier back flat with his good arm, careful to only touch cloth.

She still lay unmoving.

Palmer looked up at Nico, who looked back. Neither was willing to speak.

Without a sound, Rosette came up to the body, looking down at it sadly. "Her Nothing's gone."

Palmer just looked up at her.

"She needs it back." Kneeling next to them, Rosette reached out and placed her hand on Brier's chest.

A rush of wind swept over them, and the black vines around Rosette's feet contracted, rolling over her small body. They pulsed, shooting out, diving into Brier.

Rosette fell back, her gasp mixing with Brier's.

Brier coughed, her eyes shooting open. She looked at Palmer, then Nico, then back to Palmer as she panted. Closing her eyes again, she groaned. "Since when have you two hung around with each other?"

Palmer laughed, pulling her up into a hug.

Nico pulled her toward him, catching her between the two men.

"Ow, hey, ow." She pushed back, her eyebrows rising as she looked around. She met Palmer's eyes. "What the hell happened?"

"Short answer," Palmer said, "you did."

She continued to frown, and her eyes fell on Rosette's small body, lying motionless beside them. "Rosie?"

Palmer let her scramble up, leaning over the girl.

Rosette shifted, and Brier relaxed visibly. "What are you doing here, Rosie?"

"Helping." Rosette sat up, blinking as she pulled her skirt up off her ankles. The vines were gone, but something like black ink appeared to have worked its way under her skin, leaving an intricate pattern around her thin calves.

Brier frowned, touching it lightly. "Does that hurt?"

Rosette shook her head then threw herself into Brier's arms. "I'm glad you're not dead."

Brier gave a surprised laugh. "I'm glad I'm not too, *piccola*."

They all pushed themselves up to their feet, examining the cracked wall that sheltered them. Palmer watched Brier's eyes widen as she looked around. He turned to look himself, unsure if the destruction had been that bad when they had gone underground—if he had just missed it in their focus—or if all hell had broken loose while they'd been in the tunnel. In any case, if he hadn't known better, he would have thought they had survived the end of the world.

Then again, perhaps they had.

No building seemed to have escaped entirely intact. The once-impressive structures of the Augarian were coated in red crumbling roofing that still fell now and again onto the piazza, off balance on cracked walls. Bodies covered the piazza, all slick with blood. Some were fresh, some entirely decayed, all piled over the open expanse, unmoving.

"The dead have stopped walking," Nico murmured.

"Walking?" Brier's head snapped toward him.

"While you were…" Nico didn't seem able to finish the thought, and he caught her hand. He motioned out toward the piazza. "That happened."

"Me?" She looked at him and then shifted to Palmer, seeking his confirmation.

"I think Nothing was trying to keep you from dying," Palmer said.

"I helped." Rosette nodded happily.

Brier glanced at Rosette and looked back at Palmer. "Can we *never* do that again?"

He gave a weak laugh. "Believe me, Bri, I will do my very best."

"And mine," Nico cut in.

She squeezed Nico's hand lightly.

Something rumbled.

They looked as a sinkhole opened under a building, half of it disappearing down into the smoke and dust as flames began to lick their way out.

"The library!" Brier squeaked, her hands flying to her mouth.

Palmer pulled her to his chest as she cried, ignoring the dark look Nico shot over her head. "It's all right, Bri. It will all be all right. It will."

CHAPTER THIRTY-TWO

BRIER SAT HEAVILY, DRAPING HERSELF over the one chair—the Augur's throne, she supposed—that had made it unscavenged through the week. Somewhere in the distance, she could hear people working. Craftsmen were taking down unsafe walls, and masons were already starting to replace them. New gravediggers had come out in swarms, drawn to General Gully's very generous offer of gold for each body buried. With the destruction that had covered the entire city, Brier couldn't imagine many other jobs were available for those who had chosen to remain. And in the political vacuum the lack of an Augur or council left, the order Gully and his men brought at least kept the city working. They all had to be grateful for that.

A gold symbol on the side of the throne jutted out awkwardly, bent so it no longer fit its mount. Brier picked at it, and the symbol came off in her hand. She lifted the disk to study it. Staring at the intricate gold work, she ran her fingers over the Augur's crest, now bent, misshapen, barely recognizable in the precious metal. She turned it over in between her palms, looking at it one way and then the other. It seemed somehow fitting. Something that had been so well known, so important to the place, was still there but destroyed. Even the best goldsmith wouldn't be able to fix it, not without melting it down and starting over.

Still, she could feel the weight of it. Damaged or not, it had to be worth a year's wages to some of the craftsmen out there. Hell, it could pay for all the graves that still needed to be redone, likely twice over. She looked at the half-destroyed room around her. Even damaged, the money in it was still obvious: slabs of marble, tons of precious metals and gems. The gold alone—half of it melted, the other half bent—had to be worth more than most people out in the world would see in their lifetimes. If the money Gully received from his supply wagons dried up, he'd likely still be able to pay the workers as long as he was willing to dig through the rubble.

Wrapping the gold in her hand carefully with a stray piece of cloth—no doubt part of a great tapestry or cushion at one point—she slid it into her pocket, the weight feeling jointly comforting and appalling.

Shouts echoed down the hall, making her jump. However, they were happy voices, joking, someone having fun as they played cleanup. She watched two boys run past the doorway, not even looking in to see her.

Bootsteps on marble followed them, echoing as they advanced. Brier didn't move, continuing to watch the threshold.

General Gully's broad form finally appeared. Looking from side to side, he finally spotted her. Picking up his pace slightly, he moved into the gaping room. "There you are. The boy has been looking for you."

Brier raised an eyebrow, unable to care enough to stand. "Which boy?"

General Gully laughed. "*The* boy. Kosmos."

Brier looked away. "Palmer could find me if he really wanted."

General Gully didn't speak again, but neither did he leave. Brier traced the pattern in the arm of the throne, pretending much more interest in it than she actually felt. Slowly, the boots began to move again, coming closer. She put off acknowledging them as long as possible, only looking up when Gully stopped directly in front of her.

He reached down and tilted her chin up, his large fingers seeming far too big on her small face. Still, he looked at her, the same kind eyes shining down at her, a small smile evident behind his thick beard. "War is an awful, awful thing, little Miss Chaos. I have yet to meet a man who escapes from it unscarred. If there are some who leave the battlefield and can go back to their daily lives as though nothing has happened, I'm not sure I want to make their acquaintance."

Brier just looked up at him.

"That doesn't mean we should stop living, however." He finally dropped his hand, still studying her with the same kind-yet-serious gaze. "Don't punish those who care about you because you have seen horror.

Don't push away those who will help you just because you feel you have broken. That is when you need those people the most." One side of his mouth curled up into a half smile. "Take it from an old war-hardened general."

Brier still didn't answer but finally reached out to Palmer. *Here.*

General Gully released a heavy breath. Laying his broad palm atop her head—nearly covering it—he mussed her hair. "It will all be all right. It may take a while, but it all will be."

"So people keep telling me," Brier said, bending away from him.

"Well, then, it must be true." The other side of his mouth turned up, ending in a wide smile. "You're a strong little thing, Miss Chaos. I wouldn't worry about you in the slightest."

"Brier?" Palmer popped around the corner. "Oh, sorry, General."

"I was on my way out." General Gully winked at her, his boots slowly retreating across the room. "As you were."

Palmer gave a halfhearted salute, waiting for General Gully to leave before moving toward Brier. "I've been looking for you all day."

"Weren't looking hard enough, I guess." Brier put her legs down and leaned toward him.

"Or you're blocking me."

She shrugged.

Palmer let it go and just sighed. "They found Reinhald's body today."

Brier nodded. "They were bound to eventually."

"You don't sound surprised."

"If he were still alive, do you really think he *wouldn't* be here trying to snap up whatever power he could wrestle away from the general?" Brier cocked an eyebrow.

"Fair enough," Palmer said.

They fell silent. The voice of a workman calling to someone in the distance echoed from somewhere and drifted away into nothing.

"I don't think Cerise has spoken since she heard, if you can imagine," Palmer continued.

"She's a big girl," Brier said. "I'm sure she'll manage."

Palmer started to say something but apparently thought better of it. He shut his mouth again and finally dropped down to her eye level. "What happened to you, Bri?"

"What do you mean?"

"There's something wrong with you. Something you haven't been telling me."

She looked at him for a long moment, waiting for him to squirm away and apologize. He didn't. She released a long breath. "I died, Palmer. That's what happened."

"Not the first time," he said. Then he added, "For either of us."

"It was different this time," she said. "Everything just feels... wrong."

"Wrong how?"

She shook her head, unsure how to explain the pressure that had slowly been building in her head, the disconnect she sometimes felt between her mind and reality. She ended up repeating, "Just wrong."

Palmer placed his hand over hers on the arm of the throne, curling his fingers around hers. "We'll get through it. I promise."

She didn't answer but didn't pull away either.

"Do you trust me?"

She met his eyes, struck by how warm they were. Something good shone from deep inside him, calling to whatever good was still in her. He didn't look away. She didn't expect him to. She finally offered a smile. "Should I?"

He smiled back. "At least I'm not asking you to run off into the night this time." Squeezing her hand gently, he stood again. "Now, come on. Rosette wants to show you something."

"What?" Brier asked.

"You'll have to come and find out."

Brier's smile grew, his good mood easing her bad one. Standing, she looked up at him. "Lead the way."

Palmer took her hand, warmth traveling up Brier's arm as he led her through the one roundabout route the workers had cleared in what was left of the palace. They turned a corner, slowing as they reached a stretch of rooms that had somehow escaped in good repair.

Rosette looked up at their footsteps, a wide smile taking over her small face. She ran up and grabbed Brier away from Palmer. "There you are! I thought you weren't coming!"

"Took me a little while to find her." Palmer let Brier's hand slip away, smiling back at Rosette.

"We've all been waiting." Rosette continued forward with a vengeance, moving toward a set of doors at the end of the hall.

"We *all?*" Brier furrowed her eyebrows, looking from the back of Rosette's head to Palmer.

He just smiled at her.

Dropping her hand, Rosette turned the handle and pushed the double doors open.

Brier's jaw dropped. Books stretched out on shelves around the entirety of the small room, dark spines sticking out on white shelves. Putting a hand over her mouth, Brier stepped inside, looking around slowly, only half aware of the others in the room—Nico, Cerise, and Goebel—watching her.

Rosette pulled at Palmer's sleeve, speaking in what only a child could consider a whisper. "I told you she'd like it."

"We couldn't save everything, of course." Nico stepped forward. "But it's what's left of the library."

"And I'm doing my best to figure out what burned," Palmer said. "See if I can replace them."

Brier looked between the two of them. "This is for me?"

"Well, who better to take care of them all than you, Bochard?" Nico stuck his hands in his pockets. "With the rest of the librarians gone, we thought you might like to fill in."

"Oh." Brier pressed her fingers to her mouth again for a split second before turning and hugging him. "Thank you."

Nico hugged her back.

She turned to Palmer and hugged him as well before picking Rosette up into her own hug. Rosette felt heavier than Brier remembered, nearly hard to lift. She was finally putting on weight. Brier held her tightly for a long moment before Rosette started squirming. Brier set her down and looked at Goebel—the gray in his hair more obvious than before, his face more drawn—looked at Cerise—dark circles under her eyes, beautiful hair looking lackluster—and looked back at Nico and Palmer, standing and watching her.

She took Palmer's and Nico's hands, one in each of hers, looking back at the beautiful room. "We're going to make this all work, aren't we?"

Palmer smiled at her, squeezing her hand gently. "We're going to do our very best."

ACKNOWLEDGMENTS

This book would not have been possible without a myriad of help. I would like to thank the entire staff of Red Adept Publishing, including my amazing editors, Suzanne Warr and Kelly Reed, who have likely read this novel nearly as many times as I have while making the entire manuscript immeasurably better. Several thanks also belong to Streetlight Graphics, who managed to make a cover beyond anything I could imagine.

As always, I need to thank my endlessly patient husband, Niles, for all his late nights listening to me go on about my plot and characters and offering historical consult when needed. I never knew how lucky I was to marry an historian. For this book, he—and my parents—deserve a special accolade for allowing me to turn our family vacation to Italy into a research trip.

Last but not least, all of my family and friends who have provided immeasurable support through my work on this book and my entire writing career deserve sincere thanks. Hans, Carolyn, Ryan, Jeanne, Michael, and everyone else, thank you, and I hope you enjoy.

ABOUT THE AUTHOR

Jessica Dall finished her first novel at the age of fifteen and has been hooked on writing ever since. In the past few years, she has pub-lished novels such as *The Copper Witch* and *The Paper Masque*, along with a number of short stories that have appeared in both magazines and anthologies.

In college, Jessica interned at a publishing house, where her "writing hobby" slowly turned into a variety of writing careers. When not buried under her own world building, character sketches, and manuscripts, she works as an editor and creative writing teacher in Washington, DC.

She can most often be found with her overworked laptop and too often ignored husband wherever there is wifi.

www.ingramcontent.com/pod-product-compliance
Lightning Source LLC
Chambersburg PA
CBHW032114180726
48284CB00002B/568